Shattered Lies

Book Three: The Unraveled Trilogy

Theresa Sederholt

Shattered Lies
Copyright© 2015 by Theresa Sederholt

The author acknowledges the copyrighted or trademarked status and trademark owners of the following wordmarks mentions in this work of fiction: Nutella. Starbucks. Jammie Dodgers. Doctor Who. Bon Genie. Raider's Inc. MI6. The Children's Hospital of Philadelphia. University Children's Hospital Zurich. St. Jude's Children's Research Hospital. U.S. Marshall. Filgrastim. The University of Liverpool. Chocolate Smiles. Fedex. Blood and Marrow Transplant information network. Google.

Music 'Lifehouse "Storm," 'Beyoncé "I Was Here," 'Beyoncé "Halo," 'Luke Bryan "Play It Again," 'Snow Patrol "Chasing Cars," 'James Morrison "You Give Me Something," 'James Morrison "You Make It Real," 'Empire Cast "What Is Love (feat. V. Boz)," 'Jackie Oates "Dream Angus."

This is a work of fiction. Names, characters, businesses, places, events, and incidents are either the products of the author's imagination or used in a fictitious manner. Any resemblance to actual persons, living or dead, or actual events is purely coincidental.

This book contains strong language, graphic sexual situations, and violence. It is not intended for anyone under the age of 18.

Publisher: Theresa Sederholt ©

Cover designer: Robin Harper Wicked By Design.

Editor: Jacquelyn Ayres.

Formatter: Stacey Blake, Champagne Formats.

ISBN: 978–0-9862598-3-8

Other Books by Theresa Sederholt

The Unraveled Trilogy
The Unraveling of Raven
Darkness Into Dawn
Shattered Lies

Uniquely Mine

The Letter: Dear Michael

The Bench

Dedication

For Josiah Garcia, you are a brave and beautiful boy. I know you will survive and go on to do great things. Your kind and gentle way is an inspiration to everyone. It has been said that everyone comes into your life for a reason, even if it's only for a brief moment. I am honored and blessed that you have come into mine. Your faith and inspiration is a shining light. Thank you and God bless.

To everyone who has fought cancer, your battle has not been in vain. That moment in time, no matter how brief, will never be forgotten.

Chapter One

James Phillips

THE DAY HAS FINALLY come, the one I've feared the most. The day my oldest son comes to find me. I knew it'd be only a matter of time before my past would collide with my future. His family . . . murdered because of me. My grandson and daughter-in-law gunned down like animals. How can I face him, knowing what I've done? I've stayed away for their own safety, but what did that get me? They are *still* dead because of me. I have managed to keep the rest of them safe, but, for how long?

A knock on the door startles me out of my thoughts. I'm expecting my valet. "Come in, Reynolds." Reynolds has been my valet and confidant for twenty years; the keeper of all my secrets.

"Sir, I just received word their plane has landed. It's only a matter of time now. What would you like to do?"

"Well, Reynolds, what we won't do, is run anymore. The time has come to face my demons. I must own up to what I've done. They are not children anymore, and they deserve the truth, no matter how ugly it is."

"Sir, what about their safety?"

"Well, the better question should be, what about ours? When Maxwell finds out my role in all of it, I venture to say, I'm a dead man."

"Sir, you did everything you could, I'm sure he will understand."

I squeeze my eyes shut, trying to get that image out of my head.

"Everything but save them," I whisper.

Ten Days Earlier

Raven

AS I WATCH JAX sleep, I see such anguish on his beautiful face. I wish I could take away his pain; I would bear it for him, if I could. I lean in and tenderly kiss him. I don't want to wake him, but I want him to feel me and know I'm always with him.

"Hmm . . . I'm awake, sweetheart."

"I can never tell if you're really asleep."

He tilts his hips and I can feel how aroused he is. I know he sleeps best when he's buried deep inside of me, but I haven't made it to my six-week postpartum checkup yet; my body's not ready. He keeps a tight grip around my waist while I snuggle up against him. For now, this will have to do.

"Jax, you know I'm not going to disappear; you can let go of me."

"Raven, you are so strong and so positive, even after all you've been through. How? How do you manage to do it?"

"I believe in us. Our daughter is a beautiful product of that belief. *And* I've made you a promise. A promise to be your companion, forever; beyond this lifetime. But most of all, I have given you my heart and my soul. I will fight to the bitter end for *us*." I lay a trail of soft kisses down his neck.

"I really am dreading getting on that plane tonight," he groans lightly. I lift my head up to catch his eyes. "Please don't look at me like that, you know I have to do it—I need answers. Now Bella has decided she is going with us. I think she blames herself for his leaving, and no matter what I've told her, she won't listen. She's so stubborn."

"Really, Jax? I wonder where she gets that from." He says nothing, only closing his eyes tightly.

"Sweetheart, Max and I have put extra security in place. I don't expect to be gone very long, however, I don't want you to be alarmed with all the extra guards."

At just the mention of his leaving, I feel his whole body tighten, his eyes still tightly shut. My heart is breaking for him. One of the many facets of this man is his need for the truth. "I understand having questions, but do you really need to know the answers? Will knowing change anything for you? Will it change any part of who you are?" I ask as he strokes my back in a rhythmic pattern like he's trying to find comfort.

"Raven, I've never shared any of this with anyone. I thought by keeping it buried, it would be gone. But things never stay buried, do they? Eventually, everything comes to light." He mindlessly twirls my hair around his fingers.

"I would sit by the window every Saturday, waiting for him to come home. Sometimes, I would set up our peanut butter and jelly sandwiches on a TV tray, hoping he would come back to watch *Doctor Who*. He never came back, but I kept setting it up . . . hoping. As I got older, I made sure I worked hard in school and helped my mum with Bella. I always protected my mum and my sister. I never gave into my fear that one day, I would wake up and they would be gone, too. I wanted to make him proud of me, just in case he came back to us. Instead . . . he just moved on to the next family. No matter how hard I tried, it was never good enough. *We* were never good enough," he barely whispers, "When is it ever good enough?"

Right now, my heart is breaking for this man. He's been through so much and yet all he ever wanted was his dad to love him, as he should have. "Jax, you were a little boy, trying to protect your mom and sister, the only family you had left. You did everything right. You carried so much of the burden. Anyone would be proud to call you 'son.' Don't ever think that you're not good enough; it's your father who's not good enough. He didn't deserve any of the wonderful children that he created."

"Sometimes I would make up stories about him. I would have him out, saving the world. I would pretend he was like *Doctor Who*, traveling through time and space, to save everyone like a superhero. It would ease the loneliness, especially for Bella. I thought I was helping her, but, maybe I didn't. Maybe I made things worse for her."

"Why would you think that you made it worse? It doesn't seem that she has put him on a pedestal or that she has any hate for the man. She seems almost . . . indifferent."

"What about her remark about dad leaving after she was born? That sounds like she blames herself and she shouldn't. For Christ's sake, she was just a baby. She wants to confront him, and honestly, I can't say I blame her."

"What about Max?"

"What do you mean?"

"Well, I understand why Bella wants to meet James and I even understand why you do, but why Max?"

"Sweetheart, I think he's going for Bella and me . . . to support us. I really think he has no desire to have any kind of relationship with him. He told me that when he married Samantha and had Elliot, he finally made peace with it all. I think in the beginning, he blamed dad for his mum's death. It's only with age and maturity that he's come to realize we are all responsible for our own actions."

"Your mom doesn't want any of you to go. She told me *'the past can't be changed and it's best to keep it buried.'* I think she is speaking as a mother, trying to protect her children. I know I would lay down my life to protect Antonia. Now that I'm a mom, I can understand that bond so much more. I think she chose to bury the past for survival purposes. It wasn't just for her survival, but for the survival of her children."

"My mum acts like she doesn't care one way or the other, however, I'm not so sure. What else did my mum tell you?"

"Nothing more about your dad. She does talk fondly of Max's grams. I think they became good friends over the years. Did you ever meet her?"

"Yes. I met her right after he came on board at Raiders. She passed soon after that. She always seemed like such a strong lady."

"Having lost a child and then having to raise her grandchild, I would think she was very strong." I stroke his face, "How long do you think you'll be gone?" I ask. His grip gets tighter, "Jax, really, if you need me to go, I will, but we will have to take Antonia with us."

He leaps out of bed and begins pacing and pulling at his hair. I'm watching his struggle boil to the surface. I'm shocked at his reaction; I never expected him to get this upset.

"Fucking bloody hell, woman! I can't do this. What the fuck has happened to me? Do you even realize what you've done?"

"Jax, calm down. Please, sit down and talk to me rationally."

"Calm? Rational? You can't be serious. Calm and rational flew out the window the day I met you. In one year's time, my entire life has changed. I have real love for the first time ever. I have a daughter, who I have to protect. I have a family that is growing daily. I've come alive, Raven, and it's all because of you. Now I have to leave this and confront the demons from my past. A past I thought was dead and buried. I really thought he was dead, and honestly, I didn't give a royal fuck until Antonia. Now everything I say and everything I do, matters. Every second, without you both, matters. What if she forgets me? Have you even thought of that? I know I have!"

"Jax, stop right now! You're not going to be gone that long."

"Raven, one day is too long. What if it takes a while? What if he doesn't want to see us? There are so many *what ifs*. I don't do *what ifs!*"

I need to keep it together for him, but he knows I'm just as apprehensive about him leaving. "Realistically, how long do you think you'll be gone?"

"I don't know. All I do know is every minute away is too long. I planned for two days; get in ask my questions and get out. Then, Bella demanded that she go. What if she wants to stay longer? I can't leave her behind—no one gets left *behind.*"

I open my arms, "Come back to bed."

He stops. His eyes gaze up and down my body as he seemingly struggles with his decision. "You're not going to tempt me with that beautiful body. I have enough to deal with, and not being able to go to the happy place for the past six weeks is fucking killing me!"

"You need me, Jax, but more importantly for you is the fact that I need you." He slowly walks toward me and just as he crawls back into bed, I hear the baby monitor come to life. I reach up and kiss him gently. "I'll be back in a little bit; Antonia needs to eat." The look on his face haunts me as I leave, so troubled and my heart is breaking for him.

Jaxson

I WATCH MY WIFE sashay out of the room and *now* my cock decides to come to life. Bastard has a mind of his own. I watch her on the monitor tending to Antonia and it's such a beautiful sight. It's pure and natural, which only makes me want her more. Right . . . like that's even possible. I head into the shower, trying to get my mind off of her, but it won't. As I go about washing, I look down at my cock and he's hard as stone. *Bastard.* "Look, I told you we are adults here and we need to have some sort of control. We don't have the all clear, yet. I told you no jumping about." I freeze—*shit* I'm so busted. I don't have to hear her; I feel it when she walks in the room. I turn around and I'm hit with those beautiful eyes. She's biting her bottom lip, trying not to laugh. "Go ahead, Raven, say it."

"Oh, my beautiful, sexy husband. I love that you have conversations with Mr. Cock. I love that you are trying so hard to follow the doctor's orders. Get out of the shower now, Jax, I think it's time you turn the reins over to me for a while."

I hesitate as I step out of the shower. "Do you trust me, Jax?"

"With my life," I say without missing a beat.

"Good, then trust me to give you pleasure tonight—my way."

"Wow. Okay, what do you want me to do?"

"Get into bed and wait for me. That's all."

As I look at my beautiful wife, I know, deep in my soul, that I am the luckiest man in the world.

Raven

I WATCH HIM HEAD into bed, and then, I begin to set stuff up for him. I gather a pair of my stockings to tie him with, some massage oil, and a glass of ice cubes. Anything I can think of that will bring him pleasure. I turned things over to him one night. I let him blindfold me, which not only ended up being very erotic, but also very therapeutic. I faced my fear and, in the end, it brought us closer. I need to do the same for him. He needs to know that he might not see me or touch me, but I will always be there. I head into the bedroom and I hear him talking to his cock, yet again. I love the playful Jax just as much as the intense one. So many facets, like a beautiful diamond; each one shining in it's own light.

"I told you, mate, if we waited long enough, it would happen."

"Good conversation, Jax?" I ask, grabbing his attention. His eyes grow wide like a boy caught swiping a piece of candy. "It's okay. I don't mind you talking to him, it's quite entertaining, actually."

"So . . . what are you going to do to me?" He presses his lips together and his hands seem to shake. He's hesitant in giving up so much control. Knowing that it's the control that grounds him makes this even more important for both of us.

"Do you remember the time you blindfolded me? I learned so much that night. I experienced what it's like to totally trust—unconditional trust. I never thought that was possible, and that's what I want to give to you. However, I want to take it a step further." I pause. "I want to tie your hands," I lay it all out. His jaw seems to tighten as he gets a wan look about him. "I know it will be hard for you. Your need to constantly touch me comes from your fear of loss. Just like I was able to put my fear of the kidnapping behind me, you can do the same with your fear of abandonment. The fear is never truly gone, but it's in a more manageable place where it can't hurt you anymore. You need to trust me. Do you trust me, Jax?"

"You know I do, but this is hard for me. I need that constant touch to keep me grounded."

"Will you try? If it gets to be too much, we can stop. If we don't try, you will always wonder *what if?*"

He bites his bottom lip and tightly closes his eyes. His skin seems to shiver and prickle at the thought of what I'm suggesting. I knew it would be hard for him; I just wasn't sure *how* hard.

He takes a calming breath, "I'll try," he whispers as he holds out his hands to me. The fact that his hands are shaking only makes me surer that what I'm doing is going to help him. I place my hand on his chest, and I can feel his heart racing. I swear it will leap out of his chest. I reach over to the nightstand and grab one of the black stockings to tie his hands together in front of him. "Breathe, Jax, it will be a good experience. If it gets to be too much, you can always tell me to stop." I take the other stocking and make it into a blindfold. "You'll need to rely on your other senses now. Take a deep breath and let it out slowly. Tell me . . . what are you feeling?"

"Fear, I can't see you or feel you."

"You know I'm still here and I'm not leaving you, *ever.*"

"My head understands everything you're saying but my heart doesn't."

I lean in and place kisses all over his chest, trying to get him to relax. "I made promises to you that I would never break." I continue kissing him gently up his neck and then kiss his lips. I can feel his jaw relax as I trail my fingers along the scruff of his beard. "I love when this scruff is between my legs. Use your other senses, what do you feel?"

"I feel your soft lips all over me. Your fingertips are following the trail of your tender kisses. I can smell our scents mixed together with a hint of sexual arousal, it's quite heady."

"That's good. Now take a few long breaths, like I taught you from Pilates . . . feel yourself relax."

I got edible, chocolate-raspberry massage oil today. I grab the bottle from the nightstand and put some in my hands. I rub them together to warm it up. I decide to start at his perfect feet. As I work his arch, he moans and the tension begins to slowly leave his body. "You're doing so good. I swipe my tongue up his arch and his cock leaps to attention. I try not to laugh—yep, Mr. Cock has a mind of his own. I work my way up his legs very slowly. Noticing his bound hands fisted, I bring them to my lips and kiss each one. Not being able to touch me or see me, is having a larger effect on him than I thought. He wants to do so much to please me and this really is one of the hardest things I have ever asked of him. I know the level of trust between us is so great, yet sometimes, the biggest struggle is with the littlest things. "It's okay, I'm here—always. Let yourself feel me."

"I can't; my hands are *bound!*"

"Feel me with your heart, Jax . . . your soul. You don't need your hands, I'm all around you." I reach down and plant a kiss over his heart. "Even if I left the room, I would still be in here." I tap gently with my finger before placing another kiss. "I will always be with you; that will never change."

His rapid breathing seems to be calming down. "Jax, are you okay now?"

"Yes, I'm good."

I take the glass of ice and pull out a cube. I slowly rub it around his nipples followed by my warm tongue. Hot and cold; back and forth. He's beginning to relax under my touch, ever so slowly. I massage every square inch of him—my tongue darting out to taste him—trailing with feather-light kisses. "Turn over, Jax." He complies and I begin the process all over again. I reach his ass and freeze. He has the most beautifully sculptured ass. I straddle him and try to continue, but as my hands work over this perfection, I moan. I reach down and kiss each cheek. My God, he takes my breath away. I swirl my tongue in circles and up his spine. I swear, I could have an orgasm just from the sight of him. My breathing has become rapid and I'm close to the edge. I can feel my body begin to tremble with every kiss. I know he can feel it too. He's always so in tune with me. He senses my needs before I do, knowing when to slow me down or let me have control. I hope tonight I'm doing the same for him.

"Sweetheart, are you okay?" he asks.

"More than okay." I climb off of him. "Roll onto your back and lift your hands above your head. Hang onto the headboard and no matter what happens, don't let go." God love him, he does it without question. I climb on top of him and kiss the tip of his cock before sliding my tongue up and down.

"Raven, I don't know how much longer I can last without touching you. I'm aching for you." There's a plea in his voice.

"Lift your head up, Jax."

*J*axson

I DO AS I'M told and I know exactly where I'm headed. I thank God for her and her willingness to explore the unknown with me. Her understanding and grace befuddles my own logical mind. What did I ever do right in my life to have been gifted with her? I lift my head up and my lips land right between her legs just as she takes my cock even deeper in her mouth. I know I have to be gentle with her right now, but it's hard to concentrate when she's working her magic on me. I lightly kiss her sweetness, followed with the swipe of my tongue. Still bound and blindfolded, I realize she's right; I don't need to see her or touch her. She is in my heart and my soul. As she gets to the tip of my cock, I beg her—no, I plead with her—to please do the nip that I love so much. She swirls her tongue around the head, then stops, hums, and goes right back down. *Sweet Jesus, and all that's holy, I'm gonna die.* When she gets to the top again, I hold my breath. I don't have to beg; she squeezes me and nips the head of my cock. She knows just how I like it. I explode with a force that I never thought was possible. Not having the sense of sight and touch makes my orgasm so much more intense. I shake uncontrollably and let out an animalistic groan that sounds foreign to my own ears. I know I should be giving her what she needs, but right now, I can't move . . . or even think, for that matter. Right now I'm just trying to breath. She climbs off of me and quickly begins to remove my bindings. "Jax, are you okay?"

I feel as if I'm in a daze. "Raven, I've never experienced anything like that before. It's like all of my senses were magnified." As she crawls into my arms, I glance down, taking a quick peek at my cock.

"His head didn't blow off, Jax; he's fine."

I laugh, "I can't get anything past you, sweetheart." My fingertips stroke her back slowly, "Let me love you tonight. I know we can't have traditional sex, but I can love you in so many other ways."

She reaches up and pulls my forehead to hers. "Nothing about us has ever been traditional."

I throw my head back laughing. "Oh, my sweet, sweet girl, let me show you exactly what I'm talking about."

Raven

I KNOW I'VE TOUCHED upon a fear in him that he's tried to keep buried. I can only hope that in time, he will see that I'm not going to disappear. Together—we're both unraveling—one day at a time. I reach up and run my fingertips down his face. " Love me tonight, before you go; slow and gentle, please."

"My beautiful girl, you'll never have to ask me twice." He plants a sweet kiss on my lips. "Now, let me show you something different tonight." He pulls the sheets over us, holding me tight. As he begins to lose himself in me, I feel a calm that wasn't there before. I know we will face whatever is thrown at us, together.

Chapter Two

Maxwell

I DECIDE TO GO over the file again before we have to leave. Something is bugging me but I'm not sure what. I know I don't want to leave, but I would never let Jax and Bella go alone. I wish I could figure out what is making my tingle sense act up. I had it that day I went after Vincent. I didn't listen to it, and I paid a heavy price. I thank God I listened and we didn't go to that island. We would have been sitting ducks, waiting to be plucked off. Sometimes, I can't seem to bring things to the surface of my mind, it's like a salmon trying to swim upstream. I close my eyes and rub my temples. I sense her before I hear her, I always do. My whole body seems to come to life when I know she is near. I turn around and what I see stops me dead in my tracks. Jackie is standing before me with fire in her eyes. I've only seen her this mad one time, *right before the condom broke.*

"Hey, baby, what's up?"

"Maxwell Fleming, don't you 'hey, baby' me!"

Holy fuck—full name; I'm in deep shit here. "Um, are you mad at me for something?"

She has one hand on her hip and she's pointing her finger at me. "Let me tell you what happened today. Maybe—just maybe—you will understand why I'm so pissed off. I went to see Mick today. I wanted to surprise you, so I asked him to teach me how to defend myself. I know you're going away, and you know I don't like guns, so I thought if I knew some self-defense moves, you would be more at ease. He informed me that he is not allowed to teach me because that would mean he would have to touch me. He said, and I quote, *'No one is allowed to lay a finger on you, Jackie.'* Really, Max, have you lost your ever-loving mind? I'm not a child, and you can't act like a crazy ass lunatic—that's Jax's job!"

"I could tell you that at the time I wasn't in my right mind, but in all fairness, that's not true. Honestly, the thought of anyone putting a finger on you makes me see red. If you want to learn how to protect yourself, I'll be the one to teach you."

"You don't see anything wrong with this, do you? Your fear is smothering me. I love you, but you're the one driving a wedge between us. My whole damn life has been turned upside down. I've constantly had to be the giver. I've given up my teaching career and my freedom. I'm only twenty-five and I'm being isolated yet again! My father isolated me, and I fought so hard to be free, but that's never going to happen for me is it, Max?"

"Please calm down, Jackie, whatever you need, please, just tell me."

"I need a life, Max, a normal life. I need to feel self-worth. I want to grow and be able to teach."

"I thought you loved your riding academy?"

"I do love it. You don't get it." She brings her hand up to her forehead and shakes slightly as if in disbelief. "I feel like I'm living in your fear." Her hand darts off, emphasizing her point. "Your fear that's overpowering me. I don't want to see doom and gloom around every corner. I want to love life. Maybe it's a Pollyanna way of thinking, but damn it, it's what I want."

I feel my heart constricting in my chest. If she leaves, I'll die—I know it. "Please, I need to leave tonight, but I can't leave you like this. I can't let them go alone. Please don't leave me."

"I'm not leaving you. I need you just as much as you need me. I need you to stop smothering me, though. Let me live and let's experience life together. I know you will always be overprotective—I get that—but let's work together as a team, Max. Love me like the woman I am, and not like the child you're afraid of losing."

I lift her up and she wraps those beautiful legs around my waist. I rest my forehead on hers. "Please, give me a chance, I'm really trying."

"Yes, you are, Maxwell."

"Well, at least you can still joke. Now let me be the one to teach you some self-defense."

"Is this going to be something I can really use?"

"Of course. But I think we need to be naked."

"Naked self-defense classes? You can't be serious."

"Oh trust me, I'm serious. I need to show you all the points on the body that you can cause damage to."

"Maybe we should wait till you get back. I have other plans for you tonight."

She stops me dead in my tracks, and I gently put her back down. "Really?"

"You see, Max, you have no idea what I'm capable of. You think I'm a fragile, porcelain doll, but you couldn't be further from the truth."

"I know you're strong and yet I love that you show me your submissive side."

She sighs and looks away from me as a flush spreads across her cheeks. "I want to experiment and try new things. You're the only man I've ever been with. I want more sexual experiences, and I want them with you." She says so quickly, as if trying to get it over with.

This has been my fear, that I won't be enough for her. My eyes are piercing hers, trying to figure out what she's not saying. She seems apprehensive and nervous, picking at invisible lint on her shirt. "Do you regret not having more sexual experiences?"

"No, of course not. I want to start and end my days only with you. I want to explore every inch of your body, take on new highs with you. I promised I would be totally honest with you." Her fingers are trembling as she runs them up and down my arm. "I don't want to fall into a routine. I want to experience loving you and being loved by you. I don't want to ever regret *not* having more sexual experiences with you. Does that make sense?" She leans into me and gently kisses my lips.

I lift her up and she wraps those fantastic legs around my waist. She wants different, I can do different. I gently place her on the kitchen table. "I fully intend on being the only one taking you to new highs. It's important for you to know that I will never hurt you, but I will push the boundaries with you."

Her eyes grow wide. "Um, will I need a *safeword?*"

My jaw tightens. "What do you know about that? What would make you think you need a safeword with me?"

"I might be inexperienced but I have read books, and I've seen movies. This is the twenty-first century, Max. I can tell you I don't understand getting pleasure from pain."

Her innocence is breathtakingly beautiful. "We are lovers and lovers will never need *safewords.* If we are doing something that you're not comfortable with all you ever have to say to me is *stop.* I get no pleasure from giving or receiving pain. What gives me the greatest pleasure is when you let me love you. Everything we experience together gives me the greatest pleasure." I realize that communication is everything for us. I'm determined to keep her forever and in order to do that, I have to let her in. "I will be more open with you, however, you must do the same. If you need something from me that I'm not giving you, then tell me. I promise to try to not treat you like a porcelain doll."

"Well, in that case, before you get on that plane, I need you—bad. You and me, babe—all night."

As my eyes gaze over her body, her nipples harden and I know this is going to be hard and fast. I lift her with one arm and yank down her yoga pants. "Hold on to the edge of the table and don't let go." I drop to my knees taking her pants all the way off. I kiss each foot as I place them on my shoulders. *Oh, these legs are my undoing.* I kiss them very slowly, working my way up one side and down the other. She's using her feet to pull me in closer. When I finally reach my prize, I gently kiss her. I glance up and smile; the look on her face priceless. She's biting her lip trying so hard not to let go of the table while her legs begin to tremble. I push my fingers in deeper while my tongue never loses contact. That is until her hips begin to lift up and down. She's not going to last. I know she's going to come, so I slow it down almost to a crawl.

She whimpers, with such angst. "Max, why the *hell* are you stopping?"

"Anticipation," is all I say. She takes her hands off the table trying to push me, I stop completely. "Hands on the table or I will stop— *now!*" She grabs the table moaning, and fuck, it's hot! Very slowly, I use my fingers and gently, I spread her wetness from front to back and I feel her tense. "I will be gentle, and remember, you can always say

15

stop." I feel her begin to relax. I work my tongue in and out of her as I push through her barrier with my pinky finger, matching the pace of my tongue. Sensing she's almost there, I take her clitoris between my teeth and gently tug while flicking my tongue. She tries to move her hips but I've got a lock on her legs. Her feet are kicking my shoulders. She is screaming my name over and over again, like the song of an angel.

I stand up and drop my sweats while lifting her off the table. "You can let go now, but wrap those beautiful legs around me!" I gently slide my cock up and down gathering the sweet essence of her. I enter her very slowly. But slow is not what I need, and it's not what she wants. "We're going hard and fast, baby," I warn her before I begin pounding into her. And she's taking it all. I feel the sharp piercing of her nails breaking the skin of my shoulders. "Oh bloody hell with the fucking nails, babe!" I slow it down, trying to gain some sense of normal. There is no stopping; I can't slow down. I pull back and pound into her, all the while, pulling her hips in hard to meet mine. My legs are shaking and I feel my blood surging through my veins. I look down at the sight before me, and that's all I need. "Oh, Jackie, fuck . . . I'm coming, baby." I explode with her like nothing I've ever experienced in my lifetime; we are both gasping, trying to gain some sort of control. "Babe, you okay?"

"More than okay," she hums.

"God, Jackie, I don't think I'll ever get enough of you. I'm going to try to move as soon as I can feel my legs again." Within a few moments, my legs come back to life. I carry her into our bedroom and crawl into bed. As I run my fingers up and down her spine, the thought of leaving tonight—leaving her—is killing me. I hold her in my arms until she falls asleep. Something is still bothering me with that file. I pull the quilt over her, while throwing on my discarded sweats, before heading into my office to look at it again. Spreading the file out, I take one document at a time. What the hell am I not seeing? Jax and Raven make lists for everything, but not me. I close my eyes and visualize each piece of paper . . . every word. Finally, it hits me, the piece of the puzzle that I've been missing. I've been so focused on his other families that I almost missed the most basic thing. I need to talk to Jax. I'm about to call him, when I hear her come up behind me.

"Max, I woke up and you were gone."

"I'm sorry. You fell asleep, and something has been nagging at me."

She sits in my lap and begins lightly stroking the scar on my head. She knows this helps with the tension. "Oh no, Max, your tingle sense?" *Just the mention of it freezes her in her tracks.*

"Yeah, every time I pick up that damn file. I finally figured it out. I was just about to call Jax, but it can wait."

She picks up the phone and hands it to me. "Call him right now. I know if you don't, it will be in the back of your mind."

"I love that you get me, babe. I'm going to head up to the main house; it shouldn't take too long." I gather up the file and run out the door, calling Jax along the way.

Chapter Three

Jaxson

I HEAD INTO THE kitchen and find Max waiting for me. "Hey, mate, this better be fucking good. I was having the time of my life, you know."

"Trust me, Jax, so was I," he grumbles. "Something was bothering me with that file."

"What's the problem?" I question.

"I was so focused on the other families he destroyed, that I almost missed it. Remember your mum said he was in sales? Well, when I looked into his past, the only thing it ever said was just that. It never said what he sold, or any companies he was affiliated with. It was all very vague. How did he make so much money to be able to live the life he's living? I checked to see if he was living off any of the women he was with, but they were not well off at all. Something's missing and it's bugging me."

"Max, what the hell could he be into? Do you think it's drugs?"

"Honestly, I don't know. I have to tell you, though—I'm not thrilled about this trip. I know you need answers, but at what price?" He paces.

"I would say wait but I'm not sure Bella will go for it. Aside from being a serial bigamist, nothing in the report showed any criminal activity."

"Don't you think I noticed that? There isn't even a fucking parking ticket! No one lives that clean, Jax." He throws his hands out in a frustrated manner. He pulls out the chair across from me and tosses the file in my direction as he sits.

"What are you thinking, that maybe he works for someone or some company that's keeping him clean?"

"Wouldn't be the first person to be a front man. I just don't like it." He rocks back and forth in his chair.

"Do you think we should take everyone with us?" I ask. Max knows me, he can figure out what I'm thinking without me having to say it. He must know I'm not comfortable with leaving my family behind.

"No way, Jax. I think it would increase the danger for everyone if they did come with us. I know you're struggling, so am I. Maybe if I talk to Bella, I can get her to wait a few days, giving me some time to dig a little deeper."

I rub my temples, trying to subside the headache I feel rolling in. "Good luck with that one. You know that Bella is like a dog with a bone." I'm looking at Max and he has a blank stare—shit. "She's right behind me, isn't she? Don't bother answering, I already know. Pull up a chair, sis; we need to talk."

She takes a seat next to mine, her eyes dart to the open file. "What seems to be the problem?"

Max, being the calmer of the two of us, gestures to take the reins. "Bella, every time I picked up that file, I felt like something wasn't right, I just didn't know what. I finally realized what's off. It says that he works in sales, but there is no company listed. He is squeaky clean without so much as a parking ticket. Something is off; no one is that clean."

"Look, I need answers, but I understand if you don't want to go. I'm going and I was looking for you to see if you think I should bring Michael Jr. He could meet his grandfather . . ."

All I hear is Bella wanting to bring Junior and my blood boils over. I pound my fist on the table, instantly silencing her. "It will be a cold day in hell before I let him anywhere near Junior! Never will he have an opportunity to meet him—*never!* He hasn't earned that privilege and I doubt he ever will. Do you think this is going to be sunshine and roses? He's a low-life, Bella."

"Then why are you going to see him?" she raises her voice.

"To ask one question . . . *why?*"

"*Why* . . . is that it? Ring him on the bloody fucking phone then, Jax!"

"No. I want to—no, I need to—look him in the eye."

"Are you afraid you're like him? Is that it, Jax? You want to see if the apple really doesn't fall far from the tree? Is that why you need to *look him in the eye?*"

Maxwell

I'VE GROWN UP ALONE, having no idea about how crazy brothers and sisters can actually get with each other. Bella really knows how to push all of Jax's buttons. She just hit the nail on the head.

"Enough!" An suddenly yells from behind us, grabbing everyone's attention. "If the three of you insist on going, I can't stop you. Although you don't always act it, you're adults. I will, however, draw the line when it comes to my grandchildren. Under no circumstances will James get anywhere near them. You're all adults and can make your decisions. You can deal with the consequences of those decisions, but they are innocent children."

With the silence blaring, I decide to be the first one to speak up. "Ma'am, can I ask you a few questions?"

"Of course, what's troubling you?"

"Well, there is never a mention as to what company James worked for, or what he sold. He's squeaky clean, almost too clean. Do you know anything that's not in the file?"

"Maxwell, my head was in the clouds when I was with him. I was a foolish girl who thought the sun rose and set with James. He said sales and I never asked. When I was forced to go back home with Jax and Bella in tow, my family disowned me. My brother called my children *bastards.* I walked out that day and never looked back."

I'm watching Jax; his jaw is tight and his fists are balled. I have a funny feeling I know what has set him off. "Why did you never tell anyone about your brother?"

"The day he called my children bastards was the day he died in my eyes. I would have given him the shirt off my back if he needed it. When it comes to my children, I will go to the depths of hell to protect them."

Bella stands up and takes a deep breath. "Max, you've got two days and then I'm on that plane." She walks out leaving an eerie silence behind her.

"Ma'am, is there anything else that you've kept quiet about? I understand why and I don't blame you, but now—for safety—reasons I need to know it all."

"I have no secrets. I never told you about my brother, Rhodri, because in my heart, he died that day. I don't know whatever came of him. I do know he was very active in his church. I don't even know if my parents are still alive."

"What did your parents say when you came home?" I push. She bows her head, keeping her gaze downward. She must feel like she is reliving the humiliation all over again. Jax and I glance at each other quickly over her disposition. It stops me dead in my tracks.

Jax grabs her hands, "Mum, if this is too much then stop."

"Are you sure you boys need to hear this? As painful and humiliating as this is, if it means that my family will be safe, then I will."

I look toward Jax and nod. "Ma'am, as much as you want this to stay buried, I can't, in good conscious, let any of us go there without all the facts. Safety always comes first. Would you rather tell me in private?"

"Maxwell, what I'd rather do and what needs to be done are two totally different things. Jax, please get your sister; she might as well hear it all. I will only tell you one time, and then I never want to speak about him again."

Jax goes to get Bella as I pour An a brandy. "Drink this; you look like you need it."

I watch her take the glass and her hands are trembling. She is visibly shaken by all of this. Jax and Bella are back and I see that they notice An's struggle. Hell, you'd have to be blind not to.

Bella puts her arms around An. "Mum, it's okay, you know nothing you tell us will ever change the love and respect we have for you." Bella gives her another squeeze before she pours herself a brandy. I set up my phone to record everything. Bella furrows her brows at me. "Is that really necessary, Maxwell?"

"Unfortunately, yes. I need to record this so nothing is forgotten. Take your time, ma'am."

She takes a few slow sips of her brandy, closes her eyes, and finally finds her voice. "As you know, I was born in Wales. My father worked in the shipyard in Cardiff Bay. My mother was a homemaker. I have an older brother, Rhodri. My parents were very proud of him; he was on track to become a minister. I wanted to become a nurse, so I volunteered after school at the hospital as a nurse's aide. One day, during my shift, your father came into the emergency room in need of stitches. I couldn't take my eyes off of him; he was so very handsome. We got to talking and he told me he was in sales. When I asked him what he sold, all he said was *'importing and exporting rare things.'* I asked him what kind of things and he spun a tale about rare artifacts. I could blame my youth; I was only seventeen. But the reality was, I believed him because I wanted to." She's tearing a tissue into a million tiny pieces.

I reach over and pull out a pad from one of the kitchen draws. I begin to make notes of questions I have. I don't want to stop her, having her lose her train of thought. I hand her a glass of water, "Go on, An."

"Thank you, Maxwell. Anyway, we started dating, but I didn't dare take him home. He was older than me and I knew my father wouldn't approve. I continued seeing him on the sly. Every week, James would go away for days at a time. I should have questioned him, but it created an air of mystery around him. Every time he came back, he would bring some sort of exotic trinket."

I take her hand and stop her, "Do you still have any of them?"

"I only kept a few. Are they important?"

"Everything, at this point, is important. We can look at them later. Go on, please."

"I think I knew he was trouble, but I was a naïve girl. He talked about all the places he visited and how he wanted to take me along with him. I believed every word of the tale he spun. Sometimes, he *would* take me on day trips with him. He always introduced me as his fiancée, which I found very exciting. He had lots of money and he always spent it on me."

An lifts her glass of water to take a sip, but her hand is shaking so bad, she gives up and puts it back down. "Ma'am, if you need a break then please stop."

"No, I want this over with. I don't want to keep reliving my shameful past."

Jax takes her hand, trying to offer his support. "There's no shame here; you were an innocent girl."

"Jax, I was not that innocent. I knew he was trouble, but I was excited with the mystique that surrounded him; he was so mature and worldly. He was my first love, and I was clueless about so much. I trusted him with my heart and my body in the short time we dated. I felt like I was on a secretive whirlwind romance and soon, I found myself pregnant and unmarried." She quickly looks away, avoiding any eye contact. "I went to him and told him and he said I should handle it."

Jax slams his fist on the table, startling everyone. "He told you to *handle it?!'* Was he expecting you to get an abortion?" His voice growing louder as he runs his hands through his hair, practically pulling it out of his head!

An quickly wipes away her tears. "Jax, he never said anything other than 'handle it.' I didn't know what to do, I was too afraid to tell my parents. I went to my brother first; I really trusted my brother and felt he would understand. Rhodri flipped out on me and went straight to father. My father had a lot of friends on the docks and they went and paid James a visit. It was right after that we were ushered in to the court house. And . . . just like that . . . we were married."

It's eating me up inside, asking her to relive all of this, but I have no choice. She is always the strong one. The one that we turn to, the one everyone leans on. I clasp her hands and try to offer some sort of comfort. "Go ahead, ma'am." I nod in encouragement.

She shakes her head lightly and takes in a deep breath. "We had set up house not far from town, and everything seemed to be fine. I finished school and began my studies as a nurse. Soon, I found myself pregnant again. James said he was happy and that he rather I stay home to take care of the children. His time home started getting less and whenever I would question him, he would always claim it was business. Sadly, I believed him. Besides, I was too wrapped up in my pregnancy to dig any further, if I wanted to. Once Isabella arrived, he seemed to be around even less. Isabella had a rough first year; she was sick a lot as well as colicky. When I think back to the time right before he left, he seemed distant and preoccupied. One day, he left and never came back. I needed to pay the rent and my children needed food, so I went to my mum for advice. She told me I needed to be strong and deal with it. She said, *'you're not a child anymore. You chose this path, now deal with it.'* That was the day I decided to look for him. I went to see Garth, a friend of mine from high school. He had just opened his own investigation business and agreed to help me find James."

I have a million questions, but right now, I need to take it slow. Before you go any further, I have quite a few questions. The records show he was born in Scotland—the Highlands, to be exact. How did he end up in Wales? How long was he in Wales before you met him? How did you track him down? Did he have any bank accounts that you were able to access? Did you ever hear him talking business? Where were these 'day trips' he took you on?"

She gets a distant empty stare and her bottom lip begins to tremble. Oh *fuck,* I want to kill the bastard. I pour her some water. She is shaking so much, the water spills out of the glass as she takes it.

Jax jumps up so quickly, his chair practically knocks over, "Enough! This is not a few questions!"

"No, Jaxson, this information might be helpful. It could mean everyone's safety."

Bella grabs Jax's hand and pulls him back down. "Jax, let Mum finish, it's important to all of us."

"I told Garth everything I knew about James, which really wasn't much. James said he was born in Scotland. He said he went away to university and never went back. He said his family was deceased. He was in Wales on business, and I'm not sure for how long before I met him. He had no bank accounts anywhere. Nothing was in his name; not the apartment or any of the bills. The last week we were together, I heard him yelling at someone on the phone, but I don't remember much. My focus was on you two." She glances at Jax and Bella, then back to me. "The trips were always by train around London."

"Tell me about the cut: how did he get it, where was it and how deep?

"Maxwell, does it matter?"

"You know me, An—everything matters. Close your eyes and picture the cut. Describe what you see."

She closes her eyes and seemingly gathers her thoughts. "He walked into the emergency room holding a bandage on his right arm. I helped gather all the necessary information from him and then took him back to a room. The nurse pulled away the bandage to expose his wound. She informed him that it was deep and would require stitches. She asked him how he got it. He laughed it off, saying he was messing around with his friends. He needed twenty-six stitches. Now tell me, how does that help you?"

I get up and begin my pace. "It tells me he was in a knife fight and that he is left-handed."

"You're right, Maxwell, he was left-handed but, how could you possibly know that?"

"A wound that size was probably not from horsing around with friends. From where you described the location of the wound, it tells me he put his right arm up to block the knife, and his left hand would have reached for it. Did your friend find out anything else?"

"Yes, Garth found out he was married, but I didn't believe him. I could not imagine that the man I loved and trusted would betray me in the cruelest way possible. That's why I went to see for myself."

I stop pacing and pull her out of her chair and into my arms. This woman has become so much to me, I hope someday I will be able to express that to her. I hold her tightly as she begins to cry. "I'm so sorry that I had to put you through this. I'll need to see those trinkets now, please."

"Of c-course, Maxwell. I'll be right back." She leaves and I have a seat.

The three of us sit around the table, staring at each other . . . waiting. "Jax, believe me, mate, if there was any other way, I would never have put her through this."

He pours himself a scotch, staring at the amber liquid as if all the answers are buried there. "I know, Max. What the hell was this man into?"

Before I can answer, An walks in with a box. "Here is everything I kept. I really don't know why I kept it all, maybe to remind me of the fool I was."

Jax leaps up, startling all of us. "Don't ever consider yourself a fool; you did nothing wrong. I will have none of that, you hear?! The only person to blame is my father." Emotions are running high; we all need to dial it down a notch.

"An, maybe you could make us some tea, please." I quickly shoot a look at Jax that I know he'll understand. When An makes tea, it calms her. I walk over to the box and lift the lid. I'm quickly looking through the contents. Shock is all I can register; I know exactly what my father was into.

I begin to close the box when Bella gets up, "What's in the box, Max?"

She reaches in and lifts up one of the necklaces. I quickly take it from her and whisper in her ear, "Not now, Bella."

Jax follows An. "Mum, let me help you with the tea."

"Maxwell, is anything in the box useful?" An glances over her shoulder at me.

"It's too soon to tell, however I will go through it later. I think we've all had enough for today."

"Thank you. I would like to lie down for a bit, if you would excuse me, please."

The minute An is out of ear shot, Jax and Bella are all over me. "Max, what the fuck is in the box?"

"Calm down," I hold my hand up for emphasis. "I had my suspicion from the story An told, but I knew, from the moment I lifted the lid, what the old man was into. Both of you take a look and tell me what you see."

Bella lifts the lid and begins to pull them out. Each one is more spectacular than the last. When she pulls out the last one, she gasps. Her eyes are wide and as she opens her mouth to speak, but only silence is uttered.

Jax picks up some of the items. As he looks at them, his jaw becomes tight and his face reddens. He's going to lose it, and I might not be able to stop him. "Jax, please try and calm down; think of your mum."

"Max, are these real?" Bella finally finds her voice.

"One look at these, and even to a layperson, such as myself, I can see they are very valuable. I also venture to say that the '*day trips*' were for moving the merchandise around. I don't think An had a clue to any of this."

Jax closes his eyes and takes a few deep breaths. "Max, do you think he was a fence, a thief, or both?"

"I'm not sure. I'm going to look into some of these pieces and see if I can find out anything about them. In the meantime, I really think we should hold off for a couple of days. You've waited this long, a few more days to confront him won't matter."

Bella gets up and as she heads toward the door, she stops and turns on her heel. "I'll give you two days, but then I'm leaving. I want answers—answers that only *he* can give me."

With that, she's gone, leaving Jax and me alone. "You're very quiet, what are you thinking?"

"I'm thinking this is a big arse can of worms we've opened. I'm also thinking . . . if this is true, then there is a lot more danger than we originally thought. Are two days going to be enough? You know Bella; when she makes up her mind there's no changing it."

"I don't know what to think anymore. I wouldn't have believed it, but seeing all of this stuff with my own eyes changes that. I better get started figuring this out to meet Bella's deadline." I gather everything up and put it back in the box. "Go spend time with Raven and Antonia. If I need you, I will let you know." I leave him alone with his thoughts and head back toward my place. Right now, all I want and need is Jackie.

Chapter Four

Jackie

MAX HAS BEEN GONE a lot longer than I thought he would be. I gave up on him joining me for a soak in our beautiful tub. I'm hungry. Maybe I can attempt to cook something. Oh, who am I kidding? Unless it's salad or coffee, I'm screwed. I throw on one of his shirts and head into the kitchen just as he walks in with a box. His face is pale. "Max, what happened?" He closes his eyes and seems to be at a loss for words.

He puts the box on the table and lifts the lid. "Jackie, look at all of this and tell me what you see."

By the look of disbelief on his face, I'm almost too scared to look. I'm finally able to pull my eyes away from him and take a peek. "What I see are some very expensive pieces of jewelry thrown in a box." As I dig around some more, I find a few pictures and pull them out. They are of An and a man that I can only assume is James Phillips. "Max, what's this all about?"

"Well, I figured out what was bothering me. Nowhere in the file did it ever say what kind of sales James was in. I finally had to sit down with An and have her tell me everything she could remember about him. When she said she had some *trinkets,* I asked to see them."

"No! You think he was a thief?"

"As much as I don't want to believe it, yes I do. What other explanation could there be?"

"You don't think An knew this, do you?"

"At that time, I don't believe so; she was only seventeen when she met him. But now, I'm sure she realizes a lot more."

"What are you going to do? Are you still leaving tonight?"

Maxwell

WHENEVER SHE'S NERVOUS, SHE bites her bottom lip; her teeth are digging into it. "No, not tonight." I brush a few strands of hair off of her face. She closes her eyes, takes a deep breath, and when she opens them again, they are filled with tears.

"When will you go? Don't try and tell me you're not."

"Bella gave us two days before she's on that plane."

"That doesn't leave you much time. What's the plan?"

"Well, for starters, I need to figure out where these came from. I'm not sure if he's the middle man, the thief, or the fence."

I close my eyes and rub my temples. She knows I do this when my head starts to pound. She takes a hold of my hands and pulls them away from my head. "Max, come with me now."

"Gladly, baby." *God, she's beautiful.*

"I can't have you getting this stressed out. You know how I worry about you." She takes me into the living room and we sit by the fireplace. She wraps her arms and legs around me as I nestle between her legs.

"I think you're on overload right now. You need to organize your thoughts and make a plan."

"I think I'm going to take a picture of each piece and do a Google image search to figure out if there is any information on them. That could lead me to any reports of stolen jewelry and any insurance claims. I'm not an expert, but they look to be very expensive. An said she met him when he came to the hospital. She was studying to be a nurse and he came in with a cut. I've determined it was from a knife fight."

"How could you know that if you weren't even there?"

"He claimed he was horsing around with friends. He needed twenty-six stitches and, from where it was, it sounded like a defensive wound." I nuzzle in closer as she rubs my head.

"You only have two days and there are quite a few pieces there. I can help you with the search." She continues nursing my temples.

"I will take all the help I can get. I know Bella won't budge on the timeline. I swear, sometimes she is worse than Jax. I need to take my mind off of this for a bit. What happened with the new horses that came in today?"

"The colt seems to be pretty mellow and easy to work with. The filly is going to be trouble. I'm not sure she will work out. I'm going to work with her exclusively to see if she can be a good fit."

"You know I worry every time you go out there. All the reassurance and protective gear doesn't help me." My whole body tenses as I think about this. I close my eyes and sigh.

"I know, but I can't live in a bubble—none of us can." *If it were up to me, I would put her in a gilded cage, inside a plastic bubble if it meant she would be safe.*

I turn in her arms and kiss her so tenderly. "Babe, I love you. I love everything about you. I love how you giggle every time you take your first sip of orange juice, and I don't even know why, yet, I still love it. I love the submissive side that you're not afraid to show me. I love your strength in everything you do. I love how gentle you are with the kids when you're teaching them about the horses. I love how you calm me, yet, I love how you make my heart race. I love falling asleep with you in my arms and waking up with you still there. I love how you tuck the blankets in around us like a cocoon. I love your endless legs—God, do I love them. I heard something one of the kids said the other day by Winnie the Pooh, '*If you live to be one hundred, then I want to live to be one hundred minus one so I never have to live a day without you'.*" I reach in my pocket and pull out a box that has been burning a hole all week. "I know you said you would marry me, but I need the world to know. I need them to know that you saved me when no one else could."

She opens the box and begins to tremble. I think this just became real for her. "Do you like it? I designed it myself. I wanted a heart-shaped diamond. My heart will always be in your hands." I take the ring and slide it on her finger and then, I kiss it.

"Max, I love it. You know all I really need is you. It's all I've ever wanted."

"I know but I need it." It's just a whisper, but I know she gets it.

"The first sip always tickles my nose."

"Really?" I chuckle at this revelation, and then give her a soft peck on the lips. "I know you said you wanted a long engagement, but how long are we talking here?" *I know I can't be like Jax, but I'm done waiting.*

She strokes the side of my face and I close my eyes. "Max, this is important to you, isn't it?"

"More than you will ever know."

"Dare I ask why?"

"Cards on the table, baby. Next month I'll be thirty-nine. I've lived half my life already. I'm at the top of the slope with the skis on. If we have a child next year, I'll be fifty-eight when the kid graduates high school, and that's just the first one. I want grandbabies and I want to enjoy them all. I want to experience so much with you." *Her eyes are wide and she is chewing on her bottom lip. I hope I didn't screw myself here.*

"Exactly how many babies are you planning on?"

"I grew up as an only child. I never want that for my own. All the responsibility falls to that one kid. You said yourself that with the big age difference between you and Dylan, it was like being an only child. It's lonely most of the time. I know that Junior and Antonia are here. And, knowing Jax, he is probably trying to talk Raven into having another baby already. But no one stays around forever."

"I agree with you about having more than one child, however, please understand, I'm not a baby factory! I get that you're going to be thirty-nine and you want to enjoy life. We said early spring; how about the end of May? My understanding is that Scotland, in the spring, is spectacular."

"Little more than six months; I can deal with that. I know you're not a baby factory, but at least two, please. Think of the fun we will have."

"I love you, Max." She gives me a squeeze then pats my back lightly. "Come, we need to get started on that jewelry. Two days is not a long time, and you know Bella."

I gather her in my arms and head toward the office.

Isabella

I TAKE MY TEA and head up to my room. It was a long flight from Italy and I know Michael is already asleep. I go into my sitting room so I don't wake him. I gave them two days to get it together. Reality is—I would give them more, if they really needed it. I don't think they do. I know that Max doesn't want to go, and now with Antonia, I'm sure Jax would put it off. I need answers, though. I need to know why he left. Was I to blame? I don't think so, but I need to ask. I thought maybe I could forgive him and try to have a relationship with him. But, after seeing my mum reliving her past all over again—a past that she felt shamed by—I realize that's impossible. He put her through hell. Poor Cindy made him the center of her universe; she saw death as her only option. How could she do that to her child? This family has been through so much, I'm not sure we can take another blow. Maybe I should forget about him, but now, I have *more* questions.

"Bella?"

I leap out of my chair, nearly spilling my tea. "Michael, I didn't hear you come in."

"I called your name, but you never answered. I didn't mean to startle you. Why are you sitting here, alone in the dark?"

"Max had some more questions before we could leave." I begin to explain everything that went down: all the new information we gained from Mum, the possibilities behind the trinkets, and my deadline. He sits there in silence. "Michael, did you hear me?! He's a thief!"

"I heard you, Bella. I don't want you to go. I don't see any good coming from this. You know what the man is, and meeting him will change nothing. Do you think you're going to have a warm and fuzzy family reunion? If he wanted that, he would have gotten in touch with you years ago. It's not like we were in hiding. You need to let this go, if not for your sake, then do it for Junior."

"Don't you dare throw Junior in my face; you know I would do anything for my son. I feel like if I don't see this through to the end, then I will always wonder 'what if'."

"For Christ sake, what if *what?* He's a crook and a dead beat. He left because he wasn't man enough, not because of anything you did. I read the file, love. He finds his mark and fucks them; that's what he does. They mean nothing to him and, by what you're telling me now, he probably uses them as a front. Is that someone you want in your life? I won't have him anywhere near my son—*ever!*"

"How can you be so cut and dry, Michael?"

"Sometimes, it really is black and white—you just have to open your eyes and take off the blinders, Bella." He takes my cup of tea and sets it down. "Come back to bed, my love."

I reach for him and he pulls me tightly to his chest. I'm even more confused now than before. "Michael, I will think about it tomorrow, right now, help me forget . . . please."

Anwan

THIS HAS BEEN SUCH a difficult day, reliving the hurt and shame. My shame. A shame that I thought I kept buried for so many years. I don't know what to tell my children . . . to make them give up the idea that they will get answers from James. I know him better than anyone. I know they are going to walk away with more questions than answers. I learned the hard way how deceitful James was. It would be easy to sit here and blame him for everything, but . . . in reality, I'm just as much to blame. When Garth showed me everything, I was in shock. But, then looking back, I realize I had blinders on. I wanted this man to be all that I dreamed he was. The one positive that I took away from all of this was my children. I made them my world, and I don't regret one day of that. I have kept journals from the very first day I met James. Every day with him—documented in black and white. I can't show anyone; they are too personal. But, I still have the report from Garth. It's old; however, knowing Maxwell, he will want to see it. I go to my closet and pull out my box of journals. I haven't looked at these in so many years; *a reminder of my many mistakes.* I thought about throwing them away, but they are a part of me, a part of who I once was. I pull out the first journal and begin to look at the entries; I was so naive. His good looks and charming ways pulled me into a rabbit hole . . . an adventure into the unknown; one that became a nightmare. As I flip through the journal, I come across a flower that I pressed between the pages: a beautiful, pink Armeria. It was from my wedding day. I don't want to read any of this, but I can't avert my eyes. *"Today I married my soul mate."* What a fool. *"Today James sang to me, he has such a beautiful voice."* The day of Jaxson's wedding, when he sang to Raven, my mind flipped right back to this day, reminding me of how beautiful James sang. I can't do this, putting myself through the hurt again. I flip through some more pages and find the report. I don't think it will be of any use, but I will give it to Maxwell in the morning. As I package up the journals, a picture falls out. It's of a group of men. I remember taking the picture for James. It was from one of our day trips. I will give it to Maxwell with the report. I really wish they wouldn't go. I might be able to convince Jax, but not Bella. She is so much like James and sometimes . . . that scares me.

I go through the rituals of getting ready for bed, but I know sleep won't come tonight. As I lie in bed, I close my eyes and silently pray that my children find the peace they are searching for, the peace that has eluded me for so long.

Chapter Five

Raven

JAX FINALLY CAME TO bed, but it was almost dawn. I could tell he was upset, but when he's ready, he will tell me everything. I have to tell him that I received a package yesterday from Hage; enclosed is a letter from Duke. I'm concerned that this will only add more stress on his plate. I look over at him and, even in sleep, he seems troubled. I am trying not to interfere but I think it's time I have a talk with Bella. She is the only person who can stop this before it goes too far.

Suddenly, I hear Antonia over the baby monitor; however, I knew it was feeding time before she announced her hunger. I reach over and kiss Jax before heading into the nursery with Bo quickly following next to me. I scratch his neck and sigh, not even Bo is getting a full night sleep.

Entering, I notice that Jax had set up the *Doctor Who* night-light and I giggle. He can be such a playful little boy and I hope he never loses that. I pick up Antonia, kissing her soft curls and begin changing her. When she first starts to eat, she always makes her little hands into fists. This is my favorite time of the day; it's quiet and I can enjoy sitting in front of the window with my daughter, overlooking the fields. I swear she has the best view in the house. Watching the change of seasons from this window will be breathtaking. I haven't looked at the letter from Duke, and I'm not sure I want to. I know Jax will say information is key, but—unlike Jax—I want to be done with the past. My mom is doing so well with her therapy, I've even started going with her. I need to find a balance with her. I've been so independent for so long that I find it hard to let her mother me in any way. I don't know how she survived all that she did. I need to find a way to talk my mom out of confronting Vincent. She thinks this will help her with closure, I think it will only poke a burning fire. I wanted to talk to Jax about it but, with everything going on, now is not a good time. Antonia is done nursing and is fast asleep. I need to talk to Jax. As much as I would rather wait, I know he will get upset if I don't tell him everything right away. As I get Antonia settled into her crib, I can't help but bask in her beauty. She really is a combination of the both of us. She has my thick, black, curly hair and pouty lips. She has Jax's blue eyes and chiseled cheek bones. I'm so blessed that she survived so much before she even got here.

I head back to our bedroom, quickening my pace at the sound of strange voices coming from there. When I open the door, I see Jax in the throes of a nightmare. I know not to wake him, but my heart feels like it will leap out of my chest. He's never had one before and I know it's the stress that is triggering this. "I waited and waited. Please come back, I'll be good I promise!" he yells out while thrashing. My heart is breaking I can't stand here and listen anymore.

I go to the foot of the bed and try stroking his leg, "Jax, it's Raven, I'm here, Jax," I say softly. He leaps up and opens his eyes; he seems confused, looking around the room almost unsure of where he is. I'm still talking softly, hoping the fog clears for him. He finally hears me, and he must realize where he is.

"Raven, I'm sorry. Did I hurt you?"

"Jax, please don't be sorry and no, you didn't hurt me." I climb into bed and pull him into my arms. He's in a pool of sweat and still shaken. "Shh, don't say anything. Let me hold you, please." As I hold him and stroke his back, he begins to calm down. "I'm going to set up the tub, and then we will get cleaned up."

"I don't want to talk about it, Raven."

I pull his face up to mine and rest my forehead upon his. "When you're ready. And if you're not, that's okay too."

I get up and go set up the tub. I know it will be the best thing to relax him. He walks into the bathroom and he has dark circles under his eyes. " Come get in the tub, please." He climbs in and I climb in behind him so I can hold him for a change. I have so much to tell him about before he leaves, but now I'm not so sure.

"I'm sorry," It's just a whisper but I heard him.

"You have nothing to be sorry for."

"Sweetheart, I need to tell you what I've learned; nothing good, I'm afraid," he adds. I hold him tighter. "After a lengthy meeting with Mum, Bella, Max, and myself, we discovered some things about our father; none of them good."

"How did all this come about?"

"Max and his tingle sense."

"Oh, that's never good. What did he figure out?"

Jax proceeds to fill me in on their meeting and I'm shocked and saddened by what An had to go through, not just with James but her own family too. To know now that James is not only a bigamist but a thief as well. It's all too much to process.

"Jax, please tell me you're not going; clearly, you can see no good will ever come out of this."

"Bella gave us two days and then she is leaving. I can't let her go alone."

"Can't Michael talk to her? She has to see how dangerous this is; she's not a fool."

"I honestly don't think anyone will be able to get through to her."

"What's bothering you? And don't say 'nothing'—I know something is."

"I don't want to load you with anything else, but our deal is no secrets." I mindlessly stroke his chest.

He turns around so he can see me. "Go ahead, I'm listening."

"First, a package came yesterday from Hage, in it was a letter from Duke. Before you freak out, I didn't read it and I'm not sure I want to. Secondly, I went to a therapy session with my mom yesterday and she is talking about confronting Vincent." I wait for the storm that is coming. Surprisingly, he is very quiet. He closes his eyes and tilts his head back. He takes a few deep breaths, probably trying to gain some composure. "Jax, are you going to talk to me?" He lifts his head and opens his eyes. They are dark, very dark.

"Why? Please explain to me why she would want to confront Vincent? She is a smart woman and clearly, she can see no good would ever come of it. I know everyone is in jail. But still, Raven, you have to talk some sense into her."

"I have tried—believe me—I have. She is pretty adamant about it."

"What has the therapist said about it, or is that too personal to ask?"

"I honestly don't know; I wasn't in the session."

"What was in the package that Hage sent?"

"Besides the letter from Duke, there were some papers that Max and I need to sign. They have enough on him that Max and I won't have to testify. I really don't want to go back to the states, but if my mom goes back, I can't let her go alone."

"I understand, but your mum is not going back there. I will have to negotiate with her."

Oh Jax and his new found negotiating skills. "What if that doesn't work?"

"I will never let you anywhere near Vincent. If I have to, I will take her myself."

"I love you, but please go easy on her. Now let's get out of here; the water is getting cold and I'm hungry." I get up and give him my hand. He reaches for it and kisses the inside of my wrist. I shudder; his lips will *always* have that effect on me.

Maxwell

JACKIE AND I SPENT hours combing the Internet and the results weren't good. She finally fell asleep on the sofa. I need to head back to the main house and let everyone know what we found out. I love that we live close to everyone, yet we have our own sanctuary. I need both, more than anyone will ever realize. I look up from the computer and watch my sleeping angel. I can't wait to get married and start a family. I lift her up and carry her to bed; the bad news can wait a little longer. I need her softness, it's what grounds me. Through her, I see the good in the world. Through her, I see hope. That's what makes me want to have children again. As I carry her, she nuzzles into my neck. "Mmm, Max, where are we going?"

"To bed; I need to lose myself in your loving arms for a while."

She's kissing my neck and I might not make it to the bedroom. She begins to run her finger up the back of my neck, massaging my head. She knows I have a headache . . . she always knows. "How bad is your head, Max?"

"Nothing that an hour or two—lost in you—won't cure, baby."

"You never slept, did you? You can't keep doing this, Max. You'll be no good to anyone if your head gets worse. Promise me you will rest."

"I promise, just as soon as I have my way with you." I climb into bed with her still in my arms. She pulls me toward her and softly brushes her lips over mine. "Help me forget for a while, Jackie . . . *please.*"

She slowly kisses me softly, slowly . . . tenderly; feeling her touch relaxes me. "Lose yourself in me, Max."

I slowly peel away what little clothes she has left, leaving a trail of kisses in their wake. Gentle is what I need right now to wipe away all the harsh realities. I kiss up one leg and down the other; magnificent works of art that I will never get enough of. I lock my arms around her legs, spreading her wide for me. Her skin is so soft, and she smells so sweet as I work my way up to her core. I find my prize and she is so ready for me, but I need more. I work my tongue around her clitoris and gently tug with my teeth. She begins to shake and digs her nails into my shoulders. She knows what those nails do to me. She's there, so ready for me. I pull myself up to my knees and rub my cock up and down, stroking her very gently. When I know she's at the edge, I push my way in very slowly. When I'm all the way in, I stop. Her eyes grow wide and she bites her bottom lip. I lean down and brush my lips up her neck. I hold still—hard as stone—throbbing deep within her. I rest my forehead on hers, "Take me, baby."

"Flip me over, Max—*now!*"

My eyes grow wide with wonder. *Wow, demanding Jackie is hot.* I waste no time and follow her command. She's on top of me now and taking full control.

"Shut your mind off now, and give me your hands." She takes my hands and puts them on her breasts, helping me work her nipples, bringing her into a frenzied state. Neither of us is going to last much longer. She begins slowly gliding up and down my cock. My hips are rising up to meet her, slow and steady. Her body begins to flush and I know she's there, trying to take me with her. I start to shake and I know I can't wait any longer. I put my hands on her hips and pull her down hard to meet my upward thrust. That does it, I explode within her. She lets out a whimper and cries out my name. I pull her toward me, holding on tight, feeling her heart race next to mine . . . *beautiful.*

All I can do is whisper, "I love you . . ."

Raven

I GRAB THE BABY monitor and head downstairs to the kitchen. I told Jax to get Antonia cleaned up and meet me in the kitchen. I am going to, at least, learn how to make eggs. When I turn the corner, I find Max and Jackie are already there. *Thank God*—Max is making French toast. I grab a cup of coffee and have a seat. Before I can say anything, the monitor comes to life and what I see and hear next floors me. Max, Jackie, and I sit in front of the screen with our coffee, silently watching the show.

Jaxson

RAVEN ASKED ME TO get Antonia and meet her in the kitchen. I head toward the nursery, and I can hear my beautiful daughter cooing. I scoop her up and begin to change her. "My princess, I love being a dad. If your mum would consent, we would have ten babies. I'm realistic, knowing that will never happen, so I need to negotiate with your Aunt Jackie to get the ball rolling. After all, Uncle Max is not getting any younger. Okay, Antonia, your beautiful mum is attempting to make breakfast. Bless her for trying, but thank God we don't have to survive on what she comes up with. Now here is the plan. I need you to hang out with your Aunt Jackie, and be really good. I need you to make her want to start having babies right away. Now, I know you can do this for me and Uncle Max. Let's pick out something for you to wear that Aunt Jackie got for you. That might help the cause." I go about getting her ready and I can only hope my plan works.

Raven

I'M TRYING NOT TO laugh; even through all the madness, he can still be so playful. I look at Jackie's face, expecting to see her in total shock and instead, she is biting her lip and trying not to laugh. "Jackie, you know he's . . . well . . . he's just being Jax."

"Oh, Raven, I'm not laughing at Jax. I'm laughing because he thinks he wants ten kids!"

After hearing Jax's plan, Max silently goes back to making breakfast. "Max, you're awfully quiet. Please don't tell me you're a part of his crazy plan?"

"Raven, unlike my crazy arse brother, I don't want ten babies . . . five will do."

Jackie's coffee cup crashes to the floor. Max is on her in a second. "It's okay, babe, we can take it one at a time."

I don't think that helped her at all. It's at that moment I notice the ring. Maybe they finally set a date. I'm about to ask when I hear him coming down the hall.

Jax walks into the kitchen with Antonia. "Good morning, everyone." He smiles but it slowly fades as we collectively stare at him. "Okay, why is everyone staring at me? I've only just gotten up, what could I have possibly done now?"

I hold up the baby monitor, "Ten? Really, Jax?" I smirk. It's time for Antonia to eat, so I take her and leave Jax to work himself out of the hole he dug himself into.

Jaxson

"HOW MUCH DID EVERYONE hear?" I have to remember that damn monitor is always on.

Max hands me a cup of coffee. "Enough to screw us both; let's just leave it at that." He smacks my back. "I have information about An's trinkets." He grabs his mug and leans his back against the counter. "It appears they are all stolen. Insurance was paid, so legally, they belong to the insurance companies." he says before blowing into the cup, then taking a swig.

My mum walks in looking dog-tired. I pull her into a hug, "Let me get you some coffee, Mum." She nods then sits down and hands Max an envelope.

"Ma'am, what is this?"

" It's the original report on James from my friend, Garth, and a group picture from one of our day trips that I found in my journal."

I clench my jaw, trying to retain some control. "Mum, is there anything else you might have overlooked that you think we should know?" I try to keep my voice steady.

"Jax, All I have left are my personal journals. If I thought they would keep you from going, I would give them to you. However, I don't believe anything will stop you." She raises a brow as she takes her mug out of my hands.

I look at the baby monitor and see Raven is putting Antonia down for a nap. When I look up, everyone is staring at me. "Don't even say a word, none of you. Max, after breakfast, we have a lot to go over. We have a buyer for the company. And a package came yesterday from Hage. Where is Rose this morning?" I'm surprised Raven's mum isn't joining us for breakfast.

Max turns pale, "I don't think she is back from her daily run yet, is there a problem, Jax?" *I'm not sure Max could handle another thing.*

"I need to talk to her before we leave." I put my mug down and take a seat. Max begins serving up breakfast as Raven comes in with her mum.

"Ahh, Rose, just in time; Max made breakfast. Afterwards, I have some stuff to go over with you. How was your run?" I need to keep things light and my temper at bay.

"It was good. I've been exploring different sections of the property. I don't know if I will ever see it all," she says with exasperation then directs her attention toward Jackie. "Jackie, how are the new horses?"

"The colt will be fine but the filly will need a lot of work. Are you going to come down to the barn again today?"

"Yes, I enjoyed working with the children, that's if you don't mind."

"I would love the extra set of hands."

I take a step back and watch everyone laughing and just being a normal family and I wonder why can't we have this all the time? Is that so much to ask for?

Raven takes my hand, snapping me out of my daydream. "A penny for your thoughts?"

"I'm enjoying the normal for a change, sweetheart." I pull her tight, "Did you put the package on my desk?" I add.

"Back to reality. Yes, and go easy on my mom, *please.*"

"I will, if you promise to go easy on Bella." I lift her chin up and laugh, "I know you just as well as you know me." We finish up breakfast and I grab another cup of coffee. "Come on Max, we've got lots to discuss."

Raven

"CONGRATS ON THE RING; you did good. Now start making babies. You're not getting any younger, mate." I hear Jax talking to Max as they head down the hall.

My mom and Jackie head out to the barn, leaving me with An. "Did you get any sleep? You look tired." I shift in her direction, giving my full attention.

"Not really. I just wish there was something I could say to them to stop them from going. I have a bad feeling about all of this."

"Do you think I have a chance of getting through to Bella? I don't want Jax to go. I don't see any good coming from this."

"My daughter is more stubborn than all of them combined. She is the most like James in looks and temperament." She waves off the idea before picking her cup up for a sip of coffee. "What's going on with your mum? Something is bothering her. I tried to talk to her about it but she didn't say much."

"She wants to confront Vincent. I get why she wants to but I don't think she sees the big picture."

"Raven, do you honestly believe that my son is the best person to talk to her about this? Dear God, you know how he is; poor Rose won't stand a chance."

"I know, but he promised he wouldn't bully her. Besides, she won't listen to me."

"Well, let me know if there is anything I can do to help. I'm going to try and rest for a bit." An heads out and I'm left alone.

I need to piece together what I'm going to say to Bella. Lost in my thoughts, staring out the window, I jump as I hear a noise behind me. I turn and see one of the walls in the kitchen pop open; out steps Michael, Jax's nephew! I gasp, " How did you do that?"

"It's a secret passageway that Uncle Jax found. Come on, I'll show you." He holds out his hand.

I get up and head into the passageway. Michael turns on a flashlight and leads the way, with Bo right behind me. "Michael, how many passageways are there?"

"There are five that Miss Rose and I have explored. There is one that you can take from the main house all the way to the stables. Uncle Max showed me that one. Miss Rose and I were going through them, when we noticed strange carvings on the walls."

"You and my mom come through here?"

"Oh, Miss Rose loves to explore with me. She's the best!" he states enthusiastically.

I'm happy they enjoy spending time together, exploring. "Where does this one lead?"

"There is a spiral staircase up ahead. Once we climb that, we will be right outside my bedroom door. Isn't this great?"

I laugh at his excitement and I'm sure Jax was just as excited. "Michael, maybe tomorrow you can show me another one."

"Sure, Aunt Raven, that would be fun. If you look to the right, there is another tunnel. But, I haven't been down there yet."

We get to the top of the steps and he presses on the wall. It pops open. Sure enough, we are right outside his bedroom. "Thanks for the short cut, Michael. I need to talk to your mom."

"No problem. I'm going into my room to watch some television."

He doesn't seem to be his usual energetic self. He never wants to sit around and watch television, only if it's *Doctor Who,* of course. He seems a little off. I hope he's not getting sick. "Michael, you feel okay?"

"Just a little tired, Aunt Raven."

"Go get some rest." I watch him head off into his room and I go look for Bella.

Chapter Six

Jaxson

MAX AND I HEAD into my office to discuss business. I need to see what Hage sent and I know Max wants to tell me what he found out. However, first order of business is Jackie. "Max, what happened with Jackie?"

"Jump right in, why don't you, mate? I had the ring made and then I waited until I figured out exactly what I wanted to say. Of course when I started, it was like one giant run-on sentence. I persuaded her to get married sooner rather than later. I want a family, but I realized this morning that she's scared."

"What do you think she's scared of?"

"I don't think it's of being a mum; she is great with all children. I think it has to do with actually having the child. I need to figure out her fear and then fix it."

"Did you try asking her? I mean that just seems to be the logical approach."

"No, Jax, I haven't because I haven't had a minute to breathe."

"Well, the sooner we get this all done, the better for everyone. What did you find out about the trinkets?"

Max gets up and walks over to the window. He picks up the binoculars I keep close by and begins looking out over the vast property. "Jax, every piece was high-end and stolen. Insurance was paid on them. If he was acting as a fence, then why keep them? I think he is the thief. I don't know why he gave them to An. Based on all the reports and what An said, it's not like they were living in luxury."

"When were they stolen and from whom? Could the people or the places have had any meaning to him or Mum?"

"I don't know yet, but I do know that two days is not enough. We need to talk to Bella."

"Yeah, well, Raven was going to try and talk some sense into her today," I inform him. Max cocks his head and raises one eyebrow. "Yeah, Max, I know, but you got to love her for trying."

" How long is it going to take for the Raiders Inc. deal to go through and are you happy with the terms?"

"It should be closed in six months, possibly sooner, since it's a private company. I'm happy; I think we got a fair price. We need to look at whatever Hage sent over. Raven said there is a letter from Duke. But, we have a bigger problem to deal with, Rose wants to confront Vincent."

"Jax, we have to stop her. I know she thinks this will bring her some sort of closure, but it won't, trust me, I know. Revenge didn't help, it only added to the nightmares I have to live with."

I never asked him, but knowing Max, I didn't have to. "I'm going to try and talk to her today. I can't say it's going to be easy." I hand Max the package from Hage. "We need to deal with this. I thought part of Duke's deal was no contact ever?"

"Yeah, well, it says here that the only way Duke would agree to the terms was if this letter was sent to Raven. I'm sure, at that point, Hage would do whatever he had to do. At least Hage left Raven and I out of everything. The book with all the details of Vincent's dealings was enough for Hage to offer Vincent a plea deal; life—with no chance of parole in exchange for his testimony." I shrug. Max throws the papers on the desk, his face taking on a look of disgust. "What's the problem?"

"Who's to say that he won't be running his business from a jail cell? We have to talk Rose out of her plan to confront him. I'm sure if we explain to her that he can still be a danger to Raven, it would stop her."

"Max, I will negotiate with her. Don't laugh at me; I'm getting better at this every day. Do you think the papers Mum gave you will help in any way?"

"At a quick glance, the investigators papers seem pretty basic. It's the picture that I'm interested in. I'm not sure what it is about the picture, but I have to tell you, something seems almost familiar about it. I'm not sure, but I'm going to run it through an age progression program to see what comes up." He gathers up his stuff and heads out, leaving me to figure out how to stop Rose.

Rose

I ENJOY SPENDING TIME in the barn with Jackie. She is so comfortable to be around. She never pressures me; she just lets me be. Today, however, I can tell something is bothering her. She seems distant and troubled, quieter than usual. I take the brush from her hand and put my arm around her. "You look like you could use a hug. Do you want to tell me what's wrong?"

Her bottom lip begins to tremble and she starts to cry. "Shh, I've got you, Jackie; come sit down and tell me what's wrong. Nothing is so bad that it can't be fixed." We head over to a bale of hay and sit for a bit. I hold her in my arms, keeping my silence, I let her cry.

"Rose, I love him with all of my heart. But, I'm afraid." I'm glad that she feels comfortable talking to me. I try to be like a mom to her, knowing that she must miss her family.

"Tell me what you are afraid of? You know I would never judge you." I gently rub her back, offering her some comfort.

"Max wants a lot of children and I'm scared."

"Look at me," I demand softly and lean back as she raises her head. "It is natural to be scared of the unknown. I was scared when I was pregnant with Raven, and I'm a doctor." I wipe away her tears. "You can read all the books in the world, but until you actually do it, you won't know what to expect. That can be very scary. Gather strength from everyone around you. We are your family and we would never let anything happen to you. I promise you, every step of the way, I will be here for you, even if it's just to hold your hand. What else is bothering you, sweetie?"

"I was a twin. My sister, Madeline, didn't make it past a few hours. I was born first and apparently, I was the strongest. My mom is Japanese, Rose, and very small. The doctors were afraid she wouldn't make it to term. She went early and my sister just couldn't survive."

"Do you blame yourself for being strong? You know, logically, that's not true." She's very quiet, twisting her fingers in her lap. "Jackie, why haven't you told Maxwell?" She is biting her bottom lip, seemingly hesitant.

"What if something like that happens to me? Max will never survive and I don't think I would either."

I take her hands in mine. "Jackie, after I had Raven, I became pregnant again." Her eyes grow wide. "That's right. I was pregnant and I lost the baby at twenty-six weeks. It was very hard on Antonio, but even harder on me. I had to go through delivery and then bury my baby. We grieved, but we knew we did nothing wrong." I lift her hands up and place them on my heart. "Do you feel my heart beating? It still goes on, no matter what. The point is, you were not responsible for Madeline. Whatever happens, you will deal with it, and so will Maxwell. You can't try to stop every bad thing from ever happening; it's life. Be the best you can be and everything else will fall into place. You do, however, need to talk to Maxwell. He has the right to know your fears. You say you love him, well then trust him with your heart." I hold her in my arms and comfort her as her mother would. In the distance, I see Maxwell. "Jackie, Maxwell is on his way over here, and I think it's time you tell him everything."

"Okay," she barely whispers.

I wipe away her tears, kiss her forehead. Maxwell crouches down in front of Jackie. "Hey, babe, what's the matter?"

"I'll leave you two to talk." I'm not sure either one of them heard me, and that's okay. I start heading back to the main house to talk to Jax.

Maxwell

"OKAY, JACKIE, I'M NOT going anywhere, and neither are you, until you tell me everything. If I have to, I will lock you in the house and throw away the key!" I have to try and calm down. I can't scare her.

"Max, I'm cold; let's go inside and talk." Before she can say anything more, I put my arms around her and we head toward the house. I don't know why she is so upset, but I could never leave her like this. We get inside and she curls up on the couch, I cover her with a blanket. I light the fireplace and then make her a cup of tea. The ritual of making the tea has a calming affect. I snuggle up to her, pulling her into my arms. "Now, talk to me. Surely you know that you can tell me anything; I would never judge you."

She is chewing on her bottom lip and I gently pull it out from her teeth. "I'm afraid to have a baby." She says it so softly, but I hear every word.

"Is that what all this is about? Why now?"

"When you first asked me to marry you and said we could have a long engagement, I thought I could grow into the idea and settle my fears. It seemed so far off, but then last night, you wanted to nail down a date. You gave me a ring; it's real and it's happening. Now you're saying *five* children!"

"Why are you scared? You need to tell me everything, Jackie. I know you're holding back."

She's got a death grip on my hand. "I had a twin sister who died at birth. I thought you might have known when you ran a background check on me, but then you said you didn't look at anything personal, only what you needed for safety purposes."

"Wow, Jackie, I understand some of your fear but not all of it. Listen, you have to know it was not your fault that you lived." I squeeze her to me. "So, what else, babe?"

"Twins run in my family; what if it happens again? I'm afraid something like that would kill you." She looks up at me. Oh my God, she's worried about me . . . about my sanity.

"Babe, you are beyond words. Your kind and generous heart knows no bounds. Whatever is thrown at us, we will deal with together. Plus, medical science is much different today than twenty-five years ago. I don't expect you to be a baby factory. I would love to adopt, especially some of the children with disabilities that you work with. I love them all. But, babe, I really want to have a child with you; it would be a gift. I know how special you are and I want the world to know too. I promise we will do it together—one step at a time." I snuggle her into my arms and hold her tight. She is still so tense, and she's got a tight grip on my arm. I can sense there is something more.

"Hey, you might as well tell me everything, I'm going to find out anyway."

"I need to go home next week," she says quickly. My grip on her tightens.

"This *is* your home—for life."

"My birthday is coming up. Every year, I honor Madeline by having a cupcake at the repository where she's laid to rest. I try to spend the day with my mom, reflecting upon the last year. I have to go, Max."

"I know it's your birthday. I was trying to hold out giving you the ring until then, but it was burning a hole in my pocket. We go together—understood? I spoke to your father and asked for your hand in marriage. Now I can speak to him in person and settle any fears he might have, including that brother of yours."

"You spoke to my father?!"

"Of course, it's what any good gentleman would do. I assured him you would want for nothing in your lifetime, and that I would love you beyond the end of my days. I must say he was quiet impressed."

"What if you're not back in time?"

"I will be back, no matter what happens. I promise."

I pick up the remote and the music comes to life. As I hold her close in my arms, I know without her, I'm a shell of a man. I rock her gently and mindlessly sing to her. The lyrics are so beautiful about a man who is scared of the feelings a woman makes him feel. Stroking her back and softly singing soothes her. "I love you, baby, and I will do anything to make you happy . . . never forget that."

"Max, I've never heard that song, it's beautiful. Who sings it?"

"James Morrison. It's called "You Give Me Something." He's a young bloke, wickedly talented."

"What happened with Jax?"

"Well, we went over business stuff; nothing for you to worry about. He did say that Rose wants to confront Vincent. I don't know what the fuck she's thinking? I just want to keep us all safe."

"What was in the envelope that An gave you?"

"The original report that her friend ran on James and an old picture from one of their day trips. Which reminds me, I want to run the picture through the age progression software that I have. Everyone is so young, but something seems familiar." I sigh. "What's your plan for the rest of the day?"

"I want to go for a run and then, later this afternoon, I have a class coming in. Do you want to run with me?"

"Sure, let me load this picture and change." I get up and head to my office to load the picture. I'm staring at it and my tingle sense comes alive—*fuck!* As the faces begin to age, the locked gates within my mind open. A rage deep within me begins to boil. This can't be happening. The room is spinning out of control; down the rabbit hole, I'm falling. The program finishes, and I freeze on the face of my nightmares.

Raven

I NEED TO TALK to Bella and see if I can persuade her to give up this idea of meeting James, or at least giving her brothers more time. This house is so huge but I finally find her in the kitchen, making coffee. "Hey, Bella, do you have a minute?"

"Raven, I'm not changing my mind, so if that's why you're here, you're wasting your time."

"Bella, please don't get defensive. I would like to talk to you about the trip. Believe it or not, I do understand why you want to go. It took me a while to figure it out, but I got it. What I don't get is why the rush? If you value everyone's safety, why push them? Let them get all the information before jumping in blinded by emotions."

"How much time are we talking here? I will give them a few extra days, but nothing changes for me. I want answers that only he can give me. That man's blood runs through my veins and it disgusts me."

"If you really feel that way, then why go?"

"I look exactly like him. Mum has said many times that I have his personality. How do you think that makes me feel? Knowing what he's done, I need to know why."

"I'm not going to stop you, Bella, but give them some time if they need it, please."

"Okay, I'll go tell Jax." She gets up and heads out to find Jax. Now, if I could get my mom to agree, all would be right for a little bit.

Jaxson

I NEED TO FIND Rose and have a talk with her. I don't want to scare her, but there is no fucking way she is going anywhere near Vincent. I get up to go and as I turn around I find her standing in the doorway. "Rose, I was just coming to find you."

"I figured by now Raven told you and that you would be looking for me."

"Have a seat, please." *I need to try and remain calm.* "I need you to make me understand why you feel you have to see Vincent."

She is quiet for a bit, wringing her hands in her lap. "Jax, that man took so much from me." Her voice is soft and shaky. "I lost my soul mate. My daughter was taken from me and raised by others. I lost my career, which ultimately cost many people their lives. The procedure that I pioneered, had I perfected it, would have saved so many lives. I know that others tried to continue my research, but it was never the same. He destroyed Joseph's life. He raped and beat me. I need him to know that he didn't break me."

"How did he destroy Joseph's life?"

"Joseph was engaged when everything happened. He walked away from the relationship because he felt she would never be safe.

He made Raven and me his family. He watched me slowly fade away, and there was nothing he could do about it. He took care of me throughout the pregnancy. He was there when I delivered Duke. I realized Joseph thought there was more to our relationship and, at first, I chose to ignore it, thinking it was only his need to feel needed. Then not to long after Duke was born, he professed his love for me. He built up a vision in his mind that we could live happily ever after. He wanted to keep Duke and raise him as his own. He offered to marry me and make a stable life for all of us. That was the day I tried to take my own life. I realized how much was lost for all of us. I couldn't hurt him."

Shock is all I can register. "Does Raven know any of this?"

"No. What purpose would it serve? It won't change the past; that is dead and buried forever. I know now trying to take my life was wrong. I was overwhelmed with grief, fear, and rage. I didn't know how to deal with any of it. I've had more heartache in my life than anyone person should ever have to endure. Now you tell me, how could I not face the man that was the catalyst for most of it."

I honestly don't have any answers for her. I get up and pour us each a drink.

"Jax, you're very quiet, this is not like you."

"You're right. I'm at a loss here, part of me agrees with you and the other part doesn't. I don't know how to deal with all of this. Have you spoken to your therapist about what you're planning?"

"Yes, however, she doesn't understand the depths of who Vincent is."

"What about safety? Vincent got a deal, Rose. He got life in prison without parole. My fear is that he will continue to conduct his business from jail. Once he knows you're alive, all bets are off. I have to think of everyone's safety. I'm sorry; you're going to have to figure out some other way to come to terms with this."

"You know, Jax, I could leave, if I want to. I'm not a prisoner here."

"You're right, Rose, you can walk out that door anytime you want, however, you won't. You love your daughter and granddaughter too much to do that. Think of their safety."

"I've always put Raven's safety first. You can protect her and Antonia."

"You're right, I can. But if you go, it will break her heart, and I can't have that."

Her eyes grow wide and I know before she says anything, I don't even have to turn around. "Raven, I think you and your mum need to talk." I get up and head toward the door, "I love you and I'm here for you." I kiss her and head out to find Bella.

I MAKE A QUICK detour past the nursery to kiss my daughter. Honest to God, I don't know how I'm going to leave. I make my way downstairs and find Bella in the kitchen. "Hey, sis, I was just coming to find you."

"I spoke to Raven. I will give you a few extra days if you need them. I will tell you, no matter what—*I'm going*. But, for safety purposes, I will give you what you need."

I'm floored, how the hell did my wife do it? "You will?"

"Yes. I want everyone to be safe, Jax. If that's what it will take, then I will."

"I love you." I grab her, pulling her into my arms. "You can't possibly know how much this means to me. I need to find Max, let him know what's going on, and see if he had any luck with that picture."

As I turn to leave, Bella grabs my arm, "What picture?"

"Mum had a picture from one of their day trips. It was a group photo of dad with his friends. Max was going to run it through an age progression program."

"I'll go with you."

We head out toward Max's. I'm surprised he hasn't contacted me yet. Maybe he had no luck with it.

Jackie

MAX WAS SUPPOSED TO change for a run but he never came out of his office. I wonder if he had any luck with the picture. I head toward the office and it's very quiet. *Strange.* I open the door and it's dark. I could swear he was in here. I flip the light on and what I see stops me dead in my tracks; Max, sitting in the dark, almost in a frozen state. I rush up to him, but he's pale and shaking. "Max, please, what's wrong?" He's not saying anything. I hear Jax and Bella come up behind me. Jax takes my arm "Jackie, what the hell happened?"

"I don't know. Please, Jax, help him.

Jaxson

I CROUCH DOWN NEXT to him. "Hey, Max, it's me, mate, what happened?" *Nothing.* I look at the screen to see what he's fixated on, but all I see is the picture that Max aged. I've never seen him like this, not even when his grams died. His eyes are dark and hooded. His fists are clenched and his jaw is tight. He's shaking, pale, and as he closes his eyes, he begins to sob. For the love of *Christ,* what the hell? "Talk to me, Max. I can't help if you don't let me in."

"I told you I was a man out for revenge when my family was slaughtered. I found the murderers and got my justice. I never found the leader . . . until today."

I freeze at his words. "Max, who?"

He points to the man that our father has his arm around, and I feel my heart hit the floor. He growls out the name Miguel Dominguez. Suddenly, Max lets out a roar and in one quick sweep, throws everything off the desk. He's screaming as I try to hold him back, afraid he'll hurt himself. "Max, stop! What the hell are you saying? Who is Miguel Dominguez? Are you suggesting that Dad was somehow involved in Samantha and Elliot's deaths?"

He glares at me, "What the hell else am I supposed to think? My father has his arm around a murdering, Columbian drug lord, laughing and my family is *dead.* Don't tell me it's a coincidence. I don't do coincidences and neither do you, Jax."

I hear my mum gasp right behind me. I look and Raven has her arm around her. I never even heard them come in. I can only assume Bella must have called them.

Her knees buckle and Max catches her. "All I have ever done is love you and protect you like any of my children. I don't know much about that picture; it was over thirty years ago! Please, you must believe me."

"I do. I'm sorry. Please, calm down."

She's very pale and shaking. "Mum, please, Mum. Raven, call the doctor." Before I can finish, Rose is pushing me out of the way.

Everything is happening so quickly, yet it feels like slow motion. I step back and let Rose take over while I call the clinic.

Rose

"AN, LOOK AT ME; focus on my voice. Max, get an aspirin *now!* Focus, An, push whatever you heard out of your head and focus on my voice. Think about Antonia, how soft she is. Michael took me on an adventure today. He showed me some secret passages. Has he taken you yet?" I ask as Max comes back with the aspirin. "An, can you chew this for me, please?" I place the aspirin in her mouth and she begins to chew it. I make sure to keep her in a sitting position with bent knees. I keep talking to her about mindless stuff, keeping my voice soft and low. Trying to keep her focused on anything but what happened here. I check her pulse and it seems to be steadying. Having a clinic on the property is a good thing. Within minutes, the doctor shows up with the ambulance. Max sits next to her and takes her hand. His voice is low and steady. "You listen to me, you will not die today. Not on my watch and never because of all of this."

She seems to be getting some color back, but I know she will probably need to be airlifted to the hospital for further care. I don't know what went on in here, but someone needs to take control. "Jax, go with your mom to the clinic, she will probably have to be airlifted to the hospital."

They all race out the door and follow the ambulance to the clinic.

Chapter Seven

Jaxson

ONCE AGAIN, I'M WAITING—something I've never been good at. Finally, the doctor comes out, "Your mum's condition is stable but she will need surgery. She had a mild heart attack. She needs an Angioplasty, which will open the arteries. A deflated balloon is threaded through and then inflated. It's invasive and requires an overnight stay. It's pretty common, she is lucky whoever took care of her, when it happened, knew the right things to do; probably saved her life."

"When will you do this procedure and what are the risks involved?"

"We are prepping her right now. With any surgery, there are always risks," he rattles off the long list and I try my best to stay focused. "But this is the least invasive," he finishes then nods to the nurse who proceeds to hand me a clipboard. "You have some papers that you will need to sign before we can get started. You may see her before we take her in." He looks around the room at all of us and states, "Only one at a time and make it brief." He shakes my hand and pats my back before heading off to the OR.

"Thank you." I sign whatever they need and hand it to the nurse.

I head in to see my mum before they take her back. She looks so frail. The stress this past year has been unbearable and it's taken a toll on all of us. This however, is really bad. "Hi, Mum, you gave us quite the scare. Did the doctor explain what they are going to do?"

"Yes, how is M-Maxwell?" She begins to cry.

The monitors start beeping, *fuck.* "Mum, he will be fine. He's right outside the door, but they will only let one of us in at a time. We are all here for him, but if you don't calm down, I'm really going to lose it."

She clutches my hand, "Jaxson, I didn't know."

"Mum, he knows. Please, you need to calm down."

"Ma'am, we are going to give you something to relax you."

"Can you please give us one more moment before you give her that?" She nods and I call in Max and Bella.

I step back and let them know they need to make it quick before we all get thrown out of here.

Bella leans in and kisses Mum, "I love you, Mum."

She steps back and Max walks up to the bed. "Remember what I told you, not on my watch. I love you, Mum."

She smiles as the nurse puts a shot into her IV and she fades out. And now . . . we wait.

"I love you, Mum." I'm not sure that she heard me.

Raven

JACKIE IS ROCKING ANTONIA in her arms. I think it's more for her comfort than my daughter's. My mom is staring out the window, seemingly lost in thought. I put my arm around her and she smiles. "Raven, she will be okay, I spoke to one of the nurses and I think we got her here in time. What the hell happened to bring this all on?"

"Once again the past has reared its ugly head. I don't know all the details and honestly, I'm not sure I want to."

"Sometimes we don't have a choice. No matter how much we want to leave the past behind us, sometimes it's out of our hands. At least you can all lean on each other for support."

Her words remind me that she was alone for twenty years with no one for support.

They finally take An into surgery and the others have joined us in the waiting room. Waiting is not something any of them do well. Jax walks up and takes Antonia from Jackie's arms. He takes in a deep cleansing breath. "My salvation," he whispers. He kisses the tip of her nose. "You ground me."

"JAX, WHAT'S THE STATUS on your mom?" I ask as he heads back from the nurses' station. Before he can answer, the doctor comes out.

"Your mum did fine. She is in recovery and then they will be moving her to a private room. You can wait in there for her, if you like. Please try and keep the visitors to a minimum."

"Thank you. When can we take her home?"

"I will check her tomorrow. If all is well, she should be good to go home late in the afternoon. Expect her to be sore for a couple of days. She will have to follow up with a cardiologist. I'll give you a list when she checks out."

"Thank you."

Everyone heads into An's room, but I hold Jax back. "Before we head in there, tell me, do you think it might be possible that James could be involved somehow?"

"I have no idea and right now, I wish to God I never even saw that file, let alone the picture. I don't know what's going to happen next or how Max will want to deal with this. I just want it over with."

"It's no longer up to you; it's up to Max and how he chooses to pursue it. All we can do is support him."

"I'll support my brother as long as he makes the right decision. If not, I will negotiate with him until he does."

It's going to be a long bumpy road. "We will be okay. Come on, let's see if she's back in her room yet."

"Sweetheart, I wish I could believe that, I really do."

"I have faith, Jax . . . enough faith for all of us."

The nurses finally bring An in and get her settled in for the night. She's in and out of it, but it seems to register with her that we are there. I'm happy my daughter has no clue about anything going on around her. Life really does carry on whether we want it to or not. I put Antonia back into her carrier and take Jax's hand. We head out to the waiting room to be with everyone else. "Come sit for a bit."

He sits in the chair and I climb in his lap. I snuggle into him and close my eyes. Just breathing him in calms me. My heart is breaking for all of them. I know the worst is yet to come. I must have fallen asleep, when I open my eyes, daylight has filled the room. I look at Jax and he looks so tired, I doubt he slept. At least Antonia slept the entire time. The past few weeks she has been sleeping longer at night. "Hey, did you get any sleep?"

"No. Antonia is starting to stir, she probably needs to be changed and I'm sure she wants to eat."

"I'll take care of her." I get up, stretch, and head over to her. Her eyes are wide and she is kicking her little legs. After I change her, I begin to nurse her. I peek at Jax and he is smiling. "What are you smiling at?"

"It is so beautiful to watch you with her."

The nurse informs us that An is beginning to wake up. She reminds us that only two visitors at a time are allowed. We gather up all our stuff and head into her room.

Jax takes her hand, "Mum, you're fine. The surgery went well and we are going to try and get you released today."

"Maxwell, how is he?"

"He's fine mum, right outside that door. If you promise not to get upset I will let him and Bella in; you can only have two visitors at a time."

She waves her hand as if swatting a fly, "Nonsense, I want my family in here now."

I step outside and tell everyone to quietly slip into the room before we get into trouble.

She looks around the room at all of us, smiles, closes her eyes, and goes out again.

"Okay, everyone, she needs her rest; let's get some coffee." They all agree and head out the door. Jax takes Antonia. I kiss him and let him know I'll be out in a moment. I want to make sure she has everything she needs within reach. Her eyes open again. She is so sad and frail. She has been Jax's rock for so long. "An, look at me, please," I encourage. She begins to cry, and I wipe away her tears. "There will be none of this crying stuff. You are very strong and your family is looking to you for that guidance and strength. I know Max is hurting, we all are, but you know what? He will be okay. He has Jackie to lean on now. And I know she will support him and guide him through all of this. What this family can't deal with is anything happening to you. So pull it together and deal with the storm that is coming at us right now." I can't believe I just spoke to her like that, what the hell was I thinking?

"Raven, I could never want for a better daughter-in-law. You are all I ever wished for my son. With all you've been through, you still see the good and the happily ever after, *how?*"

"I have faith in my love for Jax and our family. It will see me through even the darkest of days. When Vincent held me captive, and I knew I was pregnant, I felt Jax all around me. I drew on his strength and now it's time this family draws on my strength and faith."

"You're a survivor, the strongest of us all."

"I don't know any other way. Now, how about I help you get cleaned up a bit. Before the others come back, I'm sure it will make you feel better."

"Thank you, my dear."

Jaxson

MICK WALKS IN. HE sees me and heads over. "Hey, Mick, is everything okay?"

He hands me two coffee carriers, "I figured everyone could use these right about now. How is Mrs. Phillips doing?"

"She had surgery and did fine. They will probably release her later today, barring no complications." I notice he's got a bag with him. "What's in the bag, Mick?"

"I know Raven grabbed the diaper bag, but I wasn't sure how long you would be here, so I brought some stuff for her. Do you think I can see Mrs. Phillips?"

I know I must have a look of disbelief on my face, but that was the last thing I expected him to ask me. He's looking down and picking an imaginary piece of lint off of his shirt. "Sure, I didn't realize you were close with my mum."

He lifts his eyes and smiles, "When you were in Switzerland, we would have tea and talk every day. She listens. She's a good friend and I respect her. I just want to see for myself that she's okay."

"Hey, you don't have to explain. My mum has that way about her. She will get you to tell her your whole life story in five minutes without you even realizing you're doing it. Come on, keep it upbeat, so she doesn't get stressed."

We head back to the room and my mum is awake, sitting up talking to everyone. She sees Mick and smiles. Wow, talk about me being clueless. "Hey, Mum, look who I found."

"Mick brought everyone coffee and some stuff for Antonia."

Raven hugs him, "You know . . . you're the best, Mick."

"Not really, Raven, I know how you are without your coffee. It's more for everyone's safety," he teases her.

I take Raven's hand and bring it up to my lips and kiss it gently. "Sweetheart, why don't we step out and give them a moment?" I glance over to Max and he ushers everyone out of the room.

"Mick, we will be out in the hall, if Antonia wakes, please let me know."

We step out of the room and Raven's speechless. "Sweetheart, I have no clue what is going on with them. All I know is, he said they talk a lot since our trip to Switzerland. I'm choosing to leave it at that."

"I don't think they are anything more than friends."

"Either way, sweetheart, I choose to keep my head in the sand on this one."

"Where is your mum?"

"She's at the nurses station, chatting up a storm."

"I have to tell you she might have been out of practice for twenty years, but her instincts kicked right in. She saved my mum's life."

"I know; I was amazed how quick and how accurate she was."

I pull her tightly into my arms, finding my comfort and solace. "I will always be grateful for all she has done."

"I love you, Jax."

"More, sweetheart, always more."

Anwan

"MICK, THANK YOU FOR coming. How are you? I'm sorry if I scared you."

"Ma'am, you can't get upset or it will set you back. If that happens, everyone will be all over me. Don't worry about me, I'm fine now that I know you're going to be okay."

I take hold of his hand for comfort. "Do you think Maxwell will be able to get past this? He was so close to having it all with Jackie, he can't let this set him back."

"I'm telling you; he will get past this. He has his family to lean on now, and, he has Jackie. Please trust me; he will be okay."

How do you know that, Mick? "

"If I can come back from the bowels of hell, he can too. Now, I'm going back to the house to get everything cleaned up and ready for your return. You need to follow doctor's orders."

"Okay, can you send Maxwell in, I want to talk to him privately."

I watch him head out the door, grateful for his kindness and friendship.

I need to talk to Maxwell alone, I know he will want to know everything I can remember about that bloody picture. I wish to God I never saved it, and then none of this would be happening. The door opens and he pops in, "Mick said you wanted to see me alone."

"I figured you would want to know everything I could remember about that picture."

"You are supposed to be resting, not getting upset over a picture."

"The sooner we get this over with, the sooner we can put this all in the past—where it *should* remain. I knew you would ask me for details. I tried to remember anything I could about it. I was seven months pregnant with Jaxson. I didn't want to go to London, but James insisted. There were four of them, and they were pretty good friends. James had me take the picture, but the man next to him, the man you called Miguel, refused to be in it. At the last minute, James pulled him in and I snapped the picture. Miguel started yelling, as did the man at the other end of the photo. James and the man next to him laughed. I don't even know their names. That is the only picture I have. I don't even know why I kept it. I have my personal journals, and the items I gave you. I assure you, I knew nothing about those men. If it will help you, I will give you the journals."

He takes my hand and squeezes it. "I don't need anything else. I know you were just as surprised as I was."

I can finally breathe a sigh of relief. I whisper, "I heard you call me mum, did you mean it?"

Before he can answer, everyone begins piling into the room. He's smiling, so I reach up and yank his ear.

"Ouch, what's that for?"

"You know perfectly well what that's for. Now, go find that doctor; I want to go home."

Everyone is laughing and right now, that is exactly what we all need. Max throws his hands up and starts mumbling while he walks out the door.

Bella begins gathering my clothes for me. "Mum, you know you really should listen to the doctor."

"The sooner I get dressed, the sooner I can get out of here."

Just then, Maxwell comes back in with the doctor. "Good morning, Mrs. Phillips, how are you feeling today?"

"I'm fine. I want to go home right now. I can assure you, we have a clinic at our estate with all the necessary equipment and a doctor on standby." That should pacify him

"You can go home. However, you need to reduce the stress in your life. I also want you to follow up with the cardiologist. He will probably recommend diet modification and exercise. I will sign the necessary paperwork, and then you will be good to go. You need to rest for this week and take it slow. You will be sore for a bit, but the rest will help. Do you have any questions for me?" He looks up from my chart that he had grabbed while he was talking.

"No, thank you so much for everything." I give him a curt smile. *Reduce the* stress—easy for him to say. No sooner does he head out and the nurse brings me my discharge papers, instructions, and a wheel chair. After all is said and done, we are out of here.

Jaxson

I MAKE SURE MAX and Jackie get back home without any distractions. When I get back to the main house, I find Bella is in the family room by the fire. "Hey, sis, how are you holding up?" She begins to shake and cry. Oh *fuck.*

"Jax, I feel like I brought this on myself. If I didn't insist on going, Max would have never found out. Mum never would have had a heart attack. What have I done?"

"Hey, stop . . . none of this is your fault." I take her hand and she immediately gives it the death grip. "It would have come out eventually; secrets always do. It's better that it came out now while we have a chance to get ahead of this. I don't want to go in there blind."

She gasps, "You still want to go?"

"Yeah, I'm going. I would feel better though, if you stayed here. Before you say anything, I *need* to go. Max will need me to stop him from doing something he might not be able to live with."

"Jax, *who* is going to stop *you?*"

Before I can answer, my wife steps into the room. "I will."

I close my eyes, knowing by the tone in my wife's voice she's not happy. "Raven, please give me a chance to explain."

Bella gets up, "I'm going to check on Mum. I will talk to you later."

She leaves us alone. Raven gives me the stare down and there is fire in those violets. Right now, I know I'm so fucked. Her hands are on her hips, her face is flushed, and—*Lord, help me*—all I can think about is how desperate I am to sink my cock deep inside her. "Jax, just so we are clear here. You will not be going anywhere without me." I'm about to object but she holds her hand up to stop me. I freeze, my eyes gazing up and down her beautiful body.

"We are a family, all of us. Max needs us to keep him from doing something that he will regret. We leave in four days; my mom will be taking care of Antonia. I've stocked enough food for her in the freezer. We will only be gone two days—no more. It's time to put all of this to bed so our family can move forward. The past is just that—the past. We can't change it. That past is what made Max who and what he is today, and we love him just the same. I will not let him make the mistake of a lifetime. It's not your job or Max's to carry the weight of this family. We are a team and we work together. Well, do you have a problem with this?"

"Am I allowed to speak, now?"

"Actually, no."

What the fuck?—she turns and walks out! "Raven, wait! Where the hell are you going?" I'm frozen in place, mesmerized by the sway of her beautiful arse. When she's halfway up the stairs, she turns, gives me a look that cuts to my soul. "Now, Jax."

As she turns to go up stairs, it hits me like a hammer right between the eyes. It's finally time, and I can't get there fast enough. I race upstairs and when I get into our bedroom, she is standing there in absolutely nothing. My heart skips a beat. "Raven, can we? I mean, I know it's only been six weeks—trust me I have counted every day—but are you okay? Did the doctor say it's okay?"

She smiles, pointing toward the chair. "Sit. *Now.*"

I don't know what happened to my wife but this is so surreal. I'm not an idiot. At this point, I'm not saying anything for once in my life; I'm doing what I'm told. She puts on the music, one of my new favorite songs by James Morrison, "You Make it Real," and I'm thinking how appropriate it is. She walks over to my chair and straddles my lap. My jaw is clenched it's been over six long weeks since I've gone to the happy place, and I'm praying I can last. She begins to slowly undress me. Every button of my shirt is sheer torture. She opens it, pulling it down my shoulders.

"Jax, you have the most beautiful neck. I love running my lips up and down it, nice and slowly. You're very tense—*relax.*"

"Sweetheart, it's easy for you to say. I'm trying to maintain some sort of presence of mind here."

"I want to take you past euphoria, past that presence of mind." Oh dear God, she's pulling my nipple between her teeth.

She stands up and bends down, pressing her lips against mine. "Take your jeans off, Jax, *now.*"

I find my scrambled brain, stand up, and, in one swift yank, I unbutton my jeans. "I'm all yours, sweetheart."

She lightly pushes me to sit again and then straddles me, slowly lowering herself onto my cock. "I want to own every one of your moans, your growls. I want to feel every inch of you. Every pleasure you experience, I want to come from me."

She puts her hands on my knees and arches her chest; those beautiful, full breast right in my face as she rolls her hips.

"Oh, Jax, *fare l'amore con me lento e facile.*"

"Oh, dear God, sweetheart, what the fuck are you saying to me?" She knows I can't take the dirty talk.

"Italian; make love to me slowly." She takes my hand and starts working it up and down her clitoris. She takes my other hand and glides it up her body to her lips. "Jax, *prendere me e fammi tuo.*"

I'm frozen like I'm in a dream.

"Jax, *take me and make me yours!*" She does the one thing that she knows will be my undoing, the one thing that will send me over the edge . . . *Clench.*

"Fuck all that's holy, Raven, please tell me I can move . . . that I won't hurt you."

"*Now!*"

I stand up and feel my legs wobble as I take her to the bed. I don't want to hurt her; I need to be gentle. "*Fuck . . .*" I begin to move slowly at first, trying for some sort of control. Oh, who am I kidding? I lost control the day I met her. I pull back and slowly glide in and out of her warmth; it's so wet. Every time I pull out, she clenches, making it snugger for my cock. My body begins to shake and I know this is going to be of epic proportions. "Dear God, please let me go longer, *please.* Raven, oh, sweetheart, I can't hold it."

She digs her nails into my arse and I'm growling endlessly. I don't care who hears. I can't stop—it's endless and mindless—it's euphoria. I look down and Raven opens her eyes and kisses me so tenderly. "Jax, I need more." It's just a whisper, but I know I what I heard.

"Really? How much more, sweetheart? Well, you know I'm not a one shot guy."

"It's been too long for me too, Jax."

"Well, you had a lot of fun teasing me earlier, I think turnaround is fair play. Will you let me bound your hands, like you did to me?"

She bites her bottom lip and pulls that ear. "I trust you, Jax."

"Okay, we will use your stockings, since they worked so well on me." I go to her drawer and get two sets, making a show of everything I'm doing. "Get on your knees, Raven." I bound her arms together and then tie them to the headboard above her head. I keep her spread wide for me. Now, I blindfold her. I take a moment to bask in my handy work, what a beautiful site. "Are you okay?" I ask her.

"Yes," she whispers.

I crawl on the bed behind her while on my knees, and rest my cock right between those glorious arse cheeks. Oh Jesus, it's like going home. Leaning down, I kiss my way up her spine. As much as I would love to reach around and play with her nipples right now I know they are too sensitive. I work my way down her back and nip at that beautiful arse. I swirl my tongue down further until I reach my goal and she lets out a low long moan. I take her clitoris tenderly between my teeth, tugging gently, followed by a kiss and a lick. I work my tongue deep inside her. She's fighting her restraints. "Raven, you still okay?"

"More than okay; please don't stop."

I spread her wetness, front to back, and slowly work my finger into her, while I unleash my tongue, quick and hard. She's right on the edge. I stop.

"*Noooo! Please, you can't leave me like this.*"

"I would never leave you on the edge." I get back on my knees and rub my cock up and down, stroking her softly. I enter her very slowly, one hard inch at a time. When I'm all the way in, I smack her arse hard enough to only tease.

"Oh, Jax, more please."

She's pushing herself back, trying to get me in deeper, harder. As much as I know she wants to, I know we still need to be careful. Instead, I reach around and run my fingers over her clitoris, applying more pressure.

"Yes!"

I smack her arse again and she is begging for more. Over and over again, right then left. "Sweetheart, are you there yet?" I don't need to wait for her answer, she is screaming and shaking. I explode endlessly within her. As I slowly bring her down, I untie her, gently massaging her wrists. She reaches up and pulls off the blindfold. I pull out of her and she turns over. She crawls into my arms and pulls me tightly. I'm holding her and trailing my fingers up and down her back. My mind flips back to why the argument started, and I need to make her understand that she should stay home. I'm about to say something when the baby monitor goes off.

"I need to feed Antonia." She gets up, puts on a robe, and goes to feed our baby. I watch her leave and I have no idea as to what I'm going to do.

Chapter Eight

Raven

I CHANGE ANTONIA AND begin to feed her. Tonight with Jax was wonderful. We finally went to our special place. I know what's coming and I will fight him on it. I can't let him go without me. I know he needs me there, even if he doesn't know it. I have to keep this family together, and I have to stop Max from making the mistake of a lifetime. I need to make Max understand that going after James will cost him Jackie. He'll never survive another loss.

I can sense that Jax is behind me, I always know when he's near. "Jax, if you think you're going to try and talk me out of going, you won't. I need to make Max understand what he will lose by doing this. We all go together or not at all. Don't think about pulling the Antonia card cause that won't work either. She needs to grow up with all her family around her. I'm making sure that's possible."

"Can I ask a question now?" he inquires as he walks around my chair so that we can see each other.

"Of course, I just wanted to make sure you're clear on where I stand."

"What happened? You've never been aggressive or domineering, yet today, I've seen a whole new side to you. Even when we were making love, you were different."

"Honestly, I don't know. What I do know is life can change on a dime. When I saw your mom go down, I panicked. I watched my mom come alive and yet, I felt myself shutting down. I won't be that vulnerable little girl ever again. You've carried all the weight of our family for so long. When your dad walked away, there was never time for you to be a little boy. You have been everything to everyone for so long. Now it's time for you to share the load." Suddenly, I realize the depth of his question and can't help but wonder if my new and improved confidence in the bedroom bothers him. I jerk my head up quickly. "Are you upset with me?"

"Well, I have to say it was hot seeing you take charge while making love to you. I love all the dynamics that make up who you are. I'm upset with the fact that you won't stay home. I'm also no fool, Raven; I know when there is no changing your mind. Tomorrow we will talk to Max, but tonight, I need my wife." He grazes my cheek with the back of his hand before helping me to get up. I put Antonia back in her crib, asleep and content. As we head toward our room, I mentally prepare myself for what I have to tell him next.

Jaxson

SHE HAS BEEN TUGGING on her ear—always a sure sign for something being on her mind. We sit on the bed, and I pull her hand from her ear. "Are you ready to tell me what's wrong?"

"I'm not on birth control. I was going to tell you to pull out but then I got caught up in the heat of the moment. My mind lost all reason."

"I thought you wanted to wait, why are you not on your pill?"

"While forms of birth control are discussed before having the baby, nothing is set in motion until after my six week postpartum visit. I can't take the pill until after I have my first cycle. The fact that I am breastfeeding might work to our advantage for birth control."

"Why were you afraid I would be upset about this? You know I want lots of babies."

"I know you do, I just didn't think it had to be right now . . . not that I think anything is going to happen, but I want you to know everything.

After all, Antonia was a surprise. I want all cards on the table."

"Sweetheart, you know I don't want Antonia to be an only child. If it happens, then so be it. I'm glad you're not taking anything that would cause any problems. Please, don't ask me to wear a condom. If you want, I will attempt to pull out, but I can't guarantee I will have the presence of mind at the time." I lift her hand and kiss the inside of her wrist. I can feel her shudder as the jolt of excitement shoots right to her core. "Are we good now, sweetheart?"

"Yes, Jax, we're good."

I pull her into my lap and kiss her tender lips. "As much as I would love to go to the happy place, I know that we can't over do it. How about I hold you in my arms all night long?"

"I know you're right and before we know it, Antonia will be up again." She tries to stifle her yawn. I roll us on our side and pull the comforter over us. "Let's get some sleep, tomorrow is going to be another long day"

I look down and she is fast asleep. I kiss her gently, "There will be plenty of time for babies." I whisper.

Maxwell

I DON'T WANT TO go anywhere near my office. I want to shut off everything that went down. "Why don't we go in the living room and sit by the fire for a bit?" I suggest to Jackie.

"Of course. Would you like some tea?"

"That sounds wonderful, thank you."

While she is puttering around the kitchen, I stare into the fire. I don't know what I'm going to do. My mind is on a complete overload. Jackie comes back and sets the tray down. I smile . . . she even has Jammie Dodgers.

"Max, can I ask you a question?"

"Babe, you know you can ask me anything."

"What is the story with these cookies? I mean, when Jax found out that An was getting them for you, he went crazy. I don't understand."

"My grams always gave them to me with my tea. It's comforting to me, like in some small way my grams is with me. Jax loves them and when they were featured in that show he watches, it made him love them more. When we were living in the states, we couldn't get them. So, An had them shipped in. When he found out, he went a little nuts . . . probably just to give me a hard time."

"Are you still going to confront James?" She shifts gears.

"Would I lose you if I did?" I watch her face for all the signs that she will leave me. I see nothing.

"Max, I want you safe, and I want you healed. That's really all I've ever wanted."

"Babe, What are your thoughts on the whole situation?"

"Tell me everything you know. Sometimes having an outsider's perspective can make all the difference."

"Are you sure you want to hear it all?"

"Yes. I know you've held back, but I figured that when you were ready to share with me, you would."

I give her a small nod of agreement, and then take in a deep breath before I let it all pour out of me. "After everything happened, I fell into a dark place, filled with nothing but hate and revenge. I was out for blood, and I left no stone unturned. When I found the gunmen, I did what needed to be done. I vowed I would never let them see the light of day." Her eyes are fixed on me, and I know this is hard to hear—hell, it's hard for me to relive it. "The thing is, I didn't feel good like I thought I would. I have to live with that for the rest of my life. I know I'm probably going to hell and all the redemption in the world won't help me. I knew who the men worked for; Miguel Dominguez, Columbian drug lord. I thought about going after him, but in the end, I knew revenge was not the way. It would make me no different from him. When I saw that picture, I knew the face looked familiar but I couldn't place it because he was very young. When I aged it, I realized who he was. The shock was seeing my father with his arm around the man, laughing. Does he know the man was responsible for the death of his grandson and daughter-in-law? Does he even care? Was he a part of it?" I've got a grip on her hand; twirling her ring around her finger. "Jackie, I need to confront him, but I'm scared."

"Scared of what?"

"Babe, I don't know if I can keep it together. It's not just me anymore. I have to think about the rest of the family. I can't lose them, especially over him. I can't lose you, you're my world."

"What makes you think you would lose your family or me? Max, at the end of the day, you know what the repercussions will be if you take matters into your own hands. He's not worth it. I can understand you wanting to confront him and call him out for whatever part he might have been responsible for. What you can't do is make him turn you into someone you don't want to be."

"How, baby? How do I do that?"

"You do what you do best, Max: gather information and facts, slowly build a case against him. Leave him to rot in jail, just like Vincent will."

"I don't know that I can do that? In my head, he is dead to me, but in my heart, he's my father. I'm so tired of all of this. I just want it over already."

"Max, you need to stop looking at him like a loving, caring father. He is nothing more than a sperm donor. He didn't make you the man you are today. Your real family is who shaped and loved you, no matter what." She kisses me and holds me tight. I know she's right.

"Max, when I was young, I had a friend that I trusted completely. She was one of my only friends. One day, she betrayed me really bad. Of course, it was nothing like this, but at that time, I was so upset and wanted to hurt her like she hurt me. My mom sat me down and told me I needed to forgive the girl. Well, I can tell you, I thought she was crazy. I told my mom she was absolutely nuts if she thought I would ever forgive her. My mom asked me if I thought I was better than Buddha. I told her, 'Of course not, what would make you think that?' She said, 'Buddha can forgive, so why can't you?' I really couldn't answer her. She gave me the best advice that day, Max. She said forgive the girl and move on. She doesn't have to be in your circle. She has to look in the mirror every day. And in the end, she has to answer to her God for what she has done. My point is, Max, if you reduce yourself down to his level, then you're no better than he is. Let him live with what he has done and let him answer for it. The more you hold onto the grudge, the more bitter you will become."

"Wow, what did the girl do?" I ask and she widens her eyes. "Don't look at me like that, you had to know I would ask."

"She slept with my boyfriend right before he came to pick me up for our date."

"So, what did you do?"

"I told the boy that I knew what he did, and I forgive him. I told him he could have her, and that he would never have me. I then went to see her, and told her that I hope they are very happy together. I wished her luck and walked out. I never spoke to either of them again. I knew if I didn't do that, I would become a very bitter person. Max, don't let James make you into a bitter person. Don't give him the power to take away what you have found here. Only you can stop this." She pulls me into her arms, wrapping those wonderful legs around me. I'm resting my head on her chest and I can feel her heart beating. It's what keeps me alive.

"Max, do you remember the crystal I gave you?"

"Yes, I carry it with me all the time. Do you want it back?"

"No, I want you to use it to help you concentrate on healing. Every time you feel that you are on the verge of losing it, rub the crystal." Her fingers are tracing the scar on my temple, and it has a calming effect on me. *Everything* she does calms me.

"I really got scared when I thought we were going to lose An. If something would have happened to her because of me, I don't think I would have survived it."

"Well, then I suggest you do whatever you have to do to put this whole situation with James to bed. He's eaten up too much of your life and, he's just not worth it. I think he should pay for whatever part he played, but not at the expense of anyone else."

I lift my head up and look at those beautiful golden eyes. "I love you."

"I know, Max." She presses her lips to my forehead. "Get some rest." I snuggle up against her, thankful that she's not letting go. Reminding myself that I need to stay focused on the present and not the past.

Jackie

MAX HAS BEEN ASLEEP for hours. The realization that James could have been a part of the darkest point in Max's life has taken a toll on him. If I was in his position, I don't know what I would do. I love this man heart and soul, but what am I willing to live with? I need to call my parents. As I try to wiggle free, his grip gets tighter. It's barely a whisper but I hear him plead with me not to leave. I close my eyes, giving in to his need to hold me tightly.

I OPEN MY EYES and realize I'm alone. I don't know how much time has passed but it's dusk outside. I get up and stretch before heading out in search of Max. I find him in his office, cleaning up the mess. "Max, can I help you with that?"

"No, babe, it's my mess, I can clean it. I'm sorry if I woke you." He seems solemn.

"You didn't wake me." I offer him a small smile. "When are you meeting with everyone?"

"I'll meet with them later. I wanted to clean up this mess, and form some sort of plan. Are you hungry?"

"Starving. Will you fix something, please?"

"Of course, babe."

I take his hand and pull him from the room. "Come, this can wait right now. I need food and you."

"Really? In that order?"

"Yes, in that order."

When we get to the kitchen, I watch him begin assembling dinner. My eyes gaze over to the table where just yesterday, I was having the time of my life. I feel my cheeks heat at the memory. I think it's time I try to turn the tables on Max, and get him out of his own head. His back is to me and I can't help but remember the first time I saw his ass, it literally took my breath away. I quietly get up and walk up behind him, slide my hands into his sweats, grabbing each ass cheek. He freezes in place. I lean in and kiss his shoulder, never letting go of his ass. He's still not moving and not saying a word. I grate my nails up his ass and then stroke them down. He drops the whisk. "If you do that again, dinner will be delayed," he whispers.

I pull my hands up but instead of stopping I grab the waistband of his sweats and yank them down. He tries to turn around. I grab his hips, "No."

He grips the counter and tries to steady his breath. I drop to my knees and begin lightly kissing his ass, all the while, admiring how sculptured it is. "Turn around," I command. As he turns around, I stand up. "Get up on the counter, hold on to the edge, and no matter what— don't let go." I giggle at hearing those words, the same words he used on me.

He's smirking and I know he is remembering too. As he climbs on the counter, I take off his sweats. Now . . . I'm going to have some fun. I have on entirely too many clothes. I take the hem of my shirt and lift it over my head. I watch his eyes grow wide and his knuckles turn white as his grip gets tighter. I slip my thumbs into the band of my yoga pants and peel them off. His jaw tightens and I know he is trying so hard to let me stay in charge. Sometimes I wish I had more experience. Hmm . . . what to do next? He must sense my apprehension, he growls. *"Touch yourself, babe."*

I glide my hands over my breasts. "Talk me through it, Max, please."

"Play with your nipples, take each one and roll them between your fingers. Pull them to the point of pain, and then stop. Tell me what you're feeling? Does it feel good?"

"It feels different, not like when you do it."

"You like when I play with your nipples? What about when I suck and nibble them, do you like that?"

"I love that, Max."

"Slide your fingers down; feel the contour of your abs. Feel how lean and long you are. Glide your fingers into the folds of your beautiful sweetness. Enter real slowly, and imagine it's my tongue going slow and deep."

As I follow his instructions, I can feel my skin prickle and my heart race. He's not even touching me, yet, I feel him all over me—*how?*

"Talk to me, babe. Tell me how it feels."

"Powerful and erotic; I feel you all over me, yet you're not touching me. I want more, Max."

"Let your thumb swipe up and down your clitoris. Make the strokes faster, while your other fingers are moving in and out of your sweetness, spreading your arousal. Now, tell me what you want, Jackie."

"I want to come with you inside of me."

He leaps off the counter and comes toward me. He begins pumping his cock and when he reaches me, he takes my hand and brings my fingers to his mouth, sucking my taste off of them. This is so erotic, almost surreal. He takes my other hand and places it on his cock, keeping his hand over it as he begins moving my hand up and down. The movement of my hand, matching my fingers in his mouth. He takes my hand from his mouth. "Do you want me, Jackie? Do you think you're ready for me?"

I brazenly take his hand and guide it down until it's right between my legs. He's trying to hold me back from pushing his fingers deep within me. My eyes glance upwards and he's smiling. "You're not going to make this easy on me are you?"

"Babe, all you have to do is tell me what you want, what you desire . . . what you *need.*"

He's watching my every move, waiting for my words. As he waits for my answer, he leans down and takes my nipple between his teeth. Oh dear God, I can't think, let alone form a sentence. "Max, I need to feel you inside of me."

He's sucking and pulling at my nipple, finally letting go with a pop. "My tongue, my fingers, or my cock?"

He's strumming his fingers over my clitoris and I think I might scream. "All t-three, Max."

He lifts me up and carries me out of the kitchen. "Where are we going?" I squeak.

"I want you everyplace I can have you, Jackie, but right now I want you in our bed."

He carries me into our bedroom and as he places me on the bed, he begins to kiss me slowly and tenderly . . . no sense of urgency. My body is wound so tight, I fear I might combust. He's kissing my neck and I know I can't take much more. "Max, please I need—" Before I can finish he slowly sinks his cock deep inside me and stops. "Why the hell are you stopping?"

His entire body blankets mine. He grips my hands above my head. His eyes are closed, and he's trying to slow down his breathing. I can feel his heart pounding. He rests his forehead on mine and I swipe my tongue over his lips. He opens his eyes. They focus intently on mine. He pulls back and finally starts to move. He's in total control as he cups my breast and pebbles my nipple. He nibbles down my neck and latches onto my nipple. It's a mixture of pain and pleasure, something I never thought possible.

"Max, I can't hold it." He nips me harder and I can't hold back. My release is so intense and I feel his body shake as his release floods me. "Max, are you okay?"

"I will be in a minute, as soon has I come back down to earth. Jesus, Jackie, what you do to me, I've never thought possible."

He begins to slowly move in and out, he's hard as stone again. He pulls out and works his way down my body, very slowly. As he nips my hip bone I giggle. His tongue circles my belly button as he continues downward. I can't take much more and I push his head down as I try to wiggle myself up further. He's teasing me, knowing what I want, what I need. He swipes me with his tongue and then works his fingers deep inside me. I'm almost there, his tongue so forceful. He pulls his fingers out and begins to work one very slowly into my rear. Oh my, it's tight but I can't focus on anything but that tongue. Flicking, nipping at my clitoris while his fingers are pushing inside of me. "Max, I'm . . . *coming!*" I'm shaking and kicking my legs as I dig my nails into his shoulders. He gets up and rubs his cock up and down, I'm nervous he will want anal sex and I'm not sure I'm ready for that.

"Not today, Babe, that takes control," he says as if he could hear my thoughts. "Right now I want to take you hard, you ready?" He hovers over me.

"Yes!"

He slams into me and God, it feels wonderful. It doesn't take long for both of us to explode. We lay here, neither one of us having to say a word. I love to mindlessly stroke his back as we both come back to earth.

"Max, are you ever going to feed me?" I ask after a few minutes.

"Babe, I'm starting to think you just want me for my culinary skills?"

"Well, that, combined with your sex skills, makes you my complete package."

He throws his head back and laughs. It's wonderful to finally hear that laugh again. "I love you, Jackie."

Chapter Nine

Raven

JAX IS STILL ASLEEP when I hear the monitor. I try to get out of bed, but I'm locked in his embrace. I hate to wake him, but I have no choice. "Jax, I need to take care of Antonia." He kisses me and mumbles something as I crawl out of bed. I get to the nursery and Antonia is her usual morning fussy. I get her changed and sit in front of her window while I feed her. This is my favorite time of the day, watching the sunrise with my daughter. I know it will be so hard to leave her, but I have to go with them to Capri. There is too much at stake here. An needs to recuperate; all the burden can't be on her. Antonia finishes and she is out cold. She always falls asleep when she is nursing. After I get her settled in her crib, I head out the door only to run into Michael.

"Hey, Michael, where are you off to so early?"

"I don't feel good, I was going to get my mum."

I feel his head and he feels warm. "What do you feel, can you tell me?"

"I'm tired and cold, Aunt Raven."

"Back to bed, little man. I will get your mom and my mom, too. Let's see if we can get you fixed up really quickly, okay?" As we head back to his room, he begins peppering me with questions.

"Aunt Raven, is it true that Miss Jackie is marrying Uncle Max?"

"Yes, where did you hear it?"

"My mum told me, she said Miss Jackie will be my aunt now. That's cool, cause she is really nice and we have lots of fun with the horses. The only bad thing about her is he doesn't watch *Doctor Who.*"

I pull him close to me and kiss his head, even when he doesn't feel well, he still makes me laugh. "I'm sure we can work on that. Now, back to bed."

I go in search for Bella and find her in the kitchen making coffee. "Morning, Bella, I was looking for you. I ran into Michael, he was on his way to get you. He has a fever and said he feels tired. I sent him back to bed and told him I would find you and my mom to come and look at him."

"Thanks, Raven, he seemed a little off last night. I was going to ask Rose to check him but she was busy with mum. I'll ask her this morning. I hope it's not that flu that's running around. You know when school starts, kids pass everything around."

"How is An doing?"

"She will never say; you know mum. I heard her tell Rose she felt sore from the procedure. Rose assured me that was to be expected. She needs to rest, and she needs to reduce the stress in her life."

"Bella, we all need to reduce the stress. I'm hoping to try and talk some sense into Max, but I doubt he will listen."

The door swings open and Jackie comes barreling in. "Hey, Jackie, is everything okay?"

"Yeah, I wanted to talk to you before Max gets here, and before my class starts."

Bella gets up to leave but Jackie takes her hand. "Bella, please stay."

She is scaring me. Something is off, and I know exactly what Jackie needs. I get up, pour her coffee, and get our stash of chocolates.

I pass her the chocolates, "This should take the edge off of whatever it is."

"Oh, Raven." She begins to cry. Oh dear God, how much more?

I get up and take her in my arms, rubbing her back to calm her down. Bella takes Jackie's hand, "Hey, no matter what, Jackie, we are family and we will get through it."

"I must be at my parents for my birthday. Max knows this and promised me that he would be back in time. He made that promise before everything happened. I don't want him to confront James. I'm scared what the result will be for everyone. He has been rocked to the core. He's afraid he is going to lose the rest of his family over all of this. There are so many emotions and now the headaches have come back, along with the night terrors. I know if I go with him, that I might be able to help him maintain some sort of control, but I have to be at my parents."

I know why she has to be home, but Bella doesn't. It's not up to me to tell her, only Jackie can. I push her hair back and wipe away her tears.

She turns to Bella and squeezes her hand. "Bella, birthdays are a happy time for some, but not for me." She goes on to explain about Madeline. "I have to be there—*no matter what!* But, I'm really worried about leaving Max."

"Jackie, I'm sorry. I never knew. Maybe we can delay the trip till you get back. I will try talking to my brothers. In the meantime, I need to check on Michael; he's not feeling well."

"Bella, I'm sorry that I bothered you."

"Nonsense; we are family." She heads out to see about her son.

"Okay, Jackie, I know something else is bothering you, so spill."

"Max and I finally talked everything out. He wants to get married and start on a family right away. I told him I'm scared, not just for me but for him, too. Jeez . . . he wants five kids! I told him I'm not a baby factory. He wants to adopt a special needs child."

I'm watching her rip apart her napkin and I know there's more. "What are you afraid of?"

"What if we have twins and that happens to us? I don't think Max will survive. Raven he's barely hanging on now."

"I know your fear is very real for you, but not all multiple births end up like yours."

"My logical mind agrees with you, but my aunt's pregnancy ended the same way. Do the math, the facts don't lie."

"I know that, but you can't go through life afraid of *what if.* Whatever happens, we will deal with it together. Max has a great support system around him and he always will."

I hug her tight, knowing that's what she needs the most right now. "You need to get Max, and tell him there is a family meeting here in two hours. Let him know I've called it."

I don't give her a chance to question me; I know she will fight me on my decision. I quickly head out to find Jax.

I HEAD UPSTAIRS TO find Jax but run into my mom leaving Michael's room. "Morning, Mom, how is he?" She seems very distracted.

"He still has a fever. I'm not sure what's going on. I'm waiting for the doctor to get here. How is Jax this morning?"

"He's still sleeping. I was just headed in there. We are having a family meeting in two hours; please make sure you are there. Mom, before the day gets away from us, I just wanted to thank you for all you did to help An." I give her a hug, and she seems distant.

"Mom, what's wrong? You seem so sad."

"Raven, I felt myself come alive, and that made me realize how much I've lost. Sometimes it's hard to keep the nightmares from surfacing. I'm happy that all my years of school and training was worth something. My whole life, all I ever wanted to do was save lives. Then, that was ripped away from me. Everything I built my life around was gone in an instant. I need to find my place in the world all over again. Everything that happened brought that need back to the surface, deep from where I buried it."

"Do you think it's possible that you would be able to practice again?"

"I wouldn't even know where to begin. My license was in New York State and I live in Scotland now. I'm sure the laws and requirements are different now. You know, I'm not young anymore. So much has changed."

"Mom, never rule anything out. We should have Jax's attorneys find out the legal end of things and then lets take it from there. You can't let what happened dictate who you are. If you do that, then all the evil wins, and that's never an option."

"You are so much like Antonio that sometimes it takes my breath away. Your quiet strength is amazing. You never fall into that pity party mentality, how is that even possible?"

"Someone told me once, 'Pity parties are for fools. You can't change the past, but you can change your path for the future. Tell that pity party to kiss your ass goodbye, as you're walking away from it.' I live by that rule."

"Great advice, do I dare ask who?"

"It was Marco. Mom, I know he did a lot of bad things, but in my heart, I also know all the good he did for me. That's what I choose to remember, otherwise, I will become bitter."

"I'm glad that you are choosing to focus on the good from that relationship. I know, from what you told me, that he caused so much pain. But, he also looked after you. Joseph must have seen something good in him if he put him in your life."

"Your right, Mom. I will always try to focus on the positive."

"Oh, Dr. McCord is finally here. I want to talk to him about Michael. I will see you at the meeting."

She rushes into Michael's room. I hope he's going to be fine. I need to find Jax. Just then, I hear Jax on the baby monitor. I look at the screen and see them both. I love watching him with her. He is such a powerful, strong man, yet . . . so tender-hearted. Sometimes I feel like I shouldn't watch or listen to them, but I can't pull myself away.

Jaxson

I LIKE TO START my day with my daughter. Even if she's asleep, she has a calming affect on me. I lean in and she begins to stir. Well, at least Raven can't yell at me for waking her up. I scoop her up and breath in her scent. She smells so sweet and pure; my beautiful girl. I love talking to her, we have the best conversations.

"Oh, my sweetest girl, I don't know how your mum and I are going to leave you. I don't know how parents do it? Your Uncle Max is going to have some really hard times ahead of him. We need to keep him grounded and strong. I think I finally got through to Grandma Rose about the potential danger she could put the family in if she goes to see Vincent. At least I hope so. Your mum is so strong; I wish I had half the strength she does. Don't you let her fool you, little one, she holds all the power in this relationship."

I nuzzle my sweet baby. "Raven, how long have you been standing there?" She never has to say a word, my blood races whenever she is near.

"Long enough, Jax. Michael is not feeling well, the doctor and my mom are in with him now."

"I should go check on Junior. What have you been up to?"

"I spoke with Jackie and Bella. I let them know that I'm calling a family meeting, and to let everyone know."

"Wow, you called a meeting? Am I in *trouble?*"

"Ha! No, for once, you're not in the doghouse. We need to organize everything before we leave. We need to have a plan. We can't go running in their half-cocked." She stops rattling off her list, cocks her head, and furrows her brow. "Why are you looking at me so strangely?"

"I'm not; everything is fine." *Fine—my arse; teacher mode makes me crazy.* "What time is the meeting?"

"In about an hour; we have time. I need to feed Antonia, and I want to talk to you . . . have a seat."

I watch her getting Antonia settled in to nurse, and it warms my heart to see such beauty. She is a perfect mum: kind and loving. "God, I hope we made a baby today." Her eyes grow wide and she is staring at me. "I just said that out loud, didn't I?"

"Yes, you did. Before the meeting, I have to tell you something. It was never my story to tell, but since Jackie has shared it, I need to tell you. Jackie's birthday is coming up, and she must be back at her parents home to celebrate it."

"Why? Can't she go in a week or two?"

"No, it has to be on that day." She shakes her head and explains to me why. "Her mom is Buddhist and follows their teachings. Madeline's ashes are in a temple repository on the property. Every year, Jackie goes to the temple and then spends the day with her mom reflecting upon the year that passed. It is a tradition that is important to both of them. She explained it to Bella, and told her if we leave for Capri, we must be back for this or, if possible, delay the trip until after her birthday. I'm going to talk to everyone and see what would be best. Max cannot and will not go this alone. I will not allow it."

"Wow, sweetheart, that is so sad. I understand she wants to be there for Max. I would much rather we wait until she gets back, that would buy us a little more time to research what we are walking into."

"I agree, plus, I don't want to leave if Michael is sick."

She's tugging her ear and I know something else is on her mind. "What else is bothering you?"

"I spoke to my mom and thanked her, her quick actions saved your mom's life and probably Max's too. She is sad that she can't practice medicine any more. Do you think your attorneys can find out what she would need to do if she decided she wants to get back into the field? She sees all the obstacles in her way, whereas I don't."

"Oh, Raven, you never do. It's one of the many things I love about you. I will give Mathew a call today." I lean in and kiss her tender lips, and then lean down and kiss Antonia. "While you finish up here, I will check on Junior. Aside from the occasional cold, he never gets sick."

I head toward the door but look back at Raven who is softly singing to Antonia, while lightly stroking her head. God I love this woman.

Maxwell

THE HOUSE IS QUIET. Jackie is probably out at the barn. I head into the kitchen to get some coffee, and I find Mrs. Osla standing at the back door. I know I'm in trouble by the glaring look on her face. I open the door, expecting her to yell, but she surprises me by throwing her arms around me and begins to cry. "Shh, please don't cry, Mrs. Osla; I'm fine. Come in and sit. I'll make you tea."

"Lad, I leave you alone for a couple of days and all hell breaks loose. Please tell me from the beginning what happened?"

It kills me that she is upset yet again because of me. I relay everything that happened, including the fact that my father was associated in some way with Miguel. "When An realized everything, she had a heart attack. I thank God that Rose was here. She quite literally saved us all," I state with widened eyes. She listens, stirring her tea and so I continue.

"Part of me wants to kill him while part of me just wants to know *why?* I know if I go after him, I might not be able to control myself. I know if I do that, it will cost me Jackie. I don't know how to deal with these emotions."

"Maxwell, only you can decide how much power you are willing to give James. How much more are you going to let him take from you? He's cost you so much, when will you say enough? Is knowing really worth the price of Jackie's love and respect? Your own self-respect? I love you, lad, but ultimately, it has to be your choice and yours alone. I'm going up to the main house to check on An." She gets up and heads toward the door. I watch her leave and think about all that has happened. I know what I have to do, what is best for everyone. I need to somehow convince them that we all need to walk away.

I'm about to get up and head to the main house when Jackie comes barreling through the door. "Hey, babe, you okay?"

"Yeah, we have a family meeting in about an hour at the main house. I need to jump in the shower so I don't go smelling like the barn."

I follow her into the bathroom, taking my clothes off along the way. "Who called a meeting?"

"Max, why are you naked? Raven, called a meeting."

"Babe, you said we are having a shower. Why did Raven call a meeting?"

"I said *I was* having a shower. If you come in, we might not get out. I don't know why she called a meeting, I guess we will find out soon enough."

"Jackie, I need to be in the shower with you. I mean, after all, you do need your back washed."

"I've been doing okay all these years, Max. Besides, we have to be at the house in an hour."

We step into the shower, and as she is about to unravel her braid, I stop her. My voice is low and my desire is high. "Not yet, babe, I need you now."

She said she wanted to try new and different things, well, now's her chance. Her back is toward me, and I blanket her with my body. I begin rubbing myself up and down her beautiful arse. I reach around to feel if she is ready for me. God, she is *so* ready. "Put your hands up against the wall and push that luscious arse toward me." She instantly takes my commands. I pick up her braid and looped it around my fist, pulling it just enough to sting. "I'm going to take you from behind. It will be hard and it will be fast, are you okay with that? Do you think you can handle me?"

"Yes," she whispers.

I smack her arse, and she yelps. "Louder, Jackie!"

"Yes, I can handle it, but if you smack my ass like that again, I might not last long."

Interesting that she likes the sting of my palm. I position my cock over her clit, slowly rubbing the head up and down, front to back. I can feel her beginning to shake and that's when I slam into her. I find a rhythm; as I push in, I pull her braid. She's almost there, but I want more. I slow it down, needing it to last. I feel my blood coursing through my veins, as my cock continues to get harder. I take a finger and work it into her beautiful arse. I want to fill every part of her. Now I work two fingers in, still going slow.

"Max, smack my ass again, please; I won't break."

Oh bloody hell! I smack her arse over and over again. It's turning pink and I fucking love it.

"Harder, Max, please."

"Oh fuck, Jackie, I'm coming." I throw my head back groaning her name, and she's following me. Beautiful . . . just *fucking* beautiful. I bend down and kiss that gorgeous, pink arse.

She pulls away and reaches for the body wash. "Max, we need to get clean or we will be late."

I spin her around and her face is flushed. "Babe, I don't care. I want to talk to you first. You said you wanted to try new things. Did you like what just happened? Did you find it pleasurable? Did it hurt at all?" I watch her face, trying to gauge her reaction. Her eyes cast downwards, so submissive—and, *fuck me*—she is so sexy. I lift her chin up so she's looking into my eyes. "No secrets."

"I liked it a lot. It didn't hurt, it stung a little, but then, it felt warm. I felt like I didn't have to be in control, yet I knew if I said stop, you would. I gave you power without giving up my power. Does that make sense?"

I pull her into my arms and kiss her long and slow. Our tongues, stroking gentle then hard. When I finally pull away, I look down at my cock and I know I need her again. I lift her up with one arm, while she wraps her legs around my waist. Slowly, I sink deep within her. I steady my legs and begin to move, taking my time—gently—until I can't take anymore and we both roll into a beautiful orgasm. When we finally come back to life, I let her down and begin to methodically wash her. Nothing needs to be said; she knows I love her more than life itself and I always will.

We finish getting ready and as we head out the door, I stop her, "Jackie, I want to let you know that I've decided that I don't want to go to Capri. I'm going to let everyone else know, but I wanted to tell you first."

"Can I ask you why?"

"Because I love you, babe . . . more than my own life. I don't trust myself in the same room with him. I'm not willing to take any chances. He's not worth it."

"What made you change your mind?"

"Mrs. Osla was here earlier and she asked me how much more power I am willing to give my father. She's right. I can't change the past, but I can protect my future, and my future is you. I will move heaven and earth for you." I look into her eyes, they are so bright. Her huge smile lights up her whole face, and I know—she understands.

"For us, Max, I love you and I will support your decision. Come, let's go find out what's going on." We walk up to the main house hand in hand. I feel good about my decision. Now I have to make Bella and Jax understand.

Rose

DR. MCCORD FINISHES HIS exam and assures Bella that it's probably the flu. I decide to step out and speak to him before he leaves. "Dr. McCord, I'm concerned about Michael. I know you said you think it's the flu, however, his fatigue has been building for days. He keeps bruising very easily and now he is running a 103 temp. I don't want to tell you how to do your job, but don't you think it would be wise to run a CBC panel?"

"Rose, I understand you are a doctor, but you have been out of practice for a long time. And so much has changed. He probably has the flu; this time of year it's pretty common. Let's not jump to conclusions. I'll check on him in a couple of days."

He storms off before I can say anything else. I'm about to go back into Michael's room when I see Jax coming and pull him aside. "Can I please talk to you for a minute."

"I was just going in to see Michael, can it wait?"

"No, please, it's about Michael."

"Of course, Rose, what's the problem?"

"You can tell me to mind my business, but I can't. Michael is fatigued. He has been bruising easily and he is running a 103 temp. I suggested to Dr. McCord that it might be wise to run a CBC panel. Michael never gets sick and he's usually so full of energy. Why not play it safe and run the panel?"

"What did he say?"

"He blew me off, telling me to leave it to him. I would, if I thought he was doing his job. He thinks it's the flu and I hope that's all it is, but I'm worried. If it is the flu, then I should have it too. I'm with Michael every day, exploring all the secret passages in this place. Why is he the only one who is ill?"

"Rose, let me look in on Junior and talk to Bella."

"Okay, I don't mean to alarm anyone. I'd rather be wrong than right." As I watch him head into Michael's room, I pray to God I'm wrong.

Jaxson

I STEP INTO JUNIOR'S room and he looks so pale. He looked tired yesterday, but nothing like this. "Hey, Junior, how are you feeling?"

"I'm tired, Uncle Jax, but I'll be okay. Miss Rose and I found another secret passage yesterday, it leads to a tunnel. We didn't go all the way yet."

"Well, when you get better, you will have to show me. Do you want to watch some *Doctor Who?*"

"I'm tired, Uncle Jax, maybe later, okay?"

"Sure, you get some rest. I'll be back later."

I step outside the room and Rose is waiting for me. I pull out my phone and call Dr. McCord. "Get your arse back here right now and run a CBC panel on Junior" I hang up, not waiting for his answer.

"Jax, you see what I'm talking about?"

"Of course, Rose, one look at him and I can tell something is off. He doesn't even have the energy to watch *Doctor Who.* Do you have an idea what is wrong?"

"I won't speculate, let's get the test run."

Before I can ask her anymore questions, McCord walks up. It takes all I have not to rip him apart. "Get in there and run the test now. One look at Junior, and you should have been able to see something is off. It's not like you've never met the kid before."

"Mr. Phillips, I think Rose is blowing this out of proportion."

Before he can finish, I grab him by the shirt. "Listen to me! This is not a fucking pissing contest. Get in there and run the test before I snap your fucking neck." I feel Rose pulling me back, and then she steps in front of me.

" Dr. McCord, I'm sorry if I offended you, please, just run the test. Thank you."

If Rose wasn't here, God knows what I would have done. McCord heads into Junior's room. I need to calm down before I go in. I don't want to upset Junior.

"Rose, how long will the test take to run?" Everyone knows I don't do well with waiting.

"It should take about two hours. Everything we need to run the test can be done at the clinic here. I will go back with Dr. McCord and oversee it. I know the nurses are capable to run the test, but I would feel better being there."

McCord steps out of the room, and I don't give him a chance to say anything. "Rose will be overseeing the test. Get me the results as quick as possible. Thank you, Rose."

I head back into Junior's room. I'm trying to avoid looking at Bella, if I do, she will know I'm worried. "Hey, Junior, I need to borrow your mum for a bit. Aunt Raven called a family meeting."

"Uncle Jax, are you in the dog house again?" At least he's laughing.

"Junior, have you ever known me *not* to be in the dog house? And stop laughing. Get some rest and I'll be back up later so we can watch the new *Doctor Who*."

We step out of the room and Bella begins to cry. I pull her into my arms and try to calm her down. "Bella, don't let Junior hear you crying, please."

"Why did you have Dr. McCord come back and run a test? You seem very worried."

"Rose asked McCord to run the test and he blew her off. She came to me and said she was concerned about Michael's fatigue and bruising. She asked me to demand a CBC be done. When I asked Junior to watch *Doctor Who* with me, he said he was tired. That was all the answer I needed. How long has he been feeling ill?"

"The fever only started this morning. Past couple of days he said he was tired. The bruising I put off to all the exploring he's been doing with Rose in those secret passageways."

"Where is Michael? Does he know Junior is ill?"

"He left early this morning before Junior was even up. He should be back by now."

"You need to keep it together, Bella, we have no idea what is going on. It could still be just a really bad case of the flu. The test should be back soon. Let's head downstairs and see what's going on."

We are about to leave when Michael comes up the stairs. Bella sees him and burst into tears again. I bring Michael up to speed on everything.

"Jax, he's been tired the past couple of days, but I figured he was getting back into the routine of school and stuff. Bella, this is just another reason why you can't leave and go to Capri."

"Michael, I already decided I wasn't going. Raven called a family meeting and I was going to let everyone know my decision."

"Sis, I'm going to head downstairs. I will let everyone know. You stay here with Junior."

She grabs my arm, "Jax, I'm not going because I can't put Max in that position. I realize that man is not my father; he donated his sperm, nothing more. Max is my brother and more important to me than that cold-hearted bastard could ever be."

I lean in and kiss her forehead, "I get it; stay with Junior."

As I head downstairs, I realize Bella is right; the past needs to stay there. This family needs to focus on the present. I have to keep my brother from making the biggest mistake of his life, no matter what it takes.

Chapter Ten

Raven

I GET DOWNSTAIRS AND hurry up, preparing for everyone's arrival. I put out some water and, of course, some Scotch. I've never been the one to call a family meeting—heck—I've only ever been to one. I silently rehearse all the points I want to bring up. I need to stress that the past needs to stay in the past. I only hope I can get everyone to listen. No one has shown up yet, and I'm about to go search out Jax when he walks in; his face is pale and his jaw is clenched. What the hell happened now?

"Jax, what the hell is going on?"

"Junior is sick."

"I know. I saw him this morning. Is his fever worse?"

" Dr. McCord thought it was the flu, but your mum doesn't think so. She had me order a test. The results should be back in couple of hours." He leans in near my ear, "I think he's really sick," he whispers.

Everyone else seems to show up at once. Before Jax can say anything more, Max and Jackie walk in. Max takes one look at Jax and freezes. "What's the matter?"

Jax brings him up to speed on what he knows so far. An is very quiet. The last thing she needs right now is any more stress.

"Son, when will the results be available?"

Jax sits down next to his mom and holds her hand. He's trying to keep her calm. "Mum, Rose is overseeing the test and will let us know right away."

I called this meeting, so it's time to get this done. "Okay, everyone, I'm just going to jump right in here and say that no one is going to Capri. Before anyone says anything, please hear me out." All eyes are on me and I have to make the strongest case. I'm only going to have one chance at this.

"There is no reason for any one of you to meet James. Nothing good will come of it. It is abundantly clear that the man is nothing but trouble. This family does not need any more drama or turmoil. We need to look to the future and build upon that. Jax, I get that there are three other men out there that are your half brothers. If you want to make contact with them, then that's a different story, but James breeds trouble."

Jax still has a grip on his mom's hand, I think more for his support than hers. "Raven, Bella already decided she is not going. She said he's nothing more than a sperm donor and I agree with her. Even though I want to know why, nothing will change. That boy will still be waiting by the window for his dad to show up. Max, if you want to go, then I will have to go with you. However, I don't think it's in your best interest to do so, but I would never let you go alone."

I can only hope we've gotten through to Max. If he doesn't go, then all this ends tonight and we can move forward. He's silent for a bit, holding both of Jackie's hands tightly in his. He lifts them to his lips and kisses them. "I decided today that I wasn't going to confront him. Nothing can change the past. I need to protect my future and the future of this family."

"Great, so it's settled then, hopefully Michael only has the flu and we can all go to Switzerland to celebrate Jackie's birthday. A vacation right about now sounds wonderful."

The baby monitor lights up and my daughter begins to stir. "I need to go nurse, please let me know when the results are back." I head upstairs praying that it's just the flu.

ANTONIA IS VERY RESTLESS today. I wonder if she can sense how stressed out I've been. I get her cleaned up and, once she starts eating, she seems to settle down. She has a great appetite and she seems to be sleeping longer at night. I can't believe she is almost two months old. I know Jax wants to have another baby right away and reality is I do too. I never want my child to be alone like I was. I look up and Jax is in the doorway. "Hey, are the results back yet?"

"Rose, just called, she and Dr. McCord are on their way."

Jax takes Antonia and gets her settled in her crib. We head downstairs and I pray it's only the flu. We sit next to Bella, and Jax firmly holds her hand.

"Sis, no matter what happens, we will get through it."

My mom walks in with Dr. McCord, and by the grim look on her face, I know it's not the flu.

Jax jumps up, "McCord, what are the results?"

I watch Dr. McCord; I notice he can't look Jax in the eye. I get up and put my arm around Jax's waist for support. Dr. McCord finally looks up from the papers he has clutched in his hands. "We just got the results back, Michael has Acute Lymphocytic Leukemia, commonly referred to as ALL."

Bella drops to her knees, crying and shaking. Michael drops to his knees stunned and silent, trying to hold his wife.

"Please, everyone, it's not a death sentence. Thanks to Rose's insistence on running the test, we have caught this early. He will need to have a bone marrow aspiration and biopsy, but that has to be done at the hospital. Once all of the tests are completed, treatment can start right away. I will outline it all for you. In the meantime, I want everyone to be tested for a possible bone marrow match. It's a simple cheek swab, but since Michael has no siblings, everyone needs to be tested. Rose will do the swabs and get them over to the lab right away."

We're all in shock; no one is making a sound. Absorbing everything being said but not believing a word of it, I look over to An and I realize, with her health so fragile, this could be her breaking point. I release myself from Jax's tight grip, grab some water, and offer it to her. Her hands are trembling so bad, she can't even hold the glass.

My mom comes over and immediately checks An's pulse. "An, please try to stay focused right now. Michael will get treatment, and he *will* survive. We have caught this early enough for the treatment to be effective. What this family can't handle is anything happening to you. I need you to calm down, take some slow, deep breaths, and concentrate on my voice." My mom, once again, is working her magic. "Raven, please make some chamomile tea," she asks me quickly then turns back to An. "Remember what we discussed; you need to focus on your health. Michael needs you to be strong and healthy."

I hurry up and put up the pot for tea. Jax finally snaps out of his shock and takes charge of the situation. "McCord, after we do the swab's, what's next? Where can he get the best treatment?"

"Mr. Phillips, the treatment is done in three phases. The first phase is called Remission induction. In this phase, the goal is to kill the leukemia cells that are in the blood and the bone marrow. The second phase is called consolidation or intensification. This starts when Michael is in remission. It's a specific therapy to kill any remaining leukemia cells that may cause a relapse. The third phase is a maintenance treatment. The best place for this type of treatment is in the USA. I have looked at the top five hospitals in the United States and I would suggest The Children's Hospital of Philadelphia. Dr. Torrence is the head of the oncology pediatric department. They are on the cutting edge of research for this type of cancer. I took the liberty of contacting them and arranged for Michael's admittance."

"What about this bone marrow that you're testing us for? When does that come into play?"

"It's not part of the initial treatment, it's used in the event of a relapse after treatment. I want to be prepared just in case. Usually a sibling is the best match, but since Michael is an only child, I want to start the search now. As long as everyone is healthy, then donating won't be a problem."

I bring An her tea and she seems to be calmer. My mom takes the swabs and begins to swab each of us. As she swabs the inside of my cheek, I'm reminded that something so simple can be a life saver to someone in need. When she gets to Jackie, she stops her. "I'm already a member of the Blood and Marrow Transplant information network. I've donated in the past, and if I'm a match, I would gladly donate again."

Max tightens his hold on her hands. "Thank you, babe."

"Max, please don't thank me. Everyone should be doing this and not just in a time of crisis. A lot of people know about donating blood, however, not everyone knows about donating stem cells."

My mom takes Bella's hand and pulls her to her feet. "Bella, listen to me, please. You are Michael's rock right now. His state of mind will be based on how you, and everyone here, react around him. It's very important to keep a positive outlook and, whatever you do, don't treat him any differently. I understand that I'm not Michael's doctor. I am, however, his friend. If it would be okay with you, I would like to go with him to the states and stay with him."

"Oh, Rose, I would love to have you there with us. I know how close the two of you have become, and I'm sure Michael would love having you there. Dr. McCord, when will we be leaving?"

"You will be leaving in the morning."

"Okay. Thank you, everyone. If you'll excuse me, I'm going upstairs to be with my son." Bella and Michael Sr. race upstairs to be with Michael.

My mom gathers up the swabs and hurries out to get them back to the lab.

The baby monitor comes to life but I already know it's time to feed Antonia, I can feel it. "An, I'm going upstairs to feed Antonia, would you like me to walk with you to your room?" I'm not really giving her an option; she needs rest.

"Thank you, Raven." I help her upstairs and let her lean on me for support, knowing the rough road ahead for all of us and silently praying we come out okay.

Jaxson

FOR THE PAST TWO days, my life has been spinning out of control. I hate the unknown, yet lately, that's all I have . . . a life filled with 'what ifs.' I don't do 'what ifs'; I don't leave things to chance. I snap out of my stage of disbelief, I need to make the rest of the arrangements. I hear Max on the phone, probably arranging security. I pour us each a scotch while I wait for him to finish his call. "Jackie, how long have you been involved with the donor network?"

"I became involved about eight years ago. My father had a friend whose son was also diagnosed with ALL. Like Michael, he is an only child, so my whole family was tested. I came up as the closest match, so when he needed the transplant, I donated. Jax, the little boy is fine. We've stayed in touch. He lives in the states and is getting ready for his prom."

"Thank you, Jackie. You are a very kind-hearted person and my brother is very lucky to have you in his life . . . we all are." I hug her. She brings so much to this family without even trying.

Max is finally off the phone. "Max, I need to get a place to stay near the hospital. I'll be leaving in the morning with Junior."

"Jax, we are all leaving in the morning. The plane is being prepared now. Mrs. Osla is setting up a place for us to live. Security is all set; we all go, mate."

I pass him his scotch, "Why did this happen to Junior? Is this something that runs through our gene pool? He has been having so much fun here."

Jackie gets up and hugs Max. "Max, I'm going to check on An and Raven."

"Jackie will go to her parents for a few days and then meet us in the states." He turns his focus back to me.

I let him know that Raven told me about her birthday. "That must be so hard for her. Birthdays are supposed to be a happy day. Can we do anything to make it better for her?"

He swirls the amber liquid in his glass; he seems distant. "I was going to go with her to her parents but, with everything happening with Junior, I'm going to the states with you."

"Go with her, and then you can both head over to the states together. It's only for a few days, and we will all be there. If you want, talk to Junior about it." I know he's torn and not just about Junior. "Max, what made you decide not to go to Capri?"

"Mrs. Osla and I had a long talk. She made me realize what I could lose if I go. I can't lose Jackie, it would kill me."

"I should have figured Mrs. Osla had a hand in it. Do you think she will ever feel comfortable letting everyone know her connection to you?"

"I told her that you know she was Samantha's aunt and practically raised her. The rest is up to her. Knowing her as well as I do, I imagine she doesn't want anyone to feel uncomfortable around her. "

"Was she upset that you told me? I've never said anything to her, I respect her privacy."

"She understood that I needed to tell you everything so that I could move forward in life. Ultimately, that's all she's ever wanted for me. When she's not scaring the living daylights out of me."

I look at him and he's really serious. I can't help but laugh. "Oh, Max, sometimes you really are my source of amusement. Let's go check on Junior, I'm sure Bella told him what's going on by now. I don't want him to be scared."

As we get up to head upstairs, Mrs. Osla walks in. "Jaxson, I need to go over the arrangements I made for tomorrow."

We both freeze in our tracks. Max is biting his bottom lip, trying not to laugh. "Jax, you stay here with Mrs. Osla and I will meet you upstairs." As he turns to leave his eyes meet hers and he stops dead in his tracks.

"Maxwell, he is your nephew also, so I suggest you both have a seat."

Heading back to the couch, I can almost swear I hear Max growl. She hands us each a folder. "I have compiled some information about the treatment that young Michael could expect, the length of time required to administer the treatment, and the possible side effects. The treatment and follow up could take up to three years. I secured an estate ten minutes from the hospital that is large enough to accommodate everyone. I understand everyone is in shock right now, however, please bear in mind this is not a death sentence. I have enclosed a packet on Dr. David Torrence, the oncologist that will be handling young Michael's treatment. If you look at the research I provided you with, the survival rate since 2005 is at 90.4%. That is something to stay focused on. It is very important that everyone stay positive and upbeat for the lad. Jaxson, I'm worried about the stress all of this is having on An. If it is okay with you, I would like to accompany her to the states and stay with her. She has been a very kind, dear friend and I would like to do the same. However, if you need me to stay here, I will."

I'm overwhelmed looking through all the research that she pulled. "Christ, Max, look at all the stuff Junior is going to have to go through. I had no idea it was going to be this much and this long." I thank God we have the unlimited resources to provide anything he needs.

"Neither did I. We will be there with him every step of the way."

"Jaxson, I also got the information from Matthew that you requested. I think you will both find this very interesting. In New York State, your medical license is for life, as long as you have not been convicted of a felony. When a physician's license is put on the inactive list, it must be updated every two years. Apparently Joseph had her license placed on the inactive list, and made sure he maintained the status for her. Matthew started the process to activate it and have her name changed on her license. If she wanted to practice legally, she could, however, she would be required to complete all updated course work and training. It won't be easy but it doesn't mean she can't do it. There are a lot of options available to her, but it is up to her to decide. Maxwell, as per your request, Matthew removed you as her legal guardian but you are still the executor of her will. Jaxson, you can't bully her to do something she's not prepared to do."

"Mrs. Osla, I wouldn't bully her." She raises one eyebrow and cocks her head to the side. "Did Matthew say how long it will take?"

"Surprisingly, once he submits the name change, only a couple of days."

"Thank you. I will sit Rose down and let her know what is going on. You can travel with my mum to the states and stay with her. I'm sure she would love the company and I appreciate that you would want to do that for her."

"If you don't need me for anything else, I want to visit with An."

"That's fine, thank you."

"What the hell are you thinking, Jax? She's been locked away for twenty years, she can't just go back to a life that doesn't exist anymore," Max pounces before Mrs. Osla even steps fully out of the room.

"Calm down. I'm not going to push her into anything. Raven, asked me to look into it. She said she spoke with Rose and it might be an option. She doesn't have to go back to being a surgeon, she could go into research. She needs to know that all her schooling and training wasn't for nothing. She still has a very full life ahead of her and we need to give her every chance possible."

"Jax, don't force her to do something she might not be ready to do."

"I promise I won't. Let's go see Junior. I promised him we could watch the new *Doctor Who.*"

"Jax, so help me, I'm not sitting through another hour of that show. Did you know Junior is trying to get Jackie to watch it with him?"

"Ha! I told you that kid is a genius."

Chapter Eleven

Raven

"AN, PROMISE ME YOU will try and get some rest. Michael needs all of us to be strong," I plead with her. I don't doubt she needs this reminder as she is still recuperating from surgery.

"Raven, I'm so scared. I've never had to deal with anything like this. How much more heartache will we have to suffer?"

She begins to cry and I pull her into my arms. "An, Michael is a very strong boy. We need to have faith. We need to be his rock to lean on." *Maybe if I tell her enough, I'll believe it myself.*

We head into her room and I get her settled in. "I'm going to feed Antonia, and then I will check back in with you. In the meantime, try and get some rest."

I'm heading toward the nursery when I run into my mom. "Hey, Mom, you're just the person I wanted to see. I'm heading in to feed Antonia, will you come with me?"

"I was going to check on An, can it wait?"

"Actually, I just got An settled in for a nap."

"Oh, okay, I will check on her later. We need to try and keep her calm. What do you need?"

"Let me get Antonia situated first."

We head into the nursery and my mom begins to change Antonia.

When she's done, I take my usual seat in front of the window and begin to nurse.

"What's on your mind, Raven?"

"Actually, I have quite a few questions. What can we expect with Michael's treatment? Should Antonia be tested? What are Michael's chances of survival? How did he get this?"

"Raven, slow down. First, I'm not an Oncologist, and neither is Dr. McCord. These are questions that need to be addressed by Michael's Oncologist. While the test was running, I did some research and found The Children's Hospital in Philadelphia has a high survival rate, in the ninetieth percentile. We've caught this early, and that's also a positive for Michael. I don't have all the answers, I'm sorry. I only thought to check for it because I worked closely with an ALL patient who also had a heart condition. This is not going to be a quick fix and everyone will have to adjust to the changes, especially Michael. He is so active and full of life. I thank God that Jax listened to me and ran the test. From what I read online, the treatments can run for three years. We will have to adjust and live our lives around his treatments."

I sit quietly for a moment, letting all of this information sink in. Suddenly, I remember the letter I received the other day. "Mom, Jax got a package the other day from his attorney. There is a letter addressed to me from Duke. I didn't open it and, to be honest, I'm not sure I want to."

"What are you afraid of? You know he can't hurt you, Raven."

"Not physically, but how about emotionally? I've worked so hard to put the past behind me only to find out I have a sibling. My whole childhood, I dreamt of having a sibling, then that dream came true, except . . . he turned into a murderer. I'm sorry if this hurts you, Mom. I don't know what to do? I would have had Max read it, but I can't put anything else on him."

"Do you feel you have to read it? Why not just burn it?—he's not in your life and he never will be."

"I thought about that, but it's because of Duke that we are free from Vincent."

"Raven, it's because of Duke that Vincent knew you were alive. Don't paint him out to be the victim. From what you told me, he had a hand in your kidnapping and the kidnapping of Michael. One good deed doesn't wipe out all the bad. He walked away with a sweet deal, never having to answer for the lives he took."

"I wish I was as strong as you, Mom."

"Nonsense, Raven, you're a lot stronger than you think. I'm going to check on An while you finish up with Antonia." She squeezes my shoulder and turns to leave just as Jackie walks in.

"Hi, Jackie, I was just going to check on An, is everything okay?"

"Yes, Rose, I just wanted to see my niece." My mom leaves and I know something is bothering Jackie. I don't say anything, I know her; she will talk to me when she is ready. I put Antonia in her crib and take a moment to watch her sleep. I'm reminded that with all the turmoil around us, life still goes on. I turn around and Jackie is sitting in the rocker, staring out into the darkness. "I never knew that you donated stem cells. What made you do it?"

"A friend of my father's son had ALL. He is an only child, so we were all tested. I was a close match. The surgery is not bad; a needle is injected into the back of the top part of the hip bone. They harvest about 2 pints of marrow, and you're sore for a couple of days. Something so simple can save so many lives. Donating cord blood is very important and also so simple. When I have a child, I already plan on donating."

"I never knew that there were uses for the cord."

"Raven, there are a number of uses for the cord blood, but you have to have the baby in the hospital."

"Funny, Jackie . . . very funny. So what's bothering you, and don't say 'nothing'."

"I told Max we could get married in May. Now with everything going on with Michael, I'm thinking of delaying it. I just don't know how to explain it to him."

I stretch out on the window bench trying to figure out a solution. "You know he is going to flip out if you delay the wedding. Plus Michael told me today how excited he is that you will be his aunt. We need to figure something out."

"I don't know what we could figure out, we are leaving in the morning for the states, and then I have to fly to Switzerland."

"Where were you planning on having the wedding?"

"I figured Scotland is very pretty in May, so I would have it here. Why, what are you thinking?"

"Now hear me out and keep an open mind."

She stops rocking and leans forward. "Okay, you have my full attention. What's the plan?"

"The plan is: you go to your parents' home and have a ceremony for them. You then come to the states and have a ceremony at the hospital, so Michael can be a part of it. When we get back and everything is settled, you can renew your vows and have whatever type of wedding you want," I declare. Her eyes are wide and her mouth is hanging open. "Well, aren't you going to say anything?"

"Are you nuts? I went from having no wedding to having three weddings. You want me to get married now?! Besides, Max is going to the states with Michael. I don't expect him to go to my parents with me."

"Look, you know you want your parents to be there. The entire family wants to be part of this day. You can't put everything on hold. Life doesn't stop, we have to adapt. This is us adapting. Max will never let you go to your parents' house alone. Face it, Jackie, he needs to feel like he is protecting you."

"Even if that's true, how do you intend on getting everything together so quickly?"

"Jackie, we have Mrs. Osla! That woman can move mountains if she had to."

"So, what do you suggest I tell Max?"

Right at that moment, Jax and Max decide to walk into the nursery.

"Tell me what, Jackie?" His voice is low and his jaw is tight, he takes hold of her hand.

I get up and take Jax's arm. "How about we give them some privacy? Besides, I need to see Michael." I pull Jax out of the room, not giving him a chance to answer.

Jackie

"RAVEN AND I WERE discussing Michael's treatment. I explained to her that it could take about three years. We were trying to figure out what to do about our wedding when you came in. Do you have any ideas as to what we should do?"

"The only thing I've figured out so far is that I'm going to Switzerland with you. Mrs. Osla made all the arrangements for Michael, and she set up a place for all of us right near the hospital. I know Michael's treatment is not an overnight fix, but I'm begging you please don't ask me to wait three years. Did Raven come up with ideas?"

"Max, calm down; we don't want to wake the baby. Raven's idea was for us to get married while we're in Switzerland. Then, we can have a simple ceremony at the hospital for Michael and the rest of the family. Down the road, if we want to renew our vows back in Scotland, we can. She suggested Mrs. Osla could pull this off." Max's face lights up and he gifts me with a huge smile. "I take it you like this idea?"

"I'll be your husband sooner rather than later, what's not to like? How do you feel about this? I know that every woman dreams of her wedding day. I want to make all your dreams come true."

"I've never dreamed of a big fancy wedding, maybe because I grew up so isolated. All I ever dreamed of was finding a man to love me honestly, heart and soul. I've found that in you. It doesn't matter how it happens, just make it happen, Max."

"Babe, I will get Mrs. Osla on it right away. Everyone leaves in the morning for the states. We will follow them over there as soon as possible. What day would you like to get married?"

"I would like to get married on my birthday. I think it's only fitting that I can mark a sad day with some happiness. My sister will be there in spirit, and that would mean so much to me."

"If you're really sure that's what you want, then I will talk to Mrs. Osla and have her make all the arrangements."

I reach up and kiss his tender lips. "Yes. Now, let's go tell Michael that I will be his aunt. I know he will be happy, even though I refuse to watch that show with him."

He puts his arm around me, and as we head out of the nursery, Antonia starts to fuss. Max walks up to the crib, reaches in, and rubs her tummy. He begins to sing very softly to her. I can barely understand what he's saying. It sounds like *hush ye, my baby, and sleep without fear.* Antonia falls back to sleep and we quietly step out of the room.

"Max, what were you singing? I could only understand part of it."

"It's an old, Scottish lullaby by Jackie Oates called "Dream Agnus." I would sing it to Elliot every night."

"It's beautiful, very soothing; she fell right back to sleep. Come on; let's go tell the others our plan."

Jaxson

AS RAVEN AND I head toward Junior's room, she fills me in on what's going on with Jackie. "So, what have you been up to since I left you alone?" she asks, changing the subject. I promptly relay all of the information Mrs. Osla gave Max and me.

"I asked my mom if we should have Antonia tested and she said we need to speak with Michael's oncologist."

"Mrs. Osla lined up the top oncologist to see Junior. It kills me that he has to go through all of this." As we get ready to step into Junior's room, I take a moment to put on a happy face and bury my anger. I know he needs only positive, upbeat people around him right now. As soon as we step inside, I notice he's upset.

"Hey, Junior, what's the problem here?" I ask then notice Bella and Michael looking grim.

"Uncle Jax, Mum told me what is going on. I don't want to leave here, and I sure don't want to get stuck with a bunch of stupid needles."

I feel like my heart is ripping to shreds. "Hey, Junior, we are all going to be there with you every step of the way. You know that, right?"

"Everyone? Even Antonia?"

"Yes, even Antonia. We are family and we stick together—no matter what. Why are you so worried about leaving here?"

"What if we don't get to come back here? Miss Rose and I have been exploring everyday and I love helping Miss Jackie with the horses. I have a lot of friends here, what about t-them?" He stutters and his lip begins to tremble. I'm trying so hard to keep it together here. I glance to Raven for help. She sits down on the bed next to Junior and takes his hand.

"Michael, look at me, please. You know this place is over a

hundred years old, it's not going anywhere. Your friends will still be your friends. I promise you will be able to Skype with them all the time. When we get back, I'm sure Jackie will have you right back down at the barn. I know you're scared, and it's okay to have those feelings, but we will all be with you every step of the way. You'll never be alone—I promise. Remember, when we were kidnapped? I promised you we would be rescued and we would be okay. I'm promising you now, we will be with you and you will be okay. Faith, Michael." She pulls him into her arms, "Faith," she whispers. The door opens and in walks Max and Jackie.

"Hey, Michael, Jackie and I need to talk to you about something."

"Sure, Uncle Max, what's up?"

"Everyone is flying out tomorrow with you to the States. Jackie and I have to head to Switzerland for a few days to see her parents. We will head out to you right after that. Are you okay with that?"

Jackie sits on the bed and takes his hand. "Michael, I promise we will be with you the whole time. I need to go to my parents for a few days, if it wasn't important, I wouldn't go. When we get to the States, your Uncle Max and I are going to get married. I was wondering if you would give me away like you did for Aunt Raven?"

"Miss Jackie, I will give you away and it's okay if you need to go to your parents. You promise you'll come as soon as you can?"

"I promise, Michael. Don't worry about the horses, I've got their care all arranged until we get back."

"There's just one thing, Miss Jackie."

"You're gonna make me, aren't you?"

"Yep."

"Michael Giaconna, I swear you are more like your Uncle Jax every day. Fine, but your Uncle Max has to, as well."

"Yes!" He throws his arms around her.

"Hey wait, what do I have to do? Jax, what's so funny?" Max smacks my arm as I chuckle.

Oh my God, I can't stop laughing. The kid is a genius. "You have to watch *Doctor Who.*" I could swear he's growling.

Raven gets up, "I'll go make the peanut butter & jelly sandwiches."

Chapter Twelve

Maxwell

THE SHOW IS FINALLY over. I don't understand what the attraction is, but Junior was happy he finally got us to watch it. At least Raven made me popcorn. "Okay, Junior, you get some rest. You have to leave early tomorrow. Jackie and I will be out in a few days. Don't even think of complaining, we held up our end of the deal." I take Jackie's hand and we head out the door.

"Hey, Max . . . Jackie, wait up." Jax catches up to us.

"What's up, Jax?"

"I just want to thank you, Jackie. I know it's not the wedding of your dreams, but you made Junior very happy, and for that, I will always be in your debt."

"I love that little boy, and I would do anything for him."

"Thank you. Is there anything you need me to do for you before I leave?"

"No, I have arranged everything for the horses."

"Max, is all the security arranged for the trip and at the hospital?"

"Yes, I've got everything under control. Get some rest, you have another long day tomorrow."

"I will. I want to check on Mum first. I'll see you both in the morning, good night."

He leaves and now I want to talk to Mrs. Osla, before it gets any later. We head downstairs and find her in the kitchen. Jackie and I explain to her what we want to do and she assures us she can get all the arrangements made.

"I'm very happy for you both. It's time this family had some good news." She hugs us both and we head out the door. I need to be alone with Jackie. It's been a very stressful day, and my heart is breaking for Junior.

We walk back to our place hand in hand; this is what's special to me. "Babe, I understand that the treatment and follow up could last three years, was it like that for the boy you donated to?"

"Every case is different; everyone's body reacts differently to the treatment. He had a setback which is why he needed the stem cells. He's fine now, and odds are in Michael's favor. His attitude is a big part of the healing. He has to believe he will beat this, as do the people around him."

"I get it, so even though my heart is breaking, I will put on a brave face and treat him no differently than I do now."

"Exactly. That is very important. Michael needs to understand that it's not a death sentence and it's not a license to do whatever he wants. Love him as you always have and always will."

As we head in the door, I turn her around in my arms and kiss her very tenderly.

"Babe, I need you slow and gentle. I need to feel your delicate fingertips trailing all over my body. I need you to make me forget."

"How about we have a nice soak in the tub, and then I'll see what I can do to help you relax."

We head into the bathroom and Jackie sets up the bath. She lights the candles, lights the fireplace, and turns on some music. I sit on the counter, watching her and I'm amazed how graceful she is . . . even doing such simple things. She shuts the water off and announces the tub is ready. I watch in a trance as she undresses and slowly sinks in.

"Are you going to join me, or are you going to ogle me all night?"

I quickly snap out of my trance and take off my clothes. I climb in the huge tub, facing her. I begin to massage her feet, and when I get to the arch, I press and drag my thumb all the way up. She tilts her head back and moans. *Fuck me,* she is so beautiful.

"Max, that feels absolutely wonderful. Now, let me return the favor. Come sit between my legs and let me massage your shoulders."

I turn around and wedge myself between her legs, looping my arms around them, feeling totally surrounded by her. She massages my shoulders and I feel myself finally relax.

"Max, have you always loved baths?"

"Yes, even more now with you." I can feel my tension fade away. "Do you think your parents are going to be okay with the quick wedding arrangements?"

"Once I explain to them why, they will understand. My mom will be happy to have something so wonderful on such a somber day. I will warn you, my brother will probably have something to say about it."

"Jackie, you understand no one will get in our way. I will be respectful of your family, however, I know what he said to you when you left. I will not put up with that type of behavior toward you—*ever.*"

"It doesn't matter to me what he thinks, it's what's in my heart that counts. Nothing will ever change that for me. Now, I think this water is getting cold and I need you to fulfill your promise to love me tender and gentle."

I climb out of the tub and get the towels off of the warmer, wrap one around my waist, and then dry her off. I don't think I will ever get tired of touching her, or caring for her. It's all the little things that make our relationship special. She tries to stifle her yawn, but I know she's tired. We've both had a long and emotional day. "Babe, let's get some rest, tomorrow is going to be another hard day for all of us." We climb into bed and I pull her close to me. I laugh as she tucks the blankets in around us. I gently stroke her back and listen to the tempo of her breathing slow down as she drifts off to sleep. "Thank you for loving me, Jackie," I whisper and kiss the top of her head.

Isabella

I SIT IN MY son's room and watch him fall asleep. I feel another wave of fear rush over me. I have to be strong for him, I just don't know how. Why did this happen—he's never been sick—*why?* Michael comes back in to check on us. I know he's scared too, but I need to focus all my energy on our son.

"Bella, come to bed. You need to get some rest. You'll be no good to Junior if you get sick."

I know he's right but I can't bring myself to leave his side. "Maybe later, right now, I need to be here with him. I know he's scared and I want to stay here in case he wakes up." He scoops me up into his arms. "Michael, what are you doing?"

"Bella, if you stay I stay; we are in this together."

He sits in the chair and cradles me in his arms. I rest my head on his chest and let my tears silently fall, careful not to wake my son.

"Hush, Bella, I've got you. I'll always have you."

In the safety of his arms, I allow myself to finally get some sleep.

Rose

I WANT TO CHECK on An again before I turn in for the night. I know what lies ahead for Michael, but the last thing anyone needs right now is to be overwhelmed with too much information. I need to make sure she remains calm. She is very lucky to be alive right now, and I mean to keep it like that. I knock and Mrs. Osla lets me in.

"Hi, Mrs. Osla. I wanted to check on An before I turned in for the night."

"She is sleeping right now, but do you have a moment to chat with me?"

"Of course, what can I do for you, Mrs. Osla?"

"Well, you can start by finally calling me Rona. You saved my best friend's life and I will always be indebted to you. I did the research for Michael's treatment, so I know what is in store for the lad. I know it's not your field of study, but I'm grateful you insisted the test be run. Again, I wanted to thank you and to let you know I will be traveling to the States with everyone. If you need me for anything, please don't hesitate to ask."

"Okay, thank you, Rona. I'm going to do a quick check on An and then try and get some rest." I head into An's room and she is asleep, however, I want to at least take her blood pressure and pulse. Exhaustion must have finally hit, she barely moved while I checked her. I head out and I see Rona is still here.

"Everything seems good. I will check her again in the morning. Rona, your name is very unusual, what does it mean?"

She smiles "Wise ruler, very fitting, don't you agree?"

I laugh, "Yes, I would say so. You should get some rest; it's a long flight tomorrow."

"I will, thank you, Rose."

I head out the door feeling very tired and overwhelmed with to-day's events. I need to get some sleep. I only hope my mind will let me.

Raven

ANTONIA IS UP VERY early this morning, which is fine since I need to pack her stuff. It's amazing how much one little baby needs. Knowing Mrs. Osla, she's probably made sure the house is well stocked. I sit in front of the window, watching the sunrise probably for the last time in a long while. *I'm really going to miss this place.* It's become home; my daughter was born here. I promised Michael that we will come back and I intend to keep that promise . . . no matter what. He is such a special boy. I spent most of the night, praying to God to please give him the strength he will need to get through this. It's going to be a long road for everyone. "Good morning, Jax," I say as I feel his presence.

"Good morning, sweetheart. Is she done eating?"

"Yeah, but she doesn't seem tired."

"I'll take her while you get ready," he offers. I hand him the baby, but I don't get up just yet.

"It's going to be another long emotional day for all of us. I'm glad my mom will be with us. Watching her take charge of everything, so effortlessly, was very comforting. She was able to keep the panic at a minimal." He sits in the rocker and slowly glides back and forth as Antonia fights to keep her eyes open.

"Raven, I had Matthew look into your mum's license, like you asked. It's still good. Also, Matthew had her name changed and requested to have it made active, but that's only the beginning. There is a lot of other stuff she would have to do in order to practice. I'm not sure of everything that is needed, but Matthew is going to look into it and let her know. In the meantime, I am going to bring her up to speed on what we do know."

"Well, I wasn't expecting it to be easy."

"That's just the first hurdle. If she decides to practice, then I'm sure she would be required to do continuing education classes along with training to bring her up to speed. Maybe she would rather go into some sort of research; I don't know what that would entail. Ultimately, it's up to her. I'm just giving her the opportunity to make her own decision."

"Thank you. Just remember to go slow when you tell her." I get up to leave and bend down to kiss Antonia. I love her smell; sweet and fresh. He takes my hand and brings it to his lips, tightly closing his eyes. I know something is bothering him.

"What's wrong?"

"The letter; have you decided what you're going to do?"

"Yes. I'm going to read it before we leave today. It won't change anything, at least for me it won't."

"I'm here for you and, if you want me to be with you when you read it, let me know."

"I love you, Jax."

"More, sweetheart, always more."

I LEAVE ANTONIA'S ROOM with Jax mindlessly rocking her back and forth. She's asleep. He could put her in her crib, but this is his special time with her. While everyone is still asleep, I decide to head straight to his office and retrieve the letter. I need to get this over with and move on. I take the letter off the desk and curl up on his oversized, leather sofa. I close my eyes and take a deep breath.

I know nothing he can say will change what happened. Jackie has always told me that the only way to move forward is to forgive and leave the past behind. *Easier said than done.* "I don't think I'm that strong."

"You're stronger than you think, Raven."

My eyes fly open and find Jax standing in the doorway. "I didn't hear you."

"I know. I didn't want to startle you, but I was worried. I'll give you some privacy, however, I won't be far away." He steps out of the room and closes the door. I muster up my courage and open the letter.

Raven,

I know you must hate me and I can understand why. I won't make excuses for what I did; I have to live with that for the rest of my life. When I first met you, I didn't know what to think. The only information I had was what Erica shared with me. I only found out you were my sister when you and Michael were kidnapped. I was not involved with Marco and Erica's plan to take you from that safe house. At that point, I was in too deep and had no idea how to get out. I thought by contacting Vincent, and telling him I was his son, that it would be a way out of that clusterfuck of a mess. When I explained to him who you and I were, and what was going on, he went ballistic. He told me not to panic, that he would help me. Little did I know the type of help he was offering would be even worse. I never killed anyone before. Hell, I've never even gotten into a fight! But that night, I took two lives. I will have to live with that for the rest of my life.

When we were in Italy, and you showed me our mother's journal, I realized what Vincent really was. I walked out of your room that day, knowing I needed to come up with a plan. I figured if I kept quiet, and let him believe that I wanted to be a part of his life, that I could figure a way out of that mess. The day the doctor came to examine you, Vincent stayed outside your room the entire time, waiting to find out what was wrong with you. That gave me the opportunity to go into his office and look around. I saw the program opened on his computer, so I downloaded everything. I knew that it must've been important, since he kept that drive with him all the time. When Jaxson and Maxwell came to rescue you, Vincent heard them and ordered the guards to go after them. He told them not to harm you, not that any of that mattered. He ran into his office and grabbed the drive. He told me to flee, and he would meet me in the states. I hid in the wine cellar until I had a chance to leave. I knew I would never get out of the country, so I took everything I thought was important and mailed it to a friend. I went to the airport, where I was picked up by the police.

Vincent sent Annabelle to see me, to try and persuade me to take the fall for everything. I knew then—I had to make a deal. I asked Hage if you were safe; I was prepared to include you in my deal if you needed me to. That's when he told me you and Jaxson were married. He assured me that Jaxson would make sure you were safe, and I knew this to be true.

Part of my deal is that I'm never to contact, or see you or any of the Giaconna family. I have no desire to see any of them, although, I would've liked to have gotten to know you better. You were always kind to me, even when I wasn't to you. I wish you and your family only the best; you fought hard for it and you deserve it.

I'm glad you're getting your happily ever after— you deserve it!

Duke

Wow, so much that I wasn't aware of. It doesn't change anything for me. I told Hage that Duke snapped that day. Anyone could see how played he was by Marco and Erica. Because of his efforts to get that drive, though, Max and I didn't have to testify. If my mom decides she wants to read this, I will let her. Maybe she can see some good in him. I take the letter and put it in the safe. I need to get ready. I want to make sure Michael is not scared. I open the door to head out and find Jax sitting on the floor.

"What are you doing?" I reach my hand down to him. He takes it, pulling himself up off the floor.

"I was worried about you and wanted to be here . . . just in case."

"I'm okay. I put the letter in the safe. He explained how he got the information and why. It doesn't matter, Jax; I closed that door for good. Now let's go check on Michael and then get started."

"Raven, you are, by far, the strongest person I know. I love you."

"It's the only way I know how to be."

As we head down the hall, he pulls me close. "You really okay with everything?"

"I really am. I know that whatever happened with Duke, he has to live with it. Jackie always tells me to forgive and then put it away. If I dwell on what happened, it would make me a bitter person. The past can't be changed, but the path we choose to move forward on can. I'm choosing only positive in my life."

"Sometimes your strength and faith befuddles my mind." We quietly head down the hall to Michael's room.

Chapter Thirteen

Junior

I CAN'T SLEEP AND I know it's cause I'm scared. My mum is trying not to cry but I can tell she's scared too. Why did this have to happen to me? I won't even have time to say goodbye to any of my friends. I wonder what the doctors are going to do to me? Vito slept with his head on my pillow all night. "Don't you worry, Vito, you go where I go." My door slowly opens and Aunt Raven and Uncle Jax stick their heads in. "I'm up; you can come in. You just missed Mum and Dad, they went to get ready to leave."

Aunt Raven crawls into bed next to Vito; he likes her. "Michael, are you ready to get going?"

I'm trying to be brave but I'm worried about Vito. I wipe my eyes as Aunt Raven pulls me toward her, which is hard with Vito in the middle.

"Michael, please tell me why you're upset. Maybe I can fix it."

"What a-about, Vito? What will happen to him, Aunt Raven?"

Uncle Jax throws his hands up in the air. "Junior, is that what this is about? I told you no one gets left behind and that includes the beast."

Aunt Raven and I start to laugh, "Uncle Jax, you know you love him."

"Whatever, Junior. Do you have everything packed? If you forget something, Uncle Max can bring it. I made sure Mrs. Osla ordered all our favorite DVDs. By the way, that was a slick move last night. You made me proud."

"Thanks, Uncle Jax, but I don't think they liked it. Oh, and why doesn't Uncle Max like peanut butter and jelly sandwiches?"

"I don't know; I never asked him. When you find out let me know."

"Uncle Jax, is Grams going to be able to come with me?"

"Just try and stop her! Now come on, you need to get ready. Be downstairs and ready to go in thirty minutes."

When they head out the door, I get up and throw on my clothes. I'm not going to some stupid hospital to get a bunch of needles. I looked it up on the Internet last night, and whatever this is that I have it doesn't look good. I grab my backpack and I'm thankful that I snuck into the kitchen this morning, using the secret passage to get my supplies. "Vito, come on, we have to go." He's not moving off the bed, but his tail is thumping. "Come on, Vito, we can't get caught." Finally he hops off the bed, and we quietly head out the door. I press the secret panel and just like that—we are gone.

Jaxson

"RAVEN, WHILE YOU FINISH tending to Antonia, I want to go over a few things with Mrs. Osla. I'll meet you downstairs."

"Ok, I shouldn't be too much longer."

I kiss her and head downstairs. I find Mrs. Osla and my mum having breakfast. "Good morning everyone. Mum, how are you feeling this morning?"

"I'm fine, son. Is everyone ready to leave?"

"Almost. Mrs. Osla, you got everything I asked for set up at the new house?"

"Jaxson, I assure you—all your favorite DVDs are already there. And, I even managed a surprise for young Michael. Before you ask, the answer is no; you'll have to wait and see."

Just then, Bella comes rushing in. "Jax, I can't find Junior! Do you know where he is?"

"I just left him in his room with the beast. I told him he had thirty minutes to be down here."

"I checked! He's not there and neither is Vito."

"Did you call his cell?"

"He left it on his nightstand. Michael went out to check the barn. I asked the guards and they said he never left the house."

"Bella, he has to be here . . . he didn't just disappear. It's a big house; let's get everyone together and start a search."

I call Max and inform him what's going on. We gather everyone into the kitchen and I hand out the two-way radios. "Rose, you've done the most exploring with Junior; is there any one of the secret passages that he likes the best?"

"He loves them all, but I know he really wanted to explore the tunnel that stretches from the backend of the house to the barn. There are so many that we haven't checked out yet."

Max comes racing through the door. "Hey, any sign of him yet?"

"No, Max, nothing. Why the hell would he do this?"

Max unfolds the blueprints and assigns each person a section to cover. "Maybe he's scared, Jax. Everyone take a flashlight along with your radio. Please check in every fifteen minutes. Mum, you and Mrs. Osla wait here in case he shows up."

Raven comes in with Antonia, ready to go. "What's going on?"

"Junior disappeared. We are going to split up to search." She gives Antonia to Mrs. Osla.

"Jax, give me a section and a radio."

We each take a passageway and head out in search of Junior.

Raven

WITH BO RIGHT BY my side, I take the passage that Michael showed me. Instead of going up the staircase, I take the tunnel to the right. There are so many twist and turns. The tunnel seems to get a little wider and then suddenly, I come to a fork in the road. I stop and look in each direction. I have a gut feeling that I should go right. I go a few feet and I see Michael curled up with Vito, fast asleep. I pull out my radio to let everyone know I found him. "Jax, I've found Michael; he's asleep. Go through the passage way off the kitchen. When you get to the spiral staircase, there is a tunnel on the right. Go through the tunnel until you get to the fork, and then, go right. I will wait here for you." He assures me he's on his way. I sit next to Michael and try not to startle him.

"Michael, it's Aunt Raven, you need to wake up," I whisper as I gently stroke his hair.

He slowly opens his eyes, and widens them as if he's shocked to find me sitting next to him. "Aunt Raven, how did you find me?"

"I remembered you told me you wanted to explore this tunnel, so I thought I would look here first. Why did you run away?"

"I looked up on the internet what could happen to me and I got scared."

I open my arms, "Michael, come here." I hug him tightly. "You can't believe everything you find on the internet. I get that you're scared. It's okay to be scared of the unknown. I promised you we would all be there with you. You will never have to go through this by yourself. I need you to fight, Michael. I need you to be that brave boy that you were when we were kidnapped. You helped me get through that and I will help you get through this."

"How did I help you?"

"You gave me strength and you reminded me that I had a lot to live for. You also made me laugh even when I wanted to cry."

"I will try to be strong. My mum is going to be really mad at me."

"I won't lie, Michael, everyone is out looking for you. I radioed your Uncle Jax, and he is on his way."

"It's okay, Aunt Raven, I will apologize to everyone."

I hear Jax coming as he rounds the corner .Vito jumps up. "It's okay, Vito, it's only Jax."

"Junior, are you okay? What the hell were you thinking?"

"I'm sorry, Uncle Jax, I really didn't mean to make everyone worry about me."

He crouch's down in front of us, "Why did you run?"

He's looking down at his hands, seemingly trying not to cry. "It's okay, Michael, tell him."

"Uncle Jax, I'm scared. I don't want to do any of this."

Michael begins to sob uncontrollably, "Shh, don't cry, Michael, you'll be okay."

Jax pulls Michael into his lap. "I know you're scared, and, I won't lie to you—we all are. But, you are the bravest boy I know. You helped Aunt Raven when you were kidnapped. You moved out of the country; no questions asked. I know you can get through this, too."

"How?"

"Faith. Now we really need to get back. How about you climb on my back and we race on out of here?"

Michael climbs onto Jax's back and I gather up our stuff. We head back out the way we came in, with both dogs trailing behind us.

"Junior, how far back does this tunnel go? It's not on Uncle Max's blueprints."

"I don't know, this was the furthest I've ever gone. Uncle Jax, blueprints are like a map right?"

"Yeah, kind of like a very detailed map, why?"

"I wonder what else we don't know about? Do you think Uncle Max will let me see them?"

"Well, after he calms down about you running away, I'm sure he will give them to you. Hell, you got him to watch the *Doctor;* I couldn't even do that."

He laughs and the sound warms my heart. We get to the panel and press it open. When we climb back into the kitchen, Jax puts Michael down. Bella is crying, she grabs and hugs him, then lets go. "Michael, what the hell were you thinking? Why would you do this? Do you know how worried I was?" she begins to yell.

"Sis, cut the kid some slack. We had a talk and all is good now." Jax nudges him a little. "Go ahead, tell them."

"I'm sorry, everyone, if I made you worry. Last night I looked up on the Internet what's wrong with me. I got scared and didn't want to go. I thought if I hid in the tunnels that you wouldn't find me. I guess I didn't really think it through."

Mrs. Osla steps up and takes Michael's hand, "Young man, I know this is going to be a long, hard journey, but you're strong. You need to ask yourself, what would the *Doctor* do?"

"Ma'am, he would accept the challenge and do his best."

"Well, then there's your answer. Now, I have a very special surprise waiting for you at the hospital, in the states, so I suggest you get ready to go." He gives her a big hug which surprises all of us, including Mrs. Osla.

"Uncle Max, do you think I can have a copy of the blueprints?"

"Why would you want blueprints?"

"They are like a giant treasure map, and I want to study them while I'm away. This way when I get back, I can search out all the secret passage ways."

"Okay, I will get a set and bring them with me next week. Now, we need to get going."

Max gives Michael a big hug "Let's go down to the barn; we will meet everyone at the plane."

"Okay, Jax, I need to feed Antonia. I will be back in a bit. Then we really need to get going."

I head out the door, and I can hear a flurry of activity behind me.

Maxwell

JUNIOR AND I HEAD out the door with Vito right behind us.

He sees the new golf cart waiting and he begins to laugh, "Uncle Max, when did you get this?"

"Okay, here's the thing. I was saving this for your birthday, but since you will be in the States, I thought we could take it out for a spin now. Do you like it?" I probably got this for the both of us, but I will never confess to that one.

"What's not to like?—a golf cart that looks like a Lamborghini! Can I really drive this?"

"Yes, you can drive this, but don't tell your mum. And whatever you do, don't tell your grams or you know what will happen. Hop in and let me show you how to drive this. You have to be careful cause I had it modified to get up to 70 mph." We hop in and he takes to it right away. I thank God he doesn't have his mother's coordination. We race toward the barn, and Vito is running behind us.

"Junior, pull behind the barn; we have to hide this." As he pulls behind the barn, we find Jackie standing there. *Oh bullocks,* I'm so busted.

"Uncle Max, looks like you're in trouble."

Jackie walks over to my side of the car, "Max, out right this minute."

I climb out; ready to make up some lame excuse, "Jackie, I can explain . . ."

She doesn't even let me finish. She hops in the car and begins to laugh uncontrollably. "Oh, Max, I wish you could see the look on your face right now. You're not having all the fun around here. Michael, hit the gas and let's take this for another ride."

Before I can protest, they are speeding away, laughing with Vito running behind them. I turn around and Jax is standing there. "Are you going to yell at me? I had it made for his birthday, and since he won't be here, I thought he should have a little fun."

"Why would I yell, he's having the time of his life. Thank God he doesn't have Bella's coordination."

"He's gotta be okay, Jax."

"He will, have faith. Do you know what Mrs. Osla planned for Junior?"

"Nope, but I'm sure it's special, she loves kids."

We watch them go around the field one more time and then they pull up to the barn. They climb out and Junior's cheeks have the most color I've seen in days.

"Okay, Junior, give me a hug. Jackie and I will see you next week. I'll hide this toy till you get back."

"Thanks, Uncle Max. Miss Jackie, I'll be ready to give you away next week."

She gives him a big hug, "I'm looking forward to it."

I watch Junior climb on Jax's back and as they head up toward the house, I feel my heart tighten, "I can't lose him, Jackie."

"You won't. We need to be strong."

I know she's right, however, it's not easy. "Hop in and I'll take you for a spin. I need to store this in the garage for now."

"You know, Max, I might want to get one of these in purple."

She can't be serious. "It will be a cold day in hell before I buy a purple Lamborghini golf cart." She reaches over and places her hand on my crotch, lightly tapping her fingers. I see where this is headed, but I'm still not buying a purple Lamborghini, it goes against everything manly. "Still not happening, babe." She removes her hand and places it in her lap. After a few seconds, she unzips her jeans, slowly shimmying them down. She slides her delicate fingers slowly into her knickers. What the hell is she trying to do, kill me?

"As you well know, Max, I've never had sex in a car before. I think it's something I might want to try."

I clench my jaw and white knuckle the wheel. I'm trying not to look but then she moans. *Fuck me.* I take a quick peek, holy hell! Her knickers are around her knees and her fingers are working in and out of her sweetness. She tilts her head back moaning. I avert my eyes from her and back on the road. I gave some thought to what she said the other day, how she wanted to have different experiences with me. I guess now is as good a time as any. Her breathing is becoming rapid and I know she is closing in fast. Two can play the same game. "Jackie, if you come without me, I will put you over my knee and spank your very beautiful arse until it's that very lovely shade of pink again. Remember how you felt the other day, the rush of power you felt. The heat from my hand . . . over and over *again?*" I glance over and she's biting her lip, her fingers are moving at a good clip. She's won't be able to take much more. I pull into the first building, which is the new distillery, and hit the brakes. After cutting the engine, I turn toward her. "Carry on."

Her fingers stop moving and her eyes are wide. "Max, I want you to—."

"You want me to what, babe?" She's practically whimpering and *fuck me* it's hot.

"I want it to be your fingers, not mine."

"Lose the knickers." I hold out my hand. She slides them down and places them in my palm. I rub the beautiful lace along my cheek and then shove them in my pocket for later. "You've been very naughty and I think now you need to understand what happens when you are naughty." I get out of the car and head toward her side. Opening her door, I offer her my hand. When she places it in mine, I can still feel her wetness. I lift her fingers to my mouth and brush them across my lips. "Place your hands on the car and stick that luscious arse out for me."

Her breathing is becoming rapid as I slowly stroke my fingers over her arse. I start out with a few alternating light smacks. She takes her hand off the car and puts it between her legs. I stop her and pull both hands behind her back. I tie them together with her knickers. "I might have to give you some extra spanks for that one, babe." I lean her over and begin spanking her, one cheek and then the other. She's wiggling, and every time she does, I spank her harder . . . just enough to sting. When I dip my finger into her sweetness, she screams out my name. I drop my pants, take my cock, and enter her from behind. When I'm all the way in, I can feel the heat from her arse. I'm using her hands, tied with her knickers, to pull her back toward me as I push forward. "Oh God, Jackie, please tell me you're there."

"Yes, Max, harder, please! Don't stop! Oh God, again."

Everything in me tightens and I explode over and over again. When my scrambled brain finally comes back to life, I untie her hands and then bend down to kiss her beautiful pink arse cheeks. "Are you okay?"

"Now can I get my purple cart?"

I throw my head back and laugh, "You really want a purple cart?"

"Of course I do, if for nothing else, but to see you driving it."

"I guess I'm ordering you a purple cart."

She throws her arms around me and kisses me hard. "Yes!"

Chapter Fourteen

Raven

JAX HAS MANAGED TO get everyone from Scotland to Heathrow without incident. It's already been a long day for Michael. Jax told me about Max's present for Michael and how much fun he had driving it. I look around the cabin and everyone seems to be busy reading or listening to music. All, except An. She's so pale. Something is still off with her, and I need to figure out what it is. She is a very strong, proud woman, and getting anything out of her won't be easy.

Jax puts his magazine down and leans in near my ear. "Penny for your thoughts?" he whispers.

"I'm still concerned about your mom. She seems pale, and before you say anything, I know that she still needs to rest. It's just been a hell of a few days for her, for all of us."

"Raven, I know this has been exceptionally hard on her, and I can see it's taking a toll. I had Mrs. Osla arrange for the top cardiologist to tend to her while we are in the States. Come with me."

He unbuckles our seat belts and pulls me to my feet. "Jax, what's up?"

He's not saying anything as he leads me down the aisle to his office. He pours himself a scotch and offers me a drink. "I have some things I need to talk to you about. With everything going on, we haven't had a minute to ourselves. There always seems to be something going on, some fire to put out."

We sit on the sofa and I take his hand in mine. "Talk to me; what's wrong?"

"I've been thinking about your mum and her medical license. Here's my dilemma: what if she wants to go back into medicine? I mean, she was very well known in that field. You saw how she came to life when everything went down. Matthew might have changed her name, but it doesn't mean she's safe. Add to that her wanting to confront Vincent and I'm not sure what to do."

"What happened when you spoke to her about Vincent?"

"I have to say, Raven, she made a very compelling argument, but in the end, it's got to be about safety."

"Did you tell her any of this?"

"No, I haven't had a chance. And now with everything happening to Junior, all my focus has been there."

"Jax, let me try talking to her. Maybe I can get a feel as to what she might want to do. In the end, it has to be her decision. Now I have something I need some advice on." I put my glass down. He gifts me with a huge smile.

"Should I have my mom read Duke's letter?"

"Why would you want her to? Do you think any good would come of it?"

"At first, I thought no, but then after I read it, I realized he was just as much a victim as the rest of us." His grip on my hand tightens. "I'm not condoning what he did, Jax. I just thought if she read it, then maybe she could come to terms with everything. She might see there was some good in him. After all, he is a part of her."

"I get why you think it might help, but honestly, looking at this from a non-emotional side, I think it might do her more harm than good. She might feel guilty for what's become of him. Even though she's not responsible, as a parent, you will always take the blame for your child—no matter what."

"I never really thought of it like that, but I guess it makes sense." I take his glass from his hand and put it on the table, and then crawl into his lap. He wraps his arms tightly around me and I feel secure.

"What else is on your mind, Raven?"

"Do you know what arrangements were made for Michael's schooling?"

"No, I didn't get that far. My goal was to get him into that hospital as quickly as possible. What are you thinking?"

"I spoke to Jackie and we want to homeschool Michael. They probably offer the services at the hospital; however, we would feel better if we did it."

"Why are you trying so hard to sell me on this?"

"I promised you that I would stay home and take care of Antonia, but if I did this, I would be away from her for a couple of hours a day. I didn't think you would mind, but I don't want someone else to take care of our daughter. If I'm not there, then I want you to be . . . not a nanny."

"Oh, I never even thought about that. Okay, I will go along with it. Besides, Max will be there to help me. Speaking of which, I know Max is stoked that he is getting married in a few days. Is Jackie really okay with everything?"

"Jackie and I had a long talk before we left and she is happy that it will happen on her birthday. She feels it will help her mom the most to have the ceremony on that day. They are Buddhist and believe life is about helping and giving to others."

"How do you think Max is going to do with her family? I have to confess, sweetheart, I told him what Dylan said."

"I figured you did, after all, you and Max are joined at the hip. You met him Jax, you know as well as I do that Max will not do well with Dylan. Jackie already called him and told him she was coming home with Max. She won't take any bull from him."

"I could never repay Jackie for what she has done for Max. She mended his heart and she stopped him from making the biggest mistake of his life. I honestly don't think I would have been able to stop him without her. I would like to make the wedding they are planning to have in the States really special for her. Do you have any ideas what she would like?"

"Simple is what works for Jackie, always has been. Don't worry, I'm sure, knowing Max, he will already have Mrs. Osla handling all the details."

"Now, I think we've done entirely too much talking, don't you? I also think you have on entirely too many clothes." I turn in his arms and lean in to kiss him; he has the biggest smile on his face. "What are you thinking?"

He runs his fingers down my cheek and then pulls me toward him, gently pressing his lips against it. "My beautiful wife, I'm thinking that no matter how crazy the world around us becomes, we will always have us. Our sanctuary; so different from everyone else's."

I begin to unbutton his shirt, leaving a trail of soft kisses behind. The intercom buzzes. He reaches behind him and hits the speaker. My mom lets me know Antonia is awake.

"Raven, I'll go get her and bring her in here." Before I can say anything, he's out the door. I know he loves tending to her just as much as I do. He comes in the door with Antonia crying in her infant carrier and the diaper bag. He seems flustered as he tries to get her out of the carrier.

"Jax, are you okay?"

"Why the hell are these seats so complicated?" He's growling with frustration.

"It took me a little bit to figure it out, too." I quickly show him how it works and then go about changing her. As soon as she is clean, she stops crying and I'm able to nurse her. I snuggle up to Jax, and he puts his arm around me.

"Sweetheart, watching you tend to our daughter takes my breath away. We really need to make another baby."

I take my time before answering him.

"Raven, I can't help the way I feel. I love babies and love making them with you. I think you are the greatest mum ever. I want to enjoy my children while I'm young."

"Have you ever thought about adopting? Jackie said that Max wants to adopt a special needs child."

"Honestly, I've never thought about it. However, I wouldn't rule it out. Do you want to adopt?"

"I'm not sure. Actually, right before everything happened with Max, I started looking into the foster care program in Scotland. I was thinking it would be a good way to reach many of the children that are considered too old for adoption. We could take the money that the government pays monthly and put that in an account for the child. This way when the child becomes of age, they will have some savings to work with."

"Obviously, you've been thinking about this for quite some time."

"I always thought about being a foster mom or a big sister, but then everything got a little crazy. I've been watching Jackie work with the kids and the horses, so I decided to look into it. I know we will be gone for a while, but maybe we can look into it more when we get back."

"It sounds like a great idea, as long as you don't rule out making babies."

"Ha! Never, Jax." Antonia falls back to sleep and I put her in her carrier.

"You take the carrier and I've got the bag. I want to lock that contraption back into the seat and check on your mom."

We head out to the main cabin, and everyone is getting ready to eat. It smells wonderful and I'm starving. Nursing seems to make me want to eat all the time. Everyone is laughing except for An. I notice she's pushing her food around but not really eating anything. I decide to wait until I can get her alone later to see how she's feeling. I don't want to alarm anyone. Dinner with all of us together is always comforting, but I really miss Max and Jackie. I hope Max is going to be okay dealing with Dylan. Jax takes my hand and kisses the inside of my wrist. No matter how long we are together, I think I will always shiver when he puts his lips there. I rest my head on his shoulder "I think I'm going to try and have a nap while Antonia is sleeping. Lately, I'm tired all the time."

"Is it normal to be this tired? Maybe we should go to the doctor." His grip on my hand gets tighter.

"I think it's all normal. The hunger and the fatigue add to that all the stress that we've been going through. I don't think we have anything to worry about." I get up and excuse myself and Jax gets up, too. "What are you doing?"

"Sweetheart, I think I need a nap. All of a sudden, I'm feeling quite tired."

If I look at him I know, I will burst out laughing, so I opt to quickly head down the hall.

We get into our room and I'm so tired. I sit down to take off my shoes, barely able to keep my eyes open. Jax crouches down at my feet and begins to take off my shoes. He's starts rubbing my feet and I feel my eyes growing heavier.

"Raven, please let me take care of you. You're always taking care of everyone else."

I lie down and give in, too tired to help myself. I feel myself slowly fade out as he's massaging my feet.

Jaxson

RAVEN HAS BEEN SO tired, and doing so much for everyone else that I'm afraid she is going to get sick. As much as I always want to be with her, it's rest that she really needs now. She gives so freely of her strength and faith, I truly have no idea how she does it. I look at my watch and realize Max must be getting ready to leave. I give him a call before he heads out. "Hey, Max, are you almost ready to go?" I ask when he picks up.

"Yeah, everything okay there?"

"We have about three hours left before we land. I wanted to talk to you before you go. Now whatever you do, make sure you don't snap the wanker's neck, cause that would not go over too well with Jackie's dad."

"Is this why you called me?"

"I'm worried about you; I know I wanted to snap that fucker's neck. You will surely want to do more. Just try to remember you're there for Jackie."

"What else is bothering you? I doubt you called just for that."

"I feel bad that I'm not going to be there when you get married. You're always there for me."

"I know, but you'll be there for me next week. I just can't wait to make it official."

"Have you thought about a gift for her? I can help with it." I'm laughing and he is probably rolling his eyes.

"Well, I really wasn't too sure what to get, but then this morning, when she went racing around with Junior, she mentioned that she want- ed a purple golf cart."

"You bought her a purple golf cart?" I'm laughing so hard, I'm crying.

"No, not a golf cart. I called my friends at Lamborghini and ordered her a purple one. They sent over a certificate with her name and delivery date. I wrapped it up."

"What about her birthday, mate?"

"When I had the ring made up, I also had a matching pendant made. Somehow, I knew I wouldn't be able to wait till her birthday. I'm going to have to get going, but before I do, how is everyone doing?"

"Everyone is doing okay, although Mum looks a little tired. Raven is keeping a close watch on her, so don't worry. I'll let you go, but make sure you check in with me." He hangs up and I'm still sad that I won't be there, but I know he's getting his shot at a happily ever after and that's all I ever really wanted for him. While Raven is still asleep I'm going to check on Junior.

I quietly leave the room, making sure not to wake her. Junior's room is right next door. I stick my head in to check on him, but he is asleep. I'm trying so hard not to let him see how scared I am for him. I close the door and go in search of my mum. She is in the main cabin having tea with Mrs. Osla. I take a minute to gather my thoughts before heading into the cabin.

"Hey, Mum, how are you feeling?" When she lifts her eyes toward mine, I notice how tired she looks.

"I'm fine, son, how is Raven? This has to be a lot for her to deal with, on top of a new baby."

"She'll be fine, Mum, it's you I'm worried about. You need to try and get some rest. I know we're all worried about Junior, but you getting sick will not help him. Bella is going to need a lot of support right now from all of us." *Oh fuck, she's crying.* I pull her into my arms. "Shh, stop crying, please."

"I'll be fine, son, really, I think I'm just tired. Plus, the realization of everything that James was into has been very hard on me. I feel like a fool—"

"—Stop, please! Just stop blaming yourself for things you never had any control over. We need to focus on the future and things we *can* control. My wife told me 'the past can't be changed, but the path we choose to move forward on can.' I believe she might be onto something." She stops crying, and I think I finally might be getting through to her.

THE FLIGHT ATTENDANT COMES over to inform me that we will be ahead of schedule and we should be landing in about an hour. The captain will make his standard announcement when we are thirty minutes out. However, she wanted to make sure I had enough time to tend to any of Junior's needs. I need to make sure everyone is up. "If you'll excuse me, ladies, I need to wake up Raven and let everyone know we are ahead of schedule."

I check on Antonia and she's still sleeping. I thank God that she is such an easy baby. I head into Junior's room and let them know to get ready to land. Now I just need to wake up my wife. I open the door and she's lying on the bed crying. I race over to her and realize she's in the throes of a nightmare. I know not to wake her. I get a wet washcloth and sit on the bed, softly calling her name over and over again. Finally, she stops and her eyes flutter open. I take the washcloth and clean up under her eyes. "Do you want to talk about it?"

"What's there to talk about?"

"Oh, I don't know, maybe the fact that I find my wife crying and thrashing about in her sleep has me worried. I know you're trying to be strong for everyone, but you need to let me in, Raven."

She sits quietly for a while, looking down, twisting her fingers. "I had a bad dream, Jax, a dream that seemed a little too real. Can we please let it go for now?"

I don't want to upset her anymore. "Sweetheart, I can let it go for now, but if they continue, you will need to tell me. We will be landing shortly and we need to get into our seats." I don't want to give her any time to dwell on it. We head out to the main cabin to check on Antonia and take our seats. As the wheels touch down, I close my eyes, making a silent prayer that Junior will be okay.

Chapter Fifteen

Maxwell

I'M PACKING EVERYTHING I think I will need, making sure I take the blue prints for Junior. The thought of him having to go through this is tearing me up inside. I just about have it together and now I need to find out what is keeping Jackie. I go in search of her and find her sitting on the floor in her closet, surrounded by shoes. I learned rather quickly that she has two vices in life: chocolate and shoes. It looks like someone took every pair of shoes she owns and piled them on the floor. "Hey, babe, what are you doing?"

"Trying to decide what shoes to bring." I'll never understand the need for all these shoes, however, I'm not an idiot—I know when to keep my mouth shut.

I sit on the floor next to her, always needing to touch her. "You could just pick a few and buy whatever you want in the States." That earns me a glare.

"Or . . . we could just take them all." Her bottom lip begins to tremble and something tells me this has nothing to do with shoes. "Talk to me, babe, what's really bothering you?"

"I'm getting married tomorrow. My mother has requested that I wear my grandmother's Kimono. My best friend isn't here, and you are going to hate my brother."

"Would you rather wait until we get to the States to get married. We can fly your parents out next week and do it with everyone there."

"I thought of that, but my mother doesn't fly."

"Wait then how were they getting here in May for the wedding?"

"They would drive."

"Jackie, that's over seventeen hours, you can't be serious. Why won't your Mum fly?"

"I asked her that once and she said she wasn't born with wings Really, after that, what could I say? The more I thought about it, the more I really want to have the wedding on my birthday, so I can have some happy memories, too."

I lift her hand to my lips, "I have one question? How hard is it going to be to get you out of this Kimono?" Her mouth falls open and her eyes grow wide.

"Is that all you're worried about?" she squeaks in disbelief.

"Babe, none of this matters to me. Out of respect for you, I will play nice with Dylan. I will have as many or as few ceremonies as you want. As long as there is one very quickly, nothing else matters. Hell, I'll even wear this Kimono thing if that will get you down that isle!" She takes my hand and begins to laugh.

"Okay, what's so funny?"

"Careful what you wish for Max. You have to wear the traditional men's Kimono."

She is now laughing so hard that she falls backwards amongst the shoes and she's holding her sides. I'm glad that through this nightmare, she can still find something to laugh about. I get up, take her hand, and pull her to her feet.

"Jackie, leave the shoes and I will take you on a whirlwind shoe shopping trip when we get to the States."

"Max, have you ever been to Bon Genie?" We head out of the closet and I begin to laugh.

"Jax told me about it when he came back from Switzerland. Not gonna happen, babe." She cocks her head to the side and gives me a beautiful smile. Who am I kidding?—*she* knows and *I* know that I'm going to Bon Genie; seven floors of shopping hell.

Jaxson

WE LAND WITHOUT INCIDENT and Max has a fleet of vehicles, with guards, waiting for us in a private hanger. We head directly to the hospital, only to find a dozen or so reporters camped out front. I've been so wrapped up with Junior that I forgot the sale of Raiders was announced today. I've been away from the press, hounding me on a daily basis, but Mick realizes what's going on and radios all drivers to go around back to the service entrance. We drive around back and there are some there, but not as many.

Before I open the door, Mick holds his hand up, stopping me. "Jax, I need everyone to go but Rose." He hands Rose a baseball cap and dark sunglasses. "Can you please put these on, ma'am? Jax, it's you they want pictures of, so I'm hoping once you're inside, I will be able to sneak Rose in without anyone noticing."

"Thank you, Mick. I almost forgot how ruthless the press can be."

We get out of the cars and make our way into the hospital with a limited amount of flashes going off. Junior grabs my hand and is squeezing it really hard. We make our way to the elevators quickly and the ride up is long and quiet. The doors finally open and we are greeted by two very kind looking nurses, Sarah and Janett. Sarah informs me that she works for the hospital, and Janett is the private nurse that Mrs. Osla has hired.

Sarah extends her hand out to Junior. "Hello, Michael. I know you are scared, but Janett and I will be here with you. There is another boy here named Josiah, he's very into superheroes and *Doctor Who*. I'm sure the two of you will become good friends. Let's get you checked into your room and then I will introduce you to him."

Junior's face lights up at the mention of *Doctor Who* and for the first time since this began, I can feel myself relax a little. As we approach Junior's room, Janett informs me to get the camera on my phone ready. I have no clue what she's talking about, but then it hits me, Mrs. Osla's surprise. Junior opens the door and steps inside. I'm so shocked that I can't even speak. Janett takes my phone and begins snapping pictures. The entire room looks like the inside of the TARDIS. Junior is laughing and running around the room, checking everything out. I finally snap back to reality, thanking Janett for taking the pictures.

Junior runs up to Mrs. Osla and throws his arms around her. Two hugs in one day must surprise her. "Mrs. Osla, you're the best! Thank you." Even the always stoic Mrs. Osla is teary eyed.

Sarah informs us that Dr. David Torrance is in charge of Junior's case and is waiting to meet with us first before he meets with Junior. While Janett and Sarah are showing Junior around, we step outside his room to meet with the doctor but find Rose and Mick waiting for us.

"Mick, were there any problems?" He's fidgeting and rocking back and forth on his heels. He seems on edge.

"Yeah, Jax, one guy was able to get a picture off. I pulled his SD card from his camera. He wasn't happy."

"Did you see anyone else? Did he try to find out who she is?" God, I can't wait till Max gets *here*.

"There were some reporters across the street, but I don't think anyone noticed us. I had her keep her head down with her hair tucked into the cap. He tried to question me about her but I cut him off. I'm going to have her change into scrubs when we are ready to leave. I will have you leave out the front and I will take Rose out the employee entrance."

"Thanks, Mick. We are about to meet with the doctor, can you please hang here with Junior?" Even though the other guards are here, I feel better with Mick around. He hangs back while we head to the meeting.

When I walk through the door of his office, I look around and I'm shocked. I was expecting a typical doctor's office. He has the usual medical books, but what surprises me the most is the wall of handmade cards. The wall has to be eight feet high and twelve feet wide, and the entire wall, from floor to ceiling, is covered in these cards. On the far wall is a shelf filled with superhero figures.

Raven is fixated on the wall with the cards. "These are amazing."

I take a closer look at them and I realize they are all survivors, thanking Dr. Torrence and his staff. The door opens and the doctor steps in, looking a lot younger than I had expected.

"Hello, everyone, I'm Dr. David Torrance, or Dr. Dave, if you will. I'm sorry; I wasn't expecting so many people; who are Michael's parents?"

Bella and Michael introduce themselves, and then proceed to introduce all of us to him.

"Mr. And Mrs. Vizzano, is everyone going to be involved with Michael's care?" He seems surprised.

"Please call me Bella. The answer is yes, and he also has another uncle and aunt that will be arriving from Switzerland, at some point. I assure you, we are a very close family." She leans her head on my shoulder and squeezes my hand. I want to make all her pain go away and handle this for her, but I know she needs to do this. I squeeze her hand back, giving her the support she needs.

"Okay then, Bella, let me lay out what I see will be our best course of action. We *have* caught this early, so that is in his favor. As far as the stem cell tests that were run, the closest match was you, however, I would have liked it to be closer. I hope we won't need it, but if we do, are there any other relatives that can be tested?" he asks. Bella is not answering and her lips begin to tremble. Michael pulls her into his arms, trying to calm her. My mum pales and Raven pulls her close.

I take a deep breath and slowly let it out. "Dr. Dave, Junior has a grandfather that we are not in touch with. If need be, I will take care of it. For now, why don't we focus on what we can do, please."

"Yes, of course. The first thing I want you to know is that his treatment will be over the course of three years due to the different phases it requires. I like to explain this to families first so that they can begin to mentally prepare for the commitment this unexpected illness will take." He pauses and looks around at every one of us in the room. Michael and Bella nod in understanding. "He will be allowed to go home for some periods of time. I understand that you reside in Scotland?"

"That's right," I speak up.

"Well, I would prefer, during treatment, that he doesn't leave the country." He grabs a folder off of his desk. "The first part of the treatment will take a month. It's called Remission induction. Remission doesn't mean he is cured, it is only the first stage." he says the name slowly as he pulls sheets of paper from the folder and hands us each one. I look down and see that it has all of the info on it for the first phase. "The goal of this first treatment is to kill the leukemia cells that are in Michael's blood and bone marrow. He will first get a blood transfusion, and then I will administer chemotherapy and steroids. I will give you a more detailed packet, outlining all the treatment. However, I would rather go over it with you before each one. It can be very overwhelming and he might not need all of it." He leans back on the edge of his desk and crosses one foot over the other as he tosses the folder down on it. His eyes soften as he looks around at all of us again. "Please know this is not a death sentence, his odds are very good. Bella, Michael . . . you did nothing wrong." He gives a nod of encouragement. "Now, what questions does everyone have?"

I put aside my fear and begin to go through my list. "Is this something that can be inherited? Should my daughter be tested? How much are you going to tell Junior? What do you need us to do or not do?" He seems to be listening intently. Not once has he treated us like just another number.

"Mr. Phillips—"

"—Please, call me Jax."

"Jax, there is no evidence that Acute Lymphocytic Leukemia is hereditary. As far as what I plan to tell Michael, I always explain the leukemia in a way a child can understand it. I also make them a part of the treatment every step of the way. Children are very smart and expect to be treated as such. When speaking with Michael, I will always refer to the cancer as ALL. What I need for every one of you to do is stay positive around him. He will sense your fear, and that is not good for him." He gives us all a slight stern look. "Now, it was brought to my attention that you will be providing his home schooling?"

"Yes, my wife, Raven, and his Aunt Jackie are both teachers."

"That's fine. I will provide you with his schedule. There will be plenty to keep him busy here. Between his treatment, schooling, and the different events we plan for the kids, I doubt Michael will get bored. Now if you don't have any other questions, I would like to go meet him."

"Actually, I have one more question. Why the superhero figures?" I couldn't help it; curiosity was killing the cat.

He puts his pen down and smiles. "Every child that comes through here gets to pick his or her favorite. That figure stays with them the entire time. They sleep with it, they shower with it, and they get their treatment with it. That figure becomes a very important friend. It's the friend that helps them fight to live. Through their journey, they learn all about the figure they chose and how and why they became a super-hero. They become that hero. How about you take me to meet Michael now?"

We all turn and file out the door. I stop before leaving and look back at the figures. I freeze, and then a smile hits my face. I know *exactly* which one Junior will choose. "Jax, are you okay?" Raven calls me, snapping my focus back. All I have to do is point to the shelf, and she begins to laugh.

I put my arm around her and we head out the door with a little more faith than we came in with.

Junior

MY NURSES, MISS JANETT and Miss Sarah, are really nice. They asked me about my home in Scotland and what hobbies I have. I can't wait for Uncle Max to get here with the blue prints so I can show them the castle I live in. Miss Sarah is showing me what everything in the room is for. Everyone comes back in and there is a man with them who looks around the room and begins to laugh. "Hi, Michael, I'm Dr. Dave and I will be taking care of you. I'm sorry to laugh; I wasn't expecting to walk into a TARDIS. I haven't met many *Doctor Who* fans; who is your favorite Doctor?"

This might not be so bad after all, "I like the eleventh, Matt Smith, but my Uncle Jax's favorite is the tenth, David Tennant. Who is your favorite?"

"I think each one brings something unique to the role, but I'm partial toward the ninth, Christopher Eccleston. So, Michael, are you ready for me to go over what you can expect while you're here?"

"I g-guess so, Dr. Dave." I'm barely able to get the words out.

Jaxson

MY HEART IS BREAKING for Junior I know he is trying so hard to be strong. Dr. Dave takes Junior into an area of his room that has a table and chairs set up and some bookshelves. He sits down with him and begins explaining everything on Junior's level. He's not demanding or dictating. He tells him fear of the unknown is natural, but ALL is not unknown to him. For the first time, I feel myself relax a little. I pull Raven closer to me; her strength and faith are my rock right now. She reaches up and tugs her ear. I pull her hand away and bring it to my lips. I lean in and whisper, "Sweetheart, are you okay?"

"I'm very proud of Michael, he is such a strong boy. I wish I could shelter him from all of this, but I know Dr. Dave is right; Michael has the right to know what is going to happen. I'm just glad he is explaining it to him in a way that doesn't scare him more. I know he will be okay, but that doesn't make this any easier."

Antonia begins to fuss just as Raven finishes her thoughts. She takes her from Mrs. Osla and heads into the other room to tend to her, with Bo and her guards not far behind her. After setting Michael up with an IV, his nurses begin to administer the first blood transfusion. I decide to step outside his room to check in with Max.

Max picks up on the first ring. "Jax, is everything okay? How is Junior holding up?"

"Calm down, mate, he's doing okay. The doctor is really nice and doesn't pull any punches. He talked to Junior directly, explaining every step of the way, what will happen without scaring him." I inform him, then continue on to relay every bit of the conversation we had with the doctor prior. In regards to our father possibly being a closer match, I know Max, if needed, he'd probably remove the damn stem cells himself. "Max, if it comes to that, I will take care of it. What is going on with the wedding?" I look at the phone to see if the call dropped, "Max, you there?" Then I hear growling. Oh no, I hope he didn't snap that wanker Dylan's neck.

"Do not laugh, Jax, or I swear I will get even with you." He then lets out a big disgruntled sigh. "I have to wear a bloody Kimono."

I try—I mean, I really try not to laugh—but the thought of Max in a Kimono creeps into my head and I lose it. I swear I'm laughing so hard, I'm crying. It is at this very moment Raven steps out of Junior's room to find me. Max is yelling something in my ear and she is looking at me like I have two heads. Maybe it's the pressure that's finally gotten to me. She walks up to me and takes my phone.

"Hello, Max, it's Raven, please stop yelling. Is everything okay?"

"So help me, if he doesn't stop laughing, I'm going to kick his arse!"

"Can I ask why he's laughing so hard, he's crying?"

"No! Please put him back on the bloody phone."

I find some sort of composure and take the phone. "Okay, mate, I'm back, but you must promise me pictures." All I get is a growl and a quick disconnect.

Raven is waiting for some answers, guess I better explain. "I was checking in with Max, and he has to wear a Kimono. Surely you see the humor in that?"

Her face lights up with a beautiful smile. "Oh, Jax, I can't believe I forgot about that. I hope Jackie gave him a heads up before time." She giggles and it's such a wonderful sound.

"Sweetheart, I have a surprise for you. Well really, it's for all of us. I spoke with Jeffery Gerhard today, explaining the situation here and why none of us can be there for the wedding. He has agreed to surprise Jackie and Max by letting us SKYPE the ceremony. I can still be his best man and you can be Jackie's matron of honor. The entire family can be there for them."

She throws her arms around me, hugging me tightly. "Jax, as if it were even possible, I love you more than I ever thought I could. Your kindness knows no bounds." She kisses my cheek enthusiastically, and then pulls back. "When is the ceremony?"

"Jeffery said he would give us advance notice, so let's go let everyone know what is going on, and see how Junior is doing."

Chapter Sixteen

Vincent

I JUST GOT WORD that my new attorney is here to see me today. That's a surprise, since I already gave the feds what they wanted or, at least, as much as I was willing to part with. There's more—hell—there's always more. I've been moved to an underground facility in Colorado. This place is considered hell-on-earth and that's not far off in the description. I'm being led out to a special visiting room that has been set up for attorneys visiting inmates. The feds might think they got a win, but this is only the first round. As long as I'm not dead, I can't be stopped. I shuffle along as best I can, being led in leg irons and cuffs. Deveno is gone and so now I will have to train my new attorney. That's okay. Unlike Deveno, maybe this one will get everything I ask for done. When we get into the room, the guards attach my restraints to a bolt in the floor and step out. There's a knock on the door, it opens and in steps my attorney. *What the fuck?!*

"Hello, Mr. Giaconna, I'm Ms. Amelia Jade, I will be representing you. I know that you already have a deal in place at this time, however, I'm here to see if I can make it better."

"Who the fuck hired you?" Damn this girl is a looker; long, red hair and tits that I wouldn't mind burying my face in.

"Your sister, Annabelle, hired me to take a look at your case."

"Well, Ms. Amelia Jade, what makes you think you can do anything for me? I already have a deal in place with the feds. My long-lost son, whom I only knew for three fucking months, threw me, along with the entire family, under the bus. The evidence against me was pretty black and white, so I really didn't have a choice. Where did Anna find you?" Let's see her work with nothing.

"Well, Mr. Giaconna, I'm not going to dispute the deal, only the evidence that was used to make the deal. I believe there was a break in the chain of evidence—the video tape to be precise. When it was obtained, copies were made. The prosecutor said it never left the chain of custody, yet, Mr. Fleming had a copy. I believe we might be able to pull the deal and have a trial. Either way this goes, you will be going to jail, I have no doubt about that. As far as Annabelle is concerned, I found her."

"So, if it's not going to change my conviction, then why bother? Why contact my sister?" Her jaw is tight and her emerald eyes become very dark. She looks down at her hands and then back up to me.

"Revenge, Mr. Giaconna—pure, sweet, and simple. I want it and you're my way of getting it."

"Wow, who pissed in your corn flakes?" I jerk my head back. "What would make you think I would even go along with any of this?"

"You want to know who pissed in my corn flakes? Joseph Adessi, when he recruited my brother, Marco, to be his spy. Cara AKA: Raven, your niece, for turning my brother into some love-sick puppy. Duke, for putting a bullet in him. I can't get to Duke, at least not yet. Joseph is dead. So that leaves Raven. My way to her is through you, plain and simple."

"You think I'm going to go along with this? What's in it for me?" Why did my sister even go along with this broad?

"Oh, there are two reasons I know you'll go along with it. I might be able to get you something better than this hellhole and I can guarantee Jacquelyn Gerhard's head on a proverbial silver platter." Now this broad has my attention.

"The entire Phillips family has arrived in the States, with the exception of Maxwell Fleming and Jacquelyn Gerhard. It appears Michael Vizzano Jr. is ill and will be here for treatment for the next three years. He just happens to be staying at the hospital where a friend of mine works, which is why I was lucky enough to receive this information so quickly. Mr. Fleming and Ms. Gerhard are in Switzerland and will be arriving soon. Once they are back in the States, the target becomes more vulnerable."

She takes out pictures of everyone arriving to a hospital and places them in front of me. I flip through them, they seem mundane until I get to the last one; I freeze. No fucking way is this possible. "Where was this picture taken and when?!"

"It was taken this morning outside the hospital in Philly. I had no idea who that was, so I had the picture enlarged. With the hat on and glasses it's still hard to tell. Is there a problem? Do you know who that is?"

This can't be, is this why Joseph never came after me? I stare at the picture and there is no mistaking that beautiful jaw line and those delicate features. "I will go along with your crazy plan under one condition. I need to see the girl in this picture, find her and bring her to me." I fold the picture and put it in my pocket.

"Mr. Giaconna, if you can tell me who the lady in the picture is, that would help?"

"The lady in the picture is Gabriella Giaconna, the catalyst for all of this; the mother of my only child. Bring her to me and you have a deal." I've always operated on the theory that my friends and associates are there for me to use. My enemies are there for me to destroy. Ms. Jade just became my new friend. I will use her and even destroy her if it means I can get my hands on Gabriella—*again.*

"First I need to get you moved out of this hell whole and back to the East coast. I will be in touch soon."

She gathers up her stuff and walks out, leaving me with more questions than answers. I can't get them from Joseph, but I will get them from Gabriella. The guards come in, unlock my chains and I begin the trek back to my cell. Once again, it's a waiting game for me.

Amelia Jade

I HATE THIS PLACE and the man I came here to see. I have no choice, though. If I want revenge for my brother's death, then I will have to deal with the devil. I'm in shock; how could this be? There was never any indication that Gabriella was alive. If Vincent is correct, then what else was Joseph hiding?

My brother ran away when I was thirteen. Joseph should have helped him come home, not make him into a babysitter for Raven. She turned him into some lovesick puppy and in the end, it cost him his life. She might not have pulled the trigger, but she was just as responsible. I need to keep my end of the bargain. If Vincent wants Gabriella, then he will get her along with Jacquelyn's head as a bonus. I pull out my duplicate set of pictures and find the one of the woman. From this picture, it's so hard to tell who the woman is. Maybe Vincent is seeing what he wants to see. Staring at this picture isn't going to get me anywhere. I pull out my phone and send a quick text to my investigator in Philly.

Just left Vincent. It's a go, but only if we deliver the lady in the attached photo. He claims it's Gabriella Giaconna. This could be why Joseph didn't use the tape. I'm heading to the airport now. Will contact you when I land.

I instruct my driver to go directly to Pueblo Memorial airport, while I try to make some sense of this. Joseph staged that accident in California to look like Gabriella and Cara died, but why put Cara up for adoption if her mother was alive? Why not relocate them both? Gabriella already gave Duke away. I just don't understand what the reason could've been to separate mother and child? I decide to head directly to, federal prosecutor, Hage's office in New York. I'm sure by now he got my motion for discovery. Maybe I can find something in his files. We pull up to the airport and I rush out to catch my plane. All of this will have to wait till I touch down in New York.

Vincent

I SIT IN MY cell and pull out the picture, stroking my finger up and down that delicate jaw line. So fucking beautiful, but this can't be— *how?* I close my eyes and remember the first day I had her. She thought she was so strong. She thought she could fight me. That was until she found out I had her precious Cara. She did whatever I asked, and when she didn't, when she fought me, it was even better. Just the thought of it makes my blood surge all over again. I can feel the tenderness of her sweet pussy like it was yesterday. I close my eyes and slowly stroke myself. What a poor substitute my hand is for her warmth. I remember thanking Antonio with every thrust inside her delicious pussy. I need to get out of here and find her again. I close my eyes and kiss her picture. I need to have her—*I will have her.* Nothing and *no one* will stop me. The thought gives me that last push I need, forcing me to finally come. *"I'm coming for you, Gabriella, you'll never be rid of me."*

Maxwell

I'M GLAD JAX CHECKED in, letting me know that Junior was doing okay. And all the information I found on the doctor seems really positive. I know Jackie is nervous about today, but something else is bothering her. She was so quiet on the ride to the airport and now, on the ride to her parents' house, she seems anxious. "Hey, babe, talk to me, this can't just be wedding jitters."

"Max, we haven't seen Sammy since the day we fled the country. I spoke to my mother and she said Dylan is in a foul mood. I thought I could do this on my birthday, but now I'm not so sure."

Fuck me, she can't be backing out now! "Jackie, I promise you everything will be fine. I will talk to Sammy about why I chose to leave him in the dark. Your brother will deal with the fact that I'm not going away. You have a lock on my heart for life and nothing he says or does will ever change that."

Her grip on my arm seems to lighten a little, that is, until, we pull up to the guard gate. As we drive up to the house, I finally get a sense of how she grew up and the isolation she had to endure for so many years. Things are starting to make sense. I look around and notice there are a lot of guards and dogs. "Jackie, is security always this tight?"

"No, Max, something must be up. My father never has the dogs this close to the house."

We step out of the car and I pull her tightly into my arms. "Until I find out what is going on, I want you close to me, understand?" Before she can answer, the door opens and Jeffery Gerhard steps out.

"So happy you're here, Jacquelyn." He pulls her into his arms.

"Papa, this is Maxwell Fleming. Max, my dad, Jeffery Gerhard," she goes about introducing us.

"Please, call me Jeff. Your mother is waiting for you. Maxwell and I have a lot to discuss. Don't worry, I promise I will go easy on him."

I pull her close and kiss her cheek, "Go, I'm fine."

When she is out of sight, I turn towards Jeff, "You can call me Max. Why don't we go sit down, so you can fill me in on what happened?"

"What makes you think anything happened?"

"Extra security and the dogs are close to the house."

"Sam is in my office, waiting for us. He has some intelligence information that he wants to go over with you." He smacks my back and leads me to his office.

"Hello, Max, I have some information to go over with you." Sammy looks up from Jeff's desk as we enter the room.

"First order of business, Sam: no hard feelings. I'm sure you understand why I did what I did. The less people that knew what we were doing, the safer everyone was."

"I understand. I didn't like it but I get it. We have more important matters to discuss. A very creditable threat has come through on Jackie's life. I know that you have bumped up security, however, I'm not sure that going to the States is the best decision."

I feel my heart constrict and pound in my chest. "Show me what you've got."

"I found out that Vincent has a new attorney. She filed a motion for discovery. My contact said she is trying to get the plea overturned due to tainted evidence."

Just the mention of his name makes me lose all reason. "Why the fuck would anyone take his case and think they would win? There has to be something in it for the attorney."

"Oh there is, Max—revenge. Her name is Amelia Jade and she is Marco Green's sister."

I freeze "Sister? Since when did Marco have a sister? There was nothing in his file about any siblings."

"Amelia Jade Esq. was Amelia Green. She was thirteen when

Marco left home. Soon after her father died and her mother remarried. Her name was legally changed to Jade and all her records were sealed."

"Sealed? Who sealed them? Please don't tell me Joseph."

"No, Marco sealed them. He was a hacker and damn good at it. Apparently, he sealed them without telling anyone. It was his way of protecting her from anything he did."

"Look, Sam, I get it. She is hurt that she lost her brother, but Duke shot him and he's gone in the wind somewhere. Why try to re-open a case that she has no chance of winning?"

"She is trying to get to Raven and to get to her; she has to get to Jackie. That is probably the only way she would get Vincent to go along with this. She knows she doesn't have a snowball's chance in hell of winning, but if she can force a trial, then you and Raven have to testify. Vincent wants revenge against you and getting Jackie is the ultimate revenge. He doesn't give a shit about you personally, only what he can do to make you suffer. You know his MO has always been about torture, Max."

"Raven didn't do anything to Marco. She honestly loved him like the brother she always wanted. I knew going to the States was a risk, but we had no choice. I have tripled security on everyone. Has Jax been informed of the latest developments?"

"No, this all came to light today when she sent Hage a request for full disclosure of every document pertaining to this case. I had MI6 dig into her past and that is when I found the sealed file. I had my contact get me a copy of the original file. That's when I found out exactly who she was. After that, all the pieces fell into place. I know Jackie and I understand leaving her here is not an option. We need to figure out the safest way to proceed. Max, understand I'm on board one-hundred per-cent. Jackie's safety and happiness is all I've ever wanted."

"Well, first thing I need to do is call Jax and bring him up to speed. If you wouldn't mind giving me a few moments to talk to him in private."

"Of course, Max, Sam and I will step outside. Let us know when you're ready for us." They leave and I take a few minutes to collect my thoughts. This is not going to be an easy call to make. I close my eyes and pray that—if there is a God—he would do what he *didn't* do before and protect my family.

Jax picks up on the first ring. "Hey, Max, what's wrong? Don't tell me one look at you in the Kimono and she ran the other way?"

"Very funny, Jax. Take Raven and go someplace quiet so we can talk. There's been a development that I need to go over with both of you."

"Give me five." He growls and hangs up.

Waiting for his call affords me the time to walk around Jeff's office. The man keeps pictures of his family everywhere. Jackie as a baby takes my breath away. All I can think of is how much I want babies with her. My phone rings, taking me out of my daydream.

"Jax, where are you and are we on speaker?"

"Raven and I are in a utility closet and yes you're on speaker. What the hell is going on?"

"Raven, did Marco ever mention a sister?"

"No, he hardly ever talked about his family; only that they disagreed with his lifestyle. Is there a problem?"

"Yeah, a big problem—for all of us. Her name is Amelia Jade and she is Vincent's new attorney, and she is out for revenge against you Raven. She knows to get to you; she has to get to Jackie. When we are locked away in Scotland, we can keep the animals at bay but back in the States, that buffer is gone."

"What kind of case could she possibly have? Vincent already accepted a plea deal; how does that get her revenge? Max, none of this makes any sense to me."

"I know, Raven. I thought the same thing but then I *really* thought about it. The first thing she did was file a motion for full disclosure of the evidence. Her focus is on the evidence, mainly that video tape. Since it is known that I have a copy, she is going to question the validity of the tape due to the chain of evidence. She will try to say it is tainted; she only has to show reasonable doubt. If she can force a hearing, that gets us out into the open and vulnerable. Killing Jackie would give her revenge against you, Raven. She would be taking away a person that you love, like she feels you took away her brother. Vincent would go along with this sick plan to hurt me where it matters most."

"Max, I didn't take away her brother, if anything, Joseph was the one who turned him into a puppet."

"Yeah, but Joseph is dead and no one knows where Duke is, so going after you is the next best thing. Raven, look I know it's a sick plan but a plan nonetheless, we need to deal with this." There is a long pause and I check to see if the call was dropped.

"Jax, are you still there?"

"Yeah, trying to wrap my head around all of this. What's the plan, Max?"

"I already tripled security, I'm not sure what other steps I want to take yet. I wanted to make you aware of what's going on. I'm also concerned about Rose. I know she wanted to confront Vincent. This threat might push her in that direction. He can't find out she's alive."

"We might have a problem, Max—a big one. When we got here, there were a slew of media. I realized the announcement came out about Raiders. Mick took Rose around back and put a hat and glasses on her, but a reporter took a picture. Mick pulled the guy's SD card, however, there were other reporters across the street. He can't say one-hundred percent that no one got a picture."

"*Fuck,* Jax! I'm going to have more security put in place. I also want to put security on Junior's doctor and nurses. I'm going to say that due to the announcement, I feel the need for additional security. Do you think they will give us a problem?"

"Not sure, mate, but I will have a talk with them. I would much rather move everyone to Scotland, but I don't think it's an option. The doctor told us that while Junior is having treatment he can't leave the state. When can we expect the additional security?"

"I will have everything in place within the hour. I'm pulling Sammy in on this; we need more people, people we can trust. Are you okay with that?"

"Yeah, I agree we need more help. Send me the files on the changes and I will update the hospital staff. What time is the wedding?"

"In a little while, but I need to get this handled first. I will send you everything and I will also send everything to Mick. Raven, hang in there. I promise you I would lay down my life to protect Jackie."

"Thank you," It's barely a whisper but I hear her. I'm barely off the phone and Jeff is back with Sammy. "I brought Jax and Raven up to speed on everything. I need to send copies of all the changes to him and Mick. Sammy, we might have another problem. With the announcement about Raiders today, there was paparazzi at the hospital. Mick brought Rose around back, one guy got a picture but he pulled his SD card. If it gets out that she is alive, all hell will break loose. On top of that, she wants to confront Vincent! Jax and I have talked her out of it for now, but I'm not sure how long that will last." I realize Jeff might not know Rose's true identity. "Jeff, have you been brought up to speed on who Rose really is?" He walks up to the window and quietly stares out, before turning his attention back to me.

"Yes, the chief filled me in—not Sam."

Sammy clears his throat, bringing our attention back to him. "So, you don't think Rose will consent to go back to Scotland?"

"Never. Look, we also need to add security on Junior's doctor and the nurses that are taking care of him. I'm leaving nothing to chance."

"I already ordered the additional security. I will send everything to Jax and Mick."

Jeff picks up one of the many pictures of Jackie that he has on his credenza. "Max, is there any way Michael's treatment can be done here in Switzerland? We have some of the finest medical facilities here; the University Children's Hospital Zurich has cutting edge research and could possibly have the treatment that young Michael needs."

"I'm not really sure. Everything happened so fast. Get me the research on what they have to offer and I will talk with the family about it. In the meantime, we have a wedding to get ready for."

Raven

"JAX, I'M SCARED. DO you think these people could get to Michael? What about Antonia and my mom? I'm so worried about your mom. I honestly don't think she can physically take another thing; she's so frail." I lean into him and begin to cry and I can't stop. The fear is overwhelming me. His arms around me are holding me up, supporting me, and I let him.

"I've got you, sweetheart, always. I think the added protection is necessary more for our own sanity. You need to pull it together, and I need to talk to the medical staff."

He wipes away my tears and kisses me so softly. "I'm okay; let's get this over with." We head out of the closet to find the staff, only to find Mick standing there, waiting.

Jaxson

"HEY, MICK, DID MAX get in touch with you?"

"Yeah, he brought me up to speed. Raven, Antonia is fussing, and there are no more bottles. Jax, I have Dr. Dave with Michael's nurses waiting to speak with us."

"Okay, Raven, go take care of Antonia; I will be in shortly." I watch my wife walk away and keep reminding myself, throughout all the madness, how lucky I am.

"Mick, how many new guards do we have coming on board?"

"Max said at least six for the family and then three for the staff. He wants me to stay on Rose twenty-four seven. He's worried she might try to confront Vincent if she finds out what's going on. Honestly, Jax, I'm not sure anyone will be able to stop her."

"I spoke with her about it before we left Scotland. I explained to her the danger she would be putting Raven and Antonia in. She is a smart woman, I think she would stick to the plan." I walk up to Dr. Dave's office and stop, taking a deep breath before entering; preparing myself to do whatever it takes to make this work.

Chapter Seventeen

Jackie

MY MOM IS IN the drawing room waiting for me, staring out the window, seemingly lost in thought. "Hello, Mom," I call out to her. When she sees me, her face warms with her beautiful smile.

"Kon'nichiwa, Jacquelyn. I didn't hear you come in. Happy birthday, and a blessed wedding day. Where is Maxwell?"

"Papa needed to speak with him right away. Come sit with me and have some tea, please."

We sit by the fireplace for some warmth and I pour the tea. "Mom, I know that everything is happening very quickly, but Papa did explain to you why, right?"

She's quiet for a bit but then she takes my hand, turns it over, and runs her delicate fingers up and down the lines of my palm.

"Of course he did, but I do have some questions for you." She usually never questions me. What she does do is make me think things through, look at all sides of a situation.

"How is Michael handling all of this?" She always thinks of others first.

"He started his treatments today. He was afraid, but we are all there for him and always will be. This family has been through so much, yet their strength is amazing to me."

"How is Raven holding up? Did you bring me pictures of Antonia?" I take out my phone and begin to show her the tons of pictures I have been taking of my beautiful niece.

"Mom, are you okay with me getting married on my birthday—"

"Stop, Jacquelyn, it will always been a double edge sword for me. I will always be sad that I lost a child. The grief is with me every day of my life, however, I will always be blessed that I have wonderful children. You and Dylan have exceeded all my dreams for you. Why don't you tell me what else is bothering you?"

How does she do it? I don't have to say a word, yet she always knows. "I love him and that's never been a question, but can I be all that he needs? He has experienced such great loss. He recently found out that his father was friends with the man behind that loss. Now Michael is fighting for his life and the threats against everyone have not gone away. Jax's mom had a heart attack. What if what happened to you happens to me? I don't know that he can survive any more. I'm scared mom, really scared for him, for all of us. I can't let him see my fear or he will lose it." I finally let it all go, I can't stop my tears and I really don't want to. I want my mom to hold me and keep me safe. I want her strength and support. She pulls me into her arms and holds me tightly.

"Oh, my sweet child, you are so brave and so very strong. A lot stronger then you ever give yourself credit for. Your father told me all about Maxwell's past. He has survived so much, don't doubt him now. He will always have your strength to draw upon. If you are blessed with children, you will love them and survive whatever God has in store for you. You love each other and you need to draw upon that. We don't always walk side by side; sometimes one must carry the other. That is what love is all about: compromise, compassion, and putting someone else before yourself."

I hear Max coming and I quickly wipe away my tears. I can't let him see me this upset or he will lose it. "Mom, let me introduce you to Max."

She gets up and embraces him. "Maxwell, welcome to our family. I hope Jeffery hasn't been to overbearing."

"No, ma'am, he has been giving me a tour of your lovely home."

"Thank you. I'm going to get ready for the wedding. Jacquelyn, I will meet you in your room shortly to help you."

My dad takes her hand, "Emi, I will go with you. Max, when it's time, I will be up to help you. Hopefully you won't need too much help getting into your Kimono." He chuckles as he heads out with my mom.

Maxwell

"OKAY, JACKIE, WHAT'S WRONG? Don't say nothing and don't tell me not to worry."

"I saw my mom and everything just hit me, hard. So much has happened in such a short time. Lately, there are never any carefree happy times. It's always so intense, and I'm worried all the time. Now I see your face, and I know something else has happened. I'm scared to even ask what's going on now."

My heart is breaking for all that she has had to endure. "I know you have been overwhelmed by everything, but you have to know that I will do whatever it takes for you to be safe. I won't give up—ever. There has been another credible threat. I'm bringing Sammy in on your protection. I have ordered more security on everyone, including the doctor and nursing staff. I won't hide anything from you, Jackie, ever."

"What kind of threat, Max?"

I update her on all of the info I had just received. "We are very well insulated, babe, and I won't let anyone get near any of us."

"You talked to Jax, how is Michael?" Of course she is worried about Junior, she is a giver and will always be.

"Jax said he is doing good, and the doctor is great. Now, I want you to put all that aside. We have a wedding tomorrow to prepare for, and apparently, your dad is going to help me get into my Kimono."

She laughs and it warms my heart. "Just the thought of you in the Kimono is funny, let alone Papa helping you." She gets up and extends her hand toward me. "Let's go. The sooner I become Mrs. Maxwell Fleming, the sooner I can have my way with you."

"Wow, you have plans for me, babe?"

"Big plans, Max." She leans in and whispers in my ear a little bit of what her plans are.

I feel the heat rush to my cheeks and Jackie giggles.

"Why, Maxwell Fleming, I do believe you're blushing."

"I might be blushing now, but your arse will be a lovely shade of pink later."

We race up the stairs. Not quite sure who is pulling who.

FINALLY MY WAIT IS over. Today, I will not only be her lover, friend, and protector, I will become her husband, too. After a quick shower, I attempt to figure out the Kimono. There is a knock on the door and Jeff comes in. "Hey, Jeff, I've got everything but this sash figured out."

He silently begins to tightly wrap the sash around me. "Maxwell, I know you love her, that's never been a question, but can you protect her? She's my life."

"Jeff, I love her more than life itself. When I pushed her away, it nearly killed us both. If I could keep her locked away, I would, but you know your daughter, hell would freeze over first. I promise you, I will lay down my life for her."

"Okay, I will give you a moment and meet you in the drawing room. Dylan is waiting for us."

I walk up to the window and look out over the estate. It really is very beautiful here and very lonely. I close my eyes, thinking about my first wife and silently pray. *Oh, Samantha, please know I loved you so much. I would have been with you for life, but God needed angels. Jackie loves me with all her heart. She is genuine and pure; I know you will be happy for me. Watch over her and keep her safe.*

I take a deep breath and head out to begin a new life. Now, I have to meet the wanker, Dylan, and try not to snap the fucker's neck.

Jackie

I RUN MY FINGERTIPS down my grandmother's beautiful Kimono, the same one my mom wore on her wedding day. It's soft and silky. The design has a thousand cranes stitched in gold thread, and when the light hits it, they sparkle like a thousand stars. I pray for my grandmother to watch over him again, just like before. *Keep him safe, all of them.* There's a knock on the door, it must be my mom to help me get ready. When I open the door, I'm surprised to see Dylan. Before I can speak, he pushes me in the room.

"I need to talk to you alone, Jac, now."

"Calm down and tell me what's wrong." I just wish he would, for once, let me have my time without butting in.

"You can't marry him, Jac. There is so much danger around him. I can't let you do this!"

He can't be serious. "Dylan, please just let it go. I love him and he loves me. He's a good man and he can protect me." He grabs my hands and tries to pull me toward the door.

"Dylan, let go of me; you're hurting me."

The door flies open and Max, along with my father, Sammy, and the guards, come racing in. Max puts his hands around Dylan's throat, lifting him off the ground. "Max, let go of him please." My father and Sammy finally pull them apart. Max pulls me toward him.

"Jackie, are you okay? Did he hurt you?" He's running his hands all over me looking to see that I'm not hurt.

"Max, I'm fine. It's just Dylan, being his usual self."

He holds me tightly into his arms, his breathing is heavy. "Please calm down, Max, I promise I'm okay." I feel his heart racing.

My father and Dylan are yelling. I've never seen my father this mad before. Finally, my mom steps into the room. Dylan sees her and immediately stops yelling. My mom then asks everyone to please leave except for Dylan and me. I feel Max tense up, and I know he's not going to leave me alone with Dylan.

"Max, look at me please." His eyes are locked on mine. "I promise you, I will be okay. I will keep Sammy in the room. You need to step outside, please."

"So help me, babe, if he touches you, all bets are off." He steps outside the room and I know he is just on the other side of the door.

My mom steps in-between Dylan and me, "Look at me, son. What has gotten into you?"

"I can't let her make the biggest mistake of her life. She might love him, but is that any reason to put her life in constant danger? He chose the life he has lived, but she has not."

I'm about to answer him when my mom stops me. "Let me ask you this. Would you feel the same way if you were marrying Raven, knowing all the danger that surrounds her? Would that be okay with you? You have had no problem letting your sister be friends with Raven as long as you thought there was a possibility that you might have a chance with her. Now that you realize that possibility is gone, can she no longer be friends with her, is that what you're suggesting?"

She steps closer to him, never giving him a chance to answer. "Since Jackie met Maxwell, she has come alive. She is growing into the woman I always knew she could be. I will not let you, or anyone stop her. I suggest you figure out how you are going to apologize to your sister, and, to Maxwell."

Dylan takes a step back "Mom, I'm sorry, but I can't be here for this. Jac, you are making the biggest mistake of your life. I love you . . . I honestly do. Quite frankly, when everything came out about Raven, I was glad that Max sent you packing. If he truly were the man you all think he is, he would have put you first. He would have never put you in so much danger. Everyday the threats get worse, and you're walking around with your head in the clouds. Jesus Christ, because of all of this, you can't even teach anymore. What are you going to do, sit around the house all day and do nothing? Or, is he going to knock you up every year to keep you locked away in that castle? I'm leaving, and if you actually live through all of this, you can call me when it's time to pick up the pieces."

He storms out of the room, leaving me alone with my mom. "Are we having a wedding here today, Jacquelyn, or am I to get Maxwell?"

"I would like a few minutes alone, please." My mom steps out of the room and I begin to cry.

"Hey, stretch, look at me." My heart nearly leaps out of my chest; I forgot Sammy was in the room.

"Are you going to let what Dylan said influence you? Don't listen to anyone but you. What is your heart telling you to do?"

I wipe away my tears. "I need to talk to Max." I open the door and he is standing there, fists clenched, and a look of angst on his face that breaks my heart.

Sammy takes my hand, "Jackie, I'm going to step outside and give the two of you a little privacy."

He is barely out the door and I throw my arms around Max. I'm trembling and I can hardly speak.

"Jackie, I heard everything he said. I don't care what he thinks, I only want to know how you feel."

I pull back and take his hands. "I want a life with you. I want to be your wife and best friend. I want to fill my days with us. I want a family with you. I want to be loved by you. I want to grow with you; into someone you will always respect. Marry me, and then I want to leave right away. I don't want to spend my wedding night here."

"That's all I need to hear. Let's go right now to the temple before anything else happens." As we race toward the temple, he notifies the pilot to have the plane ready to leave within the hour.

Raven

I HEAD INTO MICHAEL'S room, pick up Antonia, and go into the restroom. I change her and then begin to feed her. I love our quiet time together; it gives me a chance to think clearly about everything. I can't believe that Marco kept such a huge secret from me—then again—he, kept a lot from me. I wonder how much Max has told Jackie. I know that nothing and no one will stop Max from marrying her. I just pray that we can keep everyone safe.

Michael is exhausted from today; I hope he can stay awake to see the wedding. Antonia is falling asleep during her feeding as usual. I need to find Jax and make sure he didn't bully the staff. When I step outside the restroom, I see Jax lying in bed with Michael. The two of them look so tired. Bella is standing in front of the window crying. This is not what Michael needs right now. I put Antonia into her carriage and bring it next to the bed. I need to see if I can help Bella.

I walk up to her and pull her into a hug. "Hey, we need to keep it together for Michael. What's the problem, Bella?"

"Let's step outside, Raven."

As we step outside I glance over toward Jax. He's holding Michael while he falls asleep.

"Bella, what's the matter? Did something happen with Michael?"

"No, not really. It's just hard to feel so helpless. You're a mom now; imagine Antonia hurting and not being able to do anything about it," her voice trembles. "To start out in life the way he did, now this . . ." she trails off.

"What do you mean 'start out in life the way he did'?" I tilt my head, trying to think if there was something I'd forgotten about. *Was he a preemie?*

Bella takes in a deep breath before leaning in closer to me. "You're family now, so I'll tell you, but you mustn't say anything to Michael Jr.; he doesn't know." She pauses. I nod for her to continue. "Michael Sr. is not Junior's biological father. I was date raped before I met Michael. I didn't find out I was pregnant till after he and I became serious. It didn't matter to Michael; he loved me and anything that was a part of me. He talked me out of having an abortion and raised Michael Jr. as his own." She lets a small smile grace her face as she wipes her tears away.

"Wow, Bella." I shake my head in disbelief. "I'm so sorry that happened to you, but I'm so happy that Michael Jr. is here . . . that you have him and your wonderful husband." I grasp her upper arms and squeeze them gently. "Stay focused on that. We have to stay focused on the positive. There's enough love and strength in this family—*our* family—to get us through anything."

"You're right and that's what we're going to do—stay positive." She brings me in for a hug. "I love you," she says softly and she tightens the hug.

"I love you, too."

"Everything all right, out here?" Jax grabs our attention, breaking us from our hug.

"Yes, it is now." Bella reaches her hand out to him. "I've told her everything, Jax. She knows what happened to me." She squeezes his hand.

A mixture of anger and remorse flashes across Jax's eyes. "I blame myself. I was just making a name for myself. I didn't know enough to have guards on everyone. That's when I brought Max on board."

"Oh my God, none of you are to blame. What's important is everyone is safe and will remain that way. If Michael needs stem cells, we will move heaven and earth to get them. Let's try and focus on the positive. Jax, did the doctor say how close of a match you and Max are?" I try to change the subject a little, pull him away from the blame game; it won't help anyone.

"No he didn't, why? I know you, sweetheart; I can see the wheels in your mind turning."

"Jackie said something to me about donating cord blood. I don't remember what the hell she said other than the baby needs to be born in the hospital."

Bella gives me a look of utter shock. "Oh, Bella, don't look at me that way; you know this crazy man wants ten kids. If the stem cells are needed, it won't be for a while," I finish. Jax begins to laugh a deep, hearty laugh.

Bella grabs my hand, "Raven, you would do that for me . . . for Michael?"

"I would do anything for that boy and, chances are, you might not have to wait that long. You're going to have to tell Jackie everything." On that note, Jax stops laughing and his eyes become wide.

"Don't look at me that way Jax, you know that Max is just as nuts as you are. Now, I believe we have a wedding that should be happening shortly," I say as I head toward the door. I turn around and they are both standing there, looking stunned. I smile and whisper, "*Faith,*" as I head back in the room.

Chapter Eighteen

Maxwell

JACKIE AND I RACE toward the temple. The sooner we do this, the sooner we are out of here. I know that's not the way one should look at their wedding day, but I can't let anything go wrong. Sammy stops us at the door, "Max, Jackie needs to wait here."

"It will be a cold day in hell, Sammy, if you think I would ever let her out of my sight."

"It's tradition; her mom has to walk her half way and then her father walks her the rest of the way."

"Where is Dylan?" I feel my heart in my throat.

"He's already gone, Max. You're going to have to trust me. I would never let anything happen to her."

I close my eyes and silently pray for some sort of strength and courage, but I know I can't do it. I whisper her name and pull her tightly in my arms.

She kisses me so softly, "Max, let's start our own tradition. How about you walk me down the aisle with both my parents."

I open my eyes and I whisper, "Thank you, babe."

We step inside and find hundreds of tiny paper cranes hanging from the ceiling. The lights in the room make it look like they are all twinkling. Emi comes up to me and takes my hand. "Maxwell, sometimes in life, one must make changes. I understand your fears and I am willing to make the changes you need. When you love someone, you must sometimes carry their fears for them to get them through the difficult times. I wish for you both only happiness and joy, but I am realistic; I know there will be tears. Love her with all that you have and all that you will ever be. Need her and want her always. Don't be afraid to share your fears with her, your tears, and your joy. They will help you to grow not only as an individual but as a whole." I'm floored; she is so quiet and reserved yet, when she speaks to you—it is profound.

I'm about to start up the aisle when Jeff stops me. "I have a surprise for both of you." He nods to Sammy and the television screen comes to life.

"I could not let you get married without your family to witness it." I'm speechless; I can't believe they pulled this off. Junior looks tired as he has stayed awake for this.

My grip around Jackie is even tighter, "You ready, babe?"
"Yes."
The music begins and we head down the aisle. I look up at the screen and I swear Jax might be crying. Everyone is there, glued to the screen. When we reach the front, Jeff sits next to Emi and we face a man that, I'm guessing, is some sort of minister.

"Hello, everyone, my name is Bill. I will be officiating your service today. I would like to start with a modified version of the Buddhist Declaration of Intent; if you agree then both say *we will*. Will you, in every way you can, allow your deepest self to be shown?"
"We will."
"Will you both take full responsibility for your own life and all of its dimensions?"
"We will."
"Are you committed to embrace all parts of each other, your deepest fears and bring them toward the light to heal?"
"We will."
"Will you always keep your hearts open to each other, even in extreme pain?"
"We will."
He hands us each a small bottle of sand, and now I'm really confused.

"Maxwell, every grain of sand in your jar represents every beat of your heart." He hands me a larger jar, "Please pour it into this jar." I'm still confused but I do as instructed.

"Jacquelyn, every grain of sand represents every beat of your heart. Please pour your sand into the jar with Maxwell's sand."

He puts a cap on it and shakes it, and then hands it back to me.

"The sand can never be separated again. You have become one heart and one soul—for life." I roll the jar in my hands, watching the sand swirl around; something so simple, yet, so profound.

"Jacquelyn, and, Maxwell, remember these words and carry them in your heart. It's the little things that matter the most in life. You are never too old to hold hands. Never go to bed angry. Put your lover before you. Say I love you every day. Don't expect perfection. There are no halos or angel wings attached to you. We are all a work in progress, so learn to forgive and forget. Keep family close to you. Do for each other out of joy not obligation. When you have to carry the load, do so willingly without regret," he finishes, giving us a warm smile. "Who has the rings?"

Oh my God, I can't believe I forgot the rings! Jeff gets up and hands the minister the rings. "Relax, Maxwell, your brother sent them." I look at the screen and Jax has a huge smile.

"Hey, I'll always have your back, mate—always."

The minister holds up the rings, "The wedding ring is the outward and visible sign of an inward and spiritual bond which unites two loyal hearts in partnership." Maxwell, please place the ring on Jacquelyn's finger. Do you promise to always love her with all that you are and all that you will ever be in this life?"

"I do."

"Jacquelyn, please place the ring on Maxwell's finger. Do you promise to always love him with all that you are and all that you will ever be in this life?"

"I do."

Before the minister finishes, I take both of Jackie's hands in mine. "Jackie, you saved me. Everything I will ever be is because of your love for me. You've made me want to have a life worth living."

"Max, I didn't chose you, my heart did. Wrapped in my arms you will always be home. Like the sands in the bottle, our hearts beat as one. Everyday with you is a gift I will treasure forever"

I close my eyes and rest my forehead upon hers, breathing in her sweetness. "Please tell me I can kiss you now?"

"Kiss her already!" I hear Jax yell.

I open my eyes and they connect with hers, making my soul burn with desire for her. I glance toward the minister and he nods, "You may kiss your wife now."

Your wife two words that I've longed to hear. I gently kiss her tender lips. I hear clapping and laughing. We both turn and look up at the screen. What a wonderful sight; everyone is celebrating.

"Thank you, everyone, for being here with us. Junior, our flight leaves in thirty minutes. We will see you soon." He looks very tired. I don't want to be away from him longer than I have to.

Jeff and Emi step up to congratulate us. "Let's head up to the main house before you have to leave. I will keep it brief; I know you need to be with your family at this time."

"Thank you, Jeff, for being so understanding."

I pull Jackie close as we head up toward the main house. It's been such an emotional day for both of us, and I know saying goodbye will be very hard for her.

We get to the main house and I'm glad to see that there is no sign of Dylan.

"Jeff, I know this has been a whirlwind for everyone. Please, understand it was never my intention. Unfortunately, sometimes life does get in the way of living. I promise as soon as everything settles down, we will come back."

"I understand and I never would have gone along with any of this if I wasn't sure of how much you love Jacquelyn. I know you will keep her safe, but so help me if something ever happens—all bets are off!"

He pulls Jackie into his arms. "My beautiful girl, everyday you have brought me so much happiness. I tried to think of what I could give you today, but what do you give someone who wants nothing? Finally, this morning it hit me like a lightning bolt—*shoes!*"

Jackie begins to giggle and, Jesus, I love that sound.

"Max, you must know by now that my daughter has an excessive amount of shoes, but have you ever asked her why?"

I'm about to ask when Jackie gasps. "Papa, you know?!"

"Of course I know, and don't glare at Sammy; he didn't give you up. You know I love a good mystery, so I investigated on my own. Max, Jacquelyn buys six pairs of shoes at a time, all the same, all different sizes. She keeps one pair for herself and she donates the others to shelters. She has been doing this since she was thirteen years old. I will match your donation to every shelter with whatever they need."

Wow, once again she has left me speechless. She always does something so simple that can mean so much to others. *Another facet of this beautiful woman to love.* I glance at my watch, "Jeff, we need to get going. I promise, first break in Junior's treatment and we will come for a visit."

Jackie pulls her mum into a hug. "I love you, Mom, and thank you so much for everything."

"Happy birthday, my beautiful girl; safe travels and let us know when you arrive." She places a pouch in Jackie's hand. "Please give this to young Michael."

We make our goodbyes and head out to the plane, with Sammy and six guards in tow.

Jaxson

JUNIOR HAS FINALLY FALLEN asleep with Bella curled up next to him. Michael is mindlessly channel surfing while Raven is tending to Antonia. Mick has taken Rose, Mrs. Osla, and my mum back to the house. My mum was so tired. I know Rose is worried about her. I know everyone was glad to see the wedding. I didn't see Dylan there. I'll get all the details from Max when he gets back. I'm glad my sister finally shared everything with Raven. I hate secrets. Leave it to Raven, though, to find a silver lining. I stare out the window, processing everything that happened today. I feel her arms slowly wrap around my waist. She presses her warm body against mine. I need her so badly, like nothing I could ever explain. I've never needed anyone, yet she completes me. Through all the sadness and the pain, she gives me hope . . . hope for the future . . . our future.

"Jax, what happened when you spoke to the doctor about the added security?"

I turn around and hold her tightly in my arms. "He understood and so did the nurses. I tried not to focus on the unknown danger, only what we know for sure."

"How long will Michael have to stay in the hospital?"

"The doctor said for a month, and then after that, he will come back and forth as needed. We can't leave the country; he was adamant about that."

"Have you looked into treatment in other countries?"

"No, sweetheart, everything happened so fast. What are you thinking?"

"I know that Mrs. Osla pulled the best places for treatment, however, I'm sure there are other countries that might offer the same and, possibly, something new and cutting edge. I'm not saying there is anything wrong with the treatment that he's receiving, I'm just saying we should get all the facts."

"I will have Mrs. Osla look into it. I would feel safer if we were out of the States. The staff is bringing in a bed for Bella and Michael. I think we will take turns staying here; it will make it easier for all of us. When he can get out of here, I will feel better. This past year, I've grown used to having everyone under one roof."

"When can we expect Max and Jackie to get here?"

"He texted me that he was in-flight and he should be here in about six hours. I need to get you and Antonia home. You are beat, and we will be back here before you know it. Besides, I really need to lose myself in you for a while, sweetheart."

I don't need to say anything more; she gets it. She gathers up Antonia and we say goodbye to Michael Sr. We head out of the hospital, flanked by six guards and Bo, into a waiting car. The house we are renting is a quick ride from the hospital, which I thought would be a blessing until I get a look around the neighborhood. The iron gates open and we drive up a short drive to a nondescript looking home. Given the increased threats, this is never going to work for us. We get out and head inside. Mrs. Osla is waiting for us.

"Raven, why don't you get Antonia settled in for the night while I talk to Mrs. Osla."

She looks between me and Mrs. Osla, "Go easy on her, Jax."

"Raven, the bedrooms are all upstairs. Antonia's room is the third door on the right; it's attached to your room. Don't worry about me, I can handle him."

"Thank you for everything, Mrs. Osla. Jax, I will meet you upstairs."

I watch my wife walk away and my need to lose myself in her is becoming even more intense.

Mrs. Osla clears her throat, snapping me out of my daydream. "Jaxson, I know this is not the best place, but you saw the same pictures I did. The area around us didn't look like this. The pictures made it look more secluded. I'm trying to find something else, but it's not easy."

"Let's go sit down. I need to bring you up to speed on everything." She leads me into a den and pours me a drink.

"Mrs. Osla, there have been some new security developments and I know this place is not going to be secure for us."

"I'm aware of the developments; Mick has explained everything. I looked to see if there are any other hospitals that have this level of treatment for young Michael; there aren't any in this area. There is St. Jude's Children's Research Hospital in Tennessee, but I'm not sure it would be any more secure then what we've got. I also looked into other countries. Until I get the reports back, this one still comes out the best. So, what do we need to do to make it safe for us to stay here?"

"Short of locking everyone up in here, I'm not sure. We'll stay here for tonight, and then I will get with Max in the morning. How is my mum doing?"

"The trip was a lot for her, but she is resting. And Rose is keeping a close eye on her."

"How much does Rose know?"

"Nothing, we got home, and then she was making sure your mum was settled in."

"Good, I need to have Max here with me when we explain everything to her. How many guards are here?"

"There are a dozen at different points of the house."

"Okay, we should be good for the night. Get some rest, tomorrow will be another busy day."

She gets up and I'm left alone to figure out what to do about this mess. Just then, Raven walks around my chair, pulling me from my thoughts. She crawls into my lap and nuzzles my neck. "Come to bed,

Jax. Everything will still be here in the morning. Tonight, I need to cuddle up into your arms and have a peaceful sleep; we both do."

She doesn't need to say anything more; I lift her and carry her up the steps. My love, my salvation, the only place I truly have any peace is when I'm lost in her. "I love you, sweetheart, always and forever more."

Maxwell

WE ARE SAFELY IN-FLIGHT and I texted Jax to let him know.

My wedding night . . . not exactly what I was planning, but I can improvise. I take her hand and guide her into one of the large suites in the back of the plane. "My beautiful wife, God I can't get enough of that word. Happy birthday, Jackie; one of many we will share together." I hand her a small box. "I had this diamond heart made to match your ring; my heart next to yours—always."

"It's beautiful, Max, please put it on me." She turns and lifts her hair. I gently kiss her neck before putting on the necklace.

"Please, Jackie, get me out of this Kimono."

Her giggle is so sweet. "Maybe I like seeing you in this, then what?"

Her delicate fingers are trailing up and down my chest and I feel like I might combust. "Well, then I might have to get used to it, or maybe prove to you how much better it is when I'm naked."

She blushes and quickly helps me out of my Kimono. "Jackie, I need to figure out how to get you out of this. I don't even know where to begin!"

"Start by untying anything you can find. The wedding ones are more intricate, but I'm sure you will get me out of it. Keep in mind . . . this was my grandmothers, so please be careful."

Guess taking a scissor to it is not an option. There are so many parts to this, but I prevail. As the robes all fall away, I'm left staring at the most beautiful sight I've ever seen. My beautiful wife—in thigh highs, diamonds, and pearls . . . *nothing else.*

"Max, um, are you okay?"

Her voice snaps me out of my daze, okay? She is standing here like a vision and she thinks I would be okay! "I need a minute, babe. You took my breath away."

"I have something for you." She steps over to one of her bags and pulls out a small package.

"I wanted to give you something very special and it has to be now." She is chewing on her bottom lip and seems very nervous. I open the box and my eyes grow wide.

"What do you give a man who has everything? The one thing I know he really wants. I completely stopped them the day we got engaged. Honestly, with everything that has been going on, I haven't kept good track of them. I know I've missed several, so what's the point? As scared as I am, I know my life is with you and will always be, no matter what."

I pull her birth control pills out of the box. I'm speechless; she knows how much I want a child with her and she is willing to jump right in.

"It might take a while; it might not. I'm willing to go on the journey with you. We will face whatever life throws at us, together. I love you."

"I'm confused, I thought you were scared to have a baby?"

Her hand is trembling as she places it on my cheek. "Trust me, Max, I'm scared. But being around Antonia and the kids that I teach made me realize how much I really wanted one. I didn't want to tell you I stopped my pills until the wedding. I didn't want to put any more pressure on you. My hope is that, by your birthday, I will have a great present to give you. You are a very hard man to surprise, so I needed to do it this way. I knew we would be together forever; I wasn't being underhanded, Max. I wanted to make it special for you. Are you mad at me?"

With her, my needs are always first. How could she possibly think I'd be mad? "Mad? How could I ever be mad? You're making all my hopes and dreams come true. You, babe, amaze me. Come here." I pull her tightly in my arms. "You make me want a future, one that will never end. I promise you I will treasure our baby with my life."

I gently kiss her tender lips; they're so very soft. I don't want to rush this. I want to live in this moment for the rest of my life. I flutter my fingers up her sides, swirling up and around her nipples. They perk instantly to my touch. She looks down, following the trail of my fingertips. Her head is bowed but her eyes glance up to mine. She has a gift like no other, submissive and powerful in one single sweep of her eyes. "Kiss me, Jackie, *now.*"

She slowly lifts her head, her eyes keeping contact with mine. I feel desire burn deep within my soul. She softly brushes her lips over mine, followed by the swipe of her tongue. She takes her hand and glides it down her body. Slowly, she uses her fingertips to gather her wetness. She brushes her fingers across my lips and I taste her sweetness. I nip her fingertip. I consider myself a strong man, a man who is able to take a lot. When she tilts her head back and lets out a long, low moan, I lose it. I lean down and take one of her nipples between my teeth, pulling just enough to make her buck and yell. I lift her and place her gently on the bed and I wait.

She fists the sheets, "Max, what are you waiting for?—I want you now."

"Anticipation, babe, you can't always get what you want." She said she wanted to experiment and try different things. I plan on fulfilling every one of her fantasies, even ones she didn't know she had.

"Play with your nipples, Jackie." Her eyes flutter, and that shy submissive look is all over her face. She hesitates and that's what I want, that's what will intensify it for her. She brushes her fingers over them, causing them to perk. *Simply beautiful.* I kneel between her legs, lean down, and kiss each one. I slowly leave a trail of gentle kisses all over her. When I get to her clitoris, I barely let my lips touch and she gasps.

"Oh, Max, more please, I need *more.*"

Kiss, blow, nibble, and then swipe my tongue. She grabs my head, bucks her hips, trying to push for more. I've got my arms locked around her legs, holding her down. I work my tongue in and out, then stroke up and down. She begins to shake and her skin feels like it's on fire. As I work my fingers deep inside her, I keep a constant force on her clitoris. She arches her back and begins to beg me for more. "I know you want more, but not yet. I won't rush this night, our wedding night is once in a lifetime."

I need to slow her down. I slowly work my way off of her, taking my time nipping and kissing her everywhere. She whimpers at the loss of my tongue on her. Fuck me, it's beautiful. I head over to the dresser for some toys I got specifically for tonight. When I look back at her, she is rolling her nipples between her fingers.

"Does someone need a spanking?"

"No, please, Max, I need you."

I walk up to the bed and crawl between her legs. I pull her hands away from her nipples and put a remote in her hand.

"What is this for?"

"Babe, it's for your pleasure."

"What is that thing on your cock!?"

"You'll see, right now I'm going to enter you very slowly. When I tell you, slowly tilt your hand."

I enter her and she closes her eyes, I stop. "Open your eyes and watch, *now.*"

Her eyes fly open when I'm all the way in. "Oh my!" she gasps from the cock ring hitting her clitoris.

"Tilt your hand very slowly."

It begins to vibrate and her eyes grow wide. "Oh wow, what the hell?"

"Tilt your hand back and forth, you have all the power, babe. If you want more, move it more."

Every time she moves her hand, my cock grows harder. While she's having fun with her remote I roll her nipples into a perfect peak. "I have another surprise for you."

"O-oh this is so wonderful, I don't think I can handle any more surprises."

"You can and you will. Slow it down or this will end too quickly."

She slows down the vibrations and her rapid breathing is becoming more even. I reach down and grab her next surprise off the bed. I hold them up for her to see as they sparkle in the dim lighting. "What are they?"

"I had them made for you; diamond and gold nipple clamps." I need to start her slowly with these. I put them on, but make sure they are not too tight—yet.

"Wow, they are beautiful. They feel . . . different."

"Now you can use the remote again, but slow, babe."

She's getting into this and I'm trying not to explode. It's a mind game; concentrating on giving her pleasure. When she speeds up the vibrations, I tighten the clamps. Her eyes open wide and she doesn't realize it, but she's moving her hand more, which of course, makes the cock ring vibrate even more. I'm harder than I can ever remember being in my lifetime. "Oh, Max, you feel huge. I don't think I can take much more."

I tighten the clamps again and her whole body begins to shake. "Babe, you're shaking, what do you want?" Before she can answer, I release the clamps and it sends a surge through her. Right at that point, I release the cock ring and slam into her, over and over again. She finds her release and I'm right behind her—*beautiful*.

I slowly work us down as I nuzzle her neck. "I hope we made a new life tonight," she whispers.

I pull the covers over us and hold her close to my heart. "I hope so too, babe."

Chapter Nineteen

Leo Hage

THE CASE THAT MADE my career is now blowing up in my face. I'm looking at the order, demanding all documents in the Giaconna deal to go to his new attorney. Who is this attorney and why have I never heard of her before today? What does she think she can accomplish? The buzzing of my intercom snaps me out of my thoughts. My assistant informs me Amelia Jade, the current pain in my ass, is here to see me. Sending her away would be like poking a hornet's nest. "Give me a minute and send her in."

Within a moment, the door opens and in steps the most stunning redhead I have ever seen. I have to stay focused; I can't let her distract me. "What can I do for you, Ms. Jade?"

"I'm here to discuss Mr. Giaconna's case."

"Have a seat, Ms. Jade, and please enlighten me; I don't know what case you're referring to? Mr. Giaconna took a plea deal, *there is no case.*"

She doesn't sit. Her glare becomes more intense. "Mr. Hage, you must have received the order to turn over all your files in my client's case, by now. My client is requesting an emergency bail hearing and a trial. The tape was obtained illegally. You should have known that this would somehow come back to bite you in the ass. You obtained the tape without a warrant, and a proper chain of evidence was not followed.

Therefore, all the evidence you obtained from Duke never would have happened without the video. It's called *fruit of the poisonous tree,* and you knew that but chose to ignore it. Mr. Hage, my client has the right to face his accuser; he wants his day in court."

She's got to be just as crazy as Vincent if she thinks this will ever fly. "You know and I know this is never going to happen, so what's your end game?"

"Everyone is entitled to justice, Mr. Hage, even Mr. Giaconna— whether you like it or not. We all have to play by the same rules. You can't write them to fit your needs. I want him moved, via U.S. Marshals Service, from ADX Florence to Daniel Patrick Moynihan United States Courthouse for a bail hearing. On my way here, I filed the necessary papers for the emergency bail hearing."

"Look, Ms. Jade, I don't know what your game is but no judge would ever grant that animal bail. You and I both know you don't have a leg to stand on. Drop it; find another way to make a name for yourself."

She gathers up her stuff and turns to leave. "Mr. Hage, I will see you in court." Just like that, she's gone. I sit back in my chair; total shock envelops me. What is her end game? Money? Making a name—what?

My intercom buzzes again, "Mr. Hage, papers just arrived for you from the court. It appears Mr. Giaconna has been granted an emergency bail hearing. I also sent Ms. Jade the files . . . sir?"

"I'm here. Get Mr. Phillips on the line for me immediately. " This is a call I'm not looking forward to making.

Jaxson

LOSING MYSELF OVER AND over again in Raven last night was just what I needed. With her, I can release all my fears and frustration. With her, I find my safe place. I've got her locked up in my arms when my phone begins to ring. At this hour of the morning, it has to be a problem. I look at the display. And so the nightmare continues . . . Hage.

" Hage, what's the problem?"

"Vincent is being granted an emergency bail hearing." What the fuck?!

"I'll call you back in five." I don't want to wake Raven. I make my way out of bed and grab my sweats. I head downstairs where I know she won't hear me. I'm about to call Hage back when Max and Jackie come through the front door. Relief washes over me, and I pull Jackie into a big bear hug.

"Jax, you're smothering me; is everything okay?"

"Oh sorry, yeah, just very stressed out. Glad you guys got here okay." I look over to Max and nod. I never have to say anything with him.

"Babe, I'm going to go over some stuff with Jax, and then have a quick shower before we head over to the hospital. Would you mind getting everything set up for us?" he asks.

She kisses him and giggles, "If you want alone time with Jax, you just have to ask."

He is watching her head up the steps with a grin like the cat that ate the canary.

"Okay, Jax, besides this house, what's the problem?"

"Hage just called and said Vincent was granted an emergency bail hearing. I didn't ask any questions. I didn't want to wake Raven. I need to call him back now."

Sammy walks into the room. "Hey, Jax, I just hung up with my contact. The U.S. Marshal will be bringing Vincent from Colorado to New York. Hage requested that he be brought back via private plane due to the high security threat. The hearing is set for tomorrow. It's only a bail hearing so Max and Raven won't need to be present."

"Thanks, Sammy. Sorry about everything that happened when we left the States the last time."

He holds up his hand, "Don't worry, Jax; just business."

"Sammy, before I call Hage back, does he know who Amelia Jade really is?"

"I don't know, but I would tell him. Better to have all the cards on the table."

"Max, you ready for this?"

"Yeah, put him on speaker."

He answers on the first ring. "Hage, you're on speaker, and Max is here."

"Okay. As I said earlier, Vincent was granted an emergency bail hearing. He is already being processed and turned over to the U.S. Marshals office for transfer to New York City. Do not come to court."

"I personally won't be there, however, my attorney will be. My family's safety is at stake; I trust no one." I hear him growl and I really don't give a fuck.

"Hage, do you have any idea who Amelia Jade is?"

"I know that she is from Virginia and graduated top in her class. She knows she can't win the case. Vincent made a deal and now she wants him to back out of that deal. I can't figure out why. I thought maybe it was some sort of revenge but she is squeaky clean with no ties to the Giaconna family. Do you know something I don't?"

I run my hands through my hair, trying to keep my temper in check. Max holds a hand up to silence me before I snap.

"Hage, Maxwell here. Amelia Jade was formerly Amelia Greene, Marco Greene's sister. Marco, if nothing else, was a brilliant hacker and had her name changed with the records sealed. The motive very simply put: revenge. She wants a trial to get Raven out into the open. She wants to make Raven suffer the way she feels she has suffered. Vincent wants me to suffer, so there is a huge bounty on Jackie's head."

I look at the phone to see if the call has dropped as Max begins to pace. *The silence is deafening.* "Apparently, Hage, you knew none of this. My wife and Jackie will never step foot near that courthouse. My nephew is here for medical treatment and, as soon as I can make other arrangements, we will be leaving the country. What are the chances of him getting bail?"

"I didn't even think he had a chance at getting a hearing, so what do I know? I haven't been told what judge has been assigned to it yet. My understanding was that Annabelle found Ms. Jade, but now, after what you're telling me, I'm not so sure. Where is Miss Gerhard now?"

"She is safe, and that is all you need to know. When you find out who the judge is, let me know what his chances are." I don't wait for his reply—I can't or I might snap—so I just hang up.

I need coffee, but I don't even know where the kitchen is in this place. Bless her; Mrs. Osla comes in with a tray, bearing coffee and pastries.

"Welcome home, Maxwell, and congratulations. I'm sorry about this home, it's not as it was pictured. I'm trying to find something more suitable, however, getting close to the hospital is an issue."

"Thank you, Mrs. Osla. Please don't worry, we will figure something out."

"I will be upstairs if you need anything more."

As she leaves, the three of us grab our coffees and try to formulate some sort of plan.

"It's not her fault, Max, it seemed that the house was more isolated in the pictures. So, first thing we need is a safer place to stay. There are too many windows and too many neighbors. Even if I purchased every house around us, it would still take too much time to process and get them cleared out. How about a penthouse? We can isolate ourselves like we did in New York. The only thing that might be an issue is traveling to and from the hospital."

" We could ferry everyone by helicopter. I will look at the regulations, but that might not be such a bad idea. I sent Tony whatever information Sammy had on Amelia, so I need to get in touch with him and see if he found out anything else."

"How is he settling in? We gave him a sweet deal but, in the end, it's never been about material stuff with him," I ask. Max seems apprehensive as he pours himself another coffee.

Before he can answer, Sammy puts his hand on Max's shoulder. "I know more than you think, Max. You're going to have to get used to me being around and you're going to have to trust me. You know I only have Jackie's best interest at heart. I think I proved myself with Dylan."

"What the fuck happened with that wanker?!"

"That is a story for another day, mate." He shakes his head and rolls his eyes a bit. "It's not easy for me, Sammy, but in time, I will come to trust you more." He holds his mug up to Sammy in gesture before taking another sip. He puts his mug down and brings his attention back to me. "Tony is thrilled that at twenty-nine, he was able to semi-retire. But you know him; he can never be idle. He wired up the entire island, and now it's like a fort. He loves it there and has since taken up fishing. He was happy that I gave him some work to do."

"What are we going to do about Jackie? Every time she walks out that door, she is in danger. I know you want to be here, but maybe it would be for the best if you head back to Scotland."

"Trust me, I thought about that, but she will never go for it. She is the most stubborn person I have ever met—worse than you, mate. Jeff found a private clinic in Switzerland that is doing a lot of cutting edge work with ALL. He gave me the file, but I haven't had a chance to look at it yet. I'm going to have Rose look at it. I won't leave Jackie's side, Jax, ever. I just can't do it."

"I get it; I wouldn't ask you to. We will figure something out. What are we going to do about Rose? If Vincent gets wind that she is alive, he'll go crazy."

"Best case scenario, we are going to have to keep her locked up here until we can get her out of the country. We are going to have to tell her what's going on. I mean, we really don't have a choice."

"You think Jackie is stubborn? My mother in-law is worse!" I get up to get more coffee when I hear Raven scream. We fly up the steps and I find Raven with Antonia in her arms, and Bo attacking one of the new guards. Sammy pulls the guard out of the room, with Bo still trying to rip him apart. I push Raven and Antonia back into the bedroom.

"What happened? Why did you scream? Are you okay? Is the baby okay?"

"Antonia woke up and I went in her room to take care of her like I always do. When I turned around, that guard was in the room. He was staring at me and he started to close the door. I screamed and gave Bo his command to attack." She begins to shake and cry. *Fuck.*

I'm holding them tightly in my arms. "Shh, you're okay, sweetheart. Max is here now, and he will make sure we are all safe." The door flies open and Max comes barreling in with Jackie right behind him.

"Jackie!"

"Raven, it's okay, he's gone and no one will get near you. Are you and Antonia okay?"

"Yeah, Max, we are fine. I just got creeped out. Oh my God, Jackie, I'm so glad you're finally here."

"Me too, let's get Antonia cleaned up; I have lots to tell you." I watch my wife leave while trying to keep my temper in check.

"Where the fuck is he, Max?!"

"Come on, Sammy has him downstairs."

We race downstairs and find Sammy in the den with the guard strapped to the chair. Bo is sitting in front of the guy, growling. I'm about to step in and snap the fucker's neck when Max grabs me. "Don't; you and I will kill him. Sammy will get information first. After that, be my guest."

"This fucking bastard was going after my wife and child, Max!"

"Was he going after Raven because she is beautiful or because of Vincent? If you kill him, we will never know. Let Sammy do his job. After that, I'm going upstairs, and you can do whatever you want. I won't stop you."

Sammy

"I'M GOING TO MAKE this real easy on you. Tell me what you were doing up there. If you do, I will keep Jax out of here." He has the nerve to sit here and smile, *really?*

"Look, I was doing a walk through and when I got to the baby's room, I checked to see if everything was okay. She went nuts and sent that beast after me. I was just doing my fucking job."

"That would be all well and good if your job was to be upstairs, but it's not. You are supposed to be out back watching the perimeter. So, do you want to tell me the truth now?"

"I don't know what you're talking about. I was just doing my job. Look, just let me go and I won't press charges for that dog attacking me or you tying me to a chair."

"Do you really think I care about you pressing charges? You should be more concerned about staying alive and possibly being able to keep your balls firmly attached right where they are." I pet Bo as I glance down at the guy's crotch for emphasis.

"I don't know where you're from, but I have rights." Rights? Fucking scumbag I'll show him *'rights.'*

"I totally agree with you. I told you, you have the right to live and keep both your balls firmly attached. I think that's a great deal. Now, let's start again. Who do you work for?" He says nothing. The more he smiles, the more I want to unleash Jax on him. I'm done being nice. I reach in my pocket and pull out my new pocket knife. This bad boy hosts thirty-two different tools, very versatile. I make a show of slowly opening each tool, which is supposed to offer a firm grip and precision when cutting. I'm guessing it's time to find out just how precise. I take the large blade first and hold it up to the light.

"I just got this for my birthday and I've wanted to try it out. You know, the advertising claims that all thirty-two tools are very versatile. This one looks like it could cut through just about anything. The company says it's very precise; you better hope so." I slowly swipe it up his crotch, cutting through his jeans and boxers, still leaving his balls intact. He's breathing very heavy and beginning to sweat. Seems perfect to me.

"Wow, I guess their advertising is correct; one upward sweep and you still have your balls. So, are you ready to talk to me yet?"

"Go fuck yourself, pretty boy."

"Have it your way. No skin off my balls; just yours."

I take the little saw blade out and hold that one up to the light. His eyes are following my every move. I smile as I reach down and make a small, jagged slice right up the center of his balls.

"Are you fucking nuts? I don't know anything!"

He seems to be trying his hardest not to scream, but then I pull a bottle of booze off the shelf and he gets where I'm going with this. One pour of this on the torn up skin of his balls and he will either hit the roof or pass out.

"Are you going to talk to me now?" I unscrew the bottle and slowly walk up to him, holding it over his lap. I tilt it slightly, and his jaw is tight, as his eyes stay focused on the bottle.

"Okay, I freelance for a private detective firm. He hired me to find out everything I can about the girl with the baseball cap. I was upstairs looking for her when I saw the other one and she was so hot. Then she started nursing that baby and I lost it, I swear that's all I know."

"What is the name of the firm you work for?"

"Look, if I tell you that, I'm a dead man."

I look down at his balls, and blood is starting to pool around the jagged tears in the skin. I tilt the bottle a little bit more and his eyes grow wide. "Who?"

"Johnston Investigations; I swear that's all I know."

I tilt the bottle and watch the liquid land all over his balls. He is screaming and begging me to stop. "That's for being a filthy fucking pig." As I walk out, I see Jax with his fists clenched and Max trying to hold him back.

"I got what we needed. When you're done, if there is anything left, I will have him put into the prison system and his paperwork lost for quite some time."

Max let's go of Jax. "Don't go past what you can't live with. I'm going upstairs to check on everyone," Max growls. Jax heads into the den and closes the door as Max heads upstairs. I walk away, listening to the sound of the man begging. *All the begging in the world isn't going to help him.*

Jackie

RAVEN HAS ANTONIA TIGHTLY in her arms as we head into her bedroom to get her cleaned up.

"Let me take care of my beautiful niece," I offer. She gives me Antonia, sits in the chair, and begins to cry. I don't tell her not to—hell—I want to cry, too. The pressure is getting to all of us.

"I'm sorry, Jackie; this should be a happy time for you."

"Stop apologizing for something that is out of your control." Just then, Mick steps into the room. "Welcome home, Jackie, and congratulations. What went on here this morning?" He quickly turns his attention to Raven. "Are you okay?"

Rose, An, and Mrs. Osla come rushing in. "Raven, what happened? We heard yelling and Bo barking."

"Oh, Mom, one of the new guards freaked me out. Everything is fine now."

Swaying with the baby, back and forth, I glance up to Mick. He nods. "Ladies, I'm going to leave you all to catch up on the wedding while I find Max and congratulate him."

"Okay, Mick, thanks." I smile as he heads out.

An gives me a big hug. "Jackie, we all watched the wedding ceremony; it was breath taking. It looked like you were standing under a thousand twinkling lights."

"Thank you, An. It is a custom in the Japanese culture for the mother of a daughter to begin making paper cranes from the day she is born. They are then used to decorate for the wedding. She hung them from the ceiling; with the lights, and the breeze hitting them, they twinkled. The Kimono was my grandmother's wedding Kimono. I felt very honored to wear it, but I have to tell, you getting in and out of it was a challenge!" I laugh as I look down and notice Antonia is out cold. I swear she will sleep through anything. I put her in her crib and it hits me; I'm really ready. Not just for Max, but for me. I want a baby with Max.

"Come on, ladies; let's give them some time to catch up. An, it's time for your meds. I'll put up a pot of tea." Mrs. Osla barks out orders, ushering everyone out of the room.

Before she leaves, she pulls me into a hug, "Thank you," she whispers, and then wipes away a tear and rushes out of the room.

"Jackie, you okay?"

"Yeah, I wasn't expecting that from Mrs. Osla. She is usually very stern and reserved."

"She loves Max—hell, we all do. So, how did he react when you gave him the gift? Don't even think about holding out on me. Hell, I couldn't stop thinking about it all through the ceremony!"

We both begin to laugh and it feels good. "He was surprised and thrilled. I did warn him that it might not happen right away. He was okay with that."

"What happened with Dylan; don't think I didn't notice he wasn't there."

"Ugh, it was really bad. He tried to physically take me from the house. Max grabbed him by the throat and lifted him right off the ground! My mother stepped in and called him out on his feelings for you."

"Oh my God, you can't be serious?"

"He said I'm going to be isolated and waiting to get *knocked up.* Max knows how I feel about the isolation and I understand, right now, there are not a lot of options. I can see past that, though. Once all this craziness dies down, we will be able to have the life that we want and not the one we are forced to have at this moment in time. I was never able to see past any of that until Max. That's what Dylan doesn't get; with Max I see the future, not just the moment."

"Maybe in time he will come around. Don't give up on him. What happened when you saw Sammy?"

"Max apologized to him and he said he understood that it was business."

"Did Max bring you up to speed on the latest threats?"

"Not all the details; we were trying to get the wedding done, and then get here as quickly as possible. So, fill me in."

"I don't know all the details but, apparently, Marco had a sister who is now Vincent's new attorney. I know that was the reason for the increase in guards. That's really all I know." She shrugs then lets out a big sigh. "I think we should get ready and get over to the hospital."

"How is Michael doing? I bet the room cheered him up."

"He's brave and strong. You knew about the room?"

"I helped Mrs. Osla get it all together but you better never let Jax and Michael know, otherwise, I will get sucked into watching that ridiculous show."

"Your secret is safe with me. I'm going to get ready; will you stay with Antonia?"

"Of course, go."

Raven

I HURRY TO MY room to get ready. I want to get to the hospital as quickly as I can. I hear the water running; Jax must already be in the shower. I head in and find him with the water running over his hand. He has a grim look on his face. The sink is full of blood. What the hell? "Jax, what the hell happened?!"

"I think I broke the guy's jaw and possibly my hand. He was working for a private investigation firm, trying to find out who Rose is."

I can't panic, my husband needs me now. I rummage under the

sink and find a first aid kit. I open the peroxide and pour it over his hand.

"Can you move your fingers?"

"Yeah, barely, but I can. Please bandage it for me." His plea breaks my heart. We are both silent as I clean and bandage his wound. I'm so afraid this is going to break him, his spirit.

"Where's the baby?"

"With Jackie, she is fine. Now talk to me, tell me everything."

He sits down and fills me in on everything that he found out. "How the hell was he given a bail hearing? Wouldn't he be considered a flight risk?"

"Sweetheart, my head is spinning from all of this. If he's granted bail, the last thing I would be worried about is him being a flight risk. He's fucking crazy and that's what scares me. This house is not safe; too many neighbors and windows. Jackie's dad found a private clinic in Switzerland that might be a good fit for Junior. Mrs. Osla is going to check that out today. If it's possible, I would like to move him there."

"Do you think Max and I will have to go to court?"

"I told Hage it's never going to happen."

"Maybe I should confront Ms. Jade, let her say what she needs to. Maybe all she wants is her day in court."

"Have you lost your mind?! She wouldn't go through all of this for a conversation. She wants revenge, not a fucking cup of tea and social chat."

"Beating people up might make you feel good, but it doesn't solve the problem. Maybe using something other than physical violence might help defuse the situation. Maybe a *fucking* cup of tea and social chat is just what she needs." I'm not about to fight with him about all of this. I go turn on the shower and step in. I hear him growl and he slams the door. I go about my shower, trying to calm down, when I hear him come back in. He puts the music on pretty loud and then steps into the shower.

"Jax, what the hell are you doing and why is the music so loud?"

"The walls in this place are thin and I want to negotiate with you."

Jax's version of negotiation is a lot different from mine. "You're getting the bandage wet."

"I don't give a *fuck* about the bandage. I need you to understand every move we make can be life and death. Think about the price that is hanging over Jackie's head. Think about your mum . . . our daughter. What would happen to Antonia if you were gone? This girl is out for revenge. She wants you to suffer, just like she feels she is suffering. That guard was hired to find out who the lady in the baseball cap was. If Vincent finds out, then all bets are off. Even if you try to explain to her that you are not responsible for what happened to Marco, she won't believe it. You can't reason with crazy. Please, I'm begging you not to fight me on this."

"Okay, I will not fight you on this, but understand I want Vincent held accountable for all the heartache he has caused me. I won't back down on that. Do you have a plan?"

"Yes, if the Swiss clinic can offer Junior what he needs, then we are out of here. I don't feel safe in this house or this city. Maybe I'm wrong, but I would feel better if we were not in the States."

"I agree. Now, let's get out of here; I need to re-bandage your hand." We begin to towel off and something he said just hits me like a brick. "Wait a minute! If the guy was here to find out about the lady in the baseball cap, what was he doing in Antonia's room?" His jaw gets tight and his body instantly goes ridged.

"He saw you begin to nurse and decided he wanted to see more." I barely make it to the sink and heave. He holds my hair back and hands me a wet washcloth.

"I feel violated, and I want to leave here."

"I know, sweetheart. I'm working on it. Let's get ready and get to the hospital. Max can't wait to give Junior the blueprints. How is Jackie holding up with all of this?"

"Honestly, we talked about the wedding and stuff. I did tell her the increase in guards is because of Marco's sister. However, I ended the conversation pretty quick since I'm not sure how much she knows."

"Well, now I need to talk to your mum and explain what is going on. I'm not looking forward to *that* conversation."

We finish getting ready and head out to face everyone.

Chapter Twenty

Maxwell

I NEED MY WIFE—*bad*. I go in search of her and find her singing and dancing with Antonia in her arms. I stand in the doorway, taking it all in. They are a beautiful sight; Antonia is giggling and Jackie is singing a song I've never heard before. Jax and Raven come up behind me and they are trying not to laugh.

"She was like, come here boy, I wanna dance."

Jackie spins around and notices the three of us. "Oh my, um . . . how long have you been standing there?"

"Long enough, babe. What song were you singing; quite the catchy tune."

"Max, don't tell me you've never heard Luke Bryan? That was one of his most popular songs, "Play it Again." He's a country music singer. Anyway, I was entertaining my niece. Are we ready to go to the hospital?"

"Not just yet, I need to talk to you about some stuff before we leave." I take Antonia from her arms and give her a kiss before passing her to Jax.

"Max, you're scaring me; what's wrong?"

"I promised you no secrets. Vincent was granted an emergency bail hearing. He is on his way to New York right now. I can't keep you here and safe. We are going back to your parents' compound."

"You're 1-leaving me?"

"Oh, babe, never—I promise. I'm going with you. Remember your dad gave me that file on the Swiss clinic? We think it might work. Your dad said we can all stay there, and that way I'll know you're safe."

"What if you have to testify? You're not coming back here without me."

"I promise you I won't."

"What about Michael?"

"We will talk to him about it today after I talk with his doctor to find out how quickly we can leave."

"Raven, are you okay with this?"

"Everyone's safety is the most important thing. I don't see any other options."

"Okay, can I at least see Michael before we have to leave?"

"Yes. Jax and I just told everyone else what is going on."

"Oh my God, Rose." Of course she would put someone else before her own safety.

"Yeah, we haven't spoken to her yet. She had wanted to confront Vincent even before all of this happened. We can only hope she goes along with the plan. For now, let's go see Junior."

We head out to the waiting car; Sammy has us in one large Dartz Kombat. It's basically a bulletproof tank with two cars in the lead and two cars bringing up the rear. I'm glad we had brought him into the fold. He is proving himself with all the small details. Everyone is very quiet and I fear this is taking a toll on An's health. She seems frailer than when she came home from the hospital. I reach over and take her hand. "Mum, it will be okay, we will get through all of this." Oh bloody hell, she's fucking crying.

"Oh, Maxwell, hearing you call me 'Mum' . . ." she trails off.

I pull her into my arms. "Is that why you're crying? If you don't stop, I swear I will go back to calling you ma'am."

She reaches up and yanks my ear. "Manners, Maxwell." Everyone begins to laugh, and I'm glad.

We finally get to the hospital and pull around back to the employee entrance. Jax is about to open the door, but I stop him. "Don't."

He freezes. "What is it, mate?"

"Not sure. Mick, please drive around the block to the area that has the freight elevators." Even though the windows are limo tinted, I pull Rose down and throw my jacket over her. Sure enough, as we pull out, the paparazzi are running toward the car, trying to get off a few pictures.

Mick gets through security and to the service elevator, which is designed to carry large equipment. He backs up into the elevator and we are able to exit the vehicle right into the elevator. "You went through the employee entrance yesterday, so they figured you would come back the same way today. I'm not psychic; it's what I would have done."

Rose leans in and kisses my cheek and I swear I must turn a millions shades of red. "Thank you, Max."

The doors open, and I can't wait to see Junior. I race to his room and swing the door open. "Oh hell no! Jax, did you do this?"

"Nope, I was just as surprised as you when I saw it. Mrs. Olsa all the way, Max."

"Uncle Max, you made it! Did you bring them?"

He throws his arms around me and it feels like home. "Yeah, buddy, I got them. How are you feeling today?"

"I'm a little tired but I'm okay, promise."

"Good, I'm going to talk to your doctor." I hand him the blueprints and he quickly loses himself in them.

I pull Bella and Michael aside. "We need to meet with the doctor, we might be moving from here."

"What do you mean moving? Michael has already started his treatments."

"Bella, for safety reasons, we need to get out of here. We are going to be moving to a private Swiss clinic. Mrs. Osla checked it out and Michael can get the same treatment there. They are also developing some new treatment that won't be available in the States for years."

"Max, how safe is it to move my son?" Michael looks like he is about ready to blow a gasket. I can't have him getting upset, it would only upset Junior.

"Michael, the safest thing for Junior is to move him. Staying here puts us all at a very high risk. In the last twenty-four hours, there have been a lot of developments. We need to remain calm, not only for Junior's benefit, but for everyone's safety. You need to continue to trust me."

Bella grabs me by my shirt collar. "You get us out of here in one piece—all of us—Max, or so help me; there will be hell to pay."

" That's my Bella. I'm going to talk to the doctor and let him know that Junior is being moved."

I head out to meet with the doctor, my mind trying to figure out how I'm going to get everyone out of here and then safely out of the country.

Vincent

IT'S FIVE AM AND the guards are already outside my cell. They inform me that I'm being transported by U.S. Marshals from Colorado to New York City. I'll be damn, that broad actually pulled it off; she got the bail hearing. Now let's hope she can argue my release. The Marshals shuffle me along to a private airport. When we're finally off the ground, I'm offered breakfast. Airline food has to be a step up from the prison shit they've been feeding me. In my mind, I can think of a dozen ways to escape, but then that won't get me what I want, at least, not yet. I can wait for now, enjoy the perks of a real chair and hot coffee. I close my eyes remembering all my time spent with Gabriella. The anticipation of possibly seeing her again sends the blood surging to my cock. I don't know how much time has passed, but I'm pulled back into the present when I'm told we are landing. When we finally land, we are at the furthest most point of the airport and waiting for us is an armor tank, along with six other vehicles. They fear me, and that's what will cause them to make mistakes. When we finally get to the courthouse, I'm shackled to the floor and given a moment alone with my new attorney.

"Well, well, well, Ms. Jade, not only do you have a great rack, but also some pair of coglioni."

"I'll take that as a compliment, Mr. Giaconna. When we get inside, please keep your mouth shut and let me do the talking. If the judge should ask you anything, look to me first before answering. Please remember to address him as 'your honor.' Prosecutor Hage will be there along with Mr. Phillips' attorneys. Whatever you do, try not to look so cocky. I'll let the guards know we are ready."

Like I said, some pair of coglioni.

Hage

I SPENT ALL NIGHT looking for some way of having Ms. Jade removed as Vincent's lawyer—nothing. There is no conflict of interest, since Marco was never directly involved with Vincent. I can't prove her motives—nothing. The stars seem to be aligning in Ms. Jade's favor, as she drew Judge Jepson, the bleeding-heart liberal, to rule on this. That's not good for me. Jax has a team of attorneys here, which I'm sure the judge will be pissed about. He finally steps in and we all rise. *Let the show begin.*

"Why are there so many spectators in my court house?" I knew that was going to happen.

Jax's attorney stands up. "Your Honor, I'm Matthew Turner, I represent the victims in this case."

"This is only a bail hearing Mr. Turner; no case has been presented. That is for another court at another time. I will give you a little leeway today. You can sit and observe, but only you." Matthew's colleagues get up and leave.

"Before we begin, there are a few rules to discuss. This is my court. This is not a trial." He eyes us all then turns his attention to the defendant's side. "Ms. Jade, tell me why you think your client should be granted bail."

"Your Honor, Mr. Giaconna was presented a deal while he was still recuperating from a gun shot wound to the head. He was not fully cognitive of what was being presented to him. My client still has the bullet lodged in his brain and must have access to better medical care than he is receiving now. His original council was also arrested, so he had no time to prepare with his new one. In question, is whether or not key evidence in the case was legally obtained and if the proper chain of command was followed. Basic *fruit of the poisonous tree,* your Honor."

"The issue of the evidence, Ms. Jade, is not for this court to decide." He peers over the rim of his glasses at her, slides them back up his nose with his finger, and then turns to me. "Mr. Hage, you're up."

"Your Honor, Mr. Giaconna was cognitive when he was arrested for his crimes. He was presented with a plea or the death penalty. He was advised by his counsel to accept the deal. He had ample time to secure new council, had he chosen to do so. He is a major flight risk and a risk to the community around him. He was not the only one who went to prison on the deal he agreed to. All of those cases would be in question if bail were granted. This would cause a major upheaval in the justice system, your Honor."

"The court will take a thirty minute recess while I review everything." He slams down the gavel. Now . . . we wait.

Every minute feels like an hour. If he grants bail, every case will be reopened. It will be a nightmare for everyone. I look over to Amelia and she is keeping herself busy, never once speaking to Vincent. It's past thirty now. I turn around to Matthew. "What do you think?"

"Well, Hage, I think you just got fucked. It's past thirty; she argued a good case. As far as judges go, you drew every defense attorney's dream judge. He is the most liberal judge in the circuit. Plus he couldn't take his eyes off of Jade's tits. Yep you're fucked, and I'm not looking forward to calling my client." Before I can answer him, the judge returns.

"Will the defendant please rise? I have reviewed all the information before me. Mr. Giaconna, I am granting bail in the amount of twenty-million dollars. You are to be under house arrest and will be required to wear an ankle monitor. You may only leave your residence for religious expectations, medical appointments, and court appearances. Since the federal government has seized all of your residences in this country and abroad, you will be put up in a safe house at the expense of our federal government. Mr. Giaconna's passport needs to be turned over to this court until any other action is taken."

He slams his gavel and Matthew is already racing out the door, I'm sure to deliver the bad news. All of Vincent's assets were seized; maybe it won't be so easy for him to come up with the bond. That is until Amelia tells Vincent the bond is being wired as we speak. He turns toward me with that Cheshire cat look and I want to rip his fucking eyes out.

"Don't get too comfortable, Mr. Giaconna, I'm like a dog with a bone and this is far from over." I head out the door to start damage control; it's gonna be a long day. RICO, Patriot Act, Treason—basically any and everything I can throw at this fucker, I will.

Jaxson

MAX IS BUSY WITH Sammy, making arrangements to secure our living arrangements for the time being and then get us all out of here. The meeting with Dr. Dave went great. He was already aware of the work being done at the clinic and he doesn't see any reason Junior's treatments can't continue on schedule, once the initial thirty day treatment is done. That means we have to stay put for another three weeks. Jackie is sitting with Junior and his new friend, Josiah, going over the blueprints. She brings such happiness to everything she does. Max told me about the shoes and it makes sense. She silently does so much, like this room. I know that she helped Mrs. Osla and her secret will always be safe with me. The alert on my phone goes off. It's a text from Matthew:

Get some place quiet. Make sure Max is with you. Call me NOW!

This doesn't sound good. "Raven, I need to make a call; have everyone stay put."

I pull Mick aside. "Hey, no one leaves this room; Max and I need to make a call."

I step outside the room and find Max finishing up a call. "Hey, we have to call Matthew now. There is a supply closet across the hall." Max seems apprehensive about neither of us having Jackie in sight. "Don't worry, Mick is with them and they've been instructed not to leave the room." We step into the closet and I ring up Matthew. "We're here and you're on speaker, what's going on?"

"Vincent made bail. The judge set bail at twenty-million, house arrest, and an ankle bracelet. He can only leave his residence for religious expectations, medical appointments, and court appearances. The money has already been wired and he will be released within the hour. Hage is having the feds keep detail on him. I would suggest you do the same." He then goes on to give us the breakdown of what happened. "Hage has a lot of ways he could go with this, all of which will take time, but will ultimately get him his conviction. Unfortunately, time is not your friend. Ms. Jade is going to push for a trial and she is going to subpoena Raven and probably Max. She wants her day in court. You never heard this from me, but get out of the country, sooner rather than later."

"If you find out anything more, let me know." I hang up and I can feel my heart pounding.

"Max, have you figured out how we are getting out of here?"

"I'm working on some different ideas. I need to get with Sammy on some of it. We need to let everyone know what is going on. They need to understand the extreme danger."

We step out and head back to Junior's room. My mum and Mrs. Osla are playing with Antonia. Jackie and Michael are playing with Junior and Josiah. Raven is in a heated conversation with her mum. "Where the *fuck* is Bella?!" Everyone turns to me as the bathroom door opens and she steps out.

"Oh thank God." I pull her into my arms.

"Jax, I can't breathe." I loosen my grip and try to calm down.

"What happened, bro, you're more than your typical crazy self."

"Come on, I need to tell everyone what is going on." The nurse comes in to take Josiah for his treatment; her timing is perfect.

Amelia Jade

THE BAIL HEARING WENT better than I expected. I need to play nice now with Hage. I leave the feds to sort out Vincent, and try to catch up to Hage. I find him right before he steps into his building. "Mr. Hage, do you think I can have a few minutes of your time?"

His glare is very intense. "Ms. Jade, how much more do you want to fuck me and the good people of this country? You just aided in putting a ruthless killer back on the street."

"Don't you think you're being a bit over dramatic?"

"Over dramatic! Do you even know who your client really is? If revenge is your game, Ms. Jade, or . . . is it Ms. Greene?—you are sadly mistaken. Did you think I wouldn't find out? I've already filed to have you removed as council. The emergency Special Grand Jury hearing is scheduled for tomorrow at one, so I suggest you get to work. The sooner I get that animal off the street, the better," he growls. Bingo—*just what I wanted!*

"You can try to have me removed as council, but I have no conflict. Mr. Giaconna did not shoot my brother in the head. That was Duke; a man, whom *you* gave full immunity to. I will see you in court, Mr. Hage."

He turns on his heels in haste, leaving me to line up all the pieces of my plan. Next up, I need to contact my investigator to see if the lady in the baseball cap really is Gabriella Giaconna. I call Johnston Investigators. Apparently, they lost their man on the inside. Still nothing, but I can string Vincent along until they find out something. Right now I need to prepare for the hearing tomorrow. The quicker this goes to trial, the sooner I can have my revenge.

Hage

WHAT THE HELL IS wrong with that woman? She can't possibly think I would just lie down and let her walk all over me. I'm sure Matthew already called Jax, however, I still have to make the call. He answers on the first ring.

"Jax, by now you must know Vincent made bail. I got an emergency Special Grand Jury hearing for tomorrow at one."

"Hage, just so we are clear, my wife and my brother will not be there." I knew this was going to happen; the man is over the top protective, and personally, I don't blame him.

"Look, Jax, I don't want to put either of them through that, but if the evidence gets thrown out, then we might not have a choice."

"There's always a choice, Hage." The bastard just hung up on me. Someone has to reason with him and I know it won't be me. Maybe his attorney can talk some sense into him. I'm about to call Matthew when my assistant steps in.

"Sir, I'm leaving for the night and Matthew Turner is on line one for you. Do you need anything else?"

"No, thanks for staying."

"Matthew, I just hung up with Jax or should I say he hung up on me? You need to try and talk some sense into him."

"Look, I know he is intense, but the risk to his family is very high right now."

"If he pushes me, I'm going to order a Material Witness Warrant for the both of them. I can detain Mrs. Phillips from her husband for quite some time."

"Hage, do you really think you're going to get anywhere with me by threatening my clients? You can prove that the chain of evidence was not tampered with. When that video was obtained, the letter of the law was followed. As far as the deal with Duke, that is also iron clad. Look, Ms. Jade is throwing up shit to get my clients out into the open. You're playing right into her hands. They will not, under any circumstances, be anywhere near that courthouse. Enraging my client is the worst possible thing you could have done. If you have any questions, feel free to contact me, but under no circumstances are you ever to contact my clients again. Goodnight, Hage."

Matthew is right; I need to keep in mind Ms. Jade is out for revenge. I can't play into her hands. I can prove my case. I look up at the clock, it's gonna be an all-nighter.

Jaxson

I NEED SOMEPLACE TO work and the storage closet is getting old. Unfortunately, I really have no choice; it's that or the washroom. I pull Max aside. "We need to talk to Matthew now. Hage called and had the fucking gall to threaten me. He told me he might not have a choice; you and Raven might have to testify."

"Get Matthew on the line." He shuffles his hand at my cell.

I hit Mathew's number. "Matthew, you're on speaker with us. What's the status?"

"Hage is at a loss as to what to do. Honestly, how the fuck this guy got where he is, is beyond me." He quickly catches us up on his conversation with Hage. "The special grand jury must first say there is enough for a trial. They are meeting tomorrow at one. This is the fastest I've ever seen anyone pull this off. If they say there is enough for a trial, then they have to do a jury selection before it begins. We are talking months. What is the status with Junior?"

"We have to stay here for a month for his initial treatment before we can head to the clinic."

"Maybe that will work to our favor. Let me tell Hage that you are not leaving the country. You need to stay here for Junior's treatments. He doesn't need to know that as soon as the kid can travel, you will be leaving. I will tell him that Raven and Max will be available to testify, this way he doesn't order the warrants."

Max grabs the phone, "Matthew, there is a big problem with your plan. After everything happened the last time, and I enlisted help from the Queen's grandson; I was made active in MI6. I can't, and won't testify; I have immunity. I wouldn't be surprised if Ms. Jade tries to file civil charges against me for shooting the fucker. I will refuse to answer."

"Can I ask why I'm just finding this out now?"

"With everything going on, I forgot all about it until now. While we are full disclosure, Jackie and I are married, and she will not be going anywhere near the court house."

"Okay, well, congratulations on the marriage and I don't think that will be a problem. Like I said, I think the less we say the better we are. I will let Hage know that you're not leaving the country. That should keep him calm. Max, keep your mouth shut about your status. I will keep everyone updated."

"Matthew, you're sure Raven and Max shouldn't leave tonight?"

"Yes, Jax, please don't poke the bear. I'll keep you posted."

He hangs up and all I can think about is Hage trying to separate me from Raven.

"Max, I need my wife now."

I walk out of the closet and head right into Junior's room. Everyone is sitting around watching television like nothing has happened. If only . . .

Chapter Twenty-One

Amelia Jade

S O HAGE FIGURED OUT who I am a lot quicker than I thought he would. I wonder if it really was him that figured it out. Doesn't matter—he can't stop me—no one can. I will get my revenge. She will suffer a loss greater than she can ever imagine. *You took from me, now I will do the same . . . an eye for an eye Raven.* I've combed through the all the boxes that Hage sent over, looking for mistakes. He is very thorough, but I might be able to convince the Grand Jury that the tape was compromised. If they agree, I get my trial. I can then subpoena Raven to tell what she saw. After all, she is the only living witness to the events that day. That will put her in the same room with me. I can argue that when Maxwell Fleming and Jaxson Phillips rescued Raven from the villa in Italy, they planted that thumb drive for Duke to find. Thanks to Hage, Duke's not here to say otherwise. The puzzle piece I can't figure out is the lady in the hat. Still no word back from my investigator. Hopefully, he will have something for me before court tomorrow. In the meantime I need to check on Vincent to make sure he doesn't do anything crazy. I'll bring him dinner and prep him for court tomorrow. I also need to make sure he has the proper clothing, I can't have him looking like the animal he really is. I'm reduced to a glorified babysitter. But if that's what it takes, then I will do it. I head out and notice that I'm being followed. Chances are it's the feds, they are not very subtle. I pick up everything I need to bring to Vincent and head over to the safe house. He ratted so many people out, I'd be surprised if he lives to even see the inside of a courtroom.

Maxwell

I step out of the closet and find Sammy waiting for me. "Max, what's the problem?"

I bring him up to speed on what I know. "Have you come up with any options for housing while we're here for the month?"

"Well, we could stay at the hotel downtown, which means a car ride everyday. We could fly by helicopter, but everyone can't go at one time. The helipad is not big enough for anything very large. I think we should stay where we are. We can board up some of the windows so it's not like a fish bowl." He rubs the scruff on his chin then his eyes widen as if he's thought of something. "The chief contacted me. Apparently Gerhard is applying pressure, which I suspected he would. More men will be arriving within the hour." I hear what he is saying but something is bothering me.

"Max, are you even listening to me?"

"Yeah, something is bothering me and I'm not sure what—tingle sense."

"Oh hell, talk it out. When did it start?"

"It's like a giant chess board; the pieces are floating around in my head." I close my eyes and rub my temples like Jackie usually does for me. The fog starts clearing. I need to talk to Jax *now.*

"Sammy, can you quietly get Jax for me. If I go in there, they will know something is wrong."

He goes and it gives me a little bit more time to clear my head. Jax steps out of the room. I'm just now noticing how pale his face is and I wonder when the last time he slept was. This is going to put him over the edge, but I have to tell him.

"Hey, what's the problem?"

"Well, something has been bugging me. In order for Jade to get Vincent to go along with her twisted plan, she needed to offer him

Jackie. Now, I'm not saying that Jackie is no longer a target, I just think she was never the original target. The target has always been Raven. Raven's brother killed Jade's brother. But since Duke is no longer in the equation, she needs someone else. She doesn't know about Rose, otherwise, she would not only be in Vincent's crosshairs but Jade's too. That leaves you and Antonia. Losing a child cuts to your soul, it's a loss that not everyone can come back from. Think about it; when will Antonia be the most vulnerable? I know she has guards around her twenty-four seven, however, a mother's worst fear is that something will happen to her child when she is not there to protect her. Jax, I need to stop thinking like a normal person and think like the sociopath Jade is. Once she has Raven in that courthouse, she will taunt her and make her believe she can and has gotten to Antonia. It's a chess game of sorts. Personally, I don't think Vincent realizes what he's gotten himself into, or maybe he just doesn't care. I'm sure she will do something to make sure in the end, Vincent rots in hell. After all, his son did murder her brother."

Jax is quiet and that's bad for everyone. Sammy finally breaks the silence.

"I have an idea. You may not like it, but hear me out. You've seen Gerhard's compound. You know it's locked up tighter than your *Fort Knox*. I say you take Rose, your mum, and Antonia out of the equation, move them to the compound tonight. Gerhard's plane is like *Air force One* and I can have it ready within the hour. Once they are in that compound, they are locked up tight."

He's still not saying a word, his jaw is tight and his eyes are closed. "Jax, talk to me, mate. What are you thinking?"

"When I think with my head and leave my heart out of the equation, what you're saying makes sense. It's sick and twisted, but that's what Jade is. I need to talk to Raven and Rose. I'm sure I can get Raven to go along with the plan, but Rose . . . I'm not so sure about. We will need to let everyone know what's going on. What are we going to tell Junior?"

"The truth. He can handle it. He would never believe that his grams just left for no apparent reason. Come on, Jax, let's go talk to everyone while Sammy makes the arrangements." We head back into the room and everyone is still sitting around watching television.

The best thing right now is honesty. I don't think sugarcoating the situation will help anyone.

Jaxson

WE ENTER THE ROOM and everyone is still engrossed in a movie. I pull Raven close to me and whisper in her ear, "I love you." She pulls back and searches my eyes, she can read so much.

"What's wrong, Jax?"

Before I can answer, Max flips the television off and announces a family meeting.

"There has been a change of plans. Junior, your doctor said we have to stay here for a month, so you can finish your initial chemo treatment. Unfortunately, not everyone can stay here for a month and remain safe. There is some danger and I need to move some of us to Jackie's parents' house ahead of schedule. Rose, An, and Mrs. Osla will take Antonia to Switzerland tonight, along with Jackie."

Jackie leaps up, "Max, you said I wouldn't be without you!"

He begins to explain the plan and I can feel Raven tense up. Rose is showing no emotion whatsoever and I just can't get a read on her.

"I know I did, but the more I take my heart out of the equation, the more it makes sense. You and Antonia are the triggers for a whole lot of pain for all of us. Knowing that the both of you are safe will help us do what we need to make sure everyone survives this nightmare."

Raven has a death grip on my arm. "Jax, you're asking me to be separated from my baby for three weeks?!" She can barely get the words out.

"Yes, sweetheart, I am. Ms. Jade wants you to pay the ultimate price and hurting our daughter would do it. Vincent wants Max to pay, and what better way than to hurt Jackie? I'm sorry it's come to this, but there is no choice for any of us." I hope Rose understands that includes her, too.

"When will they have to 1-leave?" I pull her tightly against me, bracing for what's coming. "Within the hour." She begins to tremble and cry and my heart is breaking.

"Why can't I leave with my daughter and not come back? There is nothing legally keeping me here."

"Matthew is trying to pacify Hage by guaranteeing him you will not leave the country. He threatened to serve you with a Material Witness Warrant, which means he could detain you and keep us separated indefinitely."

"Max, can't you have a passport made for me under another name?"

"Oh, Raven, I wish I could, but this is not the movies and things like that don't happen overnight. You are the only living witness. You and everyone around you are in a world of danger. You're going to have to do this to protect your daughter . . . *I'm sorry.*"

Sammy's phone rings. Max and I get a text all at the same time. I look down and then to Max, will this madness ever end? A text from Matthew:

Vincent escaped and took Ms. Jade hostage. Your men and the two feds are dead. Get the hell out of the country, be safe. I will keep in touch.

I grab Max by the arm, "What do we do?"

Sammy hangs up and stuffs his phone back in his pocket. "Vincent's escaped! We need to get the hell out of here. Some of you will be taken to the roof where a helicopter will take you to the plane. We can't all go together, but Michael Jr. needs to go first," He starts barking orders. "I've had a medical team on stand-by in anticipation of any type of emergency. They have informed me that we must secure that he has minimal exposure to anything that might cause an infection. I have a Huey helicopter on the roof next door with some of my men on stand-by. They will shadow the transport helicopter to and from the airport. The first set to go: Michael, Bella, Junior, Antonia, Mick, and An. The next set will be: Rose, Jackie, Raven, Jax, Max and me. We need to move now," he finishes out his commands, none of us getting a word in otherwise.

He hands Max an ear bud. "Put this in so you can hear everything that is going on."

Raven grabs Antonia and holds her tightly in her arms. "Jax, please, I can't leave my baby."

"I don't like it any more than you do, but we have to protect her no matter what. Mick, so help me God, this is my family . . ."

"Jax, I promise you; I would lay down my life for any one of them—you know that. They are like my family and all I have."

Bella secures a mask on Junior as we head to the rooftop heliport. Once again, we are running for our lives. It's like being in a time warp over and over again. We reach the roof, and the first group is loaded. Raven and I are kissing the baby, trying desperately to let her go. Finally, Mick takes her and secures her in her seat. Raven gives Bo the sign to go with Antonia and protect her. Sammy closes the doors, and they take off. My wife collapses in my arms, hysterical. My heart is in my throat as I watch them fly away, not knowing if I will ever see my daughter again. I don't know how much time passes, but I realize alarms are blaring and lights are flashing.

"Max, what's going on?" He's got Jackie tightly in his arms.

"There has been a breach in security. They are reporting that a man with a gun has entered the hospital. They are evacuating the patients that can be moved now." He holds the ear bud in tighter, and then looks to Sammy. "Sammy, how much longer before the chopper is back with the guards?"

"At best—fifteen minutes. We were limited to space and we wanted the heaviest protection on Antonia."

"We are on our own up here. I want everyone to do exactly as I tell you," Max takes his turn at barking out orders. "Head to the far west corner of the building. There are stairs there leading to the landing below, take them *now!*" Before any of us can move, the door opens and Vincent steps through with Ms. Jade at gun point. Sammy turns and puts himself between Vincent and Jackie. Sammy gets a shot off, but his focus is on shielding Jackie. His shot is wide, but Vincent's is not, and he hits Sammy in the chest. He collapses to the floor. Jackie is screaming as Max tries to hold her back, shielding her with his body. I'm trying to hold Raven back as Rose steps out from behind me. She drops to her knees and tries to stop the bleeding. The rage that takes over Vincent is like nothing I've ever seen before.

"Gabriella, it's true; you're alive, you cold-hearted bitch. You fucking gave my son away! I never had a chance with him. Was it because of Joseph? Were you in love with him and he didn't want your bastard son? Is that why you gave away that bitch daughter of yours, too? Where have you been hiding?" He's waving his gun around with one hand and has the other fisted in Ms. Jades hair. "Answer me, God damn it. Where the fuck have you been for the last twenty years?"

Rose lifts her hands from Sammy's chest and, at the same time, takes the gun from his hand. I see it, but I don't know if Vincent does. "He's dead. Another kind man; dead by your hands. You want to know where I've been? I've been in a clinic—silent—for twenty years, all because of *you*. I had to give my daughter up to protect her from *you*. I gave up your bastard son because I couldn't look at him without being reminded of *you* raping and torturing me on a daily basis. You always looked for someone else to blame for who *you* are. You blamed Antonio because *you* couldn't measure up to him. I could have saved your father if you would have come to me sooner, but you purposely waited until it was too late. Did you think I didn't know? It was so obvious, but he told me right before he went under that *you* withheld his treatment. It was all about money and power for you. You think fear brings you power? You have taken so much from me, but so help me God, with all that I have, you will never take another person from me ever again." Before any of us can react, she lifts the gun and shoots him in the chest. He lets go of Ms. Jade and drops to his knees.

"I loved you, Gabriella."

"The only one you ever loved, Vincent, was yourself. I hope you rot in hell for an eternity." She drops the gun and we are stunned as we watch the life fade out of him.

Ms. Jade reaches behind her back and pulls out a gun, aiming it at my wife! "Well, that's one less person I have to deal with. Did you really think I would have let him live or even rot in a tiny cell for the rest of his life? He was just a means to an end; a dead man the day I met him. Raven, my brother dedicated his life to you. He took you in and made sure you were safe. He loved you, and how did you repay him? You skewed his way of thinking. You got him mixed up in things that he never would have. You should have tried to get him to go home, to make amends with his family."

Raven has a grip on my arm and I can feel her trembling. I try to pull her behind me but Ms. Jade points her gun at Raven's chest, making me freeze. Raven tries to calm her down. "Don't you think I tried? I loved Marco like a brother. I even offered to go home with him, but he said his parents disowned him. If he was such a loving brother then why did he never mention you? You have some twisted idea in your head that I'm somehow responsible for Marco's death. You have no clue what he did to me. He lied to and betrayed me, pretending to be my friend. He used me, had me kidnapped twice. He hit me, and then claimed to love me. He knew I had a brother and withheld that information from me. He kept your existence hidden away because he knew how twisted he really was. You have these dreams of the type of brother you wanted. They are the same dreams I had about the friend I wanted. Those where just that—dreams. Dreams that Marco could never live up to. Don't become like him. Put the gun down. Please think of what you're doing."

I see Max in the corner of my eye inching his way toward her, but she sees it too. "Take another step, Mr. Fleming, and I will shoot her." He freezes as she's waving the fucking gun around like a mad woman.

"Raven, you may have gotten your daughter out of here safely, but I can guarantee you that your husband will not make it out of here alive. You will know what it feels like to suffer great loss."

As she lifts the gun toward me, police storm the roof, but she doesn't flinch. I look at her eyes; they take upon a darkness that is unexplainable. Just as I pull Raven behind me, Max tries to go for her gun . . . she pulls the trigger. It's at that moment that Rose steps in front of me, taking the bullet that is meant for me. The police shoot and Ms. Jade is dead.

Raven drops to her knees and is screaming over and over again. "Mommy, please, please don't leave me again. Please don't die. I only just got you back. Help! Please, someone help her! God, no please . . . no."

I drop to my knees and apply pressure to her wound to try to stop the bleeding. "Rose, why? Why did you do this?"

"I've known great love, my daughter and granddaughter need to know that, too. I know you will love them with all that you've got."

She takes Raven's hand. "I love you. I'm so proud of who you've become, my *Cara.*"

The hospital staff finally gets to us. They are trying to start her heart again as they are rushing her down to emergency. Raven is screaming she wants to go with her, but the police are trying to ask her fucking questions now. I grab her hand and we run toward the exit, trying to keep up with the doctors.

The police try to stop us. "Get the fuck out of our way, so help me if you don't—." They get the hell out of the way. We make it to the emergency room and they are still trying to restart her heart. I stare at my hands covered in blood . . . blood that was shed to save me. I watch the seconds on the clock tick away. The wait seems like an eternity. I finally see the doctor coming and the look on his face is grim. I pull Raven into my arms; she needs me to be her rock right now. I only hope I can.

"I'm sorry, we did all we could. The nurse will come and get you so you can have a few minutes alone with her before we have to move her."

I hold her tight and we fall apart. I don't think I will ever be the same again. Someone gave up their life for mine. How can I live with that?

Maxwell

I TRY TO EXPLAIN to the police as best as I can the events that unfolded here tonight. Jackie is sitting on the floor next to Sammy's body, crying. He always said that he would protect her at all cost. He paid so dearly, giving his life to protect my wife.

"Jackie, you need to let the police do their job. Please come with me." She's shaking and crying uncontrollable.

"I can't leave him, Max. Please, I need to stay with him."

"You can't and right now, Raven really needs you. Rose is fighting for her life.

Jackie, please, we need to find Raven." I finally get through to her. We head downstairs to find out Rose's status.

Jax is very quiet, probably still in shock, as we all are. Knowing that someone took a bullet for you and might not survive is overwhelming. We find Raven sitting in Jax's lap, crying and rocking back and forth. I don't need to ask the question, I already know the answer. An answer I'm dreading.

Jax looks up at me. "She didn't make it," he whispers.

Time stands still for all of us.

A nurse comes out and escorts us back to say our goodbyes. If only it were that easy. How do you say goodbye to someone who, in such a short time, has done so much for you? How was that even possible? We thought we were saving her, yet she saved each one of us when no one else could. Hell, Junior wouldn't be getting the early treatment if it wasn't for her insistence. She helped Jackie get over her fear of having a child. She saved An when she had a heart attack. She helped me through the realization that my father, quite possibly, had a hand in killing his grandson and daughter in-law. She saved my brother by taking a bullet meant for him. I can only hope if there is a God, he has reunited her with Antonio. I reach down and brush my fingers along her cheek. "Fly with the angels, Rose."

Jackie bows her head, reciting some sort of prayer in Japanese. I have no clue what she is saying, but it sounds almost musical. She buries her face in my chest and sobs.

"Raven, Jackie and I are going to step out and give you some privacy." I don't even know if she heard me. I look back and Raven crawls into the bed, curls into Rose, and loses it. I know none of us will ever be the same again.

My phone buzzes, it's Mick. I need to get him updated on everything. "Hey, Max, what's going on? The pilot radioed and said something big went down. The heliport is full of police."

"Vincent made it to the roof with Ms. Jade. He shot Sammy. Rose tried to help him but he didn't make it."

"Oh, I'm sorry——."

"There's more. Ms. Jade was not a hostage as first thought; she pulled a gun on Raven." I hear him gasp. "There was a heated confrontation. She had every intention of shooting Jax. I tried to get to the gun before she could shoot him, but Rose jumped in front of him. Rose didn't make it, Mick. She's *gone.*"

"R-rose, is gone? Oh my God, no, she was so much to so many. Never asking for anything in return and now she's g-gone."

"Mick, I need you more now than ever before. You need to get the family to Gerhard's compound and whatever you do, don't let them watch the news. Tell them that we have some stuff to follow up with and then we will be there in a couple of days. I don't want Mum to hear any of this right now. I know the stress is taking a toll on her. Junior can't find out either, he needs to focus on his treatment."

"Max, you can't keep everyone in the dark for too long. Within a couple of hours this is going to hit the press. You know Raven and Jackie are not leaving there without Rose and Sammy. Shit that can take weeks and tons of red tape. I have an idea, let me call Gerhard and have him arrange to have a doctor at the house, just in case. You know An and I are pretty close, I promise I will be with her and support her through all of this."

"Mick, thank you, I'm proud and honored to call you my friend."

"Let everyone know that they are in my prayers and if they need me to do anything else, let me know."

"I will. Check in when you get to the compound."

I hang up just as Hage comes rushing in. I don't think I can deal with another thing right now. I know if Jax sees him, he will unload on him.

"Hage, why are you here?"

"Why wouldn't I be here? What the fuck went down?"

"I'm sure by now you know, so again, why the fuck are you here?"

"You know, Max, I'm not the bad guy here. I'm sorry for your loss, but you should have told me that Gabriella was alive. I might have been able to protect her."

"Don't go there, Hage. You really need to shut the fuck up right now."

Every man has a breaking point. We always think we can take just a tad more, but then it happens, that point when your mind snaps. I try everything I know to get myself past that point. I slowly count down from ten, trying to block out his irritating voice.

"Maybe if I knew she would still be—."

Oh bloody hell no. I snap. I'm done. One swift move and he's down on all fours. "I fucking told you not to go there, now shut the fuck up! If you have any questions contact my attorney. Now, I suggest you get out of here before Jax and Raven get back."

"You just assaulted a federal prosecutor. You can't order me around. I can have you arrested. I'll leave when I have all the answers and, if need be, I will detain you."

"Good luck with that." I take Jackie's hand and we head in search of Jax and Raven.

Chapter Twenty-Two

Jaxson

MY WIFE IS CURLED up next to her mum, begging her to come back to life. I can't stop staring at my hands that are covered in blood . . . Rose's blood. How do I go through this life and not feel her blood on my hands every day? I close my eyes and all I see is Rose, leaping out in front of me. Everything happened so fast, yet it seems like slow motion. I stand over the sink and try to wash the blood off; it will never truly be gone. *Nothing ever is.* I need to snap out of this and tend to my wife. "Raven, we need to let the staff take care of your mum now." I don't even know if she hears me. I try to lift her up in my arms, but she is fighting me.

"No, I'm not going without my mom . . . *please.*" Her arms are clutched around her mum and she is begging me to help her.

"Sweetheart, the sooner we let them do their job, the sooner we can bring her home. Our daughter needs you, too, Raven." Finally, she puts her arms around me and lets me carry her out of the room. Max and Jackie are waiting for us, and I notice Hage is down the hall barking at someone.

"Give me an update, Max. Where is the family? How soon can we get out of here?"

I put Raven down and Jackie pulls her into her arms. "Come on, Raven, let's go wash up."

I watch them leave and realize they both have blood all over them.

"I called Mick and told him everything. I had them leave without us. I'm not sure how long this is going to take, and I know Raven and Jackie will not leave here without Rose and Sammy. Mick is going to have a doctor at Gerhard's when he tells mum. I think we should be the ones to tell Junior." I'm looking down at my hands and I keep wringing them, hoping to will the image of all that blood out of my head. I focus my attention back to the problems at hand.

"I agree. What the fuck is Hage doing here?"

"I lost it on him. He really said the wrong thing. I reached my breaking point and knocked him out, so he threatened to detain me. I already put a call into Matthew."

"Don't worry; you did what I've been wanting to do." He is mindlessly rubbing his knuckles, no doubt sore from punching Hage.

"What happened to the other helicopter?"

"By the time they got back, everything was over. The pilots dropped off the few remaining guards to take care of us until we get to Switzerland."

"How long do you think this is going to take? I think getting Raven back with Antonia, would be best for everyone."

"Matthew is working on it now. We have to wait for the coroner to finish an autopsy and issue a cause of death."

"Oh bloody hell, we know they were both shot." I'm about ready to punch the wall but he grabs my arm, stopping me.

"Standard procedure they have to follow. Rose really loved the estate in Scotland and I was thinking, if it's okay with Raven, we could have something built there in her honor."

"Do we even know what her wishes were?"

"Actually, I do. When I had myself removed as her guardian, she came to me and asked me to be the executor of her estate. She wanted all of her assets dissolved and given to certain charities. She made all her own arrangements. She told me when her parents died, she had no one to turn to. She had to make all the arrangements herself and she never wanted Raven to go through that. She kept it simple, requesting to be cremated and have her ashes scattered in the ocean. She named a beach in North Carolina, where Antonio asked her to marry him, called Topsail Island." I'm feeling anxious without Raven, and I begin to pace.

"Okay, let me know if you need me to help you with any of it. I'm not surprised that she made all her arrangements. She never wanted to burden anyone. Thank you for handling everything so quickly. I know it must be hard on you too." I stop pacing and pat his back. Acknowledging that I'm grateful for all he has done.

"Do we have someplace to stay for the next few days?"

The girls come back looking a little bit better. "Yeah, come on, I got us a couple of rooms downtown while we wait."

We go out the back, taking the few remaining guards with us. Unfortunately, the press has gotten wind of what happened. Max and I take off our jackets and use them to shield Raven and Jackie. I get it, better than anyone, that everything that went down here is newsworthy but for Christ's sake, give people a chance to grieve.

When we pull up to the hotel, there is a crowd waiting out front. We try the back entrance and it's just as bad. "Max, get us to the nearest helipad. We can easily fly to the rooftop of our New York penthouses. We will hold up there until we can make arrangements to leave the country."

Within minutes, he has everything lined up for us.

Mick

I HANG UP THE phone and the realization that she's gone begins to sink in. How could this possibly have happened? I was able to get everyone safely from the heliport to the plane, but I can't stop now to grieve. I need to get everyone safely to Switzerland and keep them from seeing the news. I step out of the onboard office and find An waiting for me. "Hey, is everything okay?"

"You tell me, and don't say 'nothing.' I'm strong, Mick, please tell me my children are okay." I take her hand and squeeze it up to my lips.

"They are fine, we, however, need to get to Switzerland, so please get into your seat and buckle up. I'm going to meet with the captain." She cocks her head and glares at me. Before she can say anything more,

I guide her back to one of the chairs. I head into the flight deck and give the captain the go ahead to take off. I also have him disable the Wi-Fi and television. I strap into the additional jump seat in the flight deck. I know that the crew is more than capable to do their job, but it gives me some sense of peace being in there. It's the one place I can totally relax, letting the world go by. The captain, informing me that Mr. Gerhard is on the line, interrupts my few moments of bliss. I know I need to bring him up to speed and I've been dreading it. I've never even met the man and now I have to greet him with this type of news. "I will take it in the office, and thanks again for letting me in here for takeoff." I head to the office, avoiding An's stare.

"Hello, sir, I'm not sure how much you know but I will start by telling you your daughter is safe."

"Who the hell are you?! Where *is* my daughter and Max? Why is Sammy not taking any of my calls?"

"Sir, my name is Mick and I'm one of the guards. I'm sorry, sir, Sammy was shot while protecting Jackie . . . he didn't make it . . . neither did Rose, Raven's mom. We are on our way to you, however, Jackie, Max, Raven, and Jax are still in the States. They are waiting for the bodies to be released and then they will be on their way. I have not told anyone yet what happened. I was hoping to hold out until we got to you. Is it possible to have a doctor on hand when I do tell them? I'm afraid An's health is frail and the shock might be to much for her, not to mention Michael Jr."

"Of course. How is my daughter and Raven? When can I speak to them?"

"The only thing I know is that they are safe. I've only spoken to Max, but I'm sure you will hear from them today. We should be to you in about seven hours. I will keep you posted, if I hear anything else."

"Thank you. I will have everything ready for your arrival," he states before ending the call. I hang up and pray that I can make it through the next seven hours. I hear the tap on the door and I know it's An. My hopes of avoiding telling her anything have just been squashed. I open the door expecting An but it's Mrs. Osla.

"Mrs. Osla, is everything okay?"

"Yes, Mick, everyone is asleep so I figured now would be a good time for you to tell me what you're trying to hide. This family has been through so much, I don't know if they could take anything else. I know you care deeply for An; she is my best friend. If there is a problem, I want to be there for her . . . to help in any way possible."

"Please, ma'am, have a seat. I really don't know where to start? So much has happened."

"Did something happen to Maxwell? Is that what you're afraid to tell u-us?"

For the first time since I met this woman, I see a look of dread and fear come over her. "Oh no, Maxwell is safe. There was a confrontation on the roof of the hospital after we evacuated. Sammy and Rose were shot, neither of them made it."

She gasps, "Oh God, no." I rush to give her a glass of water but she pushes it away.

"I spoke with Mr. Gerhard and he will have a doctor at the house. I would rather wait to tell An until we get there, if that's possible."

She gets up, walks to the bar, and, pours herself a whisky. "You might not have that luxury. This is a long flight, and you can only hide out in here for so long. She is sleeping right now, so you have some time. When she wakes, I think we should tell her together. If you try to wait, her mind will run rampant, which could be even worse for her health."

I close my eyes, trying so hard to keep the fear at bay—sometimes, it's a losing battle. I get up and pour myself a whisky, feeling the burn as it goes down. My grip on the glass is so tight, I'm afraid it might shatter in my hand. I feel her hand on my shoulder and I nearly jump out of my skin. She squeezes my shoulder even tighter. I know she can help, but it's not easy for me to share my fear with anyone but *An*.

"I know what you've been through; let me handle some of this. Please, Mick, it's what I do best. What are you not telling me?"

"I haven't heard from Max since they left the hospital, no one has. He had a reservation at a hotel downtown but he never checked in. They are probably lying low due to the press, but I just wish he would check in."

She takes out her phone and sends a text. "Ma'am, he hasn't answered my texts, believe me I've tried."

Just then, her phone begins to ring. "Maxwell, where are you and is everyone safe? I know about Sammy and Rose." She listens and then hangs up without even a goodbye.

"They are at their New York flats. He said they are resting as best they can and he will call you later."

I feel the tension release from my body and wipe the sweat from my brow. "I have to ask you how on earth did you get him to respond to you so quickly when no one else can?"

She takes another sip of her whisky. "Maxwell's first wife, Samantha, was my niece. We were always very close and, after her death, we remained very close. He gave me a word and told me when-ever I need him right away, no matter what time of day or night, all I had to do was get that word to him. Page, text, voice mail, email—any-way possible, and he would always find me."

"Wow, and to think, we all thought he was afraid of you."

She chuckles, "Oh he is, and you might keep that in mind. I'm going to get some rest before An wakes up. Unless you need me for something else?"

"No, ma'am, and thank you."

I feel a little bit better that I know where everyone is and I won't have to tell An by myself. I only hope that everyone doesn't have to stay in New York too long.

Maxwell

WE LAND IN NEW York and head right down to my place. I'm not sure Raven will want to go next door; there is so much of Rose every-where. Jax lifts her up and carries her to their flat anyhow. My phone beeps with a text from Mrs. Osla; one word—Piglet. My heart stops. That's our word for immediate contact. I should have contacted her so she wouldn't worry. I quickly call her to make sure she is okay, and as-sure her I will call her later. Right now, I need to take care of my wife. I gently lift her and carry her to our bedroom. I need to get her clothes off; they still have blood on them. I quickly set up the tub for a soak and begin undressing her. I want to burn these clothes so she never has to look at them again. The huge tub is finally full, and I hold her in my arms as we slowly sink in. The hot water warms her and she slowly stops shivering but she is vigorously wiping her hands. I take them in mine and kiss them. "Babe, there is no blood, I promise. It's gone."

I hold her close so she can feel safe and she begins to sob. My heart is breaking for her—hell—for all of us. Neither of us say a word, we don't have to. I'm not sure how much time has passed, but the water is getting cold and her fingers are pruned. "Babe, let's try and get some sleep. We have some long, emotional days ahead of us."

"When can we leave? There are so many arrangements that have to be made and Sammy's partner, Ian, needs to be told," Her voice trails off and she's crying again.

"I will talk to your father and see how he would like to handle it. This is not something one should hear over the phone. Besides, Sammy was active MI6 and there are certain protocols that need to be followed. Right now, let's try to get some sleep."

When we get into bed, I tuck the blanket tightly around us, just like she does every night. We lie there in silence. Finally, she begins to drift off to sleep. I can only pray it will be a restful one for her.

Jaxson

RAVEN IS IN SHOCK and I'm numb from everything that went down. I need to get her out of these clothes; they are stained with blood—her mother's blood. She sits on the edge of the bed and allows me to take care of her. It's what I do best, what I've always done. I need to do this and she needs me to do this for her. I put her in one of my shirts, knowing that she will find comfort from it. I climb into bed and wrap my arms and legs around her. As I gently stroke her back, I keep reminding her that I love her and need her . . . our daughter needs her. She finally falls asleep. It's only then that it really hits me; Rose will never see Antonia grow up. My daughter may not remember her, but I will make sure she knows how much she loved her. The sacrifice that she made so Antonia would have a mum and a dad. I can't fall apart, my family needs me, and they need my strength. I close my eyes and drift off, praying I can be strong.

The constant rattling awakens me and I realize it's my phone, bouncing on the night stand. I grab it, trying not to wake Raven.

"Hello."

"Hey, Jax, sorry to wake you so early."

My brain is not really functioning. "Matthew?"

"Yeah, like I said, sorry to wake you, but I pulled some strings. The bodies are being released today. They will be delivered to the hanger at Teeterborough by noon today. All the arrangements have been made. Make sure you inform your pilots."

"Thank you, man. How the hell did you get this pulled off so quickly?"

"Well, Sammy was MI6, so I went to them and they want this wrapped up just a quickly as you do. They were able to pull some strings with The State Department."

"Thank you. The sooner we get out of here, the happier I will be. Will we have to come back here for anything?"

"I don't think so. I have everything I need to execute Rose's will, and Hage should be able to wrap everything up without you."

"Okay, I will let Max know what's going on, thanks."

I'm about to call Max when Raven begins to whimper in her sleep. All I can do is hold her tighter to me. "Shh, I've got you, sweetheart, and I always will." She finally falls back to sleep. I wiggle out from under her, being careful not to wake her. We've got two hours before we need to head to the airport and I've got calls to make.

I walk into the living room and take a minute to watch the sun rising over the city. Reflecting can be like a piece of wood. Run your finger with the grain and it's silky, almost soft. Run your fingers against the grain and it can be rough and painful. So much like life, itself. Time moves on whether we want it to or not. I have to put all of that aside and concentrate on my family and what they need now. I grab my phone and call Mick.

He answers on the first ring. I'm sure the added stress is taking a toll on him, too. "Hey, Mick, how is everyone?"

"I'm glad you checked in, Jax. I'm sorry about Rose and Sammy."

"Thanks, what's your status?" I need to keep my mind focused on business.

"I told Mrs. Osla, she really didn't give me a choice. I was going to wait till we got to Mr. Gerhard's house to tell your mom, but I don't think she will wait. Antonia is fine, she only woke up once and Bella took care of her."

"Mick, get my mum, Skype me, and I will tell her. She will take this better coming from me."

"Okay, give me ten minutes and then call me back."

While he takes care of that, I put a call into my pilots and inform them of our plans. I want to have wheels up as soon as possible. I would like to have Max with me when I tell Mum but I'm not leaving Raven, and I don't expect him to leave Jackie. I take a few deep breaths and dial, the screen comes to life and it's Bella.

"Hey, sis, how's Junior doing?" I have not seen my sister look this bad since that day at the hospital in Vegas.

"Mrs. Osla went to get Mum. Mick told me everything; He wanted to make sure I try to keep it together for Mum when you tell her. I'm so sorry. She was a great friend to all of us. Hell, she probably saved my son's life. Raven must be destroyed, she just got her back in her life and now she has to mourn her all over again." Before I can answer, Mrs. Osla arrives with Mum.

"Hey, Mum, how are you feeling?" Oh no, I'm getting the look. Damn, I'm so busted.

"Jaxson, please stop worrying about my health and tell me what everyone is trying to hide from me."

"Mum, there was a confrontation with Vincent and Ms. Jade. Vincent tried to shoot Jackie but Sammy was shot. Rose tried to help him, but he didn't make it. She picked up Sammy's gun and she killed Vincent. We thought it was over, but Ms. Jade pulled a gun. Raven tried to talk her down—to explain—but she was hell bent on making Raven pay. Her plan was to go after Antonia, but since that failed, she was going to shoot me. Rose stepped in front of me and she was shot. Mum . . . Rose didn't make it."

"Oh, son, I'm so very sorry. She was such a wonderful lady. She saved my family and I will forever be grateful for that. How are the girls holding up?"

"They're destroyed, Mum. The feeling that someone sacrificed their life so you could live is overwhelming."

"What about Maxwell? I know him and he is probably blaming

himself." I didn't even think that.

"Why would he blame himself? He did all he could possibly do, Mum."

"*Why?* Because that's Maxwell; he thinks he can save the world and that he's invincible. He will always think he should have done more." She shakes her head and pushes away a few whispers of hair that have fallen out of place. "When are you coming home?"

"We will be leaving in a few hours. How is Junior? I don't think we should tell him just yet."

"He's fine, but tired. I think when we land we should get him to the clinic right away. There will be plenty of time to tell him what happened. Let him concentrate on getting better."

"Okay, I need to get going. I love you, Mum."

"I love you too. Safe travels."

I hang up and take a moment for myself. "*I will love them and protect them with all that I am, Rose,*" I say softly as if she could hear me.

"She knows, Jax." I nearly leap out of my own skin.

"I'm sorry, sweetheart, I didn't even hear you."

"I know. What's the plan?"

"I need to call Max, and then we have to be at the airport in two hours. Matthew worked his magic and got them to release your mum and Sammy. I spoke to Mum, and Antonia is fine. Everyone knows, except Junior. I think it's best to wait and tell him later. Max is the executor of your mum's will and Matthew said we don't need to be there to execute it. If I'm overstepping the line, please tell me. I just want to help." I've never had to deal with anything like this; all I can do is take my cues from her.

"You are fine, Jax, it's what I need right now. Besides, I don't even know what her wishes were. I did know she wanted Max as the executor. I was one of her witnesses when it was notarized. She said she didn't want to burden me. I never wanted to think about it. I always thought we would have more time." That thought hits home. Time is a precious commodity that we fight so hard for, but always seems to slide through our fingers like grains of sand.

"Max told me her wishes, and we will make sure they are followed. She was an amazing woman, and I'm lucky to have known her." I hug her, not sure if I'm trying to comfort her or myself.

"While you call Max, I'm going to have a long, hot shower. Join me when you're done."

I call Max and it goes to voicemail, so I leave him an update. I head off to the shower to join my wife.

Anwan

"I WOULD LIKE TO get some rest before we land," I announce before I get up and head into one of the cabins to be alone. It's only then, in the privacy of my cabin, that I let myself feel. I know everyone is worried about my health, but I don't need to be sheltered. The thought that I will never see my friend again is overwhelming. "Oh, Rose, we will meet again, my friend. I could never repay you for saving my family, but I promise you, I will find a way. Your death will not be in vain. This world will know what a beautiful and wonderful person you were." I curl in a ball and, in the privacy of my own world, let my tears fall.

Chapter Twenty-Three

Maxwell

I WATCH JACKIE SLEEP and it's very restless. When I look at my phone to check the time, I notice I have a voicemail from Jax. I hit the message and put it up to my ear to listen as I turn away from Jackie. *Thank God* . . . Matthew was able to pull some strings. The further we are away from all of this, the happier I will be. As many enemies as Vincent had, he had just as many friends. I never want to come near the States again, but we will have to come back one more time to execute Rose's will. After that, I'm done here. I slowly stroke Jackie's cheek, trying to gently wake her. Her eye's flutter open and she pulls me tightly against her.

"Max? Oh thank God you're safe! Please don't leave m-me."

"Shh, babe, I'm here. I'll always be here. Matthew was able to get Sammy and Rose released. We're leaving for the airport soon; we need to get ready. I never had the flat packed up, so I'm sure you have some clothes here. I want to check in with Mick before we leave." Her arms are tightly around me and she's not letting go.

"The sooner we get to the airport, the sooner we can get home. I promise you, I'm not leaving your side."

"I'm s-sorry, Max, it's just so much . . ."

"Hey, don't be sorry. You've been through a lot. It's okay to be scared. I would worry more if you weren't. Come on, I'll get ready with you, and then I can call Mick."

"Thank you." She tenderly kisses me and I feel the tightness in her body relax.

We silently go about getting ready which doesn't take too long. I wish I knew what to do for her . . . to help her.

"Would you like some tea while I call Mick?"

"If only tea could solve everything, Max. Make your call; I'm fine."

I kiss her and head out to make my call.

Jackie

I SIT AT THE vanity and begin side-braiding my hair. I know Max likes it this way. My thoughts are all over the place. I can't believe Sammy is dead because of me. I know Max would say otherwise, but he died protecting *me.* How do I live with that? How do I face Ian and try to explain what happened? My thoughts stray to Rose and I feel my heart in my throat. She was like a mom to me, giving me hope and the strength to face my fears. I know Raven will go on; she's the strongest person I've ever met, but it will be hard. "Ah!" I gasp, remembering how much Michael loves to explore with Rose. "I promise you, Rose, I will never let him forget you." I look in the mirror and find Max in the doorway. "How long have you been there?"

He doesn't say a word, only opening his arms for me. I get up and head right into them, my home, my sanctuary. "I love you."

"I love you and I know we will get through this. We will be strong for each other."

"Did you get in touch with Mick?"

"Yes, no worries, everyone is fine. Jax told An via Skype. They opted not to tell Junior right away. Let him get settled in at the clinic and continue his treatment. When we are all together, then we will tell him. I also put a call into your dad to let him know you are safe. Mick had already contacted him and made all the arrangements. I called the chief and requested that they let your dad and I tell Ian."

"I would like to be there when you do."

She looks down, averting her eyes away from mine. "I figured you would. Jackie, look at me please." I lift her chin, so I can see her face. "None of this was your fault. I know you and you're acting like you are to blame. Sammy's job was to protect you. That's what he was trained to do. It's sad—very sad—that he lost his life at the hands of a madman, but he knew what he was signing up for when he took the job."

"That sounds so cold and harsh."

"Yes, to you, it does. But to someone like me, it's the only way to survive. When I did protection detail, I had to leave my heart out of it. If not, I would have made mistakes. That's why I agreed to have Sammy come on board."

"Can I ask you a hard question?"

"Of course, you can ask me anything."

"After everything that went down, doesn't it make you question our decision to have children? After all the loss you have suffered, and the continued craziness that always seems to surround us, do you really feel that bringing a child into this world is such a great idea?" His jaw ticks with tension.

"If every good person in the world thought like that, there would never be a balance. Am I scared? Oh bloody hell, yeah. Will I let that fear rule me? Never again, Jackie, never. That fear almost cost me you. You're the one who taught me to fight to live life and not live to die. If we give up, then evil will win. I know it's not that simple. And I know we will have hard times, but I know together, we can make a difference. I will fight for us until my last breath."

I wrap my hands around his collar, pulling him closer to me. "I'm going to tell you this only one time. You will *never,* in my lifetime, do any of this cloak and dagger type of work again. So help me, Maxwell Fleming, if I have to tie you to a chair to stop you, I will!"

"Oh, now that could be very interesting, babe. Maybe when we get home I can teach you some rope tricks."

"Ah, Max, you are such a sex feign. Let's go get Jax and Raven. I want to go home."

We head out into the living room where Jax and Raven are already waiting. As lost and hurt as I feel, I realize that Raven must feel ten times worse. She has to mourn her mom all over again. "Max, why don't you and Jax give us a few minutes, please."

"Come on, Jax, I want to hear what happened when you told Mum."

They leave and I wrap my arms around Raven. "Let it go. I know you're trying to be strong." We drop to the floor and I rock her in my arms, letting her cry. Holding her and taking care of her like she did for me when Max was shot.

"Jackie, I just found her and now she's gone. How can this be happening to me again, why? I'm not a bad person; at least, I don't think I am. I try to do the right thing even when it's not always easy. Why?"

"It's not you, it was never you. There are evil people in this world. You can't give up. If you do, then evil wins. I think we need to honor her by doing good things in her memory. Don't make her death in vain." I stop rocking her and rest my forehead upon hers. I take both her hands and hold on tight.

"We are married to two of the wealthiest and most powerful men in the world. They want nothing more than to make us happy. Let's take this world by storm and kick some ass. Rose didn't die; she lives on in all of us. In such a short time, she made a huge difference. Let's show her what we've got."

She looks at me, and finally, I see a smile. "Does Max know yet that he's married to the most stubborn, strong, obstinate woman I've ever met?"

"Shh, some things are best left alone. He's liking the discovery as much as I am."

"Oh, Jackie, thank you. I love you so much, please never change. Come on, let's go get the guys; I'm ready to go home."

Jaxson

MAX AND I HEAD into the office. It seems like a lifetime ago that we were last in here. What happened when you told mum? I wished you would have called me, mate, you know how she worries."

"She handled it better than I thought she would. Mrs. Osla, Bella, and Mick were with her. Of course she was worried about Raven and

Jackie. We are going to wait to tell Junior, he needs to concentrate on his treatments."

"That's all well and good but you know he's going to want to see her. He's too smart to put off for too long."

"I know. I honestly don't know how he's going to handle this. I didn't realize how close they were until that day he hid in the tunnels." I slump down into one of the chairs, feeling overwhelmed by all of this.

"I know you reviewed the research on the clinic, are you sure it's going to be okay for him?"

"Yeah, it's cutting edge research that's not available in the States. I feel comfortable sending him there. Junior's doctor and Rose looked over everything and they thought it was a good fit."

He closes his eyes and begins to rub his temples. This usually helps him, but I notice his jaw is clenched and I know there's more he's not telling me. "Max, what is it? Please just tell me and I'll deal with it."

"The clinic's research is done with stem cells early on in the treatment. The hospital in Philly doesn't bring that in until the end of treatment and only if they feel that it is warranted. Bella is only a seventy percent match. You know that Michael is not a match. I thought about cord blood, but that takes time—"

"—Stop. I know where you're going with this. If we need him, I promise you, I will be the one to go. I would never put you in that position, Max—ever." We sit quietly for a bit and it's these times with him that are the best for me. "You know what Jackie gave me the night of our wedding? Her birth control pills. She stopped them before the wedding."

I begin to laugh so hard, tears are falling.

"Jax, you want to tell me what's so funny?"

"Oh, yeah, Raven is subscribing to the let-the-chips-fall-where-they-may method." I lean back and prop my feet up on the desk right next to his.

"Well, Jax, you just might get your wish for ten babies."

"One at a time, Max. Let's grab the girls and go home." I get up. Max follows suit and we head out to the living room only to find the girls waiting for us by the elevators. "Hey, I guess everyone is ready to go."

Jackie puts her hand out to Raven. "Are you ready to go live that life we talked about?"

"Ready as I'll ever be." She puts the key in the elevator.

"Well, I believe the helicopter is waiting on the roof to take us to the airport. Are you guys coming?" Jackie raises her brows at us. Raven is giggling and it's such a beautiful sound and so rare.

"Max, who is this woman you married?" I cock my head toward him and ask out of the side of my mouth.

"Every day is a new experience with her." The elevator doors open, we step in and head up to the roof.

The guards are waiting and escort us to the helicopter. Within minutes, we are on our way.

Isabella

EVERYONE IS FINALLY ASLEEP, so I pull out the file on the clinic to see what it's all about. It seems they are pretty advanced in their research. Oh my God, the words are staring me in the face: *stem cells*— used in the early stages of treatment. What the hell am I going to do? I'm not prepared to tell my son. Jax said he would go to Dad if we need them. I know he thought we might be able to use cord blood but that was down the road. He's my son and if I have to, I would make a deal with the devil himself to save him. Why couldn't one of us be a better match? Why is God doing this to my son, to our family? I lie down and curl into Michael.

"Bella, what's troubling you now?" he whispers.

"Nothing, Michael, go back to sleep."

"I read the file. I will find a way. He's my son in every way that matters. Please never doubt that."

"I love you, Michael."

"Per il cielo e amore indietro. Now try and get some sleep."

Mick

WE ARE ABOUT TWO hours out and I still haven't seen An. I know she wanted some time to be alone and rest, but I need to know she's okay. I'm about to knock on her door when she opens it.

"I'm sorry, I need to know that you're okay, and then I will leave you alone. I'm sorry I can't help it—"

Before I can finish, she pulls me inside her cabin.

"I'm sorry; I should have told you I was okay. I needed some time to rest and think." She reaches up and brushes her lips across mine. "Mick, I made some tea, have a seat."

Tea? What the hell?!

"I think we need to talk."

Talk? Tea? She kissed me!

"You seem surprised, Mick. Can I ask why?"

"Surprised? Yeah, you could say surprised. We're friends, An. I feel comfortable talking to you. I don't want to lose that." My whole body becomes tight and I feel like any movement might make it snap.

"You would never lose my friendship, that's a given. I know I'm a little older than you, is that a problem?" Her voice has a quiver to it, and I realize she's worried about what I think.

"Honestly, I've never thought about it. Whether you were eighteen or eighty it wouldn't matter. It's about trust with me, you know that. I care about you a lot. You are the one person I can be myself with and not worry. I don't always have to be perfect; you accept me for who I am, scars and all."

"Then, why were you so shocked that I kissed you?" She sits down next to me and takes my hand. Rubbing her fingers over one of the scars on my hand. "I already know the answer, Mick. I need you to say it out loud . . . to own up to it. You'll never get past your fear if you don't."

I close my eyes tight, I can't look at her. "My body is very marred up, An, I can barely look in a mirror. How can I expect you to look at me without disgust? This family is all I have. I can't lose any of you; I won't survive it."

"Do you think so little of me that you feel a few scars would push me away? Look at the shame I've lived with for all these years. The mistakes I've made. Mick, no one is perfect. My point is, we all have scars; some are just more visible than others. Those scars make up who you are and all you've been through. But, they shouldn't decide where you're going. They shouldn't define you as a man. You need to let yourself feel again. Look what happened to Rose; that should be a wake-up call for all of us. Life is too short, Mick, and I don't want to spend the rest of my life alone."

She reaches up and rests her hand on my cheek. The fear makes me want to run, but she makes me want to stay. I pull her hand away and gently brush my lips across her knuckles, as I tightly squeeze my eyes shut. "Give me time to wrap my head around this. Time to deal with the fear, please."

"Open your eyes, Mick, and look at me." My eyes immediately open and look into hers, and all I see is kindness.

"One day at a time, one step at a time. Never be afraid to talk it out with me. First and foremost, we will always be friends. Now, I think we need to get ready, we should be landing soon."

I get up and pull her to her feet, "Yes, let's get seated and ready for landing."

"Thank you," It's just a whisper but her beautiful smile lets me know she heard me.

We head out to the main cabin and everyone is already seated. I feel like all eyes are on me. I hurry over to the inflight phone and check with the captain that everything is still on schedule. He assures me it is and that Mr. Gerhard is personally at the airport awaiting our arrival. I know I will feel a little bit calmer once we are all safely tucked away at the Gerhard compound. The captain asks if I would like to come into the flight deck for landing. I quickly take him up on his offer; it's the one place I find peace.

Maxwell

THE FLIGHT FROM THE Tower to Teeterborough is quick. I was hoping the caskets would have been loaded before our arrival, but no such luck. As we are approach, Raven and Jackie stop, frozen in place. I feel Jackie sway in my arms. *Fuck,* we're almost there; please hang on.

"I can't do this, Max." She closes her eyes and her tears are falling. She is shaking in my arms.

"Yes you can. You're a lot stronger than you think. That's not them in there anymore, you know that. Your faith tells you they are already with the angels. Be strong, babe, I know you can. Raven needs you to be . . . we all do." I finally get through to her and she steps forward, taking Raven's hand.

"Come on, Raven, we will do this together. Their death will not be in vain, let's prove it to the world." They walk up to the caskets, kiss each one, then walk up the steps, and enter the plane arm in arm. With a bond this strong, I know nothing will break it.

"Come on, Jax, we need to go." I watch my brother trying to be strong, but I know this hit him hard. Watching someone die for you is not something he will ever get over. I know . . . it stays with you for life. We head up the steps and give the customs agent our documents. When we are all cleared, we buckle up and head out. I, for one, am happy to be getting out of the States. Raven and Jackie are curled up together, each gaining comfort from the other.

I grab a bottle of water and nudge Jax to get his attention, "Let's go in the office, we have lots to discuss." I need to get him out of his head for his own good.

" Have a seat; I need to talk and you need to listen." He sits down and I pour him a scotch.

"I know what you're going through; I've been down this road before." He looks at me wide-eyed and shocked.

"Yeah, my partner took a bullet that was meant for me. It almost broke me, made me second guess myself. I felt doubt all the time. Was it my fault? Did I provoke the shooter? Maybe I didn't do my job properly? It was eating me up alive, and making me a danger to everyone around me. No one wanted to partner with me. My mind wasn't in the game." I pour myself a drink, my mind instantly flashing back to that day.

"So what did you do? I mean, how do you live with it, knowing that person's life is over, but you get to live on?"

"You just said it, Jax. You live. You do your best to be the best you can be. Don't make that person's death be for nothing. Don't waste your life doing nothing or wallowing in self-pity. Do something to honor that person. Make a difference in the world. Jackie asked me why I wanted to bring a child into this world that is so full of evil. I told her there has to be a balance or evil wins. I have hope, even after all I've been through."

I hold my glass up toward him, "Here's to grabbing life by the bullocks, mate."

We toast and finish our drinks. "Now, on to business, we need to check in with Mick. They should have arrived there by now."

"Raven spoke to Bella right before we left. She said everyone was doing okay. I know Bella is eager to get Junior checked into the clinic. Did you get a chance to read the file from the clinic?"

"Yeah, Jax, do you have a plan?" I know him and he thinks he has this all figured out.

"As a matter of fact, I do. After everyone is safely tucked away, I will be heading to Capri—alone. I told you I would handle it. I won't put you in that position."

"Cold day in hell, mate. Never gonna happen, so get that shit out of your head. We go together and we cover each other's arse. That's what brothers do."

"What if you can't control yourself, have you thought of that?!"

"Have you thought about what you would do if you can't control yourself?"

"You're. Not. Going. With. Me. Max!"

"You're. Not. Going. Without. Me. Jax!"

We are just about to come to blows when the door flies open. Jackie and Raven are both standing there, hands on hips, glaring at us. We let go of each other and sit back down. Raven steps forward and I swear she's about ready to explode.

"What the hell is going on in here? You are fighting like kids on a playground! You're grown adults, what the hell is the problem?"

"Um, sweetheart, we had a difference of opinion, nothing more." I'm trying not to laugh as Raven is tearing into him, that is, until she turns her attention to me.

"Max, why do you push his buttons? You know how crazy he can be, but you're like a dog with a bone. What is the problem? And don't tell me nothing!"

I look to Jackie for help, but my wife is not budging. "Don't even think that I'm going to help you out of this one, Max. Nope, you are on your own. Now, what the hell is going on back here?"

"Jackie, It's all Max's fault."

"Oh, bloody hell—no! Don't you dare throw me under the fucking bus!"

Jackie leans on the desk, her face only inches from Jax's. "Spill, Jax, all of it and *I mean* all of it."

"Okay, all I did was tell Max that I would go see Dad as soon as Junior is settled in and get the test for the stem cells. He is insisting that he has to go with me. I don't think it is necessary. That's all, just a little difference of opinion."

"Ah!" Raven gasps. "What happened that Michael is getting stem cells now? Why didn't you tell us sooner? Jackie, did you know any of this?"

"No, this is all new to me. Why now?"

"This clinic does things differently; they treat early on with the stem cells."

"Well, isn't Bella or Michael Sr. a close match?" Jax and I look at each other and I realize I need to tell Jackie everything. It's always been so hard for Jax and me to talk about.

"Jackie, Bella had every intention of disclosing this to you, she just never had a chance. Michael is not Michael Jr's biological father. Bella was drugged and raped at a convention in Las Vegas. She didn't think she would ever have to deal with this again, but then everything happened. She is only a seventy percent match. I mentioned to her about the cord blood you told me about. I really couldn't remember much, only that the baby needs to be born in a hospital. We figured we had three years, that one of us would have a baby by then."

"Well, Bella and Michael are the best parents—biology has nothing to do with that. Now, as far as going to see James, we either all go, or no one goes. No more fighting, no more yelling, and no more secrets—ever. We have a long flight ahead of us and I'm tired. Is everyone good here now?" she asks, hand on her hip.

"All good, babe, I'm going to come with you."

I rush out the door after her, hoping to finally have some alone time with my beautiful wife.

Raven

"HEY, YOU OKAY?" I know he needs me just as much as I need him. He seems a little distant. Usually, he is all over me. I wonder if there's something more with Michael that he hasn't told me?

"Yeah, I'll be okay. With everything going on, I didn't get a chance to talk to you about the clinic. I looked at the research and I think it will be a good fit for him. Raven, I'd go to hell and back if it meant he would get better. I just worry about Max going with me."

"One thing at a time; let's get through today first."

I get up and lock the door. "Jax, I need you, more than you will ever realize. I need to lose myself in you. I need you to take away the pain and the hurt. I miss my mom and I miss our daughter. I miss you and all your crazy intense ways. I need you . . . please."

"Are you sure?"

"Yes." I remember the day in the washroom and how much he loved to watch me. I lift off my shirt and shimmy out of my jeans. His eyes follow my every move.

He leans back and props his feet on the desk. "Carry on, sweetheart."

I turn around so my back is toward him as I reach behind and un-hook my bra, letting it fall to the floor. I'm left in nothing but a thong. I take my hair down and let it tumble down my back. I turn around and he hasn't moved. He's letting me take the lead. I run my fingers up and down my neck and chest. My breasts are still producing milk but I ha-ven't pumped today, so I need to tread lightly here. I glide my fingers down my ribs and pull at the thong. I know he loves to snap them. I let go and continue running my fingers down into my thong until I reach, what he calls, cock heaven. I throw my head back and let out a long, low moan. "Oh, Jax." My fingers are moving faster. I look at him and his eyes are wide as he takes his feet off the desk. He's almost ready to pounce. "Oh, Jax, please now."

That's all it takes, he leaps out of his chair and in one quick move he snaps my thong. He drops to his knees and his lips and tongue are all over me. "I can't hold it, Jax." He's not stopping. He reaches his hands up and rolls my nipples between his fingers. I'm screaming and I don't care if the world hears me. All of my emotions are flooding to the surface; every nerve ending is on fire. "Jax, I need more—now!"

He gets up and his jeans are around his knees. I don't give him a chance to even get them off. I jump into his arms and wrap my legs around his waist. In one swift move, he's inside me. He's pounding into me, it's—hard and fast, love and lust—a release beyond compare. He tilts his head back, and I know that he's close. The most beautiful sight in the world—his unraveling within me. "Yes, Jax!"

"Show me. Oh God, Raven. Violet to blue . . . yes!"

He falls to his knees and lays me down, slowly working us down. I finally catch my breath, but he's not stopping. "Jax?"

"Never enough, sweetheart."

He's taking is time, kissing my neck and moving his hips in and out. I'm clenching and he begins to do that swivel thing I love. I'm there and I want him to feel my release, like I can feel his. I drag my nails over his nipples and that's his undoing. That's my tipping point. I reach up and kiss him and then everything I've kept bottled up inside me rises to the surface. I start to shake and cry. I can't seem to catch my breath. He wipes away my tears and gently kisses me.

"You're okay, sweetheart. I've got you, I always will."

Jackie

"MAX, DID YOU REALLY think either one of you would go to see James without us?" I ask him as I undress. He opens his mouth about to answer but I hold up my hand. "Wait. Don't even answer that, because in some strange part of your brain, I really think you believed you would go it alone. Maybe I should just chalk it up to the after effects of being shot in the head. You know, the more I think about it, the more pissed off I'm getting. Let me tell you something, Maxwell Fleming, we are part of a large family. We work together or not at all. Your days of going off half-cocked, on your own, are over! We all have a say in what goes on. That's what a family does, so you better learn to start playing by the rules."

He's leaning against the wall with his arms crossed and his feet crossed at the ankles. He's got a smirk on his face and damn I feel my heart flutter. "Well, are you going to say anything?"

"I was waiting until you were done, babe. First, I have to say right now, while you're getting all pissed off, I'm getting turn-on—it's hot. Second, I don't want anyone in danger and, no matter what happens, I will always be over-the-top protective with everyone. Lastly, you standing there, in nothing but your knickers, is driving me crazy. Come here *now*, but leave the braid. Fucking sexy as hell."

I step up to him and begin to slowly undress him, starting with his shirt. When I trail my fingers over his nipples, he takes a few deep steadying breaths. His eyes are watching my every move, but he's not touching me. I undo his jeans and slowly slide them down, taking his hipsters with them. He steps out of them and I remain on my knees. I keep my eyes cast downward, knowing how much he loves it. I don't want to look up; if I do, it will be over before we start. My fingertips are gliding up and down his legs. I reach for his cock and rub my thumb over the tip. I can hear his breathing become rapid. The heat coming off of his body is unreal. I slowly trail my tongue up his cock and then take him in my mouth. At first, I give a little tease with my tongue swirling gently around the head. I glance up and notice his eyes have darkened. I quickly look back down.

"Take me deeper, Jackie . . . *please*." I relax my muscles and give him what he wants. I might be on my knees right now, but I hold all the power. It's heady to realize that I can do this to him. I know he's close. I don't want this to end. I stop and stand up, his eyes on me. "Make love to me, Max."

He lifts me up and carries me to the bed, kissing me the entire time. His lips are so soft, yet the heat they leave in their wake is so intense. I feel the heat rising in my body; all my nerve endings feel electrified. He lays me down, his mouth slowly working its way down to my legs. Every inch—covered . . . up one side and down the other. I listen to the sound of him groaning and mumbling as he pulls my panties off. Positioning himself on his knees, he slowly enters me. He then stops and leans down, resting his forehead on mine. Our eyes gaze intensely into each other.

"Babe, are you okay?" He's always worried about me, making sure that he's pleasing me.

"Yes, love me, Max." He begins to move, slowly at first, but then I can feel the build-up in me, rising to the top. I dig my heels into his ass, trying to push him, but he's fighting me . . . holding back. Then, he tilts his hips and with each thrust I swear he gets harder. Every emotion rushes to the surface, a rush that is so intense, I feel lightheaded. I let go and let the rush wash over me.

"Oh, babe, yeah." His voice is deep and raspy and his release seems endless. His eyes never leave mine. He gently presses his lips to mine. I wrap myself tightly around him and close my eyes.

As I drift off to sleep I hear him whisper, "I love you."

Chapter Twenty-Four

Maxwell

I COULD SPEND MY whole life with Jackie tucked safely in my arms, and I know I would be happy. It's so different with her; she feels what I feel. She knows my fears and she accepts me just the same. We fit each other's needs, yet we challenge each other. She's finally asleep, so I tuck her in tightly and check in with Mick.

He answers on the first ring and sounds a little off. "Hey, you okay?"

"Yeah, everything is fine. Mr. Gerhard was waiting for us when we landed. We went directly to the clinic and got Junior settled in. Heads up—he's upset that he doesn't have his *Doctor Who* room. Let Raven know that Mrs. Gerhard is in love with Antonia and refusing to let anyone hold her."

"What about An? How is she doing?"

"She is fine, all settled in and she is getting along wonderfully with Mrs. Gerhard. When can we expect you to get here?"

"We should be landing in a few hours. I'm sure we will go straight to the house. Where are Bella and Michael?"

"They stayed at the clinic with Junior. Mr. Gerhard has arranged for transport when you land. Do you need me to do anything else?"

"No, get some rest. Thanks for everything."

I crawl back into bed, trying not to disturb Jackie but no such luck. "Hey, we have time yet, go back to sleep."

I stroke her back and twirl her braid around, as she drifts off to sleep. There are going to be many more emotional days ahead for all of us. All we can do is rely on each other for strength and support.

Jaxson

I HOLD RAVEN IN my arms and somehow manage to get us into bed without breaking my neck. Lately, everything has been so intense. Even making love to her feels like it's laced with a fear of great loss at an extreme intensity. I mindlessly twirl her hair around my fingers and she seems to be calming down.

"Sweetheart, when we land, I want to check on the baby and then head to the clinic to check on Junior. Are you okay with that?"

"Of course, do you want me with you when you tell him?"

"Actually, I'm going to talk to his doctors first and see what they think is best for him. I know Bella wanted to shield him from any hurt, that's what mums do. But Junior is like me, he wants everything up-front and honest from the get go."

"You go; I'll be fine. Besides, I really need to spend some quiet time with our daughter. Make sure you let Michael know that we will all be there in the morning."

"There's something else I need to talk to you about." Even though I'm trying to hide it, I can hear the dread in my own voice. "Jackie will probably want to be there when Sammy's family is told. She is going to need you for support. I know that you're grieving also, but you're her best friend. I don't know what to do for her." We are both silent for a bit, her fingers tracing hearts on my chest while I twirl her hair mindlessly around my finger.

"You're right, she is my best friend and I will do whatever she needs me to do. She is a lot stronger than you think."

"Oh trust me, sweetheart, I learned that one today. I do believe my brother is going to have his hands full with her."

She giggles again and it's music to my soul. "We need to get ready; we should be landing in thirty minutes."

We get up and move about the room, getting ready for the next hurdle. I watch her doing all the simple things: brushing her teeth, pulling her hair up, and I know she's the total package—the real deal. As crazy and fucked up as things have been, I'm still the luckiest man in the world. I've grabbed that brass ring and I'm holding on tight with both hands. I'm never letting go . . . ever.

Isabella

MY SON IS AMAZING; so resilient and strong. Through everything, he always remains so positive. I admire his strength and wish I had more of it. I know the next few months will be difficult to deal with. I thank God that I have my family's unwavering support. I know, in that sense, I am very blessed. After speaking with my mum and my son's doctors, Michael and I think it's best to wait and tell him about Rose later. I can't wait till the rest of the family gets here; I offer Michael a smile as he finally comes back in with coffee.

"Where is Junior?"

"The nurses took him for his treatment. I know he wasn't too happy about giving up that room, but this is like a small apartment for us. It will be better in the long run, don't you think?" He doesn't answer me. Hell, I don't even know if he heard a word I said.

"Michael, what's wrong?"

"I've come to a decision. I am going to see your father and ask him to be tested."

"What?! Have you lost your mind? Jax said—."

"—He's *my* son, Bella, in every way that counts. I know what Jax said and, believe me, I do appreciate that he wants to spare all of us, but when it comes to my son, I will move heaven and earth for him." He puts his cup on the table, sits down, and squeezes my hand.

"Everyone at the winery has volunteered to be tested. I've also contacted my family. They have agreed to be tested." I'm totally floored.

"Michael, your family? The same family that wanted nothing to do with us once you told them everything? Why would they agree to this?

Michael, what did you do?"

He closes his eyes, looking beyond stressed. "I agreed to let them meet him, and I agreed to be a part of the family again."

"What?! What if they aren't even a match? They wanted nothing to do with us, Michael! Hell, they called my son a bastard! How could you want to have anything to do with them?"

"For the same reason I will go to your father and beg him to try and save my son's life. That's what a parent would do to save their child. He's my world; the sun rises and sets with him. We have no idea who or what he will become, but I know that he is destined to do great things. I will make sure that he is around to do them."

I put my arms around his waist and hold on tight. He's right—no matter what happens—we will do all that we can possibly do for him. "I love you so much. You're the best dad any child could ever dream of having."

"Well, don't praise me, yet. I haven't found a match and I still have to figure out how to explain to Junior why he never met his grandparents or any of my family."

"We will tell him that not all family is as crazy close as ours. Sometimes, there is a difference of opinion and families separate. What matters is that all of that is in the past. If he chooses, he can get to know them now. We keep it simple, and show him it's not a big deal."

"Okay, I can do that. Have you heard from your brothers?"

"No, but they should be landing soon. I, for one, will feel better when everyone is all in one place. Just because Vincent and that crazy lawyer are dead, doesn't guarantee that everyone is safe. There will always be someone out there trying to take the easy way out to get money."

"I would love it if we could live at the vineyard in Italy. Even though it would be very safe, I know it would be a lonely life for Junior. In a lot of ways, he's like Jax—always wanting lots of family around."

"Well, if my brothers get their wish, Jackie and Raven will both be pregnant soon." Before I can say anything more, the nurse wheels Michael in the room. He is finally back from his treatment.

He gets up and sits on the couch between Michael and me. "Mum, when is everyone getting here?" His voice is tired and raspy.

I need to keep it light for him. "They should be here soon, do you need something?"

"Take a look around this place—it's boring; not even a *Doctor Who* DVD. I hope Uncle Jax remembered to take them."

"Don't worry about it. If he didn't, then Dad will replace them."

He pulls out his cell phone. "Michael, who are you calling?"

"Miss Rose, I want to make sure she comes here as soon as possible. I found a tunnel in the blueprints that Uncle Max gave me and I want to show it to her."

His words twist like a knot in my stomach. I'm about to answer, when the door opens and Jax walks in . . . alone.

"Uncle Jax!" He jumps up and runs into his arms. "Where is everyone? Did you remember the DVDs? They have no clue who the *Doctor* is. How long do I have to stay here?"

"Slow down, buddy, it was a long flight and everyone was very tired, so when we landed, they went directly to Mr. Gerhard's house. I will order everything and have it sent here tomorrow. You know me, Junior, I always tell you the truth. Your health is not worse. You know bad people were trying to hurt us." Jax puts his hand on the back of Michael's shoulder and guides him over to the couch to sit.

I know my son needs to be told. Michael and I sit next to them. "Jax, please, let me." I take a deep breath and take a hold of his hand.

"Michael, I need to tell you something, and I need you to be really brave for me. The bad people that were after us were trying really hard to hurt Aunt Raven and Antonia, and even Aunt Jackie. They were finally stopped, but not before they hurt Miss Rose and Sammy."

His eyes fill with tears and my heart is breaking for him, for all of us. "Mum, they d-died?"

"Yes, I'm so sorry." I hold him close to me, rocking him in my arms as he cries. Michael wraps his arms around both of us, trying to comfort us.

Junior finally pulls away from us and looks to Jax. "You promised me we would all be together. You said you would be right behind us. How could you let that happen? How could you let her die? I trusted you!" he yells at him and I think I can safely say that we are all shocked. Jax sits there and doesn't say a word, taking everything that Michael is throwing at him. I see a tear escape Jax's eye and he quickly wipes it away. I can see that he's holding back; there must be more. He tries to wipe away Michael's tears but he pushes him away.

"Answer me, Uncle Jax, how could you let this happen?!"

"I tried to stop it. I was pulling your Aunt Raven behind me when Rose stepped in front of me, taking the bullet that was meant for me. She gave her life for *me.*" He opens his arms and Michael leaps into them. The two of them are rocking and crying. My brother keeps saying he's sorry over and over again. They have a bond like nothing I've ever seen before. It's being tested and rocked to the core, but it will never break. I sit here stunned by what Jax has said. Mick said Sammy and Rose were shot and didn't make it, he never went into detail. Then it hits me, the guilt is what Jax has been hiding. He feels responsible for Rose's death. I can tell him till I'm blue in the face that he wasn't, but he will never believe me. From when he was a young boy, he always felt responsible for us. He thought he had to be the man of the family. My rape almost destroyed him, but we survived. This, however, is something that he needs to come to terms with on his own.

"Let's give them some time alone," my husband whispers near my ear. Even though I don't want to, I know he's right. "I'm going to give Raven a call and check in." We get up to leave but I don't think either of them notices.

Jaxson

JUNIOR FINALLY SEEMS TO be calming down. I look around and realize Bella and Michael left. I need Junior to stay focused on his treatment and getting better.

"Hey, I know you and Rose were close but the one thing she wouldn't want is for you to get sick over all of this. She fought for you to get tested, and it's because of her that we knew very early about your cancer. You need to fight harder than you've ever fought for anything before. Do it for Rose; become a man she would be proud to always call her friend."

"I will, Uncle Jax, I promise. How is Aunt Raven?"

"She is doing the best she can. She will be by here in the morning to see you. Try and be strong for her, too, okay?"

"Yeah, I will. Now . . . about this place . . ." he trails off, eyeing the room.

I begin to laugh and it feels so good. "How about we start with a quick tour and then we can talk about what we are going to change."

Raven

JEFF MADE SURE THAT my mom's and Sammy's caskets were already removed by the time we got off the plane. Jackie held it together until she saw her dad. I know we have so much more stress coming our way, I just don't know how any of us are going to deal with it. The pain I feel can overtake me, if I let it. My daughter is my salvation, my lifeline. As long as I keep my focus on her, I can and will survive. We finally pull up to the house and I can't get out of this car fast enough. Everyone is here, offering their condolences, but all I want right now is my daughter.

Mrs. Osla embraces me, "Up the steps, second door on the left. Good luck getting her away from Emi; go."

I don't think I will ever understand why anyone is afraid of her. "Thank you." I race up the stairs to be with my daughter. I need her to comfort me. I open the door and freeze in my spot. Jeff and Emi had a complete nursery set up for Antonia. They even took the cranes from the wedding and hung them from the ceiling. It's like being under a giant mobile. Emi is holding her and singing, the site makes me realize all over again how much my mom will miss. My daughter will never know her, the price she paid for Antonia's happiness. Emi puts her in my arms and the emotions are overwhelming.

"Raven, your mother's spirit will live on forever. She is within your heart and around you always. It is never goodbye forever."

"Thank you, Emi. And thank you for all you have done for her."

I lean down to kiss her little hands and breathe in her scent. It's sweet and all her. "Oh, my beautiful baby girl. So much has happened and, through it all, you still go on, we all do. Your grandmother gave her life so you could be happy. Live it to the fullest, and be all that you can be—the best of the best."

I watch Emi leave as I take a seat with my daughter securely in my arms. I let myself feel all the emotions and the fears that I've been keeping bottled up deep inside of me. I rock my daughter and let my tears wash over every thought.

I don't know how much time has passed. Antonia is fast asleep and everyone has kept their distance. I'm grateful for that. I needed the stillness that comes with the quite.

Jackie and Max were going to see Ian today. I know I should go with them, but a part of me feels like I'm to blame. I know I'm not responsible for Sammy's death, but I can't stop what I'm feeling, I don't know how. I keep running through the events on that roof over and over again. My mom new that Vincent withheld my grandfather's medicine until there was no hope. She understood, better than anyone, the depths of his hatred and jealousy for his whole family. So many lives lost at the hands of a madman.

By tomorrow night, I'm sure we will be off to Capri; another huge emotional hurdle to deal with. I wish we could have found a donor and avoided the entire thing, but no luck, so far. We might go through all of this for nothing; James might not even be a match. As a parent, I understand why we must go. But it doesn't make it any easier.

I get up and put Antonia in her crib. She needs to rest and I need to put away my fears and emotions; my family needs me now. I lean down and kiss her little cheeks. "Watch over her Mom and Dad, be her angels. I love you."

Jackie

MAX AND PAPA ARE waiting for me, but I needed a few minutes alone. Time to gather up my courage to see Ian. How do I face him? How can I make him understand when I don't understand myself? I have to be strong. Sammy would want me to be strong for Ian. I wipe away my tears and open the door, only to find Max sitting on the floor.

"What are you doing on the floor?"

"I didn't want to bother you, but I wanted to be here for you."

I reach down, take his hand, and pull him up off the floor. "I know that you are my strength when I need it; always there for me, no matter what. I will always be here for you, too, Max. Now, let's go find Papa; we need to get going."

"We will be okay; one day at a time."

We head into the drawing room and find my father and Dylan in a heated discussion.

I feel Max's grip around my waist tighten. "Max, please let me go. I'm asking you to remain calm and let me handle my brother."

He lets me go of me but remains at my side. "Dylan, why are you here? What are you two arguing about?"

"Why the hell wouldn't I be here? You're not that naive to think that none of this is your fault."

"How is it my fault, Dylan? Sammy was doing his job—the same job he has done for the last *ten years.*"

"It's your fault because you put yourself in danger. You brought all this on yourself by hooking up with him. I warned you, but you were too blinded by lust to think about anyone but you."

I snap. I smack Dylan so hard across the face, that I've left a handprint. In my whole life, I have never hit another person—*ever.* "Don't you *ever* talk about my husband *ever* again. You are being judgmental about me and my decisions. You're upset because I've decided to live my life and not sit on the sidelines. Sammy was doing his job, a job he was proud to do. I will not have you taint it. Get out of my life, stay away from me and my family." I feel myself beginning to shake uncontrollably and then I hear Raven behind me yell at Dylan.

"Leave her alone, Dylan!"

"You can't make me stay away from my sister. I'm entitled to my opinion. This nightmare began with you. Maybe you need to step up to the plate and take some responsibility for the bloodshed," he barks back at Raven.

Raven turns pale as Papa steps between them. "I think you've said enough, son. You gave your opinion, now put it to bed. We need to move forward. We have guests and they will be remaining here with us until young Michael's treatment is done. Now, we need to get going."

"We won't be staying here." All of us turn to find Jax in the doorway.

"Dylan, out of respect for your parents and your sister, I have put up with your bullshit, but you just crossed the line. You've done nothing but talk out of your arse the entire time I've known you. Jeff, we will be moving out tomorrow. I appreciate your help and your hospitality, but my family's safety and well-being is my top priority. You and Emi are always welcome to my home. Now, if you'll excuse me, my wife and I have a lot to discuss."

"This isn't over, Jax, you can't just dismiss me like some servant. If I want to see my sister, I will. You can't stop me—no one can."

Jax stops and looks back over his shoulder towards Dylan. "Watch me!"

I'm holding onto Max, trying to keep him calm. Jax totally ignores anything else Dylan is saying.

"Max, while you and Jackie go talk to Ian, Raven and I will be getting everything firmed up on this end." Their eyes lock and then he excuses himself, taking Raven's hand and walking out.

"Papa, are you coming?" I ask.

He looks at Dylan and then back to me. "Tell Ian that Mom and I will be by tomorrow." I feel like a little child again, being dismissed. I hated it then, and I hate it even more now.

We head out to the car and Max is very quiet . . . too quiet. We get in the car and I tell the driver where to take us. "Are you going to tell me what the hell is going on?"

"Honestly, I have no idea. One minute your brother is flipping out on us. The next minute, Jax is cueing me to shut up and get out."

Before I can ask any more questions, he gets a text. He allows me to lean over and read it with him.

Jax: Pay your condolences and then get back here. Say nothing. I'm making other arrangements now.

Max: Call Tony; he can handle it all.

Jax: Done.

"Now are you going to tell me what is going on?" I slap his knee.

"I really don't know anything."

I'm not going to fight with him over this. I need to mentally prepare myself on what I'm going to tell Ian. We pull up to Ian's and I can tell from the surprised look on Max's face, it's not what he was expecting. "Ian's parents left it to him. Sammy enjoyed doing all the renovations himself. Ian, on the other hand, wouldn't know which end of the hammer did what."

"The grounds are impeccable, who takes care of them?"

"Ian does all that. He finds it very relaxing. When I first moved to the States, Ian came over with Sammy and helped decorate my flat. The week after he left, I killed the plant. He never lets me forget it."

Before he can ask me anything else, Ian comes flying out the door. He grabs me, hugs me, and then pulls away, his eyes on mine. He begins to cry, I don't need to say a word.

"Let's go inside, please. Jackie, I need to hear it all."

We head in the door and Ian leads us right into the kitchen. That's his comfort zone. "Ian, this is my husband, Maxwell."

Max places a hand on his shoulder try to offer him comfort. "Sorry to meet you under these circumstances. I'm sorry for your loss; Sammy was a good guy."

Ian grabs onto the counter for support, and I wipe away his tears. "Were you with him when it happened? Oh what a stupid question, of course you were, tell me what happened? I need to hear it all."

"He jumped in front of someone that tried to shoot me. Raven's mom tried to save him but she couldn't. In the end she was also shot and killed."

He begins to sway on his feet and Max tries to steady him. "Please, why don't we sit down?" He guides him to a chair.

"How is Raven? Is she going to be okay?"

"It's going to be very hard on her; she just got her mom back into her life only to lose her again."

"Did my Sam suffer? Was it quick?" He puts his head in his hands and cries. Max grabs some tissues off the counter, clearly not knowing what to do to help Ian.

"It was very quick. I held him, Ian. He wasn't alone."

He stops crying and lifts his head. He offers me a tissue. "I hope you're not blaming yourself for any this. Just like the last time, Jackie, it wasn't your fault."

Max sits down next to me and squeezes my hand, "Last time?"

"When Sammy first became my guard, he didn't know how to

ride. I was jumping and competing, I was being very stubborn at the time and I refused to change my routine. He thought it was no big deal; just get on the horse and go. Needless to say, he fell off and broke his leg. In the end, I changed my routine so I could stay here to look after him."

"You should have seen him giving her a hard time and ordering her around. But she got even with him. As soon as the doctor said he was okay, she put him right back on that horse."

Ian takes my hand, "Oh, Jackie, I always knew this day would come. I worried every time he stepped out that door. He would tease me, always saying he would outlive me. I don't even know where to begin. I want to see him, Jackie. Please, I need to."

I get up, go to the fridge, and grab a couple of bottles of water. I don't know how to answer him. Max takes one of the bottles and hands it to Ian. "My attorney has already contacted MI6 on your behalf, letting them know that he will be handling everything so you won't have to. I can set up a viewing and I will go with you."

"Thank you. You're very kind."

We get up to leave and Max stops. "Ian, I would like to do something to honor him, if it would be okay with you. Think about what you would feel comfortable with and let me know."

We make our goodbyes and head out, promising to keep in touch. We head toward home; both of us are very quiet.

"Max, we need to create a project for Ian. He is going to be very lost without Sammy. I can't leave him all alone in that huge home. We need to come up with something."

"Well, we are not going to be leaving the area for the next three years, so how about some sort of garden sanctuary. It could be set up like a memorial garden for Sammy."

"That might work. I'll talk to him when we get back from Capri. Don't even think of telling me we're not going."

The quiet that envelops us is extremely deafening.

Chapter Twenty-Five

Jaxson

RAVEN AND I HEAD upstairs and into Antonia's room. While Raven is tending to the baby, I send a quick text to Max letting him know to keep his mouth shut. Next, I shoot one off to Tony.

Jax: Are my text messages secure?

Tony: Yes, they are encrypted to the outside world. Is there a problem?

Jax: Maybe. We are at the Gerhard compound. I'm uncomfortable with the situation here. That wanker, Dylan Gerhard, is here and causing trouble. I need a safe place near the clinic for the family. We need to head out to Capri, can't leave until I know the family is safe.

Tony: Stay calm and don't use your tablets. If you have to, use the new iPhones I gave you. They have enhanced security in place. I will take care of everything on my end.

Now we wait, something I've never been good at. I don't trust Dylan and knowing that he would have unfettered access to my child—never gonna happen. I watch Raven playing with Antonia and I wish all our days could be like this very moment. "Sweetheart, I want the baby to sleep in our room tonight." She doesn't question me. She knows I need to feel like my family is safe. My phone vibrates with a group text to Max and me.

Tony: I have secured a place near the clinic. The information will only be sent to your phone. I have a friend in Geneva who is headed to the new place now. He will have everything wired up before morning. I ordered all the stuff you requested and had it sent overnight to the clinic. I also threw in some new stuff that just came out. I'm sure he will be very excited. All new electronics will be waiting at the new place. Have the old ones shipped to me; don't leave them behind.

Jax: Thank you. Have you informed Mrs. Osla?

Tony: No, I'm not telling her. You or Max can tell her.

Max: Jax can tell her. :)

Jax: Max, where are you?

Max: Just pulling up now. I'll meet you upstairs.

I hand my phone to Raven, so she can read what is going on while I lie on the floor and play with the baby.

"Jax, do you really feel this way?" Before I can answer, Jackie comes storming in.

"Jax, do you seriously think my brother would hurt us? I get he's an ass, but he would never lay a hand on any of us."

"Jackie, you are probably right, however, I just can't take a chance. I can't leave for Capri and not feel like my family is safe. If your parents want to come over and visit with you and the baby, I would never stop them. Your brother, well, that's another story."

My phone beeps with an urgent message from Tony.

Tony: Not sure if this will matter to you or not, but Dylan is in financial trouble. He has closed up his shop in Japan. He is in debt to some nasty men. Mr. Gerhard is giving his son money. You know desperate men do desperate things. Stay safe.

I hand Jackie my phone. "Maybe you should read this."

"How could this be? Can I confront Dylan and Papa?"

"I would rather you wait until we are back from Capri."

She hands me back my phone and I know this has hit her hard. She always sees the good in people. "I'm sorry, Jackie, I don't know what to believe anymore."

"My head is spinning. I need some food and sleep. I promise I won't confront them."

"Well, I, for one, am going to take my daughter downstairs and make myself something to eat." All heads turn toward my wife and I start laughing. Maybe it's the stress, but the thought of her in the kitchen makes me lose it. Jackie is trying not to laugh and Max is laughing so hard, he's crying.

"Oh come on. People! I'm not that hopeless in the kitchen."

As I guide her out the door, I can hear Max tell Jackie it would be a bloody cold day in hell before he eats a peanut butter and jelly sandwich. I would pay big bucks to see that, but right now I have to talk to Mrs. Osla, since everyone is afraid of her.

"I will meet everyone in the kitchen. I want to talk to Mrs. Osla before she turns in for the night."

I find Mrs. Osla in the sitting room, by the fire. She is working on her needlepoint; bless her and her patience. "Mrs. Osla, I need to speak to you about some things."

"Pull up a seat and tell me what's troubling you."

I show her the text messages and when she reads the one about Dylan's financial situation, she takes a deep breath and her eyes are wide.

"Lad, let me work with Tony. I promise not to scare him too much."

She takes my phone, pulls up notes, and then proceeds to type away. I lean over, watching as she does so.

Don't speak about any of this in this house, it could be wired. If Mr. Gerhard is as security conscious as he seems, then it wouldn't surprise me. Tomorrow we leave to go see young Michael, and we don't come back. Anything we need, I can make arrangements for.

I nod. "So how is my mum feeling? She took Rose's death very hard."

"We all did. But she seems to be gaining her strength back a little bit every day. Have you decided what type of arrangements you are going to make? I could handle them for you, if you would like."

"Max is the executor of her will but she had everything already planned out. She never wanted to burden Raven with anything. Matthew will handle it all."

"What about you? How are you dealing with everything?"

"I'm dealing. It's not like I have a choice. I have a family that is counting on me. I have to be the strong one. I still need to get to Capri and deal with that whole nightmare."

"So, you are going? What about Maxwell?" She is mindlessly playing with the strings of her needlepoint.

"I tried to go it alone, but we almost came to blows over it. Raven and Jackie stepped in and now the four of us are going. We don't even know if he's going to be a match. I wish they would let me go alone, but they are all so stubborn."

"Ha, yeah look who's calling the kettle black. Do you want me to try and talk to Maxwell?"

"No, he won't listen and then he will get mad at me for having you talk to him. I'm in a no-win situation here."

"I would offer to handle James for you, but I fear I would be worse than Maxwell, if put in that situation. What if he refuses to be tested, have you thought about that? Not everyone is willing to do this, and—let's face it—we already know he has no conscience."

"Sometimes in life, Mrs. Osla, we don't have a choice."

"So be it. What time would you like us all ready tomorrow?"

"Right after breakfast. Now I need to find my wife, she was headed to the kitchen acting as if she could cook us something."

She makes the sign of the cross, "Lord, have mercy. You better go rescue everyone."

I laugh as I head out the door in search of my wife.

Raven

I HAVE NO IDEA why everyone thinks I will poison them. I take Jackie's hand, "Come on, we can do this."

"Have you lost your mind? I can make coffee and a salad."

"I know, but Max is such a good cook, surely you learned something being in the kitchen with him all the time."

She turns fifty shades of red. "Okay, never mind; I don't think I want to know what you've learned in the kitchen."

Max hands me Antonia, "How about you and Jackie play with my beautiful niece while Jax and I make dinner?"

Jax comes in just at the right time. "Okay, hit me, mate, what are we cooking?"

We let them get started while we play with the baby. Jackie takes Antonia while I set the table. "Raven, are you ready for Capri? I want all of this to be over with, so we can get on with our lives. I want Michael to get better, so we can get back to Scotland. I love it there. I don't think I ever want to leave the castle. What about you, are you ready?"

"Oh, Jackie, I want to be done with this, too. I had an idea that I talked to Jax about before we left Scotland and he was all for it. Maybe you and Max might want to be a part of it, too?"

Max comes over and puts the plates down. I don't know what it is, but it smells wonderful. "It's a potatoes and eggs frittata on Cuban bread and a salad; simple, comfort food."

"Amazing what you two can do in the kitchen. Alright, Jackie, I'll admit it, we are very lucky."

Max pours everyone craft beer, which goes perfect with the sandwich. "So, Raven, what is this idea that you came up with?" he asks.

"I would like to set up some sort of foster child program. Young kids get adopted a lot quicker than the older ones. I think if we can give them a safe place to learn, and have Jackie introduce them to working with the horses, they might excel. The money that the government pays us to take care of the kids can go into a fund that we could match, if they keep their grades up. When they turn eighteen, they can use that money for a start in life. It would be a way of giving back. I haven't worked out all the kinks yet, but it's a starting point."

"Scotland's foster care program is complex, but I'm sure we can figure out some way around it. What do you think, babe?"

"Well, I would love to teach more kids on the horses. It really is good therapy for them." She can barely keep her eyes open as she tries to stifle a yawn.

"Jackie, get some rest. Jax and I can clean up here. We have a long day tomorrow."

They leave and we begin clearing the table. I know the housekeepers will do this for us, but I've never been comfortable with that. Just then, Antonia starts to fuss. "Jax, why don't you change her while I get her bottle ready? I'll be up in a few." I smile as I throw the rag I was using in the sink. They leave and I go about getting Antonia's bottle ready so Jax can feed her. Mick comes in, announcing the need for a snack.

"Hey, Mick, how are you feeling?"

"Shouldn't I be asking you that? I'm so sorry about your mom. She was a very brave, kind woman. Very easy to talk, too. I will miss her."

I'm trying not to cry but isn't easy. "In such a short time, she touched so many people."

"What do you need me to do for you?"

"Just keep my family safe. We are leaving for Capri and I need you to be with Antonia twenty-four seven. I trust you with her."

"I promise I will protect her, you don't have to ever worry about that."

I hug him and he no longer pulls back from it. "Thank you. There are some leftover potatoes and eggs, if you want it. Don't worry, I didn't cook it. I need to go feed Antonia before she wakes up the entire house."

I head up the stairs, but then I stop when I hear Dylan and Jeff arguing in the drawing room. Normally, I wouldn't eavesdrop, but after the last few days, I realize, lives are at stake. The argument is confirming what Tony said about Dylan being in financial trouble. I feel so sorry for Jackie. On top of everything we've been through, now she has to deal with this. I head up the stairs reminding myself, *only one more night here.* The sad part is, I used to love coming here. Now, I just want to get as far away as possible.

Maxwell

WE HEAD UPSTAIRS AND she can barely keep her eyes open. She slept a lot today; I hope she's not getting sick. The stress we've been under has taken a toll on all of us. I scoop her up and carry her the rest of the way.

"I can walk; you don't have to carry me."

"Nonsense, it gives me great pleasure to take care of you." She snuggles into me, seemingly too tired to argue.

When we get into our room, I begin to undress her. "You know, I can do this myself."

"I know you can, but I want to feel like I'm doing something, besides it calms me down." I get undressed and climb into bed with her.

"Max, I can't have sex with you in this room . . . it's creepy." I spoon up against her and tuck the covers tight, just the way she likes them.

"I wouldn't dream of it, babe. Besides, you're exhausted and tomorrow is another busy day."

"My body is so tired, but my mind keeps racing. I can't seem to shut it off."

I run my fingertips gently up and down her side, singing Beyoncé's "Halo" softly to help her relax.

"You're everything I need and more." I look down and she is fast asleep.

I could watch her sleep all night long; her golden hair, shimmering in the moonlight.

Yeah, I definitely have my angel now. Oh how true. We just need to get through Capri. I wish Jax wasn't going. I know he's reached his limit, and I fear what he might do if James declines to be tested. We need to be strong and support each other. I haven't seen An and I'm sure she doesn't know we are going. I'm not looking forward to that conversation. At least Bella isn't going, so we might have a shot of getting out of there quickly. Jackie's tossing around in her sleep. Usually, she barely moves. I sing a little more, and she falls back to sleep. I just realized that I gave her the pendant for her birthday but I never gave her the wedding present I got her. I will give it to her first thing, so she can tell Junior all about it.

I close my eyes and try to fall asleep. *Fuck*—tingle. Why? What the hell did I miss? I'm going through all the events in my mind and then, it hits me. Sometimes something is right in front of you, but you never see it. I shoot a quick text off to Tony with my question. I need to see Jax right now. I text him one word: tingle. Slowly, I wiggle out of bed, not wanting to disturb her sleep. I grab my sweats and race out the door. I find Jax and drag him into the kitchen.

"What the fuck is going on? Can't we have one night of

uninterrupted sleep?"

"Trust me, I would love nothing more, but that damn tingle sense kicked in. Look at Tony's last message; it was staring me in the face the whole time."

He pulls out his phone and scrolls through his messages. His eyes look from the screen to mine a couple of times and then it hits him, just like it hit me. "Max, Who?"

I pull up the notes on my phone, not sure if it's safe to talk here. I feverishly begin to type my answer, however, my mind is moving faster than my fingers can.

Yeah, that's my question. Tony is looking to see if there is a connection. Remember what Hage said, Vincent's reach was all over the world. The drug business usually is like that. What if he was in business with Vincent?

Raven said that Dylan and Jeff were arguing about money when she came up to bed.

Seconds seem like hours as we wait for Tony to get back with us. "Jax, I don't feel comfortable not having one of us stay at the hospital tomorrow."

"Then maybe you should listen to me and stop arguing all the fucking time. Let me handle this. I promise you, I will not kill him . . . only because we might need him."

Tony's message finally comes through.

Tony: I went as far back as I could find, which was early into Gerhard's career. There is no connection between them. Dylan dealt with Yakuza only. Jeff Gerhard has never had any connection to the Giaconna family. The Yakuza make Vincent look like a pussycat. It looks like Gerhard made a payment, but they want more. I don't see this ending well for them. I suggest you tighten security around Jackie.

"Well, that settles it, you are staying here. I'm going alone. Don't argue with me on this, please."

"Okay, Jax, I agree with you; one of us needs to stay here. You must stay in touch with me the entire time. Better yet, I'm going to have you wear a wire."

"I'm not wearing a fucking wire. Go to bed, tomorrow is going to be a long day and I'm not looking forward to telling Mum what is going on."

"Either way, you know we will both get in trouble with her. Try and get some rest, I'll see you in a few hours."

I quickly head back to Jackie's old room. I need to be with her, even if it's just to hold her. She comforts me without even trying. Hopefully she didn't wake up while I was gone.

Jackie

THE SUNSHINE IS PEAKING through the curtains and Max has a grip around my waist. I tilt my head up and he's smiling at me. I should have known; *this man never sleeps.* "Good morning, how long have you been up?"

"Not that long. I've been waiting for you to wake up. I have a present for you."

"For me, why?"

"Well, I got it for our wedding, but in all the confusion, I forgot to give it to you."

He pulls an envelope off of the side table and hands it to me. He has the most joyful smile on his face and I know this must mean a lot to him. I open it up and inside is an official certificate from Lamborghini stating that a purple Lamborghini Huracán GT3 is being custom made for me! "Oh my God! No way. Oh my God! Really? You really did this? A real car and not the golf cart?"

"Yes, I really did this, and yes, a real car, not the golf cart. You have to promise me you will be careful."

"Oh my God! I'm speechless; a real purple car!" I guess now might be a good time to make a huge confession.

"Max, I have to tell you something and you have to promise me that you will not blow a gasket. You have to swear, Max."

"Okay, what's the problem?"

"I don't have a driver's license."

"What do you mean, you don't have one? You mean a current one or one for Scotland?"

"Like . . . I never had one in my life."

"Wait, how can that be? I've never met anyone who didn't have their license. Do you even know how to drive?"

"Of course I know how! Sammy showed me in case there was ever an emergency and I needed to drive to safety. I never had the need for a license, since I was driven everywhere by security. Then, when I moved to New York, I took trains and cabs. Will you teach me the right way to drive?"

"Well, I guess so, since you're getting a purple car and I have no intention of driving it."

I leap out of bed, clutching my certificate. I can't wait to show everyone. "Oh, Max, my very first car and it's purple!"

"Come on, babe, we need to get ready. I can't believe you don't have a license." He shakes his head.

We go about getting ready and I can't think of anything else but my gift. I watch him shave as I finish side braiding my hair. "You are very handsome."

"You're just telling me that because I bought you a purple Lamborghini."

I whip his towel off from around his waist and smack his beautifully sculptured ass. "Oh, trust me, it's a lot more than the car. Hurry up and finish. I can't wait to tell everyone."

We finish up and quickly head downstairs. I can barely contain my excitement. Everyone is gathered in the dining room for breakfast. I notice my brother is absent, which is good. I don't think I can deal with him today. Everyone is lost in their conversations and I just want to shout from the rooftops. "Excuse me, everyone, I have a very important announcement to make." The room falls silent.

"Max ordered me my very own purple Lamborghini!" Why is no one saying anything? I'm so excited and they are acting like it's no big deal. "Excuse me, did everyone hear me? My very own car and it's purple!"

Raven starts laughing, "You know you need a license, right?"

"Yes, and Max is going to teach me."

Jax finally stops laughing, "Jackie, I only ask one thing of you, please take a picture of Max driving a purple Lamborghini for me."

The two of them start bickering back and forth until An pulls

Max's ear. "Ouch, what was that for?"

"Jackie, am I to understand that you've never had a license?"

"I never had the need for one until now."

"Well, it's settled then. I will be the one to teach you how to drive."

Jax drops his fork and Max almost chokes on his coffee.

"Why do you get to teach her? Jax and I are both capable."

"Jax has no patience, and you taught Bella how to drive; need I say anything more?"

"She has a point, mate."

"It's not my fault that she has no coordination."

They continue bickering throughout breakfast; I'm too excited and hungry to care. Besides, we need to get to the clinic. We finish up and head out to the waiting cars.

Jaxson

WE PULL UP TO the clinic and the security that Tony arranged is waiting for us. "Before we go inside, let's head into the garden area to talk." I point in the general direction.

Mick checks the area to make sure it's clear, and we all have a seat. "I can't get into details, but we will be moving into a private location this afternoon. Everything is already arranged and I need everyone to give your tablets to Mick. He will ship them to Tony. There are new ones at the house waiting for you. It's just a precaution; everything is fine. Junior's set up here is like a two bedroom apartment, so Bella and Michael have decided to live here. When Junior is not having treatments, he will be at the house with us. I will be leaving in a few hours for Capri—alone. Max will be staying here with everyone. I will not be gone very long; for all we know, he might not even be a match. Junior knows about Rose, I told him last night. As you can imagine, he took it very hard. We need to stay upbeat and positive for him."

Jackie's upset, apparently Max never told her about the change of plans. "Jax, why are we staying behind?"

"Jackie, I need to know that Antonia is safe. I also need to make the arrangements for Junior. I trust my brother; I know that my family will be safe."

My mum is not saying a word but she is giving me that look; it's never a good thing. "Come on, everyone, we need to see Junior before his next chemo treatment." I don't give them time for any more questions. I hurry up and head into the clinic.

When we get into Junior's room, it looks like a toy store explosion. He is so happy to see everyone. He is going on and on about all the stuff that showed up in the middle of the night. I take Bella by the hand and go outside.

"What's wrong, bro?"

I give her the quick rundown on the move and then tell her I'm leaving.

"By yourself? Why?"

"Safety reasons' I need Max here with everyone. It's quick and easy if I go alone. Don't worry, I will be safe. I promise to touch base when I get there and when I leave. Now, I need to talk to Raven before I leave."

"Be safe. I love you."

"I love you too, sis." We head back in the room and Jackie is telling Junior all about her purple car. Poor Max, he is going to have his hands full with her. I lean down and whisper in Raven's ear. "Step outside."

"You're leaving, aren't you? Will you reconsider and let me go with you?"

"No. I love you; please don't make this harder on me. I promise I will come back to you. Take care of Antonia and watch over Junior." I close my eyes and try to keep it together. If I see a single tear from her, I'll lose it. I kiss her, turn around, and run out before I change my mind.

Chapter Twenty-Six

I HEAD TO THE airport with my heart breaking. Having to leave my wife and daughter behind is killing me, but I have no choice. If there is a possible threat to my family, then the only person I would ever trust is Max. I need to do this for Junior. No matter what, I am determined to get this done and over with. The crew is getting ready to close up the cabin, but there is a commotion just outside the door. I hear her threatening everyone from the pilot to the guards . . . my mother.

"Jaxson James Phillips, you might as well let me on here. You will not be leaving here without me."

She barrels her way past the guard and onto the plane. "How did you even know where I was?"

"Your sister can't lie her way out of a wet paper bag. There is no way you are doing this alone. Now, let's get going; the sooner we get there, the sooner we get back."

Mick comes racing in the door, his hands tied together with ropes. "Jax, do you see what she did? An, you can't tie me up and run away. I'm here for your safety, this is not a game! How did you even learn to make these knots?"

"My father worked on the docks, you would be surprised what he taught me. I'm sorry, but my son needed me."

"Mum, get him out of those knots and then both of you buckle up; we need to leave. Oh and how the hell did you get away from Max?"

"You know when I put my mind to something, there is no stopping me. I assure you, the only thing that's hurt is probably his pride."

She makes quick work of the ropes, and they both buckle up. "Jax,

I swear she just doesn't listen. She is going to be the death of me."

"Yeah, Mick, welcome to my world. It's a quick flight, so we shouldn't be too long. Any sign of trouble, you are to get her out of there. I don't care if you have to throw her over your shoulder—you protect her, no matter what." I close my eyes and reel in my temper. God only knows what she did to Max.

James

Present Time

NO MATTER HOW MUCH I try to wipe the images from my mind, I never can. This is my daily cross to bear. I open my eyes and Reynolds is still standing there, waiting for me to make a decision.

"So if we are not running, sir, then, what exactly are we going to do?"

"I am going to wait right here and face the music. You are free to go."

"Sir, we have been together all these years. Besides, I have no place to go."

The doorbell rings. Reynolds leaves, closing the door behind him. Old habits die hard. I get up and look out the window. The view from here always takes my breath away. There is a light tap on the door.

"Come in, Reynolds."

"Sir, your guests have arrived."

I turn around and in walks An with Jaxson and a man I've never seen before. He appears to be a bodyguard. "An, you look beautiful. I wasn't expecting to ever see you again."

"Who were you expecting to see, James?"

"The rest of my children; you must be Jaxson." I extend my hand out but he doesn't take it. "Where are Maxwell and Isabella?"

"This is not a social visit. My grandson is undergoing cancer treatment. He needs stem cells and we haven't found a match. You need to be tested to see if you are a close enough match."

"Always the bossy one, An. Would you like a drink?"

"A drink? James, please, for once in your life, please, do the right thing. He's your grandson; you already let one boy die, are you going to let another one?"

"Have a seat, everyone. Please, I have some questions." I'm watching Jax and he is wound up real tight, to the point, he could be dangerous.

"Tell me about the boy."

"My grandson is nine years old, very smart with a heart of gold. What else do you want to know? What do I need to tell you to make you have some compassion?"

"So he is Isabella's son from when she was raped." Her eyes grow wide, shocked that I know.

"I have followed all my children's lives; some of them I'm a part of and some of them I chose to stay away." I'm watching Jax's eyes as I tell my story and, there it is—I hit a nerve with him. He leaps out of the chair so fast, I don't have a chance to defend myself. His hands are around my throat, and the body guard steps forward, trying to pull him back.

"You *chose* to stay away? Did you choose to let your grandson and daughter-in-law be slaughtered in the street? Do you care that Cindy killed herself because of you? You've left nothing but destruction and mayhem in your path, and for what, money? Is money that fucking important to you? If it's money that you want, I will give you one million dollars in cash to be tested. If you're a match and you donate, I will give you an additional fifty million in cash. Does that make you happy?"

He finally lets go of my throat and I'm able to talk. "Maybe you should let me explain before you go off half-cocked, son."

"Son? Don't even think you can call me that. You are nothing but a sperm donor. My mum wore both hats; she carried the load for both parents. You are nothing to me."

"An, if you want me to explain, I will . . . but you need to calm him down."

"Jax, please let him explain, and then we can leave."

I'll say one thing, no matter how much of a hot head he is, he listens to her.

"Do you really want him here when I explain everything?"

He sits back down next to her. "I'm not leaving, so deal with it." She doesn't seem to mind if he knows all the details, so why should I?

"Have it your way. An, you were so young when I met you and I never expected to fall in love. I had a great set up with Cindy; she let me have my space. I'm sure, by now, you've figured out that the trinkets I gave you were stolen. You remember that day we took the train and met up with my friends?"

"How could I forget, I was very pregnant with Jax. I wanted to stay home, but you insisted that I had to go with you. That was the day I took that picture."

"That picture was like the start of a bad dominos game. Miguel was very upset over that picture. It's one of the few pictures of him in existence. He was also upset that I left you with those trinkets."

"You pulled him into that picture. It was very clear he didn't want any part of it."

"He is the reason I was in that hospital the day we met. He was a violent, vicious man."

"If you knew this then why did you hang out with him?"

"He was family, my cousin through marriage. We went into business together; I was the thief and he was the fence. Women flocked to me, making it easy for me to steal from them. They were always married, so they never wanted to press charges. Then you came along and I got caught up in a whirlwind romance. When you told me you were pregnant, I panicked. I was already married, but your father's friends really didn't give me a way out. I figured I could somehow juggle you and Cindy, but then you became pregnant again. I realized I was in too deep, so I walked away. I felt it was best for everyone. You were young and pretty; you would find someone. I told Cindy everything in hopes that she would forgive me. Honestly, I would have stayed with her and continued doing what I was doing, but she finally stood up to me and said she had enough. She said her son deserved better. I don't believe she killed herself. I think her overdose was accidental. Then again, maybe that is wishful thinking."

"Let me get this straight," Jax speaks up. "You thought it would be okay to stay with Cindy and continue to steal from other women, pretending to love and want to be with them? You thought it was fine to toss *my* mum and *your* children aside for money? What kind of sick monster are you?"

"If you are done criticizing my choices, I will continue."

He waves his hand, "Oh, please go on, the sooner you finish, the sooner we are out of here."

"After Cindy died, I went to Miguel and told him I wanted out. I thought I could take Maxwell and beg you to forgive me. Miguel had other plans for me. It was always one more job. He was always threatening me with one thing or another. He threatened to hurt Isabella if I didn't get that picture back from you. I convinced him I destroyed everything before I left you. Going back to you would have put you in even more danger. The best thing you did was move to the States. Maxwell was living with his grams. I continued to work with Miguel, but then he got into drug dealing. That's when his business took off. He couldn't get the drugs cut and sent out fast enough. Money was coming in so quickly and he needed to turn it as fast as possible. At one point, he had storage units filled with cash, waiting to get back into circulation. At that point, I wasn't sleeping with women and stealing their jewels, I was laundering drug money." I pour myself a scotch, feeling the knot in my stomach. I know this is the part they want to know, the hardest part for me to relive.

"More time passed and then Maxwell joined the police force. Of all the things he could have become, he chose the worst possible thing. Miguel flipped out; he wanted me to do something. He wanted me to turn him, but I knew there was no way that would ever happen. The threats went back and forth until I got wind of what he was planning to do. I raced to the park that day, but I was too late—they were dead. I was there when Maxwell showed up. I saw my son fall apart that day; watched silently as his world crumbled around him. At that moment, I knew there was no redemption for me. Miguel went into hiding, and surrounded himself with layers upon layers of very bad men. It took years, but I finally found Miguel; he paid for what he did. However, the damage was already done. I will live with their blood on my hands for the rest of my life."

"Was Miguel responsible for my daughter's rape?" She was always too smart for her own good.

"I could never prove it, but I had my suspicions. "

"I've listened to your story, now will you be tested?"

"Will you let me see the boy?"

"Will you be tested?"

I go to the desk and get out the test results. "I've already been tested and the information has been sent to his doctors. I don't want your money, Jax. I want to see the boy, will you let me?"

Jax leaps up but An takes his arm. "Jax, please let me handle this."

"James, I have to do what is best for my grandson. Learning about you and what you've done will not be in his best interest. He needs to stay focused and positive on his recovery. He just lost someone very close to him. I don't think he can take anymore."

I know I won't get anywhere with her. Once her mind is made up, there is no changing it. Maybe I can get through to Jax.

"Jax, as you know, you also have three brothers that you've had some business dealings with. I contacted them and they have all been tested. The results have been sent to the doctors. I'm not the bad guy here. I want to help."

"If you're a match, will you donate?"

"Of course I will. All I want is to meet the boy."

"My work here is done. Come on, Mum, let's go."

He gets up to leave. "That's it? Not even a thank you?"

"You want me to thank you?! Have you lost your fucking mind? I hate you! I'm not here for your approval or to make friends with you. You have no fucking clue what you've done; all in the name of the almighty buck. I was a little boy when you left. I had no one. I had a mum and sister to protect. I never had a normal childhood. I was too busy doing your job so you could go out and fuck the world. Well, I hope it was worth it. Oh and while were on the subject, if you come anywhere near my family, I will fucking kill you. Stay away from all of us; you've done more than enough. Come on, Mum, we are leaving *now!*"

I watch them leave and Reynolds comes back in. "Sir, did you tell them you're a match?"

"No, let them digest everything I told them. I'm sure they will be back again when they find out."

Jaxson

WHAT THE FUCK IS this man thinking? Like I would ever let him see Junior. I've got the papers clutched in my hand but I don't need to look at them, I already know what they will say. It's like a chess board that I'm looking down on. Of course he knew we were coming; he was expecting it. He's been watching all of us for a long time. How much did he know? Did he know about Raven, her kidnapping? Did he know where she was for three months, while I was going out of my mind searching for her? The more I think about all the pieces to this game, the more pissed off I get. He's a match and he will use it for leverage to see Junior. Bella will let him if it means her son will survive; what parent wouldn't? The problem is, once he gets his foot in the door, there's no turning back. He'll be like a cancer, leaving death and destruction in his wake.

We board the jet and everyone is very quiet. I'm glad Mick is here to take care of Mum. I can't even begin to understand what she is feeling right now.

"Jax, is he a match?"

"Of course he is. Why do you think he made it so easy to see him? He wants Junior for his redemption. What he doesn't get is that there is no redemption for him. He will go to hell with Cindy, Samantha, Elliott, and God knows how many others' blood on his hands. All those lives destroyed for what—money? How is that worth anything?"

"So, what do we do?"

"What we always do, Mum; we survive."

I turn my phone on and there is a message from Max.

Max: So help me God, when she gets back here, there will be hell to pay. Is everything okay?

Jax: Everything is fine, he was already tested and he's a match. I will give you all the details when I see you. Should be back in an hour. How is everyone?

Max: Everyone is good. Safe travels.

"Mum, what did you do to Max?" She's picking imaginary lint off of her pants, it must be bad.

"He's a stubborn man and when I told him where I was going, he was yelling. You know I don't like when he gets upset. I went to the ladies room and climbed out the window." I know I must have a shocked look on my face. Part of me wants to yell and the other part can't help but laugh.

"Oh please, Mum, don't stop there. Go on, I really need to hear the rest of this."

"I got outside and the Gardner was there. He was very gracious and offered to drive me to the airport. I saw that Mick was following us, so I asked the man for some of his rope. When I got to the airport, I thanked the man and got out. Mick pulled up and was demanding I get in the car. Rather than make a scene I did."

"So when did the ropes come into play?"

"I held Mick's hands and pretended I was crying. I leaned against his chest and tied his hands to the shift stick. I jumped out of the car and ran. There, now you know the whole story. I'm not proud of it, but I had to do this. I needed to understand why."

"And do you? Was it worth it?"

"As a matter of fact, yes, it was worth it. It confirmed what I knew all along, I was a fool. He made me believe I was the great love of his life. I know now that he is a con artist and I was a pawn in his games. I also learned that I'm so much better off without him. I learned that while I was pining away for an unrealistic love, he was using people. I learned that no matter how much I despise the man, he still gave me the greatest gift of all, my children. For that, I will always be thankful to the man."

"I like to believe we are who we are because of the person who raised us and not who donated their sperm; nature versus nurture." I put my seat back and rub my temples, trying to squash the raging headache. "You will have to deal with Max when we get back. Good luck with that."

I close my eyes for the rest of the flight. I don't think I can handle anything more without saying something I might end up regretting later. I need to mentally prepare myself for the next hurdle, dealing with Bella.

Maxwell

I'M PACING AND I swear, if Jax doesn't get back soon, I will wear a hole in the floor. What the hell was she thinking?! Climbing out the bloody window like some sort of teenager! Why the hell did Mick let her get on that plane? I love her, I respect her, and hell, at times, I even fear her but right now, I want to tear into her.

Jackie takes my hand and squeezes it, pulling me toward her. She kisses me. "Max, I know you're upset but you might want to try and relax a little before you see her. She did what she felt she had to do, granted, it was a little extreme, however, it's done and she's safe. If you flip out on her, you will hate yourself for it later."

"I know you're right, but why does she continue to do things that will upset me?"

"No one is perfect and neither is the world we live in. Free will doesn't always mean people will make the right choices."

I rest my forehead on hers and close my eyes. She calms me like no one else can. "You're smart *and* beautiful; I'm so lucky."

"I'm also hungry . . . very hungry, actually. I ordered lunch for everyone, it should be here shortly. You need to eat something, and try to calm down before they get here."

"No such luck, babe, they're here," I announce as I watch them walk through the entrance. I'm holding her so tight, I'm afraid I might break her.

Before I can say a word, Mum walks up to me and wraps her arms around Jackie and me, damn it!

"I'm sorry, Maxwell, I know what I did was wrong. I should have told you my intentions, however, in my defense, you never would have gone along with it. I know it was foolish and reckless, but I needed to do it."

"I really want to yell at you right now, but I know it won't change anything. It's over, but never again, in my lifetime, will you ever pull such a crazy arse stunt."

She yanks my ear. "Language, please. I promise I will try not to."

"Mick, you have a lot of explaining to do, like how the hell did you let her get that far?"

He's about to explain when Jax stops him. "In Mick's defense, Mum tied him to the stick shift in his car. You've seen her when she is determined, Mate, there is no stopping her."

Jackie starts laughing so hard, she can barely catch her breath. "Oh my God, I can't believe she tied you up!" She says as she watches the food being wheeled in. "The lunch I ordered is here. Come on and tell me all about it. After lunch, Michael has a treatment; you can tell us what happened with James."

Everyone heads into Junior's room but Jax and I stay back. "Okay, what the hell went down?" Before he can answer, Mick comes out of the room.

"Here's my cell phone; I recorded everything for you. I knew you would be overwhelmed."

"Thank you. Mick, Can you make some excuse for us while we go listen to this, please?"

"Sure, Max, I'll take care of it."

"Come on Jax, let's grab a cup of coffee."

We head into the lounge and I don't think I've seen Jax this bad since Raven was kidnapped. I'm almost afraid to listen to the recording.

"Max, are you sure you want to hear this? He talks about everything, even your mum."

"Yeah, I don't see that I have a choice." He gets up and walks over to the window while I hit play. I have to stop it a few times to catch my breath. To hear him talk about my mum, so cavalier like, makes me sick. When I get to the part about my family, I know I won't be able to be in the same room with him; I'll kill him with my bare hands. He was there; he knew what was going to happen. He never called the police, hell—he could have called me. I was five fucking minutes from that park. I close my eyes and try to gain some composure to finish listening. Being a match, I know he wants to come swooping in at the end, like a white knight, saving the day. This isn't a fucking fairytale, he doesn't get to ride into the sunset and all is forgiven. I don't even hear Jax come back to the table.

"Max, what are we going to do? I have the paperwork; he's a ninety-seven percent match. I think the only way he's going to donate is if we let him meet Junior. Our other three brothers aren't a match. I can run with this if you want, but I need to know what you want to do. Max, are you listening to me?"

"He was there, Jax . . . in the park. He knew and he could have stopped it. He's the reason I never found Miguel. Was my mum's death really an accident? I can't see him. I'm barely hanging on as it is. I think if I do, I will snap."

"Well, ultimately, it has to be Bella's decision. But, if it were Elliot that needed to be saved, you would do whatever you had to. How do you think she is going to react when she finds out about the rape?"

"He said Miguel was a cousin by marriage but there is no record of that. If I were Bella, it would make me sick to think that the rape could have been some sort of warning for James. No matter what happens, Jax, we need the stem cells. I will not have Jackie or Mrs. Olsa anywhere near him. He breeds death and destruction."

"Bella needs to listen to this recording. I will be with her when she does. I don't expect you to listen to it again. I won't have my family anywhere near him, either."

"She's my sister too, and I need to be there for her. I'll be okay . . . I have to be."

"Come on, let's get back before they send out a search party for us. I still can't believe Mum ditched you and climbed out the bathroom window."

"Not funny, Jax, and what's up with her and Mick?"

"I'm choosing to not go there. Sometimes, in life, ignorance really is bliss."

We head into Junior's room, ready as I'll ever be, to face what I know are going to be some very difficult times ahead.

Chapter Twenty-Seven

Jaxson

WE HEAD INTO JUNIOR'S room and seeing him laughing and playing puts everything into perspective. I know I have to do this for him. Antonia is sitting in her baby recliner, laughing and kicking her feet, not a care in the world; as life should be. I feel her arms wrap around my waist and it's a comfort, it's home.

"I'm glad you made it back safe, I was worried."

"I was never in danger, sweetheart, only James was. We got what we needed. He's a perfect match and will be donating stem cells."

"At what price, Jax?"

I turn around so I can see her eyes, they ground me. "What makes you ask that?"

"Any man, who could do the things he has done, would never do a kind act without wanting something. So what price are we going to have to pay?"

"He wants to meet Junior." I can barely get the words out, my stomach in knots at the sheer thought of it.

"Oh."

"Yeah, oh. Mick recorded everything, which I'm glad he thought to do. Max already listened to it, but Bella still has to. In the end, she will have to go along with it. Sometimes, in life, there really is no choice. When the day comes that they have to meet, I don't want you or Antonia anywhere near here. Please don't fight me on this, allow me a little peace of mind . . . please."

"Okay, I can do that. Why don't you go spend some time with Michael? Tony sent him something very special that he's been bursting to tell you about."

I make my way further into the room and Junior sees me. He comes running and leaps into my arms. "Hey, guess you're excited to see me."

"Oh, you are not going to believe what Tony sent! Hurry up, I have to show you. He designed a gaming system and he wants me to test it out for him. And guess what, Uncle Jax, the very first game he made is a *Doctor Who* game. It's so cool! I know it's going to be a big hit." I put him down and he's still going on and on about the wonders of the game. It doesn't matter who Junior's real father is, it's the love and nurturing that's made him the fantastic kid he is.

"Uncle Jax, are you okay?"

"Yeah, now let's see what this bad boy can do."

Isabella

JAX MADE IT BACK okay but he looks really bad, I'm worried. What if Dad isn't a match or what if he won't agree to be tested, what will I do? Playing with Michael always seems to bring him back to life.

Max puts his arm around my waist and kisses may forehead. "Bella, let's go get a cup of tea." He says low enough so only I can hear.

"Are you going to be delivering bad news?" He doesn't say anything as we head to the cafe.

"First, I will tell you the good news is our father is a perfect match. He has agreed to the donation. The paperwork is being processed now."

"And the bad news? He cocks his head, lifts his eyebrows, and tightens his grip around my waist. "Don't look at me like that, Max, we both know he's got to want something."

"Mick recorded the entire conversation. I know that—no matter what—you will do what you have to in order to save Junior. If you don't want to listen to it, you don't have to. The choice is yours," he offers.

"I want to listen to it, but will you stay with me?"

He hands me a headset. "I will, if you put these on. I don't know that I can listen to it ever again."

Max gets tea and I know it's that act not the tea that is comforting. I press play. His voice is deep and raspy . . . not what I was expecting. My poor mum having to listen to him, reminding her of her naivety. I understand why Max can't listen to this again. He could have saved them. "Ah" I gasp and drop my cup, my whole body begins to shake. Max races over and pulls the headset off.

"Shh, I've got you."

"M-max, could it be I was raped because of him? He wants to meet my son. That's the price I have to pay? He's a sick and twisted person." He lifts me up and carries me out of the cafe. I can't stop shaking. What kind of person would ever let their child go through what I did? If he knew Miguel was that crazy, why didn't he protect his family? Instead, it's like he threw us to the wolves. Oh dear God, how can I do this?

I finally stop shaking. I open my eyes, but it's dark and I have no clue where I am. I only know that I'm in Max's arms and he's rocking me like a child.

"Were are we?"

"A quiet room off the solarium; you're safe."

"How am I going to do this? I have no choice, I know that, but . . . how can I look at him? Why does it have to be him who can save my son?"

"Bella, look at me. Jax and I will be with you the entire time. We will explain to Junior what is going on. We will get through this, and then, we never have to see him again. Meeting Junior is not going to give him redemption. In his eyes, he's doing something good. But, one good act doesn't erase all the bad. When you do something good for someone, you do it because you want to, with no ulterior motives. He will always be damned to hell and nothing he does will ever change that."

"What about you? Are you going to be able to do this without killing him?"

"I will do whatever I have to for my nephew and if it means I have to deal with him, then so be it. We need to get back before we are missed. Are you ready?"

I get up and wipe my face as best I can. "I am a very lucky girl to have two of the best brothers in the world."

"Jax and I want to tell him in the morning, if that's okay with you."

"That's fine. So what happened that everyone moved out of Mr. Gerhard's home very quickly?"

"Can't get nothing past you, can I?"

"Nope, eventually I find out everything. I'm worse than Mum."

"Dylan came back and was causing a scene. The whole thing didn't feel right. Then we found out that he is in financial trouble and dealing with some shady characters. Best to be in our own place. Besides, that was just a place to regroup after fleeing the States."

We step back into the room and find Jax and Michael asleep with the remotes in their hands. Raven comes up and gives me a hug. "Are you okay, Bella?"

"Yeah, I will be. I see they are out cold. I can't tell you how many nights I've found them like that. If you take the remote out of Jax's hand, he will wake right up." I walk over, take the remote, and just like always . . ."Bella, I'm playing."

"Jax, go home; everyone is tired. I promise you can come back tomorrow and play again."

Everyone makes their goodbyes. Now I have to explain everything to my husband. I'm not looking forward to this conversation. Once again, I have no choice.

I crawl onto Michael's lap and begin to tell him everything. He surprises me by remaining calm and agreeing to everything. "What happened? Why are you so calm?"

"I told you, I would do whatever I had to do to save my son."

"What about your parents? Are you still going to have them meet Michael?"

"Yes, it's time, Bella. I am willing to let them try. In the end, it's my son's decision if he wants a relationship with them."

I snuggle into him, "You are such a kind man. I love you."

"Ti amo più della vita stessa e amerò sempre."

"It sounds beautiful, whatever it means."

"Oh, Bella, someday you will learn my language. I said, I love you more than life itself, and I always will."

Raven

WE FINALLY GET TO the estate and it's extremely secluded, even more so than the Gerhard compound. Electric fence and armed guards; God only knows what the house is like. Jax has his head on my shoulder and he is asleep. He hasn't given me any details of what happened today only that James is a match. I can't believe that An climbed out the bathroom window. She is always surprising me, but she probably knew that was the only way she would get to go.

"Jax, wake up; were here." He opens his eyes and throws his arms around me.

"Hey, we're safe. I'm here." My heart is breaking for him. God only knows what went down today. It's eating him up inside.

He grabs Antonia's carrier and we all head inside. The place is huge and fully staffed, something I'm never comfortable with. Max is already going over all the details with the head of security. Mrs. Osla must be able to tell that I'm at a loss here. She takes out a chart and begins assigning rooms.

"Thank you, Mrs. Osla, we would be very lost without you." She doesn't take compliments well and shoos me away.

"Jax, I'm going to get Antonia ready for bed, and then I'm going to soak in the tub. When you're done here, please join me."

"Of course, I'll be up in a minute. I want to go over some stuff with Max before we turn in."

Jaxson

MRS. OSLA DIRECTS EVERYONE to their rooms while I drag Max into the den. "Okay, what happened with Bella? I wanted to be there when she heard the recording."

"You can't be everywhere, Jax. You were gone for a good portion of the day and Junior really wanted to spend some time with you. I stayed with Bella the whole time. She was destroyed to find out about the rape. In the end, she knows she has to let him meet Junior. She wants it to be very quick and she was going to explain everything to Michael tonight. She also wants you and me there when she tells Junior about James."

"I'm not sure the kid can take much more. Rose's death hit him really hard. Michael's family will be coming sometime soon. Not only will he be meeting them for the first time but also James. You know how important state of mind is; I'm worried."

"I understand what you're saying, but we don't have a choice. James attached a condition on giving the stem cells. Granted he didn't say he would withhold them, but after listening to that recording, there is no doubt in my mind that is his intention."

"Maybe we can get him in and out very quickly. Do we know how long the procedure is?"

"I spoke to the doctor and he said they do two different procedures. The one like Jackie had where then remove the stem cells from the bone marrow in the hip. The other is a procedure called peripheral blood stem cell donation. The donor is given injections of Filgrastim to aid in cell reproduction. He said he uses both, especially after chemo. From the sound of it, I don't think it's a quick thing. Look, whatever it is, we will have to deal with it."

"How the hell are we going to do this without losing it? You don't know how hard it was."

"Mick told me you had him around the throat. You're a better man than me; I would have snapped his neck."

"That's my point, Max. How the fuck are we going to do this? I think I've spent what little control I had. You're talking about being around him for days. I don't want my family around him at all. I think his meeting with Junior should be hi and goodbye."

"That's not realistic. What will you do if Junior says he wants to get to know him, have you thought about that?"

"Get to know him?! Have you lost your bloody mind?"

"He's a nine-year-old boy who knows nothing about James or

anything that he's done. All he knows is what he's been told; keep that in mind."

"I'll negotiate with Junior, he will listen to me."

"Look, it's been a long, emotional day, let's get some sleep and we can deal with this in the morning."

"Okay, except I have no clue where my room is, so lead the way." He's right, it's been a long day and the only thing I'm looking forward to right now is getting lost within my beautiful wife.

Raven

I HOPE JAX WON'T be too long. When he's with Max, they tend to lose track of time. I like this house. Tony did a good job of finding it and getting everything set up so quickly. We have access to Antonia's room right through ours, which is perfect. Hopefully, this will be our last move for quiet some time. I peak in her crib; I could watch her sleep all night long but I want to get the tub set up for Jax. He's had two emotional days back to back and he needs to unwind. I go about setting everything up when I hear him come in. My God, he looks like a beaten man. My heart is breaking for him.

"Jax, let me take care of you tonight, please. We will have a nice soak in this beautiful tub, and you can just close out the world for awhile."

"That sounds good to me. I really need to be alone with you."

I pour him a glass of wine, and then help him get undressed. "Climb in and I will sit behind you so I can massage your shoulders."

"Wow, take-charge-Raven is here tonight. It's okay; I need her to help me forget my horrific day."

"Is that your way of telling me you don't want to talk about it?"

"Part of me wants to yell and punch something and the other part of me wants to close my eyes and forget this whole week has ever happened," he groans. I keep massaging his neck and shoulders. I know if I wait long enough, he will tell me everything.

"When Bella came back with Max, she was very upset. You were sleeping, but do you know what happened?"

"Yeah, she listened to the recording."

"What recording?"

He takes in a deep breath, and then tells me about Mick recording the whole confrontation with his father. Both Max and Bella have listened to it. "How bad was it?"

"Bad, sweetheart, really bad." He leans his head back and continues to tell me what happened. He admitted a lot of stuff that made it seem like he just used my mum and Cindy. He thought Cindy's death was accidental. Then he wanted to take Max and hook back up with my mum but she was already in the States. Apparently that photograph with the four men was a bone of contention for Miguel who by the way is James's cousin."

"Ah, no Max is related to the man that killed his family?"

"He's a cousin through marriage. When Max became a cop, Miguel wanted our father to turn him. When he couldn't, he killed Samantha and Elliot. Our father was in the park that day and knew what was going to happen. He could have stopped it and he didn't."

"Oh, how sick is that?"

"Wait, there's more. He believes that Miguel was behind Bella's rape."

"That's why she was so upset. Bella knows this now. Oh, how sad. All these years she blamed herself, like she did something wrong, but, in essence, it was all planed."

"You want to know what the kicker is? He is a perfect match for Junior. I offered him fifty-million dollars in cash for his donation, but the only thing he wants is to meet Junior. Bella has no choice; she's going to have to do it. I'm telling you now, Raven, I don't want you or Antonia anywhere near my father."

I pull him tightly up against my chest. "I have no desire to ever meet James and he will never get near our daughter. I'm worried about Michael Jr., though. I don't know how much more that boy can take. Bella told me that Michael's parents are also being tested and want to finally meet their grandson. This is an awful lot for a nine-year-old to deal with."

"Max told me tonight about Michael's parents. I give Michael a lot of credit. I don't know that I could be as strong as he is. When he told his parents what happened to Bella and that he was marrying her, they said some pretty harsh stuff. They weren't dating very long and I admire him for his choices. I was prepared to take care of her and Junior for the rest of my life. I told you that Max was part owner of Raiders, but what I didn't tell you is that Junior owned a higher percentage than Max. It's all in a trust for him. He has no clue, but if he never wanted to work a day in his life, he wouldn't have to. The only person who knows about it is Max and now, you. Not even Bella knows. I never wanted money to get in the way of their lives."

"Why didn't you tell Bella?"

"Can you imagine the creeps that would have come out of the woodwork if they knew that a single mum has a son who's worth a fortune? Michael came to me when Bella was about seven months pregnant and asked for her hand in marriage. I told him no and sent him away. The next day, Bella came to me crying and begged me for my blessing. Again, I said no. So, she said she would get married without it. The fight was huge and finally, my mum sat the three of us in a room to hash it out. I offered to pay Michael to go away."

"Wow, I know you can be tough, but that was very harsh."

"Maybe, but there was a lot at stake and I'm not talking about money. Whomever she chose would be around Junior and that was my sticking point. I didn't doubt that he loved her, he showed her in so many ways. I had blinders on when it came to the baby. Finally, I agreed to the wedding, but there were certain things that had to happen. A prenup had to be in place. He had to agree that the baby would be brought up Catholic. He had to agree that if they split up, he would have no legal rights to the child. He had to agree to it all before I would say yes. His parents said if he married her, they would disown him. They said Bella was using him for his name and for money. He walked away from his family, and they got married. Then Bella had major complications with her pregnancy. It was so bad that, at one point, we called in a priest. She's tough and pulled through, but she can't have any more children. Michael stood beside her the entire time, even though he knew he would never have a child of his own. I admire him for that more than I could ever explain."

"I didn't know that she went through all of that, she never really talked about her pregnancy. I wonder why Michael is forgiving his parents now."

"Max and I tease Michael all the time, telling him that he is up for sainthood being married to Bella. In reality, he is a very kind man and maybe after all of this, he realizes, like the rest of us, that life is short, and it can change on a dime."

"Do you feel like you got the answers from James that you were looking for?"

"Actually, yeah, I did. It had nothing to do with me or Bella. He never wanted us; we were his mistake. His attitude made me sick—we had his wonderful DNA and everything we accomplished was because of it. You can imagine how well that went over with me."

"I'm sorry you had to go through all of that, but maybe it's put everything into prospective for you. Now you can believe what I keep telling you, that none of it was your fault. You are a good son and brother." I kiss his neck before tapping his shoulder. "Now I think we need to get out of here."

"Thank you. I know life with me can get a little crazy, but I promise I will always love you as fiercely as I did from the first day you doused me with your coffee."

We get out and we wrap each other in the warm towels. "Make love to me, Jax, softly, all night long."

He lifts me up and carries me into the bedroom, climbing into bed while he kisses me. He slowly enters me and stops. He takes my hand and places it on his heart. "I will love you, with all that I am, for the rest of my life. Nothing will ever change that." He kisses me and begins to move slowly at first, but then he flips over so I'm on top, our lips never breaking their connection. His hands on my hips, guiding his every move, I can feel him so deep, with each upward thrust. He's holding back, I know he's there. "Don't hold back, I want it all."

He slows me down and then holds me tightly so I can't move. He begins to tilt his hips back and forth without pulling out. The sensation as he hits my clitoris is so intense, that my whole body begins to tremble. A tingling wave rushes through me like hot lava. As he flips me over, I clench; it's his undoing. His release is so powerful. He tells me he loves me over and over again. When I finally find my wits, I open my eyes and he's smiling. "That was different and intense, are you okay?" He's twirling my hair and still smiling.

"I'm fantastic, sweetheart, I'm in cock heaven." He tilts his hips up and he's ready again.

I can't help but giggle and his smile gets brighter. "Aimez-moi à nouveau avec tout ce que vous avez."

"Oh, dirty talk—French. More . . . *please*."

"Nothing dirty, Jax, only love. Je espère que nous faisons un bébé ce soir. Je te aime."

I clench his cock and begin to move faster, driving him crazy. Over and over again, he's begging for more. He reaches up and rolls my nipples between his fingertips. My body flushes, my release is so strong and so powerful, my heart skips a beat as I call out his name. I collapse onto his chest and try to come back to earth. He's stroking my back, soothing me. "I hope so, too," he whispers.

Jackie

MAX HAS FINALLY FALLEN asleep but it's not a peaceful one. An told me a little of what happened, but I need to hear it from Max. I wrap my self around him and gently rub his temple, it always seems to help. "I love you so much, and I'm so sorry you have to relive this nightmare. Whatever I have to do to help you, I will."

Whenever he's restless he pulls me tightly against him. His fear comes through more when he's asleep. His eyes open and he pulls me even tighter. "Jackie, oh thank God! I dreamt you were gone."

"I'm safe, Max, but ease up a little, please."

"I'm sorry, did I hurt you?"

"No, tell me what happened yesterday. Bella looked destroyed last night. An said James is a match and he wants to meet Michael. Does this mean that James will be around us?"

"The way the doctor explained it, he does it two different ways. I'm not sure how much time that will take."

"Max, hold on; let me put your mind at ease here. While you were talking with Bella last night, Mrs. Osla and I did some research. James needs to get injections of Filgrastim to aid in cell reproduction. They are usually given over the course of a few days, but he doesn't have to get them here, he just has to get them. The actual procedure is anywhere from two to four hours. It's not a big deal; he's playing upon everyone's emotions. He wants to be the white knight coming in to save the day. Well, guess what?—never going to happen. If he insists he wants to meet Michael, then he gets five minutes and that's it. We are not about to bow down to him."

"Wow, you never cease to amaze me. So, he doesn't need to be here until he has to donate."

"Even the donation can be done elsewhere. Have you thought about what you're going to do? I would rather you weren't around him. I know Mrs. Osla said she can't be anywhere near him."

He's quiet for a bit, playing with my braid. He then tells me about the recording.

"Are you sure he knew?"

"Miguel was his cousin. He wanted my dad to turn me into a bad cop. He knew that he wouldn't be able to, so Miguel was teaching him a lesson." I'm trying to be strong for him, but I can't stop my tears.

"How will everyone be able to face him? Michael needs him, but can our family survive this?"

"What choice do we have? I don't want you, or Mrs. Osla, anywhere near him. I need to know that you're both safe . . . *please.*"

"What about me? I don't want you anywhere near James! But I know you; you'll do whatever you have to do for Michael. How are you going to be in the same room with him? How the hell is Bella going to do it? Why can't we all stand strong together?"

"What are you saying?"

"What I'm suggesting is, when Michael has to meet that bastard, we stand together and make a united front. James needs to see that he can't break us. I hate bullies and we will not be bullied into doing what James wants. We are a strong, loving family and all the DNA means nothing. We did it with love and respect. I'm not running and hiding, none of us are. I'm not letting Michael meet him without all the love and support that child deserves. James might think he has us by the balls, but he doesn't. We have options." I grab my bag off the floor and dig around till I find the box I had in there for him.

"I was waiting to give you this for your birthday,

but—here—happy birthday."

He takes the top off and stares into the box. His eyes grow wide and a tear slides down his cheek. I kiss it away. "We always have options, and we always have faith. I love you and we're in this journey together. I never thought it would happen this quickly, but you know that saying: *we make plans and God just laughs,* well I think right about now he's hysterical."

"This is real? You're really pregnant?"

"Oh, it's real all right." He's on me in a second, kissing me so deeply. He pulls away and now he's staring at me.

"How pregnant are you?"

"I was using an app on my phone to track my cycle. I'm only one day late, but you can test up to five days early before a missed period with most home pregnancy tests. I wanted to wait until I was further along before I said anything but, because of everything with Michael, maybe we should discuss it with his doctor. I want to get a blood test done today." I realize he hasn't said a word. "Max, are you okay?" Now he has me worried.

"Okay? I'm in shock, Jackie. You're giving me the gift of life. I'm speechless, and you're like some kind of warrior princess. You're amazing."

"When I took that test, I cried. It's because of Sammy that I was here to even take the test."

"I will always be in debt to him. How do you feel? Are you ill at all?"

"Other than tired and my breast are a little sore, I feel fine."

He gets up and begins pacing. "All right, I can do this. I need to be calm and form a plan. I will talk to Junior's doctor today. I need to find the top OBGYN. I need to make sure she is getting the proper nutrition. I have to triple up security. I need an armor car. Oh. My. God. Jackie you're not driving that Lamborghini!"

"Remember what I told you, I'm not a child or a porcelain doll. Pregnant women drive cars all the time. I will be able to make my own doctor appointments and even feed myself—imagine that."

"Babe, we need to talk. I'm going to be calm here. No bloody way in hell I'm putting you behind the wheel of a powerhouse Lamborghini while you're pregnant, and you don't even have a fucking driver's license! I'll give you the doctor and the food, but you have got to give me the car."

"Do I get the car after the baby comes?"

"Ugh, you are the most stubborn woman I have ever met. You realize this whole car thing happened because you had your knickers around your knees! Fine, after the baby comes, you can have your car."

I leap out of bed and jump into his arms.

"Oh, for the love of all that's holy, no leaping and no jumping about."

"It's going to be a long pregnancy if you keep acting like this. Now, I think you need to feed me." I squish his cheeks with my hands, making his lips pucker. I lay a good one on him, making him chuckle.

"What would you like to eat?" he asks when I pull away.

"While I jump . . . I mean, *walk* into the shower, you can make me a three egg omelet with cheese, tomato, and toast. Please and thank you."

He smacks my ass and I giggle. It reminds me of that day with the car. "Oh, and don't tell anyone without me and, by anyone—I mean Jax. I know you two are joined at the hip, and I want to see the look on his face." I kiss him and race into the bathroom.

The shower is wonderful; four shower heads from every direction. I blast that hot water and climb in. I'm going to be someone's mom, how exciting?! I wish Rose was here; she made me realize that I'm strong and I can do this. I turn around and find Max behind me, totally naked and leaning against the wall. The sight of him takes my breath away. "I thought you were making me breakfast?"

"It won't take me too long. I got as far as the kitchen and then I realized you knew the car wasn't going to be delivered until May. You knew by then you wouldn't be driving, but you love to get me riled up. Look at you . . . biting that lip . . . trying not to laugh. One smack on that beautiful arse and your face lit up." I am so busted. I might as well have a little fun.

"Oh, Max, I've been a bad girl; whatever will you do about it?"

"Get out, dry off, and meet me in the bedroom." I watch him leave and I can barely contain my excitement. I grab a towel and head into the bedroom. He's sitting in the chair, looking unbelievably sexy. His jaw is tight, complimenting the serious look on his face.

"So, you said you've been a bad girl. How bad?" His voice is deep and my skin begins to prickle.

"Pretty bad; you might have to discipline me."

"Drop the towel."

I follow his command, trying to contain my excitement. I'm standing before him, totally naked. He's waiting and watching me. He knows what he's doing to me. His eyes never leaving mine—intense. "Over my knee—*now!*" I know how much he likes it when I seem submissive to him. I hesitate and bite my lip. He cocks his head to the side, eyes still locked on mine. "Jackie, don't make this harder on yourself. I won't ask you again."

Holy hell, I'm so turned on right now, I think I might combust before he even starts. I slowly drape myself over his knee. He moans as our bodies make contact, the sound vibrates to my core. He begins gently stroking each of my butt cheeks with only his fingertips. The gentleness and the anticipation is driving me crazy and he knows it. Finally, he gives quick alternating smacks, first right and then left. When he reaches six, he stops and kisses each cheek. I can feel his lips on my skin and it sends chills through me. I want more, so I begin to wiggle. I can feel his cock pulse against me and I know he wants more, too. He trails his fingers across the top of my legs, and then, spreads them slightly. I take a deep breath and wait, I know what he's going to do, what I want him to do, but the anticipation is the build up. "Ah!" He quickly swipes my clitoris and then begins spanking me again. I lose it. The buildup is so intense. I want to feel him deep inside of me, but my body has other intentions. I'm coming and it's not a gentle wave, it's a heart-stopping explosion. In one quick move he's out of the chair, bringing me with him to a standing position.

"Bend over and hold onto the bedpost—don't let go!" I obey. He enters me from behind, one hand wrapped around my braid, gently pulling me back to meet his trust. I want it to last, but then I hear him grunting and I know he's there. "My angel, I love you," he groans as he takes his final step to the edge. The minute I feel him explode, that feeling of warmth is my tipping point and I scream out my release. He's still moving, slowing it down but never stopping. He lets go of my braid and pulls out of me. Before I can protest, he spins me around and lifts me up. "Wrap those glorious legs around me . . . now!" He carries me back into the shower and the hot water hits us from every direction.

"Max, now will you feed me?" I ask after several minutes of collecting my wits about me.

He's laughing and I love the sound. He slowly puts me down. "I think I need a little attention first." He takes my hand and kisses my palm before guiding it over his cock. He's hard as stone and my touch brings a huge smile to his face.

"What would you like, Max." I'm playing with him and he knows it.

"Babe, I'm thinking you should tie me to a chair and have your way with me."

"Ah!" I gasp. You would let me do that?"

"I would let you do whatever you want. . . . . . within reason." He's smirking and I feel like a kid in a candy store. I shut the water off and quickly push him out of the shower. "Oh, Max, breakfast will definitely have to wait." I toss him a towel and pull him into the bedroom. I can't believe he is going to let me tie him up! I sit him in the chair and quickly hunt around the room for something to tie him up with. I hurry into the closet and find one of his belts. I also go into his valet and pull out the nipple clamps he used on me. When I come out, he's still sitting in the chair smiling.

"Put your hands behind your back." I try to sound dominant like he does. He smiles and complies. I make sure I secure the belt tightly around his wrists, and then I take a step back to admire my handy work. I know exactly what I'm going to do. I stand in front of him, bend down, and take one of his nipples in my mouth, gently pulling it between my teeth. He moans and I slip on the clamp. His eyes grow wide and he smiles. "Babe, you need to do both if this is going to work."

"Patience, Max." I reach down and do the other one. His jaw is tight as I kiss my way down his chest. I get on my knees and kiss his thighs. I start at his knee and work my way up. When I get to his cock I stop and go to the other one. He begins to growl and tries to use his feet to push me forward.

"My speed; not yours, Max." I reach my hands up and tighten the clamps. His groans are louder. I take his cock in my hand and rub my thumb over the top, followed by my tongue.

"Oh, babe, take me deep—please."

I swirl my tongue around as I go deeper and he is lifting his hips to meet me. I don't want this to end, so I stop.

"Oh bloody hell, don't stop."

I straddle his lap and lower myself on to his rock-hard cock. "Max, oh yeah." I slowly work my way up and down. His hips are following my lead. I tighten the clamps again and he grits his teeth. I'm trying to hold back, but he tilts his hips as he rises up, hitting my clitoris over and over again.

"Max, are you ready?" I don't give him a chance to answer, I release both nipple clamps at the same time. He throws his head back and lets out a long low groan, just as I find my own release. He is slowly coming back to earth as his rapid breathing begins to taper down.

"Untie my hands, please."

I reach around and loosen the belt and it falls away. He throws his arms around me and holds me close. I rest my forehead on his, "I love you. I think we need to try that shower again, and then you need to feed me."

I climb off of him and offer him my hand. Even though I would love to spend the day in bed with him, I know we can't. We head into the bathroom and quickly get cleaned up.

Max finishes up first and goes downstairs to start breakfast while I finish getting ready, basking in the knowledge that I got to reverse roles with him this morning.

Chapter Twenty-Eight

Jaxson

I DON'T KNOW WHAT the hell is taking Max so long this morning, but he better get his arse down here soon. I want to talk to him before everyone else wakes up. Raven is busy with Antonia, so now would be the perfect time to tell him my plan . . . if he ever gets down here. I head into the kitchen to make coffee and find it already done. I've never had staff around twenty-four seven, only guards, and I'm not sure I like it. Max finally comes down and grabs a cup. "Took you long enough, you're usually up at dawn."

He laughs and I get it. "Okay, don't need the details. I was thinking that you and I should talk to Junior alone."

"Hold up, Jax, Mrs. Osla and Jackie did some research on the procedure the doctor was talking about. Our father can get the shots in Capri. He doesn't have to show up here until the day of the procedure, and technically, he doesn't even have to be here for that. I get that will never happen, but we need to dictate how this is going to work, not the other way around. Oh, and my wife is pretty adamant about not staying away from the hospital. She said we are family and we must form a united front, we won't be bullied by the likes of him. I swear she's going to put me in an early grave."

"I told Raven everything that went down, and knowing my wife, she won't let him bully us either. We need to have a solid plan in place before we contact him again. I won't be caught off guard again." I go fill up my coffee again. I offer Max more but he is staring into space.

"Hey, what the hell is wrong with you this morning? Get your head in the game and concentrate."

Jackie walks in with Antonia in her arms and Raven right behind her. "Cut him some slack, it's not everyday a man finds out he's going to be a father."

Raven is laughing and crying and Max is sitting here with a faraway look on his face.

"Well, that's the best news I've heard in a while. When is the baby due?"

She hands me Antonia, who is laughing and drooling. "I wanted to wait and tell Max on his birthday and then, when I was through with the first trimester, tell everyone else, but . . . with everything going on, I thought we should talk to Michael's doctor. Maybe there are other options. If I calculated it correctly, then I'm due in June. Do you think we can hold off telling the whole family?"

I begin to laugh and I can't stop. I know all eyes are on me. "Oh, Jackie, look at your husband, do you really think no one will notice? It only took me five minutes to notice his head is in his arse. How long do you think it will take Mum?"

Max gets up and begins cooking, avoiding our gawking. I know there is going to be no living with him from now until June, and I can only hope Jackie doesn't kill him before that. One of the staff members comes in and lets us know that breakfast is already set up in the dining room. Max stops cooking. I don't think we will every get used to having staff.

"Jackie, you grew up with staff around all the time, how did you deal with it?"

"Since I don't cook, for me, it was easy. You need to sit them down and tell them what you would like them to handle and what you would rather do on your own. Would you like me to take care of it?"

"You're the best, thank you." I raise my coffee mug to her. Suddenly, I hear the clickety-clack of my mother's heels, coming down the hall. "I hear mum, are you ready to face the music?"

"As ready as I'll ever be."

I put my arm around her, "You'll be fine, I will keep the family in check."

"That's great, Jax, but who will keep you in check?"

We head into the dinning room, trying to act nonchalant. Everyone is busy eating and chatting. We just, kind of, slide into conversation. I'm trying not to look at Max or it's game over. My daughter is loving the toys, hanging from the bar above and across on her baby recliner. Then I hear Mum clear her throat obnoxiously, and I can't look up. "Jaxson, what are you trying to hide from me? The same goes for you, Maxwell."

I'm trying so hard not to laugh (a dead giveaway for me) but then I make the mistake of glancing over to Max. Now we are both laughing uncontrollably.

"An, I'm pregnant. I only let them know this morning: no one is keeping anything from you," Jackie announces, putting us out of our misery.

Everyone is congratulating them; everyone—*but* Mrs. Osla. I see her wipe away a tear and quietly excuse herself. I slip out after her.

"Mrs. Osla, what's wrong? You know that no one will ever replace Samantha and Elliot. Max has so much love to give."

"Oh, Jax, I know that and I am very happy for them both. I'm happy that Max has finally let himself be loved again. Most days, I'm okay. But times like this, I'm reminded of how much was lost."

I hug her, which is rare for us. "One day at a time is all we can do. We are always here to support each other, through the good and the bad." Just then, Max comes out to look for us. "I'll give you a moment with him." I smile and give her upper arms a little squeeze before letting go.

Max puts his arms around her, and she begins to cry. I back away, giving them their privacy.

I'm not in the room for two seconds and my mum is all over me. "Jaxson what is the plan for dealing with James?"

"Max and I were going to talk to Junior today. Then we will talk to the doctors. I'm not making any decisions until after that. Right now, I just want to bask in the glory that I'm going to be an uncle again."

"I want to be with my grandson when you talk to him about James."

I'm not going to get anywhere with her. I look to Raven for help but she's busy with Jackie.

"Mum, it's what's best for Junior. I think coming from Max and me will make it easier for him. I don't even want Bella there; Junior will pick up on everyone's emotions. Right now, it has to be all about him. Please don't fight me on this."

"Of course, you're right. I just want my grandson to know that I'm always there for him." I get up and hug her.

"He knows, Mum."

Max and Mrs. Osla are back and she seems to be okay. "All right, everyone, we need to get going. We will speak to Junior's doctor first and see what he thinks we should do. Jackie, before I forget, I called your dad and told him where we are. I didn't want him to think that we weren't grateful for his hospitality. I just told him that with such a big family, we wanted to have our own place. He said he understood and knew that it was only temporary. I let him know he can come and visit whenever he wants."

"Thank you. I know things are weird with my brother, but I don't think he would ever intentionally harm any of us."

I don't say anything. I'd rather keep my reservations about Dylan to myself. I wonder how he is going to react to the pregnancy. Between Max and me, we will keep him in line.

The drive to the clinic is quick and I can't wait to see Junior, but we need to tell Bella what's going on, and then talk to the doctor.

"Max, you and Jackie can tell Bella about the baby; we won't steal your thunder."

We head into Junior's room and find him playing the new gaming system that Tony built. Michael is on the phone, yelling in Italian, and Bella is reading. Everything seems totally normal for a change. I stand here enjoying it. Michael finally hangs up and I grab Junior away from the game.

Bella looks at Max and after everything that's gone on, I'm sure, is expecting the worse. "Max, what's wrong?"

I nudge him. I swear he better get his head out of his arse or it's going to be a long pregnancy for all of us. "I'm pregnant. This is causing Max to be a little speechless right now," Jackie saves the day again.

Bella leaps out of the chair, almost knocking him over. "Oh my

God, I'm so happy for you! When are you due?"

"I just found out; probably mid-June or early July."

"Aunt Jackie, can I have a boy cousin since I already have Antonia?"

"It's not up to me, Michael; we will have to wait and see."

"Michael, Tony gave me a list of questions for you to answer about this new gaming system, so I suggest we get started." Mrs. Osla offers up a distraction for Junior, knowing that we need to speak to his doctor. She's the best and I'd be so lost without her. She pulls out her pad and starts peppering him with questions.

"Bella, we have a meeting with Junior's doctor to discuss all of our options. Max and Jackie wanted to make sure you knew about the baby before time. If we don't get going, we will be late."

THIS IS THE FIRST time I'm actually getting to meet Dr. Campbell. He seems like nice guy and is very accommodating to the fact that we are a large family with no secrets. We explain everything to him about James and about the pregnancy. We also give him details as to everything Junior has gone through. I feel he needs to understand that Junior is a smart kid, not one you can hide stuff from. He's quiet, taking lots of notes.

"First, thank you for your honesty about everything. He has been through quite a bit in such a short time. I looked at the test results and James is an ideal candidate. I would like for him to have the shots we spoke about. They can be done locally, so he doesn't need to be here. I would much rather have him here when it comes time for the final procedure. As far as the cord blood from your pregnancy, we won't know if it's a match until after the baby is born. If you were in your last trimester I would wait, but you're only in the early stages of your pregnancy. However, it is a good backup plan, if needed. At this point, you've only done a home test I would recommend a blood test. If your hcg levels are higher than they should be for a singleton, I would suggest an ultra sound, since there's a family history of multiples. We have a great OBGYN here and I can get you the number to set up an appointment." He turns his attention back to Bella and Michael. "I think before you tell Michael about James, I should contact him and discuss the injections. The injections for peripheral blood stem cell donation, or PBSC, only take four days. So next week, at this time, it can all be over. If this was my child, I wouldn't tell him about James until the day before the procedure. What if he changes his mind about donating? There is no reason for Michael to go through any additional stress."

We all agree and I give him the contact information for James. He turns back to Jackie. "I'll have my nurse give you the number for Dr. Patel. They may just send you for blood work first." He closes his folder and gives his nurse a nod. She nods back and leaves the room. "Are there any other questions I can answer for you?" he asks.

"No, thank you, Dr. Campbell," Bella says. Just then, the nurse comes back in and hands Jackie a business card. My guess—Dr. Patel's.

"Bella, can you take care of Antonia? Raven and I are going with Jackie and Max." I don't give anyone a chance to protest, something is off with Max. He wanted this badly, so I know that's not it.

Raven pulls my hands out of my hair, and then she reaches up to kiss my cheek, "Follow my lead," she whispers.

"We will be back in a minute. I need to use the ladies room." She takes Jackie's arm and they duck into the ladies room.

"Okay, what the hell is going on? Don't tell me nothing, you've had your head up your arse all morning. I know you wanted the baby, so what the hell is it?"

"I'm scared to death that something will happen to her, the baby, or both. How am I going to make it to the end of this pregnancy without losing my mind? I want to lock her in a cage, and then a big huge bubble. What happens after the baby comes? I'm working myself into a full blown panic attack!"

"Were you this bad when Samantha was pregnant?"

"No, but now I'm wiser to the danger. And now that bastard father of ours is in the picture. Jackie is so stubborn; she won't back down from him. You know she was so quiet when we first got together, and I really thought she was more submissive."

"You need to calm down. This is not good for anyone, including Jackie. You know that I will always have your back. Together, we will get through this. You need to let me handle some of the load and just enjoy the pregnancy."

The girls are back and he seems to be a little bit better. We head toward Dr. Patel's office. Jackie is offered some paperwork to fill out; they just so happened to have a cancellation this morning. I sit here and all I can think about is how much I want another baby. I don't even realize it, but the nurse already called them back.

"Jax, I would love to know what is going through that beautiful mind of yours right now."

"Honestly, all I can think about is how much I want more babies."

She hands me a magazine, "It will happen on God's time, not yours."

Maxwell

THE NURSE TAKES US back, takes Jackie's vitals, and draws some blood. She then has her head into the bathroom to give a urine sample. So far I'm doing okay. I need to keep my head in the game. I know she's scared and I know why, but the last thing she needs is to be worrying about me. Jax is right; it's time I got my head out of my arse. Jackie comes back in followed by Dr. Patel who quickly introduces herself. She seems nice enough. I'll have Tony run a check on her, just to be safe.

"I've gone over all your paperwork and I spoke to Dr. Campbell. He informed me about your nephew and your wanting to donate your cord blood, if need be. I see from your family history that multiples run in your family. If your hcg levels are suspiciously high when we get the blood work back, we'll schedule an ultrasound to see if there is more than one. For now, we're just going to touch upon your intake and go over what you can expect during your pregnancy; answer any and all questions for you." She smiles in a reassuringly manner. I'm standing next to Jackie and I know I have her hand in a death grip. My eyes are locked on to Jackie's, I can't look anywhere else.

"Why don't you have a seat? Mr. Fleming, are you okay?" I assure her that I'm fine and she continues. It all sounds simple enough. When she's done, she tells us to relax and enjoy the pregnancy. Easy for her to say. We head out to find Raven and Jax.

"Let's go get something to eat; we have a baby to feed."

"Max, I'm warning you now, if you know what's good for you, you will behave during this pregnancy."

We head down the hall and I pray that I'm able to survive this. "Why don't we go to Junior's room and I'll have lunch brought to us. I'm not locking you away I just figured everyone can pepper you with questions in one shot."

"You're probably right. Was Mrs. Osla okay this morning?"

"Yeah, sometimes it hits her hard. Trust me she is over the moon about the pregnancy, it's just every now and again something reminds her of her loss. She will be fine."

Jax hangs up the phone and he looks at me and says nothing. "Why don't you go inside and put your feet up. I'll order the food and be right in."

"If you need alone time with Jax, you only have to ask."

I pull her into a hug and whisper in her ear. "Remember what happened the last time you were naughty."

"Yeah, well remember, the road goes both ways."

They step inside the room and I know I've turned red. "Jax, what's the problem?"

"The fucker is insisting on getting the shots done here. He wants to spend some time with Junior before the treatment."

"And if we say no?"

"What do you think? Are you prepared to take that chance?"

"I think we load up security around Junior, and then we put those new found negotiating skills of yours to work."

"I can hear them going crazy from out here, poor Jackie."

"Yeah, I better get in there and rescue her; you order lunch."

I head in the room and they have Jackie surrounded. "Okay, everyone, how about we let my beautiful wife get some air."

Raven steps out of the room, leaving me to deal with all the craziness.

Raven

I GO LOOK FOR Jax. I know something is bothering him. Sure enough, he's on the phone and pulling his hair. He hangs up and kicks the chair. He finally turns around and sees me. He opens his arms and I can't get to him fast enough.

"What's going on?"

"I ordered lunch."

"You don't kick the chair over your lunch order."

"*He* is insisting he get his shots and the treatment done here. He wants to be around Junior for more than five minutes. I told him he's not welcome here."

"So, he's not going to do anything unless he gets to spend some time with Michael?"

"Exactly. On top of that, I'm worried about Max. He's trying to be strong, but he's scared to death. I know once Dylan finds out, he will cause some sort of trouble. Why can't everyone just behave, do what they are supposed to do. You know, follow the fucking rules."

"It's not realistic to think that everyone will follow the rules, or should I say *your* rules? Max will survive as long as Jackie doesn't kill him. As far as Dylan is concerned, he's an annoyance and nothing more. If he shows up here, I will deal with him. Now, as far as James is concerned, I think the best thing to do is talk to Michael. You have always been very upfront and honest with him. Why change now? Tell him who James is. Let him know that not everyone in this world is good. Then go and make the deal with the devil. If it means that Michael will survive, then we have to do it. You're driving this bus, Jax, not James."

"I have no idea what I would ever do without you. I love you."

"Well, you will never have to find out. Lunch is here and I'm hungry. I love you. Come on, let's have lunch and then we will talk to Michael."

James

HE'S GOT THE NERVE to try and dictate to me how this is going to go down. Who the hell does he think he is? I'm the one who can save the kid, not him. I throw my glass against the wall. It shatters, sending shards everywhere. I'll let him sweat it out until it works on my time. I can't clear my calendar for at least a month, so that should make him stew.

"Sir, is everything okay?" Reynolds asks as he knocks on the other side of the door.

He opens it and sees the glass. "I'm fine. I need you to clear my schedule next month. I will be gone for a week."

"Will I be going with you, sir?"

"No, this is one trip I must make alone. He thinks he can dictate to me what I can and can't do. He has no idea who he's up against."

"Maybe, you've met your match, sir."

"Or . . . maybe he's met his."

Reynolds leaves and I'm left to figure out how I can pull this off. I'm not asking for a lot, but Jax is over the top. He doesn't want me to have any contact with any of the family members. All contact is to go through him. He is out of his mind if he thinks that's going to fly. I want back in, and this is my one shot. I'll be damned if I'm going to let him stop me.

Maxwell

One month later

JUNIOR HAS BEEN OVER the top, about the baby, since we gave him the news. I can't help but laugh when he tells Jackie that if this one is a girl, then we need to have another. so the odds will be in his favor of getting a boy out of the deal. Some days he's just like Jax. Lunch arrives and Jax ordered enough for an army. He seems off. I know something is bothering him. He puts on a brave face, but I know better. He's barely eating and he keeps checking his phone, and then he quietly slips out of the room.

"Jackie, I have some stuff to check on. Stay here, please, and keep Mum entertained."

I don't give her a chance to fight me on it, I hurry out the door and smack right into a wall of guards. He's pulling his hair and pacing. What the hell is going on now?

"Jax, what the hell is going on and why so many guards?"

At the sound of my voice, he spins around and he has a look of panic on his face.

"Nothing is going on, get back in the room . . . *now!*"

"I'm not going back in the room, and call these guards off right now, Jax!"

Suddenly, the hair on the back of my neck stands up and a tingle runs down my spine.

"Listen to me, Max, please. I need you to trust me. Go back in the room, and lock the door. For Christ sake, just trust me."

"He's here, isn't he?"

He doesn't have to answer me, I feel it. My heart and my mind collide with a one big bang. I want to kill him, break every bone in his body. Make him suffer like my family suffered. My head is telling me to listen to Jax. Junior needs this bastard to stay alive. My family needs me to keep it together. My heart is telling me something else.

"Junior needs him, Jax, remember that." I step back into the room, close and lock the door.

Jaxson

WITH MAX BACK IN the room, I inform the guards that—under no circumstances—is anyone allowed to leave the room. I head down the hall, trying to intercept him, but when I turn the corner, the elevator doors open and the fucker steps out, accompanied by only one guard. I block his path, ready to snap his neck with my bare hands, but I remind myself that Junior needs this bastard to survive.

"What are you doing here? I told you that you will not be allowed to see him until the day of the procedure."

He's got a smug look on his face; I'm trying so hard not to knock it off of him.

"You don't dictate to me what I can and cannot do. You need me, so I think I should be the one calling the shots right now."

"Don't be so sure of that. I've placed an ad for a donor, offering ten-million in cash for a match. I'm sure someone will step forward."

"What if no one does, have you thought about that? Is your hatred of me that great that you would let your nephew die?"

"I could say the same to you. You're holding a little boy's life over my head, and for what? What's your end game, *James?* What do you really want?"

"I want to make amends with everyone. I'm trying to make things right."

"Yeah, and I fell out of the turnip truck yesterday. What do we have that you want? Just tell me and I'll give it to you."

He takes a few steps forward and I can't hold back, God knows I've tried. I take one perfect swing and connect with his jaw. He goes down in a heap, his guard goes to help him up, but he shoos him away.

"Be a man, James; get up and tell me what you want."

He gets up and wipes the blood from the corner of his mouth. "I want to talk to Maxwell and An—alone. "

"Never gonna happen. You nearly destroyed Max. I will never let you anywhere near him again. What could you possibly want with my mother? You've already made her feel like a fool."

"An and I have unfinished business. I assure you that I won't hurt her."

"You have no business with her. Dr. Campbell is aware that you are on the premises and is preparing your shot. You can stay in town for the next four days. When the Doctor says you're ready for the procedure, you will meet Junior. That's what I'm offering—take it or leave it."

"I'm not doing anything until my needs are met, so you take it or leave it."

I take out my phone and call Mrs. Osla. "I need you to change the ad you did for me. Change the amount from ten-million to fifty-million cash. I also want commercials run on every network and cable channel. Call Matthew to make sure everything can be set up legally outside of the US."

I hang up and grab him around the neck. His bodyguard attempts to pull me off, except Mick has stepped up next to me and put a gun to the back of the guard's head. "Listen up, *James,* my terms—*not* yours—so you can take it or leave it."

"You won't let your guard shoot him."

Before I can answer, Mick laughs. "I had orders to shoot Max and he's my friend, I could care less about this garbage."

I let go and turn to Mick, "Let him go, for now. Come on, I'm sure everyone is wondering where we are."

"This isn't over, Jax! I will get to them and you can't stop me!" James yells, following after me.

We turn the corner and there is a wall of fifteen guards with guns drawn. Max knew and told them to step up. I turn around and James is stunned into silence.

"I told you, James, don't fuck with me or my family ever again. Let me know what you decide."

Mick and I walk away, leaving James there with the guards, who are ready to take action, if needed.

I head into Junior's room, ready to do some damage control. Everyone is very quiet. Junior is playing a game with his headset on. My mum finally breaks the silence. "What did he want?"

"I can't believe anything he said, so I have no idea. He claims he wants to make amends. He wanted to talk to you and Max. He said he had unfinished business. There's nothing he could say that would make up for all the destruction he has left in his wake."

"What about my grandson? If James doesn't donate, then what?"

"I'm looking at other options, trying to offer a large cash payment for a match."

"Is that even legal?"

"As of 2011, it is legal in the US. Even though we are in Switzerland, there are always ways around it. I've already put Matthew on it."

"Don't you think this is ridiculous? I can have a conversation with him as long as Max is left out of it. You can negotiate that, can't you?"

"Why would I subject you to that?"

There's a knock on the door that makes everyone jump. Mick checks and it's Dr. Campbell.

"Sorry about the all the guards, Dr. Campbell, I needed to up security."

"I understand, however, could you have them be a little bit more discreet. Some of the other patients are nervous. I also wanted to let you know that I just administered James's first shot. He requested to stay in the hospital for the four days. I put him in our facility for plastic surgery. It's the furthest building from Michael's room. Here are the details."

I take the paper and hand it to Mick; I don't need Max seeing it. "Thank you for all of your understanding."

"Trust me, I have some family members I could do without. I would casually start bringing up to Michael who this man is and his purpose here. If you would like, I can be there to explain the procedure."

"Thank you. If I need you to explain anything, I will let you know."

He leaves and my head is pounding. I just have to keep reminding myself the end is in sight. I grab a bottle of water and decide to go for walk; I need to clear my head. Max stops me before I can make it out the door.

"We need to talk, Jax. Let's go for that walk."

"Do you promise to behave?"

He rolls his eyes and we head out the door.

"Jax, come with me. There's a quiet solarium just off of the cafe that Bella and I went to yesterday; we can talk there."

I motion Mick to come with us. "What is it that you want to know?"

"What went down, give me details."

"You heard what I told Mum, that's it." He wants details and I'm not ready to share that with him.

"Jax, you are by far the worst liar I have ever met in my life. What don't you want me to know? Look if you don't tell me I'll get it out of Mick."

"Hey, don't bring me into this. Just tell him, Jax."

"He said he had unfinished business with Mum."

"What the hell does that mean?"

"I don't know, and I don't know how to ask her."

"I think I might have an idea."

Max and I both turn to Mick at the same time, "You do?"

"Remember, I'm not emotionally invested like you both are. I was thinking back to the meeting in Capri and then I played the recording over and over again. James said that Miguel was upset that James left An the picture and the trinkets. He mentioned them twice. Max, where is everything?"

"The jewels are locked up in a safe deposit box at The Royal Bank of Scotland and the picture is in a drop box on my computer."

"When you aged the picture, I know you focused in on James and Miguel. What about the other two men, did you find out who they were?"

"Mick, you saw me that day. The only thing I could focus on was Miguel, the man whose gang killed my family."

Max closes his eyes, trying to remember the faces, I'm sure. "That's my leverage. I knew if I dug deep enough, something would come to the surface. I think the jewelry is just gravy for him, it's the picture. Remember he said that he convinced Miguel that he destroyed the picture. Why go through all of that, if the picture was no big deal? He has unfinished business with Mum; he wants that picture. Saying that he wanted to talk to you is just smoke in mirrors. A distraction for Mum; play on her heart strings. Come on, I've got a plan."

We race back to Junior's room so I can get to the computer. "Max, I need you to pull up that picture. Print out the original and the aged one. Mick, you and I are going to see James. We will take two extra guards with us and leave the rest here."

I look over at Raven and I know she's worried. I need to reassure her that everything will be fine. I walk up to her, her eyes locked on mine the whole time.

"Raven, I assure you that I will be fine. I'm going to have a conversation with James, that's all. I promise, I will be back shortly." I kiss her trembling lips and then whisper, "Please keep it together for the rest of the family. I need you, sweetheart."

"More, Jax."

I grab the picture as Mick and I race out the door. "Okay, Mick, let's get this over with. Just follow my lead."

We get to his room and there are two guards stationed outside his door. "They are ours; I had them keep a watch on him."

I push open the door and James is on the phone. He sees it's me and quickly hangs up.

"I stayed and got the shot, Jax. Now, when can I see everyone?"

I take out the pictures and throw them in front of him. "Is this what you want, these and those trinkets, as you call them?"

"Where's the original?"

"Why is this picture so important to you? Who are the other two men? I'm sure if I put the picture in all the newspapers and all over social media, I could find out rather quickly."

"You can't do that . . . not if you value your mother's life."

I freeze and Mick takes a step forward, I put my hand out, stopping him. "What does this picture have to do with my mother?"

"The man at the end of the picture is Valad Yager, the head of a major Russian Cartel. Many governments want him dead. He has information that could destroy many secret government operations. He worked both sides of the fence for years. That picture is the only known picture of him in existence. Having that picture puts An in a world of danger. I always operated very clean; flying just under the radar. But then Max started digging up the past. The guy next to me in the picture, Oliver Davis, became Miguel's right hand man. When Miguel died, he told the Valad about the picture. He knew An took the picture that day, but like Miguel, he thought it was destroyed. I loved your mother; I just wasn't in love with her. I never wanted any harm to come to her. Even now, I'm only trying to protect her."

"Were you ever in love with anyone other than yourself?"

"Yes, I was in love with Cindy. When I found out what happened to her, I realized the best thing for everyone was to walk away and never look back."

"Here's what's going to happen. You will stay in this room for the next four days. You will get the shots and then you will donate your stem cells. You will never meet Junior. You will never get to talk to Max or my mum. When the donation is complete, you will get the original photo. You will make it known to all interested parties that you are in possession of the picture, and that you always were. If anything were to happen to anyone in my family, the copies that I have will go public, along with all the details of your life."

"And if I don't go along with your plan?"

"Oh, I always have an alternate plan, James. You don't become one of the richest, most powerful men in the world by resting on one's laurels. I have the ability to keep my family tucked away someplace very safe and very quiet, while I release the photo and the details. If all else fails, I will have Mick shoot you in the balls, that is . . . if he can even find them."

"You have a deal. Just one thing, Jax. You might be more like me than you're willing to admit."

I don't even dignify that with an answer. Mick and I leave and head back to Junior's room.

We walk in the room and everyone stops what they are doing, all eyes on us. "It's done. Junior gets what he needs and no one has to see James ever again."

Bella throws her arms around me, and cries hysterically. "Shh, come on, sis, it's no big deal. Please let it go, for everyone's sake."

I look up and see Raven wipe away a tear and then I hear the most beautiful sound in the world; Antonia cooing.

I can't catch my breath; she's on the floor with Junior, playing with her toy. It almost sounds like she is singing to her toy.

"Oh, Raven, I'm telling you, she's a genius. Three months old and she's already singing."

"You're probably right. How about we go home and continue that little project we started, especially since this one turned out so well."

"I'm more than ready, sweetheart."

Chapter Twenty-Nine

Jaxson

I THOUGHT TODAY WOULD never get here. It's been a long time coming. Junior finally gets the stem cells from James and then he is out of our lives. Raven and I took a little day trip yesterday to the castle in Scotland. I wanted to make sure I had that picture in hand. I put it in the pouch with the trinkets. After talking with Max and Matthew, we decided it was best to give James everything. Keeping the jewels, or even turning them in, would open up a whole new can of worms. I need to keep my mum permanently out of this mess and although it slays me to give that bastard anything, this is the safest way to do that. It was good to go back home for the day and I can't wait till the day we can stay forever.

"Raven, will you please hurry up! I swear, I don't know what you do in the morning that takes so long."

She comes strolling in the bedroom wearing a pair of tight jeans, her bra, with Antonia in her arms. "Umm, sweetheart, I think you forgot your shirt."

"I didn't forget my shirt. I just couldn't dodge your daughter's spit up fast enough. You should try it sometime, dear."

"Why don't I take her while you finish getting ready?"

"We will meet you downstairs."

I take Antonia and go in search of Max. I know today will be another hard day for him. I thank Jackie for keeping him together.

I find Max in the kitchen, getting a cup of coffee, "Hey, I'll take one of those, too."

He passes me my coffee and takes Antonia. "Uncle Max is the best in the world. Let's practice that, my beautiful niece," Max replies to my daughter's cooing.

"Quit filling her head, mate. How's Jackie feeling?"

"Amazing, no sickness at all, but she does get tired rather quickly."

"I'm so ready for today to be over. I hope we never have to deal with him again."

"Secrets always seem to have a way of coming out. I only hope that these can stay buried forever."

"I'm happy that we never had to tell Junior any of it."

"I'm glad that Michael decided to put off the meeting with his parents until after this treatment. The less stress, the better."

"Did you run a check on Dr. Patel? Will you and Jackie keep her?"

"I had Tony run the check. Her credentials are top notch and Jackie is comfortable with her. We have an appointment later today to find out the results of the blood work."

Antonia takes my spoon and keeps banging on the table. "I think my daughter is very musically talented."

I hear that giggle that I love so much and I know Raven is behind me. "Everyone is ready to go. You left your phone upstairs. Michael called, he's nervous about today. I told him we will be there shortly."

"I don't know what to say to him. I mean, I'm probably more nervous than he is."

"Come on, guys, Jackie is going to talk to Michael about her experience with donating. That should ease some of his fears."

As we head out to the clinic, I can only focus on one thing: today is my last confrontation with James.

Junior

I TRY PLAYING MY new game, but I can't concentrate on anything. Dr. Campbell explained what will happen and I know he was trying to make it seem like no big deal. It's not him getting the needles, so what does he care? Aunt Raven said they would have been here sooner but Antonia got her good with spit up. Even though she's a girl, she makes me laugh. I wanted to go exploring, but it's kind of hard to do with so many guards watching my every move. I asked Dr. Campbell about the person that is donating their stem cells for me, but he gave me some story about confidentiality. That's okay, I know how to get around that; I have a plan. I have to go for an X-ray this morning, that's when I will put my plan in motion. The nurse is here to take me with her stupid wheelchair. Rules, yeah, we'll see about that.

"Good morning, Michael, today's a big day for you. My name is Sophia and I'm going to take you to X-ray and then we will come back here."

I hop in the chair and away we go, with my guards behind us. The guards can't go in the X-ray room, they have to wait outside. That's when I will have my chance. "Sophia, can I ask you a question?"

"Sure, what's up?"

"Dr. Campbell told me what room my donor is in, but I got lost trying to find it. I thought it was close to my room. I wanted to thank him again Do you know where it is?"

She pulls out my chart, "No he's in the plastic surgery wing, not sure why, but it's room 306. That building is two away from this one. We can take the bridgeway, do you want me to show you?"

Crap, that would ruin my plan. I'll never get the guards to go along with that. "No, that's okay. I'm sure I can find it. Thanks."

"Okay, well, you know the routine, wait here while I get the doctor to look at these."

Game on. She leaves and I sneak out the back way. I've been here enough times that I know every exit out of here. I find the bridgeway and head over to the plastic surgery wing. This was not as hard as I thought, until I get to the room and see two guards by the door. Geez, who the heck is this guy that there are guards everywhere? *I need a distraction.* I pull the fire alarm. I'm going to get in so much trouble for this one. Everyone begins racing around, trying to get the patients out. The guards go into room 306, so I run into the room next door. The room is empty and dark, I can wait it out. I look at the clock on the wall, and now I know I'm in trouble. Everyone is probably here and with the alarms going off, my uncles will freak out. I can't wait any longer. I have to just go in there. I peak out and the guards are at the nurse's station. I take my only shot and slip into room 306, locking the door behind me. I need to know who is in here and what the big secret is.

Jaxson

WE PULL UP TO the clinic and alarms are going off. Patients are being brought out of all the exits. My heart is in my throat as I see Bella frantically yelling for Junior. I yell at Mick to keep everyone in the car as Max and I race toward Bella.

"Where's Junior? What's going on?"

"He went for an X-ray, and then the alarms went off. I can't find him. Please find him."

"Get in the car with Mum and don't leave. Michael, come with us."

"I tried back searching from X-ray, but it's sheer chaos."

"Max, maybe you should wait in Junior's room in case he comes back there." I have a good idea what happened here and I need to keep Max away. He's not even listening to me, he's in his zone and running toward the bridgeway. God help us all if Max gets his hands on James. He's picking up speed; Michael and I can barely keep up with him. We get to the room and the guards are banging on the door. Max begins kicking the door—nothing. I'm yelling for Junior to unlock the door. I hear a loud crash. When I turn around, I see Max has thrown a chair at the window and is climbing outside onto the ledge! "Michael, get the key from the nurses station, I need to follow him!"

I look out and it's a three story drop. Max has a grip on a drain pipe as he's kicking in the window. I've never seen him like this—ever! He jumps into the room and I'm right behind him. The door swings open and Michael comes racing in. Max grabs Junior and pulls him into his arms.

"What the hell were you thinking?"

"Uncle Max, I'm sorry. I needed to know why everyone was keeping secrets from me. I wanted to know what the big deal was about this guy. I wanted to thank him."

"Did he touch you? Did he hurt you? What did he tell you?"

"Uncle Max, he said he's a family friend, that's it. What's going on?"

"Nothing. Everything is fine. Go with your father back to your room, your mum is worried sick."

"That's it? You came racing in here, like something out of movie, and all you can tell me is go back to my room? Why is his last name the same as Uncle Jax and Grams?"

Max looks at me and then closes his eyes. "Uncle Jax, you never lie to me. Are you going to tell me what's going on?"

"You're right, Junior, I never lie to you. Just because you are related to someone, doesn't mean that they should be a part of your life. This man is our father, your grandfather. He is not a parent, he never was. A father . . . he's the man that raises and loves you. He's there for you every day through the good times and the bad. This man has done nothing but cause problems."

"If he's such a bad person, then why do you want me to get his stem cells?"

"Because I love you more than life itself and if it means that I have to make a deal with him, I will."

Junior has tears in his eyes, trying to be brave. He walks up to James and extends his hand, and I have to hold Max back. "Mr. Phillips, thank you for your donation. You might not be a good person, but you gave me the best family."

Michael bends down and Junior climbs on his back. "We need to go; you have a lot of explaining and apologizing to do."

"Come on, Max, let's go." He's not moving, frozen in place, his eyes tightly shut.

When Junior is out of the room, James turns to me. "At least my grandson has manners."

Why can't he just *shut the fuck up?* Max finally opens his eyes and they are very dark. I know I don't have a shot at talking him down.

"What the *fuck* do you know about manners? You're a pathetic excuse for a man. You could have stopped my family from being killed that day and you didn't. How do you live with yourself?"

"I tried to get there in time, but I couldn't."

"All you had to do was make one phone call—that's it—and they never would have been in the park that day! You knew how to get a hold of me, yet you chose to do *nothing!* Don't think that you will get any redemption for what you're doing here today. You're still going to rot in hell."

"I understand that you've found another family to move on with, how does that feel, son?"

The words are barely out of his mouth and Max has him up against the wall with his hands around his throat. Does this guy have a death wish?

"Max, let him go." He doesn't hear me, or . . . he just doesn't care.

"You come anywhere near my family and you will never live to see the light of day again. You will learn what hell on earth is all about." He lets go and James falls to the floor.

"I'm done here, Jax, let's go."

I lift James off the floor, reach back, and punch him in the face. Damn, that felt good. He's lucky that's all he's getting.

"When you are finished here, there will be an envelope waiting for you with the picture and the stolen jewels. I never want to see or hear from you again."

I instruct the guards to make sure he doesn't leave this room until the nurse comes to take him. Max and I head back to Junior's room.

"I can't believe you broke the window and climbed right out there." He's not saying anything. "I can't believe you hung on a drain pipe and kicked in the other window." Still nothing. "Max, it's over, we never have to see or hear from him again. No more secrets, all the lies he told have been shattered like that broken glass. Which, by the way, you're paying for, not me."

"Thanks, Jax."

"For what?"

"For covering my arse, and knowing how to pull me back to the present."

"That's what brothers do."

"Jax, one more thing . . . you can't run for shit."

I laugh, knowing Max is back and we will be okay. We get into the room and Dr. Campbell is there with some of the nursing staff. Junior is offering up his heartfelt apology. The kid is good, by the time he's done, the nurses are in tears.

I lean into Max and whisper, "That kid is going to go far in life."

"Yeah, mate, he's a mini version of you; wouldn't expect anything less."

Everyone is very quiet as the nurses prep Junior for the procedure. That is, until, my daughter begins banging her spoon singing; music to my ears.

THE PROCEDURE DIDN'T TAKE as long as expected and Dr. Campbell thought it went well. If there is no fever, he can go home in a few days. The majority of his treatments can be done on an outpatient basis. James has been released and Mick personally put him on the plane bound for Capri.

I look around the room and I feel relief. Everyone is doing mundane normal stuff and it feels wonderful. My daughter is fast asleep, clutching her spoon. I don't think I will be getting that away from her anytime soon. Raven is curled into my side and I'm twirling her hair.

She looks up at me with those beautiful violets. "Penny for your thoughts, Jax."

"I'm happy that everything turned out okay. I'm sad that so many lives were lost to get us to this point. I'm hopeful for the future of this family. I've decided I want to do that foster care program we talked about. Even if we don't have any more children of our own, I will always be helping children; they are the future. I don't want to work, making millions anymore. I want to only do philanthropist work. We will always have more than enough and, if I learned anything this past year, it's that there really is no luggage rack on the hearse. I want to watch our family grow and see what they will achieve. I want to spend the rest of my days, loving you, like the line in our favorite Snow Patrol song, "Chasing Cars," 'Would you lie with me and just forget the world?'"

"Always, Jax. There's just one thing I have to ask you. How do you feel about even numbers?"

She has a huge smile as I pull her hand from her ear and kiss the inside of her wrist, just like I did so long ago, and I feel that familiar shiver run through her. "Sweetheart, are you?"

She giggles, "I am."

Epilogue

Twelve years Later

Jaxson

I AM SO NERVOUS and yet very excited. Today is Junior's college graduation. There was a time, for a quick second, I thought we would never see this day. I could never be more proud of him than I am today. Even after all the interruptions in his education, he still managed to graduate top of his class. He has decided to go to The University of Liverpool for his Master's Degree in Geotechnical Engineering. I'm happy that he found his niche, doing something that makes a difference. He asked to speak with me alone today, before the ceremony. He probably wants me to run interference for him with his mum. Lord knows Bella can be a handful.

Junior had so much fun showing his cousins all the different tunnels he found. He studied the blueprints Max gave him and explored each one of them. Every new tunnel, he etched Rose's name on the wall with the date. It's because of her that he's here today, and he never forgets it. Since Junior has been away at school, Antonia thinks she can run circles around everyone else. The triplets have other ideas.

They found out she was having triplets a few months after

Junior's treatment. You could have heard Jackie yelling at Max three countries over. Something about titanium sperm and a monster cock. Max barely survived the delivery but God only knows how he's going to survive the teenage years. The last part of Jackie's pregnancy, she was on complete bed rest. Raven was at the start of her last trimester and decided she would be a great best friend and stay in bed with her. I think it was their plan all along to have Max and me take care of them and their crazy cravings. Max had it worse than me. Raven craved bubble gum and oranges. Jackie had to have dark chocolate covered graham crackers from a little shop in Cary, North Carolina, called: Chocolate Smiles. The girls found this shop when we went to scatter Rose's ashes. It was such a somber day, but Rose left very detailed instructions. Raven picked a beautiful song by Beyoncé called "I Was Here" to play, while we scattered her ashes. She talked about the chocolates that Antonio had gotten her on the day he proposed. After that, Max arranged for Lissah, the sales lady, to FedEx chocolates every week.

Jackie didn't make the full nine months. She tried and fought to keep them safely inside of her for as long as possible. When there was no more room for them to grow, Dr. Patel had to do a c-section. Samuel, Jeffery, and then little Grace. It's Grace that gives Max the most trouble. She is forever pushing him to his limit. She will either keep him young or put him in an early grave. Hell, she's even got Mrs. Osla wrapped around her finger.

Raven, on the other hand, went full term. We even made it to the hospital, well, almost. We, at least, made it to the parking lot. My beautiful daughter, Gabriella Rose, made her appearance in the back seat of Mick's brand new Rover. He only had the car for three days—quite the christening.

Raven's idea to revamp the foster care program has taken off. She's even gotten some top companies around the world to donate. Jackie maintains her riding academy with the help of the foster children. A few of the kids even ended up in veterinarian school. All in all, it's been a huge success.

The knocking on my office door pulls me out of my thoughts. It's Junior, and he's not alone. He's only been home a few times this past year, and the beautiful, young lady with him explains a lot.

"Uncle Jax, I wanted to introduce you to my girlfriend, Heather Davis."

"Hello, please, have a seat. Why so formal, Junior?"

"This is important and I don't want to mess it up. Heather and I want to get married. I'm afraid when I tell Mum, she will go through the roof."

"You want me to negotiate for you?"

"Oh God, no, Uncle Jax—I've seen how you negotiate. I just need you to keep her calm, and Grams, too."

"Why the rush to get married? You're not even finished with your studies." I don't like the direction this conversation is headed.

"I'm not pregnant, sir, if that's what you're thinking."

"I'm not sure what to think, and please don't call me sir. Jax is fine. So, why the rush?"

"We're not rushing. We know this is the next step we want to take in life. I love Heather and she is willing to transfer to Liverpool to finish her Master's Degree in Education."

What is it with this family and teachers? "I'll make you a deal. Can you please give me twenty-four hours to digest all of this?"

He reaches into his pocket and hands me some papers. "I know this is why you want twenty-four hours."

I look down and see that it is the background check on Heather Davis.

"Sir, I mean . . . Jax, I'm willing to sign a prenup, and so is Michael."

Before I can say another word, Raven comes barreling through the door. "Jax, you better get downstairs and do something about your daughter. Oh, Michael, you're early, and you brought your friend, Heather. So nice to finally meet you."

"What has Antonia done now?"

"She and Grace found the keys to Michael's golf cart and they are racing around in it."

"Where the hell is Max?"

"Trying to catch them, now go!"

I get halfway down the hall when it hits me—she knew.

Raven

"MICHAEL, ANY MINUTE NOW, it will hit him that I knew about Heather. Did you give him the papers?"

"Yeah, and we told him about prenups."

"Give him time to digest it, and in the meantime, I can work on him."

"I hope you're right about this. I still have to get this past Heather's father. I'm hoping with everyone on board, it will make it a little easier."

Jax comes back into the room but before he can say one word, I hug Michael and Heather. "All your uncle ever wanted was for you to be happy. I'm sure when he sees how much you love each other, he will be reminded of what love can do."

I glance up at Jax and he's leaning against the door frame with that crooked smirk I love so much. Even after all these years, it always feels like the first time with him.

"Oh, look whose back."

"Uncle Jax, I'm going to introduce Heather to the rest of the family. I'll meet you downstairs." Poor Michael, he can't get away fast enough.

"So, sweetheart, how long have you known about Heather?"

"For a little bit. Lighten up, Jax, he came to you first. He didn't have to; he's twenty-one, he could have just gotten married. They are trying to be responsible and do the right thing."

"I need to know more about her and her family before I make any kind of decision."

"Her father owns the oldest and largest pharmaceutical company in Switzerland. She is an only child; her mother died from breast cancer when she was eleven. Her father never remarried. She is studying to be a special education teacher. I've been married to you long enough, Jax, I knew to have her checked out. Now, did you get a handle on your daughter?"

"Why is it when she's doing something wrong, she's my daughter?"

"Because that's when the Jaxson in her comes out."

"Come on, we have to go, the graduation ceremony will be starting soon."

WE ALL PILE INTO the auditorium, ready for the next milestone in this family. Jackie and I have to separate Antonia and Grace. "You know they are a younger version of us."

"Yeah, except I don't think this world is ready for them. What happened when Michael told Jax?"

"Let's just say he took it about the same way he did when Mick and An told him they went to the justice of the peace."

"Oh, well, did Michael give him the background report?"

"Yes, and it helped. I told him all about Heather's family. He agreed to at least look into them before he said no. I made sure I reminded Jax about how powerful love can be. That might work in Michael's favor."

"Did you talk to Jax about that school that Gabriella wants to go to?"

"Not yet. I can only hit him with one thing at a time. You know anything more and he'll go crazy. He already told Antonia she can't date until she's eighteen. Can you imagine what he will do when I tell him Gabriella wants to go to boarding school?"

"Grace wanted to go to a sleepover and after running a check on the family, Max said no. Apparently, the father has outstanding parking tickets."

The ceremony starts and of course, with a last name like Vizzano, Michael is always toward the end. When the Chancellor calls him to accept his diploma, he is also given a special humanitarian award for his dedication and service to others. The Chancellor talks about how Michael goes to the children's hospital once a week to cheer up the kids. He talks to the children about courage and about his journey. Knowing how far this boy has come and all that he's been through, everyone stands and cheers him on. There is not a dry eye in the house. I'm so proud of the man he has grown to be and knowing that I might have helped in that process is very humbling.

Through all my tears and all the heartache I have survived, some things have always remained constant: true love, respect, and honesty. Without that, no relationship could ever survive. I will love Jax with all that I am and all that I will ever be. He is my end all.

Violet to Blues
The end . . .

Uniquely Mine

A Fitzy Series

Chapter One

Mark Chambers

WOMEN MAKE IT SO easy for me. They think I'm broken and want to fix me. I let them try, but I'm not broken, so there is no fix for me. I have a need that only they can fill. I need to feel my hands around their throat, feel their bodies come to life with every smack on their ass. Every gasping breath makes my cock harder. If I close my eyes I can feel each pulse of my blood surging forward. Women see me as the bad boy. The boy that needs to be rescued. They are the ones that need to be rescued, rescued from me; this one tonight is no different. New York, just another city filled with desperate woman. It never ceases to amaze me how woman are so nurturing. Why do they see me as a challenge, like a little boy in need of a bandage? I'm beyond redemption, beyond repair and that suits me just fine.

Chicago, Los Angeles, they were all the same. A big city filled with lonely hearts waiting for their prince charming to come. Only to find out I'm not their dream come true, I'm their worst nightmare come to life. I've been watching this one for a couple of days. I first spotted her coming out of a gym in Chelsea. My mind wanders back to the day I met her. I pretended to be lost and she was more than happy to help me find my way. I had to go right past her place, so she offered to share a cab. Right about now she's probably regretting that decision. In a matter of ten minutes I knew where she lived. By the time she left that cab I had her number in my phone. So easy, it's laughable.

I look down at her bulging eyes, I whisper in her ear. "Do you fear me yet? Like the fear of stepping into that dark room and peeking under the bed."

I tighten my hands around her neck and with each squeeze my cock gets harder. She needs to feel what it's like to be on the brink of death and then come back over and over again. It's a rush that she will never experience again. It won't be much longer; I have to time it perfectly. The ultimate rush, followed by my release, which can only happen just as she is about to pass out. It's all in the timing it has to be perfect. One hand around her throat and one hand pumping my cock. This is the hardest part; I feel the blood racing through my veins. She's there; I release my grip and give her the air she is craving. She gasps, and then I pound my cock into her and squeeze my long fingers around her throat yet again. Even with her hands tied behind her back, this one is hardly putting up a fight. I thought she had more in her, more of a need to live. She hasn't realized yet that this is the end of the line. Her eyes are beginning to budge and roll back, I know she will pass out. That's my cue, my blood is hot and racing through me. Everything is heading to the finish line. I come and my entire body feels like it's burning, a burn I can only get right before I kill her. She's not dead, only passed out. Unlike television, it takes a long time to strangle someone. They pass out at least five minutes before they die. I don't have the time to wait around. I snap her neck. Let's face it; it's the humane thing to do.

Now comes the clean up, making sure I leave no trace of me behind. Except of course the *rose.* I leave it so I can claim the kill as my own. *Uniquely mine,* the thought makes me hard again but I have no time for that. I place the collar around her neck and stroke her beautiful cheek. I wish I could have kept her a little longer. I look around the room, making sure every last trace that I've ever been here is gone. Oh how I love the smell of bleach. So crisp and refreshing, like the dawn of a new day. I wonder how long before the city starts to panic? How long before they connect the dots? I take one last walk around before locking the door behind me, after all I wouldn't want anyone to break in and contaminate a perfect crime scene.

* * *

Fitz

I'M THE DEFENDER OF those who can't defend themselves. I'm jaded by humanity. The humanity that I see on a daily basis. I try to be the best I can be, but sometimes it's hard. Most days I look in the mirror and I'm okay with the guy looking back at me. I wonder how many people in the world can say the same. Unfortunately today is not one of those days. Today I've been called to the scene of yet another murder. The third one this month, the pattern has formed and that's why I'm here. My name is Fitzgerald S. Rodriguez. I'm a detective with a special unit dedicated to the investigation of Serial killers. I'm based out of the Sixty-first precinct in Brooklyn New York, but I go where I'm needed. Lately it seems that there is never a down time.

I get to the scene and my captain is already waiting. I haven't even finished my first cup of coffee and he's already yelling. Why can't he just shut the fuck up for five minutes? All the yelling in the world will not make my brain move any faster. Captain Jack Hart is tall, like basketball player tall yet he has two left feet. He's barking orders, to anyone who will listen, that is until he sees me. There is no avoiding him at this point. I just cleared a major case and should be celebrating but not in this city. There is never a time for celebrating, hell I'm supposed to have two weeks off between cases and I haven't even gotten twenty-four hours. "Hey, captain, do we know a time of death yet?"

Hart's jaw ticks when he's stressed and lately that's all the time. "Yeah, Fitz, this one is fresh, only a few hours old so I'm hoping we can get something more from her, maybe he left something behind. Her name is Sophie Hall and, Fitz, she's one of us."

I'm about to enter the scene, but his words stop me dead in my tracks. "A cop?"

"She was a data analyst at One Police Plaza. I explained to the chief medical examiner about the other two and he has agreed to let Gail run lead on this. She's inside waiting for you."

I put on protective booties and gloves before I head into yet another crime scene. The crime scene unit is just finishing up and Gail O'Connor the coroner for Kings County is waiting to talk to me before she leaves. Gail and I have worked together before so she knows I like to look. Yeah she calls me a creeper, but I have a way of getting inside the killers head, so no one ever tries to stop me. I like to walk the scene in silence absorbing all the little details and the smells. No forced entry, keys are on a hook by the front door. No pets to contaminate the scene. Very clean, possibly a little OCD. I head over to the body and Gail is all packed up and waiting for me.

"Talk to me Gail, what's different?"

She hesitates for only a second. "How do you know me so well?"

I smile always trying to charm her, but it never works. "It's what I do. What's got you biting the inside of your cheek?"

She instantly releases it. "You know I'm not going to say anything until I get her back to the lab, but, Fitz, look how clean everything is. It's like he feels so confident that he's taking even more time cleaning the scene and not just the body. Look around, nothing is out of place, at least from what I can tell." She waves her hand around the room trying to force her point. "Hell there isn't even a damn dust bunny. Who doesn't have a dust bunny?"

I look down at the victim and I'm taken back by how beautiful and young she is. "Are you done with her?"

"Yes, but make it quick I want to get her back to the lab while she's fresh."

I squat down and smell, the smell of bleach is over powering. "He bleached everything?"

"Yes, and it seems he even brushed her teeth with it, but CSU couldn't find a toothbrush. Could it be his trophy?"

I shrug my shoulders, "I've seen stranger things, never know what the trigger is for these guys. Tell me the truth, Gail, did you take a sniff?"

Her face flushes even though she knows I'm playing with her, trying to lighten the mood. "Yes, Fitz, I'm getting as bad as you."

"I keep telling you, Gail, become one with the crime scene."

She rolls her eyes. "What are you some kind of Zen Master today?"

I'm no longer squatting. I'm on my hands and knees, my face inches from her neck. "I see she has a collar around her neck same as the others, is the rose in place?"

"Yes, it's one of the first things I checked. And, Fitz, if you put your face there to look I will smack you."I look up and she has her hand out ready to smack me. "All right I'll finish up here and meet you back at the lab. I know you're eager to get started on this one."

I get up and wave to the tech, letting him know that I'm done with the body.

"Fitz, how about I call you when I'm ready to deliver? The pressure of knowing you're outside my door is not going to push the results through any faster."

"Yeah, yeah I get it." I wave to her as I begin to methodically work my way around the apartment. The apartment is a junior studio, which is bigger than a standard studio yet smaller than a one bedroom. By New York City standards this one is pretty large. It's a walk-up, three floors with only two apartments on each floor. The first floor is a cafe that is only open for breakfast and lunch they close at two p.m. They might be of some help depending upon what time they come in to prep. This place is directly across the street from the United Nations building. I'll make sure Hart pulls footage from all available cameras. Back to the task at hand, Sophia has her bed in the small alcove and some beads hanging in the doorway. They seem to act as some sort of divider. I sniff the wall next to the divider and smell bleach. Christ he even washed the walls. I go to the other side and sniff, no bleach. I race outside and catch Gail before she pulls away.

"Hey, did CSU take pictures of the walls? Specifically the doorway leading into the alcove?"

" I know they did a scan with the ScanStation but I'm not sure if they took actual photos of the walls, why?"

"Only one wall smells of bleach, what do you want to bet he had her up against that wall?"

She puts the car in park and reaches in the back seat pulling out a camera. "I always keep one with me, now show me what you're talking about."

Gail takes pictures of both walls while talking under her breath, which I'm sure, is about me. "You're like a bloodhound Fitz, you know that right?"

"I've been called worse. Don't suppose you want to leave me that camera?"

"You know I can't, if you find something use your phone. Chances are CSU already got these shots. Now can I please get to my lab?"

I shoo her away and go back to what I was doing. Sophia's desk pulls down from the wall. CSU already bagged her laptop, phone and tablet. She has very few personal pictures around, except for her graduation picture from the academy, class of 2011. I snap a picture of it and pull out a pad from my breast pocket to make notes, yeah I'm old school. I pull a pen off of the desk and begin to draw the wall and where Sophia was found. If he killed her up against the wall, why not leave her there and walk out? Why stage the scene? What is he showing me? I twirl the pen around my fingers as I'm running everything through my mind. The name on the pen hits me like a brick between my eyes. *Mystik* . . . oh fuck no! Mystik is a high end BDSM club own by my best friend. I need to get there right now, before anyone else gets wind of this. Coincidence maybe if I believed in coincidences.

Acknowledgements

I am so blessed to have a supportive family. Knowing they are always there to catch me, no matter what—priceless.

The following ladies have each played some part in keeping me from going too far over the edge. Claire Allmendinger, Tracy Beavers, Summer Clark, Crazy Daisy, Lisa Dowd, Janett Gomez, Jeneane Johnston, Melissa Kulis, Roseanne Lavin, Camille Novelli, Loraine Oliver, Felicia Rodriguez, Imy Santiago, Wendy Shatwell, Iris Taveras, Kizzy Williams, Sarah Williams, Shell (Purple Pimper) Williams. Thank you for your continued support and occasional arse kicking.

Robin Harper, You get me and what is in my head. This is very scary.

Jacquelyn Ayres, You make me laugh. You piss me off. You make me think for myself. You are wonder woman in yoga pants.

Stacey Blake, Your beautiful work brings my words to life.

Rick and Leif, you are more than I ever dreamed possible in my lifetime. Always and forever more.

A Little More

Thank you to the wonderful readers who came and fell in love with The Unraveled Trilogy. I know it has been a crazy ride for all of us. I laughed, cried, and yelled right along with you. Is it the end? Just like in life, sweetheart, never say never. May your days be filled with Nutella, espresso, and a love so intense, it rocks you to your core.

About the Author

Theresa Sederholt was born and raised in Brooklyn New York. She is a graduate of Campbell University in North Carolina, with a degree in Criminal Justice. Theresa now calls North Carolina home, with her husband, a professional chef, and her two dogs.

Experiencing life first hand is what she does best. Believing she can do anything has put her in many crazy situations. Whether it's babysitting a pig farm or cutting the top off of a mini truck; nothing is ever out of reach. Her list is endless, A to Z.

As a flight attendant (there's that list again), she would make up stories about all of her passengers as they came and went. It seemed only natural to put pen to paper and see where these characters led her. What started out as a single woman, having a cup of coffee—trying to make it through life—grew into a complex story of romance, mystery, and murder. *The Unraveled Trilogy* was born.

Theresa's beliefs are pretty simple. There isn't a luggage rack on the hearse, and give a girl Nutella and espresso and she can change the world.

Theresa enjoys connecting with her fans. She can always be reached through her website at:

www.theresasederholt.com